BOY'S CHOICE

BOY'S CHOICE

A collection of stories

Illustrated by
LASZLO B. ACS

HAMLYN

LONDON • NEW YORK • SYDNEY • TORONTO

First published 1965

Second impression 1966

Third impression 1967

Fourth impression 1968

Fifth impression 1971

Published 1971 by The Hamlyn Publishing Group Limited
LONDON · NEW YORK · SYDNEY · TORONTO
Hamlyn House, Feltham, Middlesex, England
for Golden Pleasure Books Limited
© Copyright Golden Pleasure Books Limited 1971
ISBN 0 601 08635 X
Printed in Czechoslovakia by Naše vojsko, Prague
51095

ACKNOWLEDGEMENTS

The publishers wish to express their thanks to authors and publishers for permission to include the following stories:

JIM STARLING AND THE PURPLE SOFA © Copyright by E. W. Hildick 1965.

AFFAIR OF HONOUR © Copyright Aubrey Feist from TOLD ON THE AIR, 1948; STORIES FOR BOYS, 1955 (B.B.C.).

GULF TIMBER © Copyright by Richard Armstrong 1965.

BRISTOW ON ICE © Copyright Howard Jones from the London EVENING NEWS, 1937.

IMPERNO STRIKES AGAIN © Copyright R. A. Martin 1965

GENTLEMEN OF THE SEALED KNOT © Copyright Geoffrey Trease from THE BOY'S BOOK OF ADVENTURE, 1950 (Evans Bros. Ltd).

THE WILD ONES © Copyright R. A. Martin 1965.

WEIRD SISTER © Copyright Howard Jones 1965.

THE CASE OF THE GILT MIRROR © Copyright Fielden Hughes from THE ADVENTURES OF BILL HOLMES, 1950 (Oxford University Press).

THE LEGACY © Copyright Aubrey Feist from THE JUNIOR RADIO TIMES, 1959 (B.B.C.).

THE TIGHTROPE by Ian Serraillier from ADVENTURE AND DISCOVERY No. 5 published by Jonathan Cape Ltd.

TODDY PROVES HIS POINT © Copyright R. A. Martin 1965.

CONTENTS

Jim Starling and the Purple Sofa

by E. W. HILDICK

'I suppose we could light part of it now, son...'

'No.'

'Just as a kind of try out for tonight...'

'*No!*'

'A kind of sample—you know... Just to make sure it'll burn all right.'

'*NO!*'

Jim Starling scowled at the rest of the Last Apple Gang. He didn't know much about the original Gunpowder Plot but he was beginning to suspect the reason for its failure. If Guy Fawkes's lot were anything like as impatient as Terry Todd, Nip Challons and Goggles Grimshaw, the poor bloke could never have had a chance.

'No!' he repeated, stabbing the ground in front of him with a pole.

The four boys were sitting on a log in Goggles's back garden. It was the biggest of a number of logs that were here that morning. The garden fell in three terraces from the house to the railway line and it wasn't unusual for these three terraces to be littered with old lumber. Today, however, they were more than littered. They were buried. Instead of three separate levels, the garden seemed to have been built on one slope and that slope to have been buried in an avalanche. It bristled with branches and legs of battered chairs. It was cluttered with so many boxes and cartons and barrels that you'd have thought the packing department of a brewery had been swept down in the same landslide. It was festooned with what looked like endless strips of unused bus tickets. It bulged in the darker corners with fat stuffed sacks. It seemed as if all that was stopping this vast avalanche of junk from sliding farther and blocking the main Liverpool—Leeds line was a ballast of bedding: a top-dressing of ancient mattresses, stained and striped and sodden with the last fortnight's rain. And there were human limbs amongst it all, too—an arm here, a scratched leg there: the limbs of Goggles's numerous younger brothers and sisters and their pals, playing hide-and-seek.

'Why *can't* we have just a little trial fire?' persisted Nip. 'A *pilot* fire? An *experimental fire?*'

Jim wasn't going to be blinded with science.

'Because before we know where we are we'll have none left for tonight.'

'We could get some more, son,' said Terry Todd, tugging hopefully at the earflaps of his leather helmet.

'Where from?' snapped Jim. 'There *is* no more. Every bit of spare wood in Smogbury was collected days ago. Every bit of old junk that'll burn. And you know it!'

'We could raid another gang's pile!' said Goggles.

'Yes—and while we're raiding theirs, they'll be raiding ours.'

'What shall we do then?'

'Wait.'

Terry glared at his watch.

'Long time till tonight. Long wait, son.'

Jim stood up. He twirled his pole.

'We'll have quarter-staff practice, then... Who's first?'

Nip stayed seated. He threw down his pole, just to make sure there'd be no mistake. He hated getting his hair ruffled, let alone having a couple of ribs staved in. Terry began to sniff.

'It's bad for me asthma, son,' he said. 'All that swingin'...

But Goggles was game enough.

'I'll take y' on, lad!' he cried, jumping up. He removed the tangle of wire, lenses, sticking-plaster and string that he called his glasses and tossed it into Nip's lap. Then he swung his broom handle. 'Have at yer, Little Jim!' he roared.

Crack!—a thin hard hand had 'at' *him* at the back of his bristly ginger head, and a voice said: 'Get them glasses on before you kill somebody!'

It was Goggles's mother. Having eight children, an excitable husband and a houseful of other relatives had made her quick at avoiding missiles, otherwise Goggles's practice swing would surely have felled her.

'If you want summat to do,' she said, 'get across to old Tommy Lodge. He's very upset. See 'f you can help him.'

And that's how the Last Apple Gang came to embark on their quest for the Purple Sofa...

Tommy Lodge was an old-age pensioner. He lived alone and Goggles often ran errands for him or took his dog, Rip, for a walk. In fact, the Gang had once spent several days helping to find this dog when it had gone astray, which was probably why Mrs Grimshaw thought they might be able to help this time.

'He's lost some money, you see,' she explained. 'It was while he was in hospital—'

'Well what d'you expect *us* to do?' said Goggles. 'Dress up as doctors an' go in there lookin' for it?'

Mrs Grimshaw gave her second son a look that suggested *he* might be going in as a patient if he didn't be quiet.

'While he was in hospital,' she continued, 'his sister's been keeping an eye on his house for him, looking after Rip and that. And she went and sold his sofa. He's only just come out this morning and he's fair upset about it and so is she. She thought it'd be doing him a favour, scruffy old thing it was.

11

She thought he'd be glad—specially when she told him she'd got five pounds for it.'

'Five quid!' said Terry. 'I remember that sofa. Purple one. Stuffing coming out. I wouldn't have given him five *pence*!'

'No, well,' said Mrs Grimshaw, 'neither would I. But this antique dealer who came must have thought different. Anyway, that's what he gave her and that's why she thought Tommy would be glad. He might have been, an' all—only there was one snag.'

'What?' asked Goggles.

'He'd got some of his savings tucked away inside it somewhere,' said Mrs Grimshaw. 'Forty-five pounds ten. In an envelope.'

Jim looked at the others.

'What about it?' he said.

'We can have a try,' said Nip.

'It'll pass the time,' said Terry.

'Our Stanley and them can guard the wood,' said Goggles.

'And it shouldn't take us long, anyway,' said Jim.

Mr Lodge wasn't as hopeful,. Jim's idea was to go straight to the antique dealer and offer to buy the sofa back. The old man shook his head.

'He wouldn't have given five quid if it hadn't been worth a lot more than that,' he pointed out. 'He'll never part with it for the same price.'

'Well, let's tell him what happened and ask him for the envelope back,' said Goggles.

The old man went paler than ever.

'Eh? Here—no!' he gasped. 'Don't do that! Too risky. He might let you have it back—yes, but then again he might not. And as long as he doesn't know about it there's a chance... I suppose...'

Jim nodded.

'You're right,' he said. 'If he'd found it already and he's

honest he'd have brought it back by now. And if he hasn't found it—well...' He turned to the others. 'I say we go round there and reckon to be interested in it. Then, while we're having a look at it—'

'—we can slip a hand inside it—'

'—an' whip it out—'

'—while he's not lookin'! Yer!'

Nobody could say that the Last Apple Gang were not optimists.

But even they began to have doubts when they reached the antique dealer's. This was no old junk shop in which anyone was free to rummage about. This was housed in one of Smogbury's finest old buildings, with gleaming brasswork on the door, thick carpets, rare old porcelain vases, richly glowing wood and a plump little man in gold-rimmed glasses and a bow tie.

He stared at the four boys as if they'd just emerged from a rubbish heap—which of course they had, in a way. Jim became uneasily conscious of a ten-inch tear in the left leg of his jeans. Terry remembered that his leather helmet had once been likened to the pelt of a bald and oversized rat, and he tried to screw it up into an invisible ball. In an attempt to conceal the state of his glasses, Goggles shaded his eyes with one hand, as if the glare from the beautiful old candelabra overhead was too much for him. Only Nip looked anything like presentable, and Jim gave him a neat tap between the shoulder blades and shoved him forward.

'Well?' said the man, suddenly smiling.

It was a pleasant smile and Jim took heart. Before Nip could say anything, he spoke himself.

'It's about a sofa,' he began.

The man's smile faded a little.

'Yes?' he said.

'A purple sofa,' continued Jim.

'Ah!' said the man.

His smile had vanished.

'One you bought the other day,' said Jim, feeling that he might as well press on, now that he'd gone so far. 'Off an old man,' he added.

'*That!*' growled the man.

He now looked positively angry.

'*That!*' he repeated. 'Don't for heaven's sake accuse *me* of buying *that* thing, *please*! That was my nephew's doing. That was Clarence.' The little man was actually trembling with indignation. 'Only a fool would have bought *that*, new to the business or not. That was Clarence. Yes. My nephew.'

He shuddered, then pulled himself together.

'Why?' he said. 'What is it you want to know about it?'

Terry gave a loud sniff and came to the front. The others fell back a little, sensing that this was a job for him.

'Poor old feller!' he said. 'While he was in hospital, too. That sofa—' Terry went on, screwing away at his helmet—'that sofa meant the world to him. It was of great sen... sen—' He left off screwing the helmet and began softly to snap his fingers behind his back.

'Sentimental!' whispered Nip.

Terry went back to screwing the helmet.

'It was of great sentremental value to him, that sofa,' he murmured. 'Poor old feller!'

'And if you really don't want it, we'll buy it back,' said Jim.

The little man looked happier all at once. He opened a door at the side of the room.

'Clarence!' he called. 'Step in here a minute. I've some good news for you.'

Clarence was a tall, thin youth with pale blue eyes. He had some straggling golden hairs on his chin that were supposed to represent a beard, but, as Goggles said later, there was really

14

hardly enough of it to make a set of eyelashes. He blinked at his uncle and smiled uncertainly.

'These lads have saved your bacon, Clarence,' said the little man. 'They've come to buy back that old junk you bought yesterday...' Clarence blinked more rapidly. 'That sofa,' said his uncle. 'That purple sofa... Where is it?'

Clarence continued to blink. Behind the golden fringe his Adam's apple had started to bob up and down.

'Er...' he began.

It was a long, low sound—half wail, half moan.

'Well!' snapped the little man. 'Don't just stand there. Take 'em to it!'

'It's—well—er—you see...' Clarence closed his eyes. 'I—well—I thought I'd cut our losses, you see, Uncle... And—well—this morning, only a couple of hours ago, maybe a bit longer, I sold it, for ten shillings, to—to Joe Walton.'

Small the dealer may have been. Pink and polite he may have looked. But the words he spoke to Clarence then were very similar to those that Jim had once heard a six-foot fighting-drunk barge skipper use on dropping his month's pay into the Aire and Calder Canal. Blushing, the boys left him to continue his lecture on the difference between running and ruining a business, and went to Joe Walton's.

Joe Walton was Smogbury's leading junk man. His premises were in an old chapel. Not that it looked at all like a chapel nowadays, apart from the inscription over the door— EBENEZER—and even that wouldn't have remained if Joe had been able to slice it out of the stonework and sell it at a shilling a letter, seven-and-six the lot. In fact, inside it looked more like an intricate system of caves than any building made by man. The junk was packed from floor to ceiling and there were narrow runs amongst it all. Some of these runs had been made into tunnels by overhanging junk. Some petered out.

Some led you back to where you'd already been. But one led to Joe Walton's office—a kind of clearing fenced with tea-chests—and there they found him.

He was sitting on what had once been the Emperor's throne in the Smogbury Operatic Society's 1929 production of *The Mikado*. His feet were on the old harmonium that served as a desk. His hands, mouth and three-quarters of his black-bristled jaws were wrapped round the newest thing in the whole place—a huge, party-sized, crisp-crusted pork pie.

'Morning,' he said, treating them to a spray of crumbs. 'What you after?'

They told him they were looking for a sofa. Knowing him, they didn't go into details. That would have been fatal. Instead, they had decided to look round themselves at sofas in general and, when they found the right one, simply take out the envelope.

'That's Heavy Furnishings,' said Joe, waving with the remains of the pie. 'Out the back. Take yer pick.'

There must have been more than a dozen sofas out there, mixed up with the old wardrobes, bedsteads, dressers, side-boards, bookcases, chests and armchairs—but not one of them was purple.

'He's probably not brought it round here yet,' said Nip. 'He only got it this morning, remember.'

Jim nodded glumly.

'It looks like we'll have to ask him after all.'

Terry sniffed.

'That's all right, son,' he said. 'You leave it to me.'

But all Terry's cunning was in vain. His story—that his mother wanted a sofa to match some purple curtains she'd won in a raffle—was wasted.

'A *purple* one?' said Joe, picking traces of pork from his teeth with a bent, gleaming nail. 'Pity... Had one in... just this morning... An hour ago... Didn't even get it off the van... This old woman saw it. Just what she wanted... We took it straight up to her house.'

Trying not to sound too eager, Jim said:

'I wonder if she'd sell it to us?'

Joe shrugged.

'Doubt it. Too good a bargain at thirty bob... Anyway, what's up with buying one of them out the back? Soon fix you up with some purple stuff. Soft Furnishings. Round there, back of them old coal-scuttles. Next that pile of Army boots. There's a very nice roll of purple corduroy there. Just the job.'

They thanked him for his help but said they'd rather try the old lady first. And, after they had promised to pay him five shillings if she agreed to sell—and had given him half-a-crown as a deposit—he gave them her address at last.

The old lady looked as if she'd been crying. Yes, she said—oh dear, yes, she had bought a purple sofa, yes—from Mr Walton—but—but...

She excused herself and went back into the house, leaving them at the door. They looked at one another. Goggles groaned.

'Don't tell me *she's* gone and sold it, an' all!' he murmured.

The old lady came back, dabbing her eyes with the handkerchief she'd been to fetch.

'Yes,' she said. 'I wanted a sofa like that for ages. Just the right size. It was dirty but—' She broke off with a sob.

The boys looked at one another again. Jim didn't like the sound of that 'was'.

'But—you see,' the woman continued, 'it—it—'

'What is it *now*, Mother? What do these boys want?'

The speaker was a younger, bustling woman. She had a face that looked as if it had been scrubbed with a wire brush. It looked as if all the gentleness and softness had been scrubbed away with every speck of dirt.

'They—they've come to ask about the—the sofa, dear—'

'*That* thing!' snapped the daughter. She said it in exactly the same tone as the antique dealer, earlier. 'I suppose they've heard I refused to allow it in the house. I suppose they want it for their bonfire... Well, you're too late!' she said. 'I gave it to some other boys.'

'Er—which other boys, man—er—miss?' asked Terry, screwing at his helmet and giving her his politest leer.

The woman glanced at the bundle of greasy brown leather and shuddered.

'How should *I* know which boys?' she said. 'They all look alike to me. They all look as if they could do with a good hot bath!'

And with that she slammed the door.

There was nothing else for it. For the rest of the morning and all the afternoon the Last Apple Gang went on with their search the hard way. They visited all the bonfire stocks within about two miles of the old lady's house. At least they *probably* visited them all. If they missed any out, it was because some gang had been keeping their wood in the safe deposit of a bank.

They peered over backyard walls. They investigated old hen-runs. They snooped round allotments, empty houses, waste-grounds, back alleys—everywhere they knew for certain that bonfire wood was being stored and everywhere they saw the tell-tale signs of stocks they hadn't heard about. A trail of broken twigs was enough to alert them, or a corner of tarpaulin, flapping over something angular and bulky just above a garden wall.

Many of the places they had actually visited before— during the dark raiding nights of the last few weeks. And if they themselves hadn't been there raiding, some other gang was bound to have. That was why they were treated with great suspicion everywhere they went.

'What *you* lot want?'

'It's O.K.—nothing to do with raiding your wood.'

'Yer—we know!'

'No, honest!'

'Well what you poking behind them old boxes for? Butterfly huntin'? Get moving before yer get hurt!'

Such challenges as this were hard to ignore. Several times Goggles and Nip had to be held back. Several times it was only with a great effort that Jim and Terry kept themselves from snatching a juicy-looking old tyre and bowling it away with them.

But they had a job to do and, as the afternoon raced on, it became more and more urgent.

'Another hour and it'll be dark, son!' groaned Terry.

'And then we'll have had it!' said Goggles. '*Woosh!* On goes the sofa and up goes Tommy's savings—in flames.'

'Not if I can help it,' said Jim.

'No, but the time, son, the *time*! There's not much time left.'

'So you keep saying. Only there can't be many *places* left, either.'

Half an hour and three stockpiles later they were still unlucky.

'What about tea, son?'

'Never mind tea! We can fill up with parkin and Plot toffee and roast spuds later. After we've got the money.'

But Jim's voice sounded a bit hollow. There was only one place left now. Only one that he could think of, anyway. Nicky Peel's.

'There's one thing,' said Nip. 'If we don't rescue it, it'll teach him to keep his money in the bank.'

'Yer! Fine!' jeered Goggles. 'But Tommy's topped seventy-five, lad. Bit old for learnin' lessons. Might never save that much again in the time *he's* got left!'

This spurred them on. Their footsteps were brisk as they made for the last place.

'It *must* be there!' Jim was thinking. 'It's *got* to be there!'

Nicky Peel's was the nearest bonfire stock to their own. Despite this, however, the two gangs were very friendly. Nicky was in the same form at school as Jim and the others and occasionally he tagged on with them. During the collecting of the bonfire wood, Jim and Nicky had made a kind of pact: you leave ours alone and we'll leave yours.

So the Last Apple Gang weren't at all furtive in their approach to Mr Peel's builders' yard, in a corner of which he'd allowed Nicky to keep his stock. And when they reached the gate and saw that nobody was about they didn't pause, wondering what to do. Mr Peel knew the Last Apple Gang well enough. If he or any of his men happened to be in the small hut next to the pile of sand and someone looked out and saw Jim and his friends, it would be all right. He'd know they were only on their way to see Nicky, down by the woodpile.

But when they reached this pile neither Nicky nor any of his gang could be seen. Jim frowned, forgetting the sofa for a minute.

'They want to be careful,' he said. 'Leaving it like this, unguarded.'

The builders' yard was at the side of the railway, a few hundred yards up the line from Goggles's place. Past the hut and the piles of material it sloped down sharply, and it was in the corner at the foot on this slope that the bonfire wood was being stored. It was well concealed and—what with the line being at one side and the yard at the other—it looked pretty safe. Still, as Jim said, you never knew.

'That's Nicky's worry, son, not ours!' said Terry. He began to go round the pile, peering, pulling branches and boxes to one side. It was getting dusk and the shapes weren't easy to make out. 'What we want to know is have they got that sofa!'

'Yer, come on!' said Goggles. 'Let's have a real good look. Nicky won't mind.'

Then it happened.

'*Won't I?*' cried a voice above them. '*Won't* I mind? Let 'em have it, lads!'

And before the Last Apple Gang could see exactly where the voice had come from, a powerful jet of water came hissing at them, over their heads, in front of them, and finally *on* them.

'Hey!' cried Jim, gasping at the coldness of it, dodging and stumbling over Nip in his haste to get out of the way. 'It's *us*! It's *me*—Jim—Jim Starling! It—*whu!*'

It was difficult to continue with a mouthful of water.

'We *know* it's you—you rats!' howled the voice from above. 'Get that other pipe going, lads—swill 'em out!'

It was stupefying. Not only the shock of cold water but this sudden attack by old allies. It was as if an American bomber had been cruising pleasantly over East Anglia and had been shot at by the R.A.F. It was unthinkable. But it had happened.

The Last Apple Gang didn't wait to argue. They didn't stop to think about the laws of trespass. They had made sure that there was no sofa there, and all that mattered now was getting away from those hose-pipes. They jumped over the wall and on to the rough ground at the side of the railway line.

'Well,' said Jim, as they stumbled along, squelching, in the dusk, back to Goggles's, 'it looks as if we've had it.'

The others only grunted. Nip was too busy wringing out the sleeve of his windcheater and wondering if at least the water had been clean. Goggles was too busy fumbling with the sodden plaster that was holding his glasses together, hoping the last bit of stickiness hadn't been washed away. Terry was wondering by what miracle his pants from the knees down-wards should have been drenched and his helmet knocked off by the jet, while everything in between was dry. Jim scowled round at them.

'Can't anybody think of anywhere else?' he asked, poking inside the collar of his shirt with a handkerchief. 'I mean don't let's forget what we se⁺ out to do!'

The others merely grunted again as they trudged on, dabbing, wringing, wiping.

Then there came a swift rushing sound, a fading scream, a crack, and a shower of bright emerald stars burst and slowly collapsed in the darkening sky. Then another rocket rushed through the air, and another, and another. Somewhere a dog began to bark. Ahead, lower in the sky, an orange-red light leapt, lapsed and leapt again, flickering.

'Well,' said Terry,s 'that' it! There's the first fire.'

'Bit early,' said Nip.

'It's after five,' said Goggles. 'Won't be long before they're all off now.'

More rockets hissed overhead. The bangs became more regular. A smell of burning rubber floated down the line towards them. The glow got brighter.

'Can anybody think of anywhere *else*?' repeated Jim, feeling suddenly weary, and wetter than ever.

'Too late now, even if we did, son,' murmured Terry.

Goggles was staring ahead. The glow was reflected in his glasses.

'I wonder whose that is?' he said. 'It looks pretty close to me. It looks—*hey!*' He stopped. They were very near to his own garden by now. 'Hey, it *is*! It's *ours*! They've gone and lit it without us!'

He was right. Up in front of them loomed the Grimshaws' house. And beyond it, a little to the side, where the waste-ground was, the fire burned bright. It was more than a glow now. They could see the flames and sparks and even the black flakes of charred paper, floating and swirling above it.

Stanley was apologetic.

'I thought you weren't coming,' he explained, lighting a banger and tossing it high in the air. 'Thought you'd gone to some other fire.'

'*Thought!*' growled Goggles.

Steam was rising from the Last Apple Gang as they stood in a menacing group round Stanley, near the fire.

'No, though,' said Stanley, lighting another firework and throwing it fizzing at Nip's feet. 'Hey! Hey! Made yer jump! 'S only a Fairy Founting... No, though,' he added, backing away from the highly unamused Nip, 'let's tell you what happened before you start blaming me. We got raided.'

This checked Nip's advance.

'Raided?' said Jim.

'Yer—your fault, leaving us like that. This gang of kids came. Big 'uns. Hundreds of 'em. Had to fetch me mother to 'em. But by then they'd got half a dozen branches—and that big log—an' three of them barrels—'

'Which kids? Who were they?'

Stanley shrugged. He lit another firework—a Roman candle this time. They stepped back. All round them the younger children were letting off fireworks, dragging fresh wood to the edge of the fire, chasing one another.

'Go on,' said Terry. 'Which kids?'

'Don't know,' said Stanley. 'Never seen 'em before.' He giggled. 'Only we got our own back!'

'How?'

Stanley smirked. He stuck a pin through a Catherine wheel.

'We raided someone else's!'

'Theirs?'

'No! I tell you we didn't know 'em... No, we raided Nicky Peel's lot instead.'

'*What?*' roared Goggles. '*Whose?*'

Stanley bent and pinned the Catherine wheel to a strip of wood.

'Nicky Peel's,' he said. 'His was the nearest. It was easy. We'd got it halfway back before they knew what had happened. Then as soon as we got back we told me mam it was the same lot comin' again an' she shooed 'em off.'

'No wonder—' groaned Terry. 'No wonder Nicky was mad!'

'You seen him then?' said Stanley grinning.

Goggles, Terry and Nip closed in on him. He gaped at them.

'Hey, what's up?' he asked, dropping the stick and backing away.

Goggles shot out an arm, grabbing his brother's collar. The arm brushed Stanley's cheek.

'Heck!' said Stanley, hoping to change the subject. 'Yer sleeve's wet! Has it been raining where you've been?'

'Argh!' growled Goggles, tightening his grip.

'Let *me*!' snarled Nip. 'I got the wettest!'

'Hey—what's up?' yelped Stanley again.

'Leave him!' snapped Jim.

'He's *my* brother,' said Goggles, 'an' I've got a right to have first bash!'

'Leave him!' repeated Jim, pulling Goggles to one side and breaking his grip. 'I've had an idea.' He turned to Stanley. 'Listen, Stanley,' he said. 'I want you to tell me something.'

'What?' muttered Stanley, suspiciously.

Some of the younger ones had gathered round. Others were still at the other side of the fire, letting off fireworks and jumping about like savages. One little group dragged some fresh fuel towards the fire.

'When you raided Nicky, what did you get?'

'I don't know,' said Stanley, sullenly. 'Anyone'ud think

I'd done a murder!'

There was a growl from the younger ones round about.

'Leave him alone, *you!*' shouted the youngest Grimshaw but two—four-year-old Dennis. 'Or I'll bash yer!'

'No—think, Stanley,' said Jim. 'I'm not blaming you. I'm not going to hit you. Just what was it you raided off Nicky? Branches?'

Stanley frowned.

'Well—yer—one or two...'

There was a cheer and a crash as two tyres were bowled on to the fire at the other side. Sparks flew. Flames licked at the huge black rings. Someone said: 'Now this thing!'—and the stoking-up group gathered round a long dark shape in the shadows. Jim was busy watching Stanley.

'What else?' he asked.

'Well—some old boxes—them flat 'uns—kipper boxes—phew!'

'And an old chair,' said young Dennis.

'Chair? What sort of chair?' snapped Jim.

'Rockin' chair,' said Stanley.

'*Yo-ho 'eave-oh!*' sang the group of stokers, dragging the long object forward.

Jim heard them but didn't bother to look.

'Anything else?'

'No—I mean yes, course there was!' said Stanley. 'I nearly forgot. There was this old couch thing.'

'*Couch!*'

Everyone jumped. Terry, Nip and Jim had all yelled the word at once—Goggles coming in about half a second later.

'Yer,' said Stanley. 'That's what we piled the other stuff on—the boxes and one of the branches. We wheeled it part of the way an'—'

'Where? Where is it?'

Stanley blinked.

'Well—'

'*Hurray!*'

This time the roar came from the stokers as, with a crash and a spray of sparks, they launched the long thing into the fire.

Jim glanced, turned back to Stanley, then glanced again. The stokers were having difficulty. The thing was stuck, half in the fire, half out.

Then, as the flames revealed more of its shape—and colour—Jim gasped.

'Hey!' he cried. 'That's *it! Leave it!*'

Even before he'd finished speaking he was there, at the other side, dragging the purple sofa out of the flames.

'Well,' said Tommy Lodge, after he'd counted the money and thanked them and they'd refused the ten shillings he offered them as a reward. 'So you traced it then?'

'Yes,' said Jim. 'We traced it.'

'No trouble?' asked the old man.

The boys glanced at one another. They were tempted. It was a good tale. But they didn't want Tommy to have nightmares. That yellow at the curling edge of the envelope wasn't a sign of old age, whatever the old man might think. Besides, if they went into details they'd be there all evening, and although Mrs Grimshaw was in charge of the potatoes and parkin and toffee you never could tell with Stanley about.

'Trouble?' said Jim, smiling.

'Trouble?' said Goggles, looking at Nip.

'Trouble?' said Nip, looking at Goggles.

'What's trouble?' said Terry.

'No, Mr Lodge,' said Jim, turning to the door. 'No trouble at all!'

Affair of Honour

by AUBREY FEIST

A patter of rain on the windows of the 'diligence'. Long lines of poplars straining against the wind. Sodden fields. An occasional peasant, trudging along with bent head and flapping blouse. Mile after mile...

Major Beverley was tired of this interminable journey. The picture of boredom, he sat hunched in his seat, staring with unseeing eyes at the toes of his Hessians, while by his side, his brother, young Julian—curly-brimmed beaver tilted over his nose and caped riding-coat muffled up to his ears—was fast asleep.

Mile after mile...

There was nothing to break the monotony until they reached the last stop before Paris. The coach rumbled into the cobbled yard of the 'Lion d'Or'. The big Norman horses were unharnessed and a new team came clattering from the stables. Noise! Confusion! Scurrying ostlers! The sudden blare of the guard's bugle...

And then, as the postilions donned their sheepskin aprons, gulped down their cognac and clambered into the saddle, there came the sound of furious bellowing and a big swarthy man in a blue frocked coat came running out of the inn. Julian, awakened by the clamour, sat up with a start and looked out of the window. He gave a low whistle.

'Latouche, by gad!'

Major Beverley frowned as the angry Frenchman began to wrestle with the door handle.

'Dangerous company, eh?' he growled. 'I've learned to like the Froggies, but if what you told me about this fellow is

27

true... Wasn't he once a fencing master in Boney's army?'

'Yes,' replied his brother bitterly, 'but now he's the most notorious duellist in the country. What they call a *bretteur*. Fights for the love of killing... You remember young Blight. He was doing the Grand Tour with his tutor, and this scoundrel killed him in cold blood. There was Spicer, too, and Ensign, Wade and...'

'The man must be mad,' said the major shortly. 'But you'd better curb your tongue. He's getting in. I'd never be able to face our parents again if anything happened to you.'

But Julian just shrugged and sat back scowling, as the door flew open and the famous bully climbed into the moving coach. Contempt was written on the boy's reckless face. It was not only Latouche's reputation: everything about the man repelled him. The little bloodshot eyes, the semi-military clothes, the ferocious whiskers and moustache. Why, even the thick black hair which curled beneath his peaked travelling cap reeked of pomade.

Latouche returned the stare with interest, for his fellow passengers were obviously English, and to him the English were still 'the enemy'... He smiled sourly, well pleased. Here was a sovereign cure for his bad temper. This little *milor*, for example! So young, so fresh—so very youthful. With such a one he could play for a long time before he sped his famous *coupé*.

For a while all went well. Latouche lit a cigar and Julian dozed quietly in his corner. Then, as luck would have it, a wheel of the coach jolted in and out of a deep rut. In an instant, Julian's beaver had fallen off and was rolling at the Frenchman's feet.

'Permit me, monsieur!' Latouche picked up the hat and handed it back with a little bow. Luck was with him, it seemed. It would be easy now to turn conversation into a quarrel. 'You are English?' he inquired politely, as Julian thanked him in his slow, schoolboy French.

'I have that honour.'

'*Ma foi!* But I have met many of your countrymen.'

'In battle perhaps?' suggested Julian curtly.

'Oh, in war—and peace,' said the *bretteur* with a grim smile. 'I remember some interesting encounters. Albuera! Salamanca! Toulouse!' His smile grew scornful. 'Ah, but you are young. You have never been a soldier.'

'No, indeed,' replied Julian, flushing. 'But my brother here was wounded at Waterloo.'

The Frenchman's insolent eyes narrowed as he shifted them to the older man. He noted the square brown face and stubborn jaw, the bright blue eyes that met his so steadily. Formidable, that one! Broad-shouldered! Strong! A quiet, kindly man, but dangerous if roused. He bowed again.

'It is an honour to make the acquaintance of an old adversary. I am Latouche. You have heard of me, perhaps. Jean-Marie Latouche. Once *maitre d'armes* of the Fifty-seventh.'

Major Beverley smiled politely as he returned the ruffian's salute. It might be as well, for Julian's sake, to humour this man. The youngster was so rash, so hot-headed.

'My name is Beverley,' he said quietly. 'I served in the Heavy Brigade at Waterloo, under Lord Edward Somerset. First Dragoon Guards. As my brother has told you, I was wounded. It was just before the Prussians came up and...'

'Ach, those Prussians!' grumbled Latouche. 'They were our downfall. If Blücher had not arrived...'

'The British line would have held!' laughed Julian scornfully.

'Impossible!'

'Monsieur, I tell you...'

Major Beverley frowned. Confound the young fool! Why couldn't he keep out of this? He knew what the end of the argument would be. A quarrel—a blow—a triumphant challenge—a rendezvous before breakfast, in the Bois. Julian would be callously murdered like all the others. His only brother! He hastened to intervene.

'Forgive me, monsieur,' he said quietly, silencing Julian with a gesture, 'but Waterloo was fought three years ago. Is it wise to discuss...?'

Latouche's strong teeth clamped on his cigar. His little eyes narrowed to pin-points.

'Listen—you!' he sneered. 'I discuss what I choose, where I choose and with whom I choose, my friend. This young cockerel and I appear to differ upon a small matter. So! Well—differences can be settled... We were talking of Waterloo, I think,' he went on abruptly, turning to Julian. 'Pray proceed, monsieur. You were pretending that...'

'I stated a fact. If you say otherwise, you lie!'

'Ah!' said Latouche, a long-drawn 'ah' that came hissing through his yellow teeth. And then for a moment there was silence, only the creaking of the coach and the sad patter of the rain. Julian was very pale, for now, too late, he saw the gulf that yawned beneath him. This was the end. He was going to die. He would never see his home again. As a gentleman, he must face this ruffian and go down gamely like the others. He threw up his head...

But it was Major Beverley who spoke first. His voice was very deep and level.

'Julian,' he said with a strange little smile, 'will you please be good enough to open the window?'

His brother stared at him in astonishment.

'The window?' he whispered. 'But—but—the rain, Tom!'

'Oh, I'm not afraid of the rain. It's the reek of this fellow's cheap pomade. Phew!' The major pulled out his handkerchief and slowly raised it to his nose.

It would seem that Jean-Marie Latouche understood a little English. He went as white as his own neckcloth and shook his bunched fingers furiously.

'You—you mean to insult me?' he said thickly.

'Ah, no. That would be impossible, I'm afraid.'

'Monsieur! I protest! As a man of honour...'

'Honour!' roared the major in a rage. 'You don't know the meaning of the word, Latouche. But your opponents do—the poor brave boys who die to satisfy your insane hatred.'

'You shall answer for this!' screamed Latouche.

'I intend to.'

'Tom! You can't...' gasped Julian.

'Hold your tongue, boy! Well, Latouche?'

The bully bowed stiffly in his seat. His words came rattling out like a formula.

'If you will favour me with your address in Paris, my friends will wait upon you tomorrow.'

'I see!' The major was very thoughtful now. One strong hand rubbed his shaven chin. 'I imagine,' he said half humorously, 'that you are challenging me to a duel?'

'Exactly! An affair of honour!'

'Egad! There he goes again. Did you hear that, Julian?' Then he became serious. 'I am not well versed in these matters, Latouche; but I understand that, as the challenged party, I have—certain privileges.'

The duellist laughed harshly and spread his hands.

'The choice of weapons is yours. As an old cavalryman, you may prefer sabres.'

'On the contrary, I shall never swing a sabre again as long as I live.'

'Pistols, then. It makes no difference to me. I can split a playing-card at ten paces.'

'Tom, old fellow!' cried Julian in agony. 'I can't let you do this. I know it's for my sake, but...'

'My mind's made up,' replied the major grimly. 'Latouche is going to have his fill of fighting.'

'Excellent, my brave Englishmen! And the time and place?'

Major Beverley considered. He took a pinch of rappee before replying. Then, flicking a few grains of snuff from his cravat, he fixed Latouche with his gleaming blue eyes.

'The time and place!' he drawled. 'I fear that I shall be somewhat busy in Paris, so, since it is my privilege to name the conditions, I intend to fight you here and now—in—this—coach!'

The cigar fell from Latouche's nerveless fingers.

'In this confined space!' he whispered. 'Without either seconds or witnesses! Why, it will be murder.'

'Then doubtless it will be all the more to your liking,' returned the major pleasantly. 'Now listen, Latouche! For once in your life you are going to take part in a fair fight. Your skill with sword and pistol will not help you to save your skin *this* time. We shall have an equal chance of being blown to blazes, an equal chance of—proving our courage.'

Latouche sat very still. His face was haggard and beads of sweat were gathering on his forehead. Twice he tried to speak and twice he failed, then out it came in a husky groan:

'We shall both be killed.'

'Oh, no,' said Beverley. 'I haven't finished yet.' He turned to his brother. 'Those new barkers I bought for you in London. Are they loaded?'

'Not yet. Tom, you must be mad!'

'Load one; then put them both into your hat, please.'

With trembling hands, Julian drew the small, silver-mounted pistols from his pocket, primed them, and rammed home a single charge. Then he placed them in his beaver while Latouche watched him, wide-eyed. The bully was shaking, and once he reached up clumsy fingers to loosen his neckcloth. But Major Beverley did not appear to notice the movement. He was icily calm.

'And now,' he went on quietly, when the operation was

complete, 'you will take one pistol, monsieur, and I the other. Neither of us knows which weapon is loaded. We shall fire from our seats across the width of the coach. If we touch each other with the muzzles, we can't very well miss, can we?'

'You're mad!' snarled Latouche with sudden fury. 'I won't be a party to such an outrage.'

'No?' Major Beverley's face was as hard as flint as he rattled the pistols in the hat. 'But has it not occurred to you, my friend, that to refuse might be even more unpleasant? You live on your reputation as a duellist. What do you think they will say in Paris when they hear that the great Latouche has turned coward? Think of the jokes that will pass round the cafés—the songs, the lampoons!'

The bully gave a hoarse sob.

'Let us get it over then, this horror.'

'That's better!' smiled Beverley. 'Please choose your pistol.'

He held out the hat and Latouche plunged in his hand. Again and again he weighed each weapon, trying to decide which was loaded. Then at last, with a despairing shrug, he drew out a pistol. The major seized the other.

'Now, Julian my boy, if anything should happen, commend me to all my friends at home.' His brother nodded (he could not speak) and the major continued imperturbably. 'You will now oblige me by counting "Three" very slowly. On the third count, we fire... At your service, monsieur!'

He raised his pistol and pressed it firmly against Latouche's chest. The Frenchman tried to imitate him, but his hand was trembling so violently that the muzzle of his weapon beat a little tattoo on Beverley's body.

'Allow me to help you,' said the major gently. 'Your hand is shaking with the cold.' And grasping his enemy's pistol barrel, he held it steady over his own heart. 'Ah, that's more comfortable. Ready, Julian? Then count away, boy!'

'ONE!' said his brother, white to the lips.

The coach creaked and jolted as it swung wildly from side to side, and with a muttered apology Major Beverley tightened his grip on the Frenchman's pistol.

'TWO!'

Latouche gave a little whimper. His head was lolling upon his shoulders, and he kept moistening his dry lips as he glared from one set face to the other.

'THR...'

Julian was about to pronounce the fatal word when a pistol rattled on to the floor. Latouche sank down in a limp heap, and the major lowered his weapon slowly.

'Egad!' he cried. 'Has the fellow fainted? Unfasten his neckcloth and give him a breath of air.'

But Julian was powerless to obey him; he could hardly trust himself to speak. He only knew that he was going to live. They would not bury him in France with the others. He would see the steep High Street of Guildford again, and gallop his horse over Merrow Downs. The nightmare was over. He was going to *live*. Thanks to old Tom!

For a little while, Julian sat very still, staring out into the rain; then, all at once, he gave a whoop of joy.

'Paris, by George!'

And so it was. The iron-shod wheels were clattering over cobblestones, and in a few minutes they had arrived at the old Barrier of St Denis. The coach slowed down, for the gateway between the two lodges was crowded with carts and cows and peasants and screaming customs-men in green, who argued shrilly with each newcomer and probed every bale of produce with their long needles.

Latouche was recovering, so, with a grin, Julian opened the door and tipped him out into the mud. He sprawled in a puddle; then, staggering slowly to his feet with the water dripping from his long hair, he passed an unsteady hand across his eyes. He was still shivering. For several minutes he seemed to

Major Beverley tightened his grip on the Frenchman's pistol

be trying to collect his thoughts. There was an almost vacant look on his face as he reeled slowly back towards the stationary coach.

'Monsieur,' he whispered hoarsely, clinging to the door and glancing furtively round him. 'Our little affair is—finished, is it not? Honour is satisfied—hein?'

Major Beverley slowly turned his head, and burst into a roar of laughter.

'Gad, yes, Latouche. I'll let you off this time. But...' he added sternly in French, '... if you annoy any more young Englishmen, I'll spread the tale of your cowardice until it is the talk of Paris.'

The great Latouche had been born a blusterer. He contrived to bluster even now.

'Cowardice, my friend!'

'That is what I said. Our chances were absolutely equal. And I'll tell you something. As a matter of fact, *you* held the loaded pistol. How do I know? Why, I could tell by the weight. My sense of touch is so acute that...'

'What do you mean?' whispered Latouche.

Major Beverely smiled. Those blue eyes of his looked brighter than ever.

'Monsieur, since the Battle of Waterloo, I have had the misfortune to be blind!'

Gulf Timber

by Richard Armstrong

Joe Cornforth's fourth voyage in the *Limpopo* was the longest he ever made, and for more reasons than one it might easily have been his last.

It took him to the Mediterranean with coal from the Tyne; to Iceland with salt from Spain; to the Cape with sawn lumber from Finland; to Baltimore with copper pyrites from Huelva; and finally to Belize, in British Honduras, with a full cargo of creosoted piles from Mobile.

She was nine months out to the day when she got rid of that lot and steamed northward into the Yucatan Channel bound Key West for orders. Nobody, not even the Old Man himself, had a clue about what their next port would be and all hands spent the day guessing; all except Corny. He pretended he couldn't care less.

Corny was a good shipmate. Jake Blyth, who was the other apprentice aboard the old scow at the time and shared quarters with him on the starboard side of her bridge-deck, could vouch for that. His one big fault was a weakness for practical jokes; and, at the supper table that evening, he had the sheepish look on his round freckled face which was the sure sign he had been up to something for laughs which had come unstuck.

'Well,' Jake demanded, 'what's it this time?'

'I don't know what you mean,' Corny hedged.

'Yes, you do! You're in trouble again. I can see it written all over your ugly mush. Come on, give!'

'All right!' Corny read the danger signal in his room-mate's eye and decided to come clean before he got scragged. 'I'm in dutch with the Mate and this time I've really caused it.

He's livid. I've never seen him so furious before.'

The Mate, of course, was their 'big shot'. It was the Bosun who ran them and taught them seamanship about the decks, and the Second Mate who supervised their studies in navigation and all the other book work; but the Mate was responsible for them. He drew the line and saw that they toed it; and his reports on character, conduct and ability could smooth the years ahead for an apprentice or make a hopeless mess of his career before it had really started. The Mate was important and Jake had warned Corny over and over again to keep to windward of him.

'You'll never learn,' Jake said wearily. 'What's he livid about?'

'The alligator.'

'Alligator!' Jake, who was a great big bull of a fellow though he was still too young to shave, sat up as if he had been stung.

'What alligator?'

'My alligator. The one I got in Belize. I bought it off a beachcomber. Gave him a dollar for it.'

'I knew nothing about this. How did you get it aboard?'

'Oh, it wasn't very big. Only a yard long, you know, including the tail. I carried it down my trouser leg.'

'You did, did you!' Jake gulped and steadied himself. 'And then?'

'Well...' Corny's face was wide-eyed and innocent. He was a bouncy little chap with a nose like a triangle of sponge rubber stuck on among the freckles. 'Then I put it in the Mate's bunk.'

'Holy smoke!' gasped Jake. 'You must be crazier than I thought. You ought to be locked up! Suppose it had bitten him?'

'Not a hope.' Corny shook his head sadly. 'This one didn't bite. It couldn't.'

'Why not? An alligator's got teeth even when it's only a yard long. It might have done, you nut!'

'Not this one. It had teeth all right but it was stuffed; you know, with little glass beads for eyes.'

'Then why did you do it?'

'For the giggle, of course. I thought it would scare him pop-eyed when his bare feet touched it under the bedclothes. Only it didn't work. Sheer waste of money. For one thing I wasn't there to see his face...'

'And for another,' interrupted Jake, 'he doesn't scare. You should know that by now. You poor sap! I've told you till I'm sick to lay off the funny stuff. I suppose he guessed it was you. He couldn't miss. Nobody else aboard is crazy enough to think up such a caper. Then he grilled you and, instead of keeping your big mouth shut, you talked till you gave yourself away?'

'Yeah!' Corny nodded with unnecessary vigour. 'Right first time. And then he tore me off a strip. There's a lot of good in me somewhere, he said, but all his efforts had failed to find it; so, for my sake and his own sanity, he is recommending me for transfer to another ship when this voyage ends. Meanwhile, I'm not to go ashore without his special permission.'

Jake let his breath go in a low whistle of dismay. This was drastic action indeed and the Mate must have been hopping mad even to think of such a thing. But there was no denying Corny had asked for it. He had been warned over and over again and now he had chanced his arm once too often.

'You've only yourself to blame,' Jake said.

'I know, I know!' Corny hacked savagely at the table leg. 'A fat lot of comfort that is!'

'Maybe he'll change his mind when he cools off a bit.'

'Not a chance. He never learned how. My only hope is that the voyage lasts for ever, and it won't do that.'

Corny was right there. Orders were received by radio over-night and by breakfast time next morning the news was all over the ship. She was going to New Orleans to load a full cargo of timber for home.

'That'll be Greenock,' said Jake round a mouthful of bacon and egg. 'Think of it! Give her a fortnight to load and twenty days for the passage—say six weeks all together at the outside—and we'll be steaming up the Clyde!'

'I'd rather be going to Philadelphia to load case oil for Japan,' said Corny morosely.

And he wasn't the only one who refused to join the cheers. The Bosun, when he briefed them for the morning's work, wore a face as long as a wet sea-boot. He had been shipmates with Gulf timber before and suggested they should wait till the voyage was over before hanging out any flags. Then he explained why.

A load of Gulf timber across the North Atlantic at the time of the equinox was just about the toughest and most dicey cargo a sailorman ever rode on. It was a mixture and only about a third of it would be small stuff—oak, sawn and seasoned, hickory, spindle-wood blocks, cedar and redwood planks—and the rest would be pitch-pine.

'None of it sawn,' he said. 'Just whole trees with the tops chopped off and the trunks roughly squared. The smallest of them will be about eighteen inches through the butt, and the biggest three foot square and up to ten tons in weight. And the catch is that it won't all go into the holds, not by a jugful—'

'That means we'll be having a deck-cargo!' interrupted Jake.

'Too true, we will. Fourteen or sixteen feet of it. And we'll spend all our days from dawn till dark crawling about on the top of it, hammering in wedges to keep it solid.'

Jake and Corny both got the point. A ship in the North Atlantic is never still; always, even in the finest weather, there is a long, slow swell running and she responds to it, sometimes with a pitching movement, sometimes with a rolling one, but more often with that combination of both which seafaring

men call cork-screwing. In these conditions the slightest stretching of the lashings on a deck-cargo would allow a motion in
the whole mass that could grow alarmingly and, if not checked,
rapidly get out of control and become terrifyingly destructive.

'Sounds as if it could be an interesting passage!' said Corny.
And because he was a great believer in living for the moment
and letting the future take care of itself, he decided there and
then to forget the sentence that hung over him at the end of
the voyage and make the most of what was left of it.

On the third morning after leaving Belize, the *Limpopo*
picked up her pilot outside the Mississippi delta and steamed
on into the river. But although New Orleans is not so very far
from the sea, there were a lot of formalities to go through
before she could enter the port. As a result, the day was almost
gone when the tugboats got her alongside the big wooden pier
and the loading didn't begin till next morning.

The logs were floated alongside in great rafts and there was
a gang at each hatch to receive and stow them. Some of the
groups were made up of white men and some of Negroes; but
they all had Irish foremen in battered bowler hats. They were
marvellous to watch. Two of them, nimble as performing
seals, and working with long spiked poles, would sort out a log
from the raft and get a chain-sling around it. Then the winches
on the ship's deck would begin to clatter and up it would
come, lifting at an angle of about eighty degrees. The gang
on top-side would be ready for it. They were equipped with short
wooden handspikes which had a large steel claw working on
a hinge about eighteen inches up from the bottom end. This
was a wonderful tool. The claw was like the thumb to a man's
hand, only all that much bigger, and it fastened on the biggest
log—no matter how slippery it might be—with an unbreak-
able grip. They also had a few rollers which were just short
lengths of galvanised metal piping. With these and their own
magnificent strength they worked the great logs—some of

them sixty feet long—down the narrow hatches, then stowed them, neat, tight and immovable, until the holds were full to the deck beams.

As a spectacle the loading had football matches and athletic meetings licked hands down, and the two boys spent every minute of spare time they could wangle just standing and gawping. Each separate log was a challenge; it presented its own special problems and seeing them tackled and overcome was a thrill they would never forget. The town was completely forgotten and the weekend was upon them before they even thought of going ashore.

'We'll go Saturday afternoon,' said Jake. 'I've got enough money left from Belize to give us a run round and take in a flick. Cut along now and ask the Mate if you can go.'

'Me! Not on your life!' Corny suddenly felt badly done by and decided to play up. 'I'm asking the Mate for nothing. And I mean nothing. If he owned all the fresh air in the world I would choke sooner than ask him for a snootful of it.'

Jake stood up and spat on his hands. 'You'll ask him for Saturday afternoon off,' he said with quiet menace, 'or else...'

'All right, you big ape, I'll go—but under protest,' said Corny and, backing out of the messroom, he went.

The Mate had not yet forgiven him for the alligator. He made that plain. Then he said he was no longer interested in Corny; he had given him up for a bad job; and Corny could do what he liked, always providing he didn't set the town on fire, start a riot or land himself by any other means in the 'cooler'.

'What sort of talk is that to give a fellow, I ask you?' Corny demanded when he reported back to Jake. 'It's not decent.'

'You bought it!' Jake reminded him.

'You're telling me!' Corny snorted. 'And if that gleam in the old coot's eye means anything, there's more to come before

I leave the old ship for ever.'

He cheered up, however, when they got clear of the ship, and resolutely set out to enjoy himself. That was easy for a youngster in New Orleans, which is one of the most fascinating towns in the whole of America. Even the site of it is odd—a swamp fifteen feet lower than the surface of the river and so wet that the dead aren't buried in graves there but put in vaults twelve feet above the level of the streets.

The river is held back from the town by huge dykes of earth called levees and even the street names—Rampart, Canal, Magazine, St Charles—are a thrill somehow.

Most American cities are raw and new, laid out in blocks with wide streets between and evenly placed intersections; but New Orleans is a fascinating mixture of old and new; part Spanish, part French, and part modern American concrete and glass.

Jake and Corny wandered all over the place, stopping now and then at a drug-store, all plastic and chromium plate, for an ice-cream or a plain glass of fresh orange juice squeezed from the fruit while they waited. They found two cinemas to choose from. One was advertised as 'an acre of seats in a palace of splendour', and the other, as big as a football stadium, was an exact copy of the ruins of the Colosseum in ancient Rome. They opted for the phoney ruin and decided that, though it was a bit of a giggle and the film a flop, it was well worth the money. The builders had even worn down the stone steps to make them look old; and inside there were artificial flowers growing along the tops of the carefully broken walls. Best of all, though, was the ceiling. It was painted like a night sky with stars set in it.

'I rather care for that,' said Corny as they came out. 'Those great big stars twinkling and the little white fleecy clouds moving slowly across them for ever and ever. Wizard!'

Somehow he managed to keep himself out of mischief,

which was quite an achievement, and they got back on board all in one piece and in time for supper. It had been a day to remember and they turned in very well satisfied with themselves. But thoughts of the Mate came between Corny and his sleep, and at breakfast next morning he was as miserable as a wet hen.

'It's all right for you!' he said when Jake tried to jolly him out of it. 'You're sitting pretty. But me..! Do you realise we're sailing the day after tomorrow?'

'So what? We've sailed before.'

'I know. But three weeks after that I'll be packing my bag. And I don't want to go. The *Limpopo* might be a lousy old ship but she is where I belong.'

'You should have remembered that before you started fooling around with alligators.' Jake leaned forward. 'Look, Corny, why don't you go and apologise to the Mate; admit you were a stupid idiot and ask him to give you another chance.'

'Eat humble pie, you mean!' Corny pushed back his plate and glared at his room-mate. 'Not on your life! What do you think I am? I'd sooner eat the flipping alligator, stuffing and all.'

Jake managed to smooth him down a bit after a while but he still refused to play, though he did, after a lot of argument, agree to think it over.

He was still thinking it over when the loading was finished and the ship, dropping down-stream, anchored below the town to make her deck-cargo secure for the long haul home. This was quite a job and important because, before the end of the passage, the life of every man aboard could quite easily depend on it having been well done.

Jake and Corny were in the thick of it and they learned as they sweated.

To start with, lengths of stout chain had been shackled to ring-bolts in the deck so as to form wide loops or bights, which were left hanging over the side during the loading. Then wooden stanchions, twenty feet long and nine inches square, were set up in special sockets inside the bulwarks. The deck-cargo had been stowed between these uprights which were spaced about ten feet apart; and now the chain-bights were brought back inboard on to the top of the load. The next step was to weave a wire rope in and out through the chain-bights like the lace in a shoe, and make the end of it fast through a stretching screw and a slip-hook to a bollard on the bridge-deck. The standing part was then thrown on to the barrel of a winch, hove bar-tight, and finally stopped off on to another bollard.

That completed the lashings, and guard rails, four feet high, were now set up along the top of the load on both sides, fore and aft. These were made of light battens set twelve inches apart and nailed to the wooden uprights.

To finish off the job, the Bosun and the carpenter, with Jake and Corny in attendance, now crawled over every square foot of the load's upper surface. They each had a maul, which is a kind of heavy hammer, and a sack of wedges, one of which they belted into every suspicious crack and cranny they could find. When they had done, the deck load was as solid and as near to being part of the ship as human effort and the seafaring man's famous ingenuity could make it.

She sailed in the night, slipping down the great river in bright moonlight, and when the boys turned out next morning she was heading south-eastwards across the Gulf, and the passage home had already begun. Tortugas, at the entrance to the Florida Strait, was her next landfall and there she picked up the Gulf Stream, most famous of all ocean currents. Keeping right in the middle of it where it was strongest, she drove past Key West, going like a bomb, then headed north and east between the Atlantic coast of the United States and the Bahamas.

The Old Man could have turned off here and, passing through the North West Providence Channel, made a course south about via the Azores; but instead he decided to stand on to the northward until he was in the latitude of Cape Hatteras.

'From there,' the Second Mate explained to Jake and Corny, 'we'll steer on a "great circle" for Inishtrahull, on the north coast of Ireland. That's what's called going north about. It's a bit of a gamble so far as the weather goes, but three times out of four it pays off.'

So far it had been a good passage; warm sun, light winds and good visibility all the way; but in the end the gamble failed for the *Limpopo* and, four hundred miles north of Bermuda, she ran into strong head winds and a rough sea.

Nine days later and only a thousand miles nearer home she was still battling, logging little more than a hundred miles for a day's work and fighting to hold what easting she had made.

That nine days had left its mark on both the ship and her crew. She had been awash most of the time and when she wasn't shipping it green, the spindrift had smothered her from truck to water-line. Consequently her superstructure was caked in salt, her boat-covers and canvas dodgers, the storm lashing on her derricks and deck gear, and even the signal halyards on her jumper stay, bleached bone white by the ravening sea. As for the deck cargo, it was still solid, still secure, but coated in green sea slime, and the Bosun's oilskin was in ribbons, the bottom edge of it up under his arm-pits.

He and the carpenter, with Jake and Corny at their backs, still prowled the upper surface of the timber, knocking in wedges from dawn till dark.

'I'm beginning to hate wedges,' said Jake as they crawled wearily into their bunks that night.

'I'm beginning to look like one!' snorted Corny. 'Worn away to a sharp edge and my feet are killing me.'

'What about the Mate?' demanded Jake. 'Spoken to him yet? About the alligator, I mean.'

'Have a heart, brother! He's got enough on his plate with this lot!' Corny rolled over and shut his eyes. 'He'd bite my head right off by the shoulders, then throw me out on my ear.'

Jake agreed it might not be the best moment for asking favours of the Mate or anybody else aboard the old scow. 'But time's running out on you fast,' he said. 'You'll have to do something about it soon or you'll have missed the boat.'

He might just as well have saved his breath because Corny was already asleep and soon began to snore fit to waken the dead.

Meanwhile, the *Limpopo* battled on through the darkness. The weather, which had eased slightly around midday, had begun to deteriorate again after sundown; then about ten o'clock the wind backed a couple of points and became fiercer in the squalls. By midnight it was blowing a whole gale from a little east of south and the ship was headed into the teeth of it with her engines throttled back.

She was throwing about alarmingly, coming up on to her course each time she lifted to a sea and meeting it square, but behaving utterly unpredictably when she thrust her bows through its crest and flung up her stern for the plunge. The night was as black as the pit with blinding squalls of rain which mixed with the spindrift and drove across her in sheets, cascading from every angle of her superstructure when she lifted.

The helmsman steered by instinct and the feel of her, and the most he could hope for was to keep her from sliding broadside on into the trough. If he failed she would be unable to rise to the next sea which would break aboard her with all its force and weight, and work terrible havoc. He knew this and somehow held her up to it; but the man who took over at eight bells was less experienced, or perhaps didn't adjust quickly enough to her mood, and just before daybreak the thing everybody dreaded happened.

Shedding spent water like a breaching whale she reared up for the umpteenth time, swung her head into the eye of the wind then thrust through the crest into the howling emptiness beyond. For a moment or two she hung there, balanced in the darkness; then up went her stern to the screaming sky; up and up until her decks were almost vertical and the Second Mate, swaying back on his flexed knees and ankles, felt the tail of his coat sweep the planks at his back. There was the clatter of heavy gear going adrift below decks; then she plunged, swinging wildly to starboard as she came.

The unlucky helmsman swung the wheel for all he was worth and kept it going until it was hard over; but the rudder was practically out of the water now and she didn't answer.

She was broadside on when she hit the trough and the impact jarred through her like the shock of a depthcharge. Something had to go and it was the stanchions holding the deck-cargo along the port side of the foredeck that broke. They snapped like twigs and the great mass of timber behind them, sliding sideways, flattened the bulwarks outboard and hung there in the lashings, holding her down on her beamends.

Nothing much could be done about it in the darkness but, to be on the safe side, the Old Man, when he had rung off the engines, called all hands and mustered them amidships on the lower bridge. Jake was among them and so was Corny, binding bitterly about being robbed of his sleep.

'If they had to smash up the old scow,' he growled, struggling to get the legs of his pyjamas stuffed into the tops of his sea-boots, 'they might have had the decency to wait till I got properly dressed for it.'

'Think yourself lucky they bothered to rouse you out!'

retorted Jake. 'You're not all that popular, you know, and letting you drown in your bunk would be a nice quiet way of getting rid of you...'

As it happened, nobody was in any danger of drowning. The timber stowed tight in the lower holds took care of that and would keep her afloat even if she turned turtle or her bottom dropped out. But any movement aboard her was perilous and everybody stayed put till daybreak.

The light when it came brought no comfort. The ship was still on her beam-ends and the timber on the foredeck, stowed so neatly and with such tremendous effort and skill in New Orleans, looked as if it had been dropped there from a great height. The huge mass had slid away completely from the starboard side; about a third of it projected outboard now beyond the flattened port bulwarks; and its upper surface, level with the bridge-deck rail, was a tangled confusion of log-butts thrust up at all angles by the pressure. The ship herself was stopped and lay broadside on to the sea, rolling crazily as she swung up endlessly from trough to crest, only to drop as endlessly and dizzily back again.

'Looks a bit dicey!' said Corny. He turned to the Bosun. 'What do we do next?'

'There's only one thing we can do,' the Bosun answered. 'We'll have to jettison the cargo off the foredeck so that she can right herself.'

'But how?'

'Remember the slip-hook on the end of the lashing? This is the exact situation it was put there to meet. We take out the pin, knock off the link, the hook flies back and straightens itself on its hinge; that releases the lashing, which then unreeves itself from the chain-bights under the weight of the cargo held in them...'

Corny got the idea and wondered what the Old Man was waiting for. But the timber on the foredeck was worth thousands of pounds and the decision to let it go was not one that could be lightly taken. It had to be worked out, weighed up and measured, and every other possibility considered first.

While the Old Man deliberated, the crew waited and Corny studied the weather. The wind was as fierce as ever and the jumper stay—a heavy wire strung horizontally between the foremast cross-trees and the top of the funnel to carry signal halyards and the whistle lanyard—was twanging like a Welsh harpist in the groove. The halyards themselves, their ends made fast to cleats on the lower bridge, stood out bar-tight and screeched like banshees in the gale. It had stopped raining but the air was still full of hard-driven spray.

It was all of half an hour before the Old Man gave the order to slip and, because it seemed longer than a month of wet Sundays, the decision brought a sigh of relief from the watching crew. Then the Bosun and the carpenter slid down on to the bridge-deck and jumped to it. While one jerked out the pin from the point of the hook, the other hit the holding-link a belt with his maul that sent it flying. The hook straightened and the wire, whipping back off it viciously, began to unreeve.

It looked like a piece of cake and the odds were a million to one against anything going wrong; but before the bare end was clear of the first loop of chain, that one chance in the million had come off. The wire kinked about thirty feet forward of the bridge, then jammed itself and held the mass of timber to the ship again just when it was on the point of beginning to slide.

'What happens now?' croaked Corny.

'Search me!' answered Jake. He could see that anybody who crawled out on that timber to clear the snag would never get back alive. Even if he made it he would be a gonner when the deck load went. 'Looks as if this is where we came in and we're back up the creek, this time without a paddle.'

But Corny wasn't listening any more. He was staring at the

kink in the wire, thinking it was such a little thing to hold up all that heavy timber and to threaten such a fine ship and the lives of so many men. His glance swept up to the jumper stay, moved aft along it to the signal halyard, took in the angle it made to the deck-load and the fore-end of the bridge, then moved down the thin double line of cordage to where it was made fast to the rail about a yard in front of his nose. All this he did in less time than it takes to tell; and while Jake was still wondering what it was in aid of, he had made up his mind and exploded into action.

Swiftly, he cast off the signal halyard from the cleat and, thrusting one end into Jake's hand, whipped the other round his waist and fastened it off with a bowline.

'Life-line! Hold it taut and pay out as I go,' he snapped.

'And then?'

'Then belay when I yell and stand by to grab me on the back swing,' he said and, snatching up a maul somebody had left on the deck, he was over the rail and prancing across the tangle of timber before a hand could be raised to stop him.

Jake watched him with his heart in his throat. The kink might hold for a thousand years but Corny's weight could easily be the little bit extra that sprang the balance; and once the deck-load started to move, his life would hang on the slender thread of the signal halyard.

In the space between two deep breaths Corny had reached the kink and checked the run of it through the bight; then, balancing himself like an acrobat on the flying trapeze, he swung the maul and walloped the little loop of wire right on the button. The kink disappeared and the wire straightened with a low *zonking* sound, like the G-string breaking on a giant fiddle, and immediately started to unreeve again.

Corny watched, ready to hit it another bash; but that wasn't needed, for a moment later the timber started to slide. All he had to do now was to get back on to the safety of the

The ship was surrounded by leaping, plunging logs

lower bridge and he had already worked out the way. He would go through the air.

'Hold on!' he yelled and, slinging the maul into the sea, he reached up and got a firm grip on the halyard above his head, then kicked off from the shifting deck-load. Hanging like a pendulum from the jumper stay, he swung outboard in a wide arc forty feet above the crashing timber; then came back in again to land light as a bird on the lower bridge, where eager hands were ready to grab him and hold him safe.

And now all eyes were on the ship. She was surrounded by a smother of broken water and leaping, plunging logs; but as the dragging weight came off her foredeck, she slowly righted herself, and half an hour later she was under control again and back on her course.

The weather continued foul and it was another five days before she made her landfall, but she made it safely and, the night before she docked, the Mate sent for Corny.

'Well, my boy,' he said after telling him he might have broken his foolish neck, 'you've got a bold mind that works quickly and the guts to go with it. I'll make a fine seaman out of you by the time you've finished your apprenticeship.'

'Yessir! Thank you, sir!' spluttered Corny. 'But what about the alligator?'

'Oh that!' The Mate's hard grey eyes looked right into Corny's and never blinked. 'That was kid's stuff and I'm forgetting about it because I reckon you've grown up a bit since then.'

This took some working out and Corny felt there was a catch in it somewhere; but in the end he decided it was fair enough. It was even rather decent of the old coot and, though they made several more voyages together after that one, he never put another alligator or anything else into the Mate's bunk.

Bristow On Ice

It's because of those two trawlers grounding off the Dogger Bank the other day that I'm writing this. It's possible, after all, that Bristow's right about this ice business, and the stranding of those two trawlers may be the prelude to a catastrophe that is going to affect you and me, and perhaps most of Europe, too.

Just possible. Mind you, I'm still not convinced that Bristow hasn't gone clean off his rocker. For the sake of all of us I hope he has. Nevertheless, the whole business is odd, very odd indeed.

Just consider the facts. According to the latest Admiralty charts the depth of water at the position 54.51 N and 2.25 E, where the *Galahad* and *Lady Eleanor* ran aground, is ten fathoms: that is, sixty feet. An ocean liner should pass there with perfect safety, let alone a trawler of six hundred tons with a draught of no more than six or seven feet of water.

You may think that some error of navigation carried the trawlers five miles or so to the east, to the shallower waters of the Dogger. You may think it, but there is not a fisherman between Grimsby and Peterhead who will agree with you. Both *Galahad* and *Lady Eleanor* were skippered by men of ripe experience, whose life work has been fishing the North Sea and, in particular, the Dogger Bank.

And in any case, trawlers and drifters have sailed over the Dogger from north to south, from east to west, since time beyond all memory; and never, never—until the other day—has a single vessel run aground there.

No, argue as you will, there is no satisfactory explanation

55

of the loss of those two fine trawlers with all their gear and equipment. Unless, of course, you accept the rather absurd idea that an eccentric fellow named James Montgomery Algernon Bristow is responsible.

I shared rooms with Bristow when he first went up to Oxford. In those days he was a monstrously tall, skinny, round-shouldered youth of eighteen, wearing thick pebble spectacles which gave him a rather owlish expression, which was quite deceptive. In fact, he was a wonderfully clever young man, and quite inscrutable, betraying nothing of the strange and startling thoughts stirring so actively in his mind.

But there was an impish and irresponsible side to his character, too. I remember that in his last term at Oxford he climbed the tower of his college during a thick November fog merely for the satisfaction of tying the Dean's nightshirt to the weathervane.

But that happened a long time ago; and I dare say the eminent scientist, J. M. A. Bristow, Ph.D., F.R.S., has quite forgotten the incident. It would be an unkindness to remind him of it; and an injustice to deny him his brilliance and originality.

Yet this last assertion of his (he read it in a paper to the Society of Antiquaries last April)—this last assertion, I say, really does seem to overstep the mark. To put it briefly, his contention is twofold: first, that mankind has existed in a civilised state for almost countless ages; and secondly, that the Fourth Ice Age overwhelmed Europe in a matter of a few weeks.

He says that 50,000 years ago Britain was shaped as it is today, and inhabited by people as intelligent and in many ways as advanced in culture as we are. It was the last great Ice Age which wiped them out, wiped out all traces of them except a number of stone tablets which Bristow dug up in Pleistocene rock near Hastings two years ago.

These tablets are covered with strange cuneiform characters to which he found the key after several months of research. They appear to be reports received by a scribe or editor of those times, and tell for themselves the story of the Fourth Ice Age in a way that must either shock the scientific pundits or make them shake with mirth.

Bristow intended publishing a treatise on them to be called succinctly: 'Bristow on Ice.' But he's out of England now, and it's possible, just possible, that he may never return. The grounding of those Grimsby trawlers has decided me to forestall him in any event.

It must be understood that I accept no responsibility for the veracity of the narrative of the tablets. I have simply translated them from the cypher supplied to me, and they must stand or fall on their own evidence, or on evidence that may accumulate, perhaps, quite soon. Nor are all of them included here. When Bristow left England he took away with him nearly a dozen I have never seen.

I have, of course, arranged them in chronological order: the era 8540, of which the scribe speaks, would seem to correspond to about 50,000 B.C. in modern reckoning. Here, then, is the story:

TABLET THE FIRST: On the sixth day of the High Summer Season of the Era 8540 there was forgathered here the yearly meeting of the Men of Science. Father Cymlwm proclaimed an astounding proposition to this great meeting.

Father Cymlwm explained that coldness was merely the slowing down of electron movement in any piece of solid or of liquid, and asserted his belief that it was possible to bring this movement to a halt, and therefore to reach an absolute degree of cold.

He had already fashioned an apparatus to carry out his purpose, but since cold induced cold, and such an experiment might endanger the common people, their crops, and their cattle, he proposed to carry it out in some place far abroad. In the far north, where a good degree of cold was already established, he would find some suitable place, and thither he would sail before the Winter Season on this Island set in.

Though his opinions occasioned disbelief and even scorn with his learned hearers, his reasoning power and temerity in proposing such an experiment called forth much praise.

TABLET THE SECOND: Though it is nigh unto two hundred and fifty days since Father Cymlwm departed to the far north to carry out his experiment, no news has been received of him or his party. It may be that he and all who went with him have perished in some unreported disaster.

In the south part of this land, near to where I write, there has been observed a curious disturbance amongst the wild beasts. Rhinoceros, elephant, and even the long-toothed tiger have gathered in numbers in the coastal forests, as if they were of one mind to leave these shores for the mainland across the southern channel. Their excitement, which may be due to the unusual coldness of the season, is occasioning unusual danger to the men inhabiting these parts.

Out in the eastern sea, where the fish generally swarm thickest, the cold is considerable. Three fishing vessels have grounded on shoals which were not there ten days back, a thing for which there is no explanation.

TABLET THE THIRD: On the twenty-third day of High Summer Season of this Era 8541, disquieting tidings come in from mariners about the coast. It would seem that in the far northern seas there is not only a great white fog spread perpetually on the face of the waters, but the waters are rushing northward at a great pace like water gushing into a bowl.

A score of ships have been sucked up and carried away to the north, and no news of them has been received. There are vast shallows where once was deepest water and the cold is intense, and increases with the passing of each day.

Fishermen of the eastern and western seas are now in despair. They, too, report this strange northward current of the waters, and say there are no fish to be had. By some it is conjectured that the fish have turned to the south where the seas are warmer.

The shallows on our fishing grounds have increased greatly. Many more vessels have grounded, and there is no wind to shift them off the banks. The fog has stretched down from the northern seas, and seems to thicken with every day. Unless some fish are caught soon, it will go hardly with the poor people, for already it is said that many are starving and all pinched up with the great cold.

TABLET THE FOURTH: Now it seems that some terrible disaster is overtaking this land. Here in the southern part the cold is so intense that it is not easy to write. And there is much worse. Within twenty-five days all the seas about this island have disappeared. The places where they were are now naught but great river-beds, vast icy stretches of swamp on which the bodies of men and many vessels lie derelict. There is no sun to penetrate the fog, and the ships and the men's bodies would seem to be preserved in the swamps.

In the north of the land there can be no man left alive. It was reported from there that great and unusual beasts such as the hairy mammoth, the hairy rhinoceros, aurochs, bison, musk-ox and reindeer had miraculously crossed the northern sea and were heading fast for the south.

But when the fog lifted quickly men saw that the northern sea was but a great ice-blocked river-bed over which the strange beasts had crossed; and far beyond it there stood a great wall of ice that seemed to be advancing, withering all

The reindeer, bison, musk-ox, hairy rhinoceros and mammoth appeared

that grew with its cold. So the men fled in terror, leaving their dead uncovered, and the aged and young to do as they may.

It is the opinion of many that all the seas that once surrounded us have been sucked up into the great ice wall, and that it will come down on us, and destroy everything before it. And some believe that it is the experiment of Father Cymlwm which is encompassing the destruction of all his brethren. On this there can be no certain knowledge.

TABLET THE FIFTH: Now there is much distress through all parts of this land that are still habitable to man, and all people are in sore straits. The great ice wall advances with swiftness, and compels men to fly before it into the south.

Besides those many who have perished from the increasing cold, the water supplies that remain to us have frozen up, and to quench their thirst men are building great fires to unfreeze the ice, or are sucking the ice, which freezes them inwardly, and brings on a sort of colic which few have the strength to survive in their hungry state.

All the cattle are now dead; the grass has become like unto rock, and goats, sheep and kine have so fallen that not one in tens of hundreds is left. All the vegetation is withering and growing black beneath the great freeze.

The fog is thinning swiftly now, so that the sun can be seen like a great earth-coloured circle in the heavens. Men who have stood on the great hills of the Midland declare the fog there has quite gone, and say they saw the ice wall coming down on them clearly, and that the strange, northern beasts, especially the reindeer, are wandering freely on the lands they had cultivated.

In the hope of holding back the ice wall the men built fires, but to little purpose, for there were too few to keep the fires properly kindled, and the ice wall is so vast that it would seem nothing can hold its advance.

TABLET THE SIXTH: The natural beasts of this country which, fifty days gone, started to cross that stretch of land which was the southern channel, have now all departed. So great was their fright and their eagerness to be away that none would attack the other, though many fell and were trampled upon, or lay in the river-bed and perished there.

For the same space of time the birds have been moving southwards, so that at times the air is wild with their cries and the heavens are darkened with them as if by storm clouds. Many have perished in their flight, and smaller ones have dropped in such great numbers that they seemed like a rain of birds from the sky.

The influx of people here is such that there are no buildings to accommodate one-quarter of them, so that they lie about in the open and die from the cold. There is much brutal crime, and some are killed for the clothing they wear or for the food they are believed to carry with them. Everyone is desperate and nobody is safe.

Many tens of hundreds of men, with their women and children, are following the birds and beasts to the south, and night and day the beat of their feet and their cries can be heard here. In the darkness great fires are lit on the marsh that was the southern channel, and at these places they stop to warm themselves and gather strength for a space. Some are so weak they drop down and lack the strength to rise again, and none will heed their cries, and so they lie and perish.

TABLET THE SEVENTH: So many have departed that the country now is quietened. Only a few, the old and the wise, remain, knowing it is fruitless to flee before their destiny. The fog has all but gone, and the air for a space seems warmer, which they say is a sign the ice wall is upon us.

The reindeer, bison and musk-ox have appeared here, and in the west it is reported the hairy rhinoceros is invading the fields. But two days since there was seen here a new form of mammoth, a great beast covered all over with red fur. It went down to the bed of the southern channel and disappeared towards the south. From the heights here the ice wall is now quite visible. It is a great blue ridge which encompasses everything from one hand to the other, and ripples in the pale light of the sun like a hungry monster writhing as it devours the lands of men. And even as the sun curves above it, it grows larger and more hideous, which shows plainly how rapidly it comes down on us.

TABLET THE EIGHTH: All here is quiet. The birds and beasts have departed, and such few men as remain do not stir and make no sound. The air about has chilled again, and it is the chill of death. It is a chill which makes men contented and sleepy, as the heat of High Summer sun.

In two nights the ice wall has reared up monstrously, and soon it will have come down and covered everything of this once fair land. Only with the utmost labour are these things recorded, for the hand is indolent, and its strength fades fast. There awaits...

There the narrative of the tablets ends. A few fragmentary scratches follow the opening words of that last uncompleted sentence, as though the scribe had endeavoured to finish off his work in the last dim seconds of consciousness. A lively imagination might read in those scratches the words 'only death', but I do not.

The text, as I have rendered it, is a tight translation of all the tablets contain. There are no imaginings.

Make what you will of it. A hoax? Well, that's possible. I still remember how Bristow climbed the college tower with the Dean's nightshirt; and the title he proposed for his treatise on the tablets, 'Bristow on Ice', seems—well, unusual for a serious scientific document. Such thoughts are comforting.

But why did Bristow keep a dozen tablets to himself, and why did he take them with him when he departed so suddenly from England? Isn't it possible that in those tablets he has discovered Father Cymlwm's secret for establishing an Absolute Zero?

Let the scientists laugh. I know my Bristow better than any of them. In his philosophy anything is possible, and everything worth trying once.

Perhaps I'm becoming old and dull-witted. But I do wish I hadn't heard that Bristow turned up at Spitsbergen three months ago with a heap of scientific paraphernalia nobody could make head or tail of. Above all things I wish those wretched trawlers hadn't run aground well off the Dogger the other day.

The Stand-in

by CHARLES KING

It took something like three years for Johnny Lane to turn into Riff Arden. The guitar and the voice came first. The guitar was bought with the money Johnny Lane saved from his first nine months as a junior in the head office of a wallpaper firm in Maidstone. The voice was Johnny's own, a pleasant voice with a beat in it that Johnny strengthened and developed night after night in his bedroom at home, with one of Sinatra's discs on the turntable and a sweater stuffed under the door to stop his father grumbling about the noise.

A year after he bought the guitar, Johnny started singing with an amateur combo at pubs and charity concerts in the Medway towns, and nine months later Tod Anderson spotted him at a talent contest in Hastings and signed him up. Tod had a stable of singers and a genius for grooming raw youngsters with their hair slicked down by water into smooth ten thousand-a-week pop stars.

It was Tod who chose the name Riff Arden. It was Tod who put the attack into Johnny Lane's voice and changed his hair style and bought his clothes and taught him how to use his hands and eyes and feet. When Riff Arden made his first public appearance three months later, it was Tod who had created him.

Until Riff made the charts with his second disc, 'You're Fetchin'', he was still Johnny Lane for most of the time. Offstage he could still go into the coffee bar around the corner from the flat Tod had got for him near World's End, and nobody would recognise him. He could still change his mind and lose his temper and act crazy. He could still go his own way.

After 'You're Fetchin'' he went Tod Anderson's way. A million eyes were watching him now. Success put him on stage twenty-four hours a day, in the glossy hotel suites and the transatlantic jets as well as in the recording studios and the night clubs. He was Riff Arden all the time, the bright docile star that Tod Anderson had polished and put into orbit, and the impulsive Johnny Lane ceased to exist.

At least, Riff thought Johnny Lane had ceased to exist, but he was wrong. He discovered that twelve flashbulb-lit months later when Tod Anderson arranged for him to make his first film.

Tod told him about the film the day they signed the contract with the Apex Production people at Shepperton. Riff was driving Tod back to London in his Jag. He had put his signature on the contract the way he did everything these days, obediently.

'In this film you play the part of a young taxi-driver,' Tod told him.

'That puts me one up on Cliff. He only drove a bus.'

'So you go on holiday to Cornwall, and you meet this girl.'

'I can guess the rest.'

'No, there's a twist. The girl's got money, she's loaded with it. Her old man's a property tycoon and he owns a fifty-bedroom mansion on top of the cliffs with a private beach and a yacht, and the girl's got her own Mercedes.'

'She sounds fascinating.'

'She is. She fascinates you, anyway. So you pretend you're the son of a millionaire and you have this romance with her. The two of you go yachting together and surf-riding together and at night you sing to her all alone on a moonlit beach.'

'With a symphony orchestra and a male-voice choir lurking behind the rocks.'

'Then the girl discovers that you're only a taxi-driver. You

66

quarrel. This happens up at the mansion, and you dash outside in a fury and jump into the Mercedes that the villain's tampered with.'

'What villain?'

'I've left him out. I'm trying to keep this simple.'

'You're doing a grand job.'

'So you drive the roadster like hell along the cliff road, and suddenly the brakes fail and you have a terrific dice with death around the hairpin bends with a sheer drop to the sea two hundred feet below... Hey, slow it down, Riff.'

'Sorry, Tod,' Riff said, taking his foot off the accelerator. 'I got carried away by the plot.' Suddenly his eyes were shining. 'So I'm dicing with death, am I?'

'You're thinking of the girl, see? You don't want to wreck her car. But at the last moment, when the car plunges off the road and hurtles over the cliff, you throw yourself out. The car smashes itself to bits on the rocks below, and when the girl comes along and sees the wreck she's heartbroken. She thinks you're dead, and she realises now that she loves you...'

Riff said, grinning happily, 'You know, I think I'm going to like making this film, Tod.'

'Of course you are, Riff boy. We've got Edie Gaynor to play opposite you.'

'You could get a monster from outer space and I'd still like it. That gimmick with the runaway car on the cliff road sounds like a lot of fun.'

'Well, of course, we'll have a pro stand-in for you on that sequence,' Tod said. 'A stunt man. He'll do all the dangerous stuff. We don't want you taking any risks, do we?'

He was chuckling pleasantly when he said that, but the chuckle was wrenched out of his mouth as the car braked. He grabbed at the door strap. Riff mangled the handbrake and glared at him.

'You're kidding, Tod, aren't you?' he said.

'What's got into you, Riff?'

'Being wrapped in cottonwool, that's what's got into me. No, you're not really going to get a stand-in for me, are you?'

'Of course we are. That car stunt is dangerous. You don't think we'd let you handle it, do you?'

'Why not?'

'Be your age, Riff. You're a star. We can't have you risking your neck.'

'I could handle the job as well as any stunt man.'

'Maybe you could, but I doubt it. These boys are specialists. That's not the point, anyway. You're the man with the face and the voice. You stick to the sweet talk and the singing, Riff, and we'll all be happy.'

'Correction,' Riff said, savagely. 'You'll all be happy except me'.

Tod stared at him, frowning. He said, 'I've never seen you act this way before, Riff.'

'I've never felt this way before,' Riff said. 'Not for three years, anyway. Not since you turned me into Riff Arden.'

'But a two-bit stunt with a runaway car, why should that be so important to you?'

'It's not just the stunt, it's doing it myself, not having a stand-in. It's a matter of self-respect.'

'But the fans won't know it's not you in the car.'

'I'll know,' Riff said.

Tod looked at him carefully. He smoothed his hair down, choosing his words. He said, in that quiet voice with the steel in it that he used at moments of crisis, 'We're going to make this film, Riff. We're going to use a pro stunt man as a stand-in for you on the runaway car sequence. You don't want me to hit you with your contract, do you?'

'I want you to look at it my way.'

'I am, Riff. I'm playing it safe for you.'

'Oh, all right,' Riff said, 'all right.'

He drove the car with a smouldering exaggerated care back into London. The speedometer needle never touched thirty all the way. Tod Anderson said nothing as they crawled through the rush-hour traffic but he asked Riff up to his flat when they got to Berkeley Square.

Edie Gaynor was there. Riff had met her at a Variety Club lunch when they were both presented with Most Promising Newcomer of the Year Awards. She was blonde and shapely and cool, and she had a nice dry edge to her tongue when she bothered to use it.

Tod poured them drinks and glanced at Riff under his sleek eyebrows and said, 'You two kids get together, while I make a couple of phone calls, will you? Riff's got this needle, Edie. Maybe you can talk some sense into him.'

He closed the door softly behind him. Edie watched Riff for a moment. She said, 'Do you want to talk about it?'

'Not much.'

'I know those kid gloves of Tod's, the ones with concrete in the fingers.'

Her voice was just the right blend of coolness and sympathy. It braced Riff. He grinned at Edie and shrugged his shoulders and told her about the runaway car sequence in the film and Tod's plan to use a stand-in for him. The queer thing was that while he talked about it he began to see a way around the problem.

Edie said, when he had finished, 'Well, you can see Tod's point of view, can't you? You're an investment, a financial asset. I mean, he couldn't let a financial asset go belting along the cliffs in a car without brakes, could he?'

'Oh, of course not.'

'And think of an investment breaking its neck.'

'Painful.'

'No, you'll have to do as Tod wants,' Edie said, 'you'll have to sit safely on the beach in the moonlight with me, and leave the heroics to the hired man.'

Riff grinned at her and stood up. He had looked all around the problem now and it was no problem at all. The thing could be worked perfectly, and it would add to the fun, and Tod Anderson need never know.

'We'll see about that,' Riff said.

The film unit had been on location in Cornwall for three weeks before they shot the runaway car sequence on the cliffs above Tregenna Bay. Riff found out when they planned the take by a casual questioning of the camera crew. He took care not to mention the subject to Tod Anderson, who had been tenderly watchful ever since their argument on the way back from Shepperton.

Riff himself behaved with all his old easy obedience through those three summer weeks. He went surf-riding with Edie Gaynor while the cameras turned, and sat on the deserted beach in the moonlight and sang to her with the help of the symphony orchestra and the male-voice choir. He even played the scene where he ran angrily from the mansion and jumped into the Mercedes without turning a hair.

All Tod said, watching him carefully as he climbed out of the stationary car after the take, was, 'O.K., Riff?' And all Riff said, with a rueful good-humoured smile that was a little masterpiece of acting, was, 'Heck, I suppose so, Tod. O.K.'

The professional stunt man turned up two weeks after filming had begun. Called O'Hara, about the same height and build as Riff, he was a lean brown man, with a crew-cut. He drove a lemon-yellow station wagon with black lettering which said Calculated Risks Incorporated on the door panels, and nattered self-importantly to the director and the camera men before going up to survey the cliff road.

As far as Riff could see, the set-up was perfect. He had surveyed the cliff road himself, secretly one moonlit night when the rest of the film unit were asleep in their 'digs' in Tregenna village. He found out that O'Hara was staying at the 'Falcon' in Truro, that he would be driving the thirty miles to Tregenna every day in the station wagon, and that he usually wore tan overalls and dark glasses on the job. All he needed now, Riff thought, was luck.

O'Hara himself obviously did not believe in luck. He spent a week sizing up the cliff road. The first two days he walked along every inch of it on foot with a tape measure in one hand and a camera in the other. The next two days he spent studying his photographs and notes. The rest of the week he drove along the cliff road in the Mercedes from dawn to dusk, rehearsing the action minutely at various speeds, working out his line around the hairpin bends, and timing the leap he would have to make when the car finally plunged over the edge.

Riff heard about all that from one of the cameramen, a spotty youth with a talent for hero worship who thought O'Hara was great. Riff considered O'Hara was overdoing the difficulty of the job, but he supposed that a professional stunt man had a vested interest in reducing the risks to a minimum. He himself kept right away from the cliff road and O'Hara while all this was going on. It was vital to his plan that O'Hara should not see him in the flesh.

On the day before the runaway car sequence was to be shot, Riff sought out Tod Anderson. He said, keeping his voice low and rather mournful, 'You're filming that cliff-road scene tomorrow, aren't you, Tod?'

Tod looked at him sharply. 'Yes. What about it?'

'Oh, nothing. I was just wondering...'

'If you're still angling to do the stunt yourself, Riff, you can forget it.'

'Please, Tod.' Riff looked hurt. 'I was only going to ask whether I could have the day off. You're not using me on film tomorrow, and with that glory boy defying death on the cliff road in place of me, I'd rather be... well, I'd rather not hang around and watch it...'

Tod was contrite. 'Don't take any notice of me, Riff,' he said. 'I was born looking over my shoulder. Of course you can take the day off.'

'I thought I'd just go for a tramp on the moors on my own. I need a break, anyway.'

'You do that, Riff boy. Enjoy yourself.'

'Oh, I will, Tod,' Riff said, 'I certainly will.'

He started early next morning. He had denims on and a sports shirt, and dark glasses in his pocket. He walked three miles inland to the little station on the railway line from Tregenna, and made sure he had not been spotted, and caught the next train to Truro.

At Truro he bought a sweater in a knitwear shop near the town hall. It had scarlet sea horses wallowing all over it and would take attention off his face very nicely, he thought, as he pulled it over his shirt and put his dark glasses on. He had a quick coffee at a tearoom and then walked around to the 'Falcon'.

The yellow station wagon was parked in the yard. He turned in under the archway and stood peering at the black lettering on the doors with a pantomime interest. He had timed it nicely. He was still standing there and goggling at the station wagon when O'Hara came out of the inn door.

Riff moved aside respectfully. This was the trickiest moment and his heart was thumping, but he controlled his voice. He put a trace of Cockney into it and said, 'Gosh, is this your car?'

O'Hara grinned at him. Obviously he saw only an admiring teenager in a home-knitted sweater, and what little he could see of Riff's face meant nothing to him. He said, 'It is that. What would be your interest in it, sonny?'

'Oh, nothing. I mean...' Riff pointed shyly to the lettering on the yellow door. 'Well, Calculated Risks Incorporated... it sounds an exciting sort of business.'

'Sure, and it has its moments,' O'Hara said. He was carrying the tan overalls on his arm, and he opened the door of the station wagon and dropped them inside. He grinned at Riff again. 'Not to be making a mystery of it, I'm a film stunt man.'

'Gosh, are you?'

'Aye well, it's a job like any other.' He paused, getting into the driving seat. 'You wouldn't be wanting a lift by any chance?'

'Well, I'd got a railway ticket, but gosh that'd be terrific... but I don't suppose you're going my way... I was making for Tregenna...'

O'Hara grinned and got behind the driving wheel and reached across to hold the door open. 'Climb in, sonny,' he said 'It's Tregenna I'm going to myself.'

He was talking hard before they left Truro behind, about the film they were shooting on location at Tregenna and the stunt he was going to do today and the way he planned his stunts. Riff just propped his mouth open and let him do the talking. He had read O'Hara correctly. The man was a glutton for a breathless audience.

They were a couple of miles short of the spot Riff had chosen on the moors, midway between Truro and Tregenna, when Riff said, flirting with danger, 'This chap you're doubling for, Riff Arden, what's he like?'

'Ah well, he's a nice enough young fellow. He's got this voice, you know, and he strums the guitar a bit. I'll not be saying anything against him.'

'He's big-headed, is he?'

'No, now I'd be wrong to say that. No, he talks a bit fancy at times but he's not above coming to a fellow like me for advice. I've put him right on a couple of things, I can tell you.

Well, me being a man of the world, you know, and risking my neck on that cliff road for him in a manner of speaking, well you can see what it is.'

'I certainly can,' Riff said, maliciously. 'He sounds chicken to me.'

'Ah no, that's pitching it a bit strong. Timid is what I'd call Mr Riff Arden. But then, you can't blame the young fellow. You need a cool nerve and plenty of guts to throw a car along that cliff road without using your brakes, and it's not surprising he's asked me to stand in for him. But there, maybe I shouldn't be speaking this way about him.'

Riff bit back the hot words and stared out of the window. They were fifteen miles from Truro and fifteen from Tregenna now, and the empty moors rolled away to the horizon all around them. He had felt sorry for O'Hara when he had chosen this spot, but he was rubbing his hands now.

He said suddenly, twisting his head round in alarm, 'What was that?'

'Eh?'

'A sort of knocking noise.'

'I didn't hear anything.'

'There it goes again. At the back. It wouldn't be the axle, would it?'

O'Hara swore and pulled the station wagon towards the verge and braked. He said, 'Now wouldn't that be just my luck, with the clouds piling up and maybe an hour of sunshine left and the cameras waiting to turn at Tregenna and me stuck out here with a broken-down car. And we haven't seen another living soul on the road all morning. Why, we'd have a five-mile walk to the nearest phone, I'm thinking, and then an hour to wait till we could get another car.'

He left the engine running and snapped open the offside door. He said, as he hurried around to the back of the station wagon, 'But maybe it's nothing to worry about at all.

Maybe it's your imagination, sonny.'

Riff was already sliding into the driving seat. He glanced over his shoulder and made sure O'Hara was still clear of the car, then he slammed her into second. 'You're right, Mr O'Hara, I've got a vivid imagination,' he said out loud with savage satisfaction as he punched the accelerator.

The station wagon roared away up the road. Riff glanced back once in the wing mirror. O'Hara was standing stock-still in the dust with his hands out before him, like a man seeing visions. Riff felt one small twinge of remorse that he stifled. At worst, O'Hara would have a long walk, and he had asked for that with his snide remarks about Riff Arden. And the plan had worked too well for Riff to feel anything but a swift, triumphant happiness.

He drove fast for ten minutes. He stopped the car five miles from Tregenna and took off his sweater and pulled on O'Hara's tan overalls which were lying on the back seat. With his dark glasses on he would pass for O'Hara at anything over a few feet, and he would have to hope for the breaks when he got to Tregenna.

He got the breaks. There was a technician with a megaphone standing by one of the film company's trucks on the outskirts of the village. As Riff slowed the technician shouted, 'Keep going, O'Hara. We've got about twenty minutes of sunlight left. They want you up at the mansion right away. The cameras are ready.'

Riff put his foot down and swung right on to the climbing coast road. He drove up at speed, keeping his head lowered. There were cameras sited in the rocks above the road at several points, and little knots of bit-players and villagers and sightseers. It was only when he got near to the mansion at the top of the road that he realised he had been using his brakes hard at every bend, and remembered that on the way back in the Mercedes he would have to do it without brakes.

He started to sweat then. He had been so determined to do without a stand-in that he had hardly given a thought to the stunt itself. He gave a thought to it now and his heart lurched. There was death waiting for him at every one of those vicious hairpin bends, an ugly death on the jagged rocks hundreds of feet below.

The station wagon was rolling up the sanded drive towards the mansion now. This was the moment when Riff Arden could have called the whole thing off. There were clusters of technicians everywhere and Tod Anderson was standing with the director by the camera on the steps of the mansion. Riff stared at Tod with a momentary regret and longing as the station wagon slowed.

He could climb out now and just swallow his pride. He could apologise to Tod and admit that Tod had been right. He could get rid of this awful aching fear in the pit of his stomach and go back to being the bright, successful, comfortable Riff Arden. He could stay alive.

Riff said suddenly, fiercely, 'No, no, no', and banged the wheel with his clenched fist. There was something deep down inside him, deeper than the fear, that would not accept the easy way out. It was something stubborn and rebellious, pride perhaps or just self-respect, but Riff had to obey it.

The Mercedes was parked halfway down the outward leg of the drive, facing the gates. There was no one near it. Riff saw his chance and accelerated past the group of people which included Tod on the steps of the mansion. He just waved his hand to them and drove fast towards the Mercedes and braked close beside it.

A couple of technicians came running along the drive as Riff climbed out of the station wagon. By the time they got to him he was crouched behind the wheel of the Mercedes. They could have seen nothing of him but the crew-cut head and the dark glasses and tan overalls that all belonged to O'Hara.

Riff kept his head down as they shouted to him. He pressed the starter and revved the engine and waved a hand to them. One of them was shouting, 'Take it away, O'Hara. We're ready to roll.'

As Riff let in the clutch, the other man shouted, 'Don't forget you've got brakes if you need them. We'd rather lose a few feet of film than a man's life.'

Riff found second gear and released the clutch. He shouted back, defiantly 'You won't lose either. And I won't be needing the brakes,' and rammed his foot hard down on the accelerator.

*   *   *   *

The road from the mansion to Tregenna village is steep and narrow. It is cut into the cliff and winds sharply with the eroded curves of the cliff face two hundred feet above the sea. There are bare slabs of rock on the inner side of the road and on the outer side nothing but a strip of wind-cuffed grass and the sheer drop.

The Mercedes took the first bend at fifty, with Riff easing off on the accelerator and holding the wheel hard over against the drift. The cameras had tracked him through the gates of the mansion and more cameras picked him up as he came out of the first bend and gathered speed with the slope of the road.

The second bend was a hairpin. He took it at sixty, coming in too close to the inner side and wrenching the wheel around at the last moment so that the Mercedes rocked against her springs and the tyres sobbed in the dust and the sightseers on the rocks above opened black mouths in the white cluster of their faces.

Riff rubbed his left hand on his chest and then his right hand, carefully. They were both greasy with sweat. The needle of the speedometer was flickering around sixty-five now and the next bend was looming in the windscreen. He realised suddenly that his right foot was hovering instinctively over the brake.

He clamped the foot viciously down on the floor. He was not going to use the brake. He was not even going to use the gears if he could help it. This was supposed to be a dice with death, and he was going to give the fans their money's worth.

He took the third bend too wide, not concentrating until it was too late and then jerking the wheel too hard. The Mercedes bucketed around with three feet to spare and Riff was still unclenching his hands from the wheel when he hit the fourth bend.

He came out of that one with his eyes shut. There had been nothing but sea and sky in the windscreen as the road curved away and the car hurtled towards the two hundred foot drop, and he must have closed his eyes instinctively. But he had leaned on the wheel as well because suddenly the rock wall was looming ahead and the Mercedes had got around the bend and was coming out too sharply.

He dragged the car back, easing his hands on the wheel, unclenching his muscles. He began to see why O'Hara had studied his speed and his line into the bends. He was only a third of the way past the cameras and already the car was getting out of control.

He just let his hands rest on the wheel going into the fifth and sixth bends, taking the Mercedes on the flattest angle across the corners and drifting from the cliff edge on one straight to the cliff edge on the next. It took nerve but he found he had it. Suddenly the panic fear had gone.

But the Mercedes was doing eighty now. The sheer speed was dragging the wheels off the line as he tried to ease the car away from the yawning drop. He was fighting the car and the wheels were skidding nearer and nearer the edge on every bend and the sky and the rock were flickering faster and faster across the windscreen.

The offside rear wheel lurched suddenly. The whole car slewed around as the wheel spun on air and gouged at the cliff edge and bit back on to the grass and road. A shower of stones dropped through the sunlight and smashed on to the rocks far below.

The Mercedes screamed on towards the next bend and the next, fishtailing violently now, snaking from side to side of the road, almost out of control with ninety on the speedometer and the tyres smouldering and Riff living a cold clear waking nightmare as he waited for the big drop and the long fall and death.

But he saw the red board on the road ahead first. Suddenly, he saw the red board that marked the end of the camera-tracked run and the corner where the script called for the Mercedes to plunge off the cliff. He fought the wheel for the last time, dragging the tortured car back for a straight run at the cliff edge, quite calm now as he came to the end of the job.

He kept his left hand clamped on the wheel and wrenched open the offside door of the Mercedes. When the tyres hit the grass verge he threw himself sideways and through the flailing door. He seemed to fall a long way, turning his shoulder, letting his body go limp. He hit the grass hard and rolled.

There was twenty foot of grass verge from the road to the cliff edge on this corner. It had been chosen because there was enough room, just enough room, for a man to dive from the car and stop rolling before he reached the edge. Riff stopped rolling with three feet to spare and his feet kicking dust over the edge and his fingers clawed into a bush.

He lay there winded, dragging breath into his lungs, listening. A long time afterwards he heard the scream of tortured metal that was the Mercedes smashing itself to bits on the rocks two hundred feet below at the foot of the cliffs, and then the thump as the petrol tank blew up. He still lay there, clutching the earth, until he heard voices on the road above.

He looked up then. A group of technicians and sightseers were running along the road, shouting and waving. They were forty yards away still, and Riff realised with a sudden shock as memory returned that it was O'Hara who was supposed to be lying here and not him.

The bush he was clinging to was the outer edge of a thick belt of scrub that ran downwards between the road and the cliff edge for a couple of hundred yards. The scrub was head-high in places and tunnelled out by paths. Riff took one more look at the people on the road above, got up stiffly on hands and knees and dived into the scrub.

He worked his way downhill fast without stopping. When he came out on the far side of the belt of scrub, the voices were calling and arguing on the cliff edge where the Mercedes had gone over. He stripped off O'Hara's tan overalls and dropped them on the grass. The bend of the road hid him from the people up there, and he just crossed the road and climbed the rocks on the far side and went on walking until he was a mile inland from the cliff and the danger of discovery.

He lay down on the grassy hillside then and rested. The dive from the car had bruised him and there were scratches on his hands and wrists but he felt good. He felt terrific. He had done the job himself. He had kept his self-respect.

*   *   *   *

Two hours later, Riff walked back towards the cliff road. He paused at the crest of the hill and looked down there. A battered old pre-war Austin was toiling up the road from the village with a wisp of steam curling from its bonnet, and a crowd of actors and technicians were gathering in the road to meet it.

O'Hara climbed out of the Austin. Riff was too far away to recognise him, but it had to be O'Hara. He must have hiked and cadged lifts all the way back to Tregenna, and from the way he was throwing his arms in the air and wagging his head, he was hopping mad. After ten minutes the yellow station wagon came down the road from the direction of the mansion and O'Hara climbed into it with a last shake of his fist and drove off.

Riff gave the crowd another ten minutes to disperse, then he just sauntered casually down to the rocks above the road and stood there looking around him interestedly. One of the cameramen saw him and shouted, and Tod Anderson and the director came running along the road.

Tod shouted, 'Riff! Come down here.'

'O. K., Tod.' Riff waved to him cheerfully. 'Have you got that stunt sequence in the can? How did it go?'

He scrambled down from the rocks to the road and stood looking from Tod to the director with a nicely-timed change in expression from friendly interest to bewilderment. Tod was furious and the director was grinning slyly and shaking his head.

'You know how it went, don't you, Riff?' Tod said, with menace in his voice.

'Do I?'

'You were in that Mercedes.'

'I was... *what?*'

'Somebody was in the Mercedes, and it wasn't O'Hara.'

Riff let his mouth drop open and stared at Tod. Then he laughed. Then he smothered the laugh and looked serious and said. 'You're kidding, Tod. What happened to O'Hara?'

The director said, 'Somebody hitched a lift from him at Truro this morning, and then stranded him on the moors fifteen miles from Tregenna and drove off in the station wagon. He was a tall kid, O'Hara said, wearing denims and a sweater with sea horses on it and dark glasses.'

'Sea horses?' Riff said.

'This isn't funny,' Tod said. 'Whoever the kid was, he put O'Hara's overalls on and turned up here in the station wagon and took over the Mercedes. We were in a hurry with the sunlight going, and nobody bothered to check that it was O'Hara, and the kid drove the car down this road and over the cliff in front of the cameras.'

Riff said, 'Holy smoke', and widened his eyes, but he must have overdone it. Tod glared at him angrily and shook his head. 'Let's cut the comedy, shall we, Riff?' he said.

'Tod, you're not accusing me of driving that car, are you?'

'Where were you today, then?'

'Out on the moors. Walking for some of the time, and just lazing, having the day off as you said I could.'

'Riff, you're lying...'

'Now steady on, Tod...'

The director rubbed an agitated hand over his head. 'Yeah, take it easy, Tod,' he said. 'All right, so Riff says it wasn't him in the Mercedes. So what does it matter who it was? We've got a hundred feet of red-hot film in the can. That was the greatest stunt I've seen in years. That car came down the road like a bat out of hell. None of your pro stunt man dodges like taking the safest line and holding her in third, no crafty braking between cameras, just whoosh around the bends at ninety with one wheel over the edge and the tyres screaming, and then wham clean off the cliff. I tell you it'll knock 'em cold in the two and ninepennies. Heck, they're still trying to bring some of the cameramen round.'

Tod took a deep breath and looked at Riff. He grinned wryly. He said, 'All right, so it was quite a stunt. But whoever drove that car took an awful risk. It was just luck he didn't kill himself and no one ought to push his luck that hard.'

'I think you're right, Tod,' Riff said, quietly.

'He must have had a pretty good reason for dicing with death like that, this kid whoever he was.'

'Maybe he did have a good reason,' Riff said.

'Yes, well I'm just a manager with a cash register instead of a heart,' Tod said, 'so I wouldn't know about that.' He looked at the ground. 'O. K., Riff. For the record, it wasn't you who took O'Hara's place. It was somebody else behind the wheel of that Mercedes.' He looked up suddenly and grinned at Riff and put a hand on Riff's arm. 'But that was one hell of a drive, Riff. I hope it got something out of your system.'

He walked away with the director. Riff stood looking after him and smiling. He was thinking about his reason for dicing with death and remembering an impulsive kid with a brand-new guitar and a pleasant voice, a kid who could still go his own way. He was still standing there when Edie Gaynor came running up.

She put an arm around his neck and clung to him. Her eyes were not cool any more. She said, 'You fool, Riff... oh, you fool...'

'No, listen, Edie, I've been thinking,' Riff said. 'I did have a stand-in for that runaway car sequence, after all.'

'But, Riff...'

'He was a kid from Maidstone,' Riff Arden said, grinning. 'Name of Johnny Lane...'

Imperno Strikes Again

by NICHOLAS MARRAT

The man was small, rat-faced, with greasy black hair and the fast jerky actions of a frightened rabbit. He grabbed the shoe-shine kit, whipped it under his arm and pelted off down Avenue Gonzales.

Imperno Quartaro saw the thief take his treasured shoe-shine kit. Treasured because with it he earned part of his living. But he didn't at once speed after the man. Imperno had learned many things since he came to the city. He had learned to think fast and to move fast, yet not to move in a panic, without thought.

Avenue Gonzales was wide, with broad sidewalks shaded by palm trees and bordered with gay umbrellas of café tables. A running man could be seen for a long way among the leisurely-strolling, well-dressed crowds. So Imperno watched and waited.

'Into the fish-sellers' quarter you must go,' Imperno muttered to himself. 'If you run far along Avenue Gonzales the police will stop you because you have no numero on your arm.'

All shoe-shine boys were licensed by the police, and a licence wasn't easy to get. In fact, it was impossible unless you knew which official to bribe. And there were streets where the shoe-shine boys were not allowed. Avenue Gonzales was one of these streets.

'You are a poor fool,' said Imperno, still watching the hurrying thief. 'You should have run the other way. Ah! Now you are turning off the Avenue.'

Only then did Imperno give chase. But not along Avenue

Gonzales. Imperno sped through a parking bay, dived across a traffic roundabout, dodging the wheels of zooming Cadillacs, and raced into a narrow alley. He emerged at the end of the fish-sellers' quarter, turned left and halted, waiting calmly for the panting thief to reach him.

'Hola!' Imperno barred his way. 'You are a stinking thief who steals the living of an honest boy. Give me back my shoe-shine kit.'

'Out of my way!' the rat-faced man snarled. 'Or I'll slice you in half!' A knife appeared in one hand.

Imperno shrugged and stepped aside. 'My miskate, señor,' he murmured.

But as the man moved on, so Imperno's foot flashed out, then his fist. His foot hit the man's knee, causing him to drop swiftly. This brought his neck level with Imperno's shoulder so that the fist, with middle knuckle extended, zonked hard on the exact spot. The man gasped and fell like a pole-axed steer. As his knife-hand touched the ground, Imperno trod on it, forcing the knife free. This he kicked into the gutter, then yanked the shoe-shine kit away and slung it over his own shoulders.

'You are stupid,' said Imperno, gazing down at the still gasping man. 'And mean — and with no brains. You are not even a clever thief.'

'Oh, my head!' the man moaned. 'Oh, my shoulder! Oh, my hand! I am dying! You are a fiend!'

'Your head will ache for a while and your shoulder will be stiff and your hand will hurt. But you should be glad I do not like violence, else you might indeed be dying,' said Imperno. 'Now tell me — what shall I do? Shall I drag you to the police, who will beat you and throw you into prison for stealing, or do you pay me for my time and trouble?'

'Not the police! No, not the police!' the man begged.

'No,' Imperno agreed, 'not the police because no doubt you

are wanted by them. So you will pay me for my time and trouble in chasing you. That is fair business, yes?'

'I have no money,' the man protested.

'Then I will stay with you until you get some. We will be amigos — but not for long as it will not help my reputation to be seen with a low-life thief like you.'

'I will pay you ten dollars.'

'Pooh! What is ten dollars! I will take fifty.'

'Never,' said the man, climbing to his feet and groping his way to the nearest doorway.

The sightseers dispersed. They weren't very interested anyway. There was no blood. No fight was worth watching unless there was blood.

Imperno picked up the knife from the gutter and said:

'This is worth two dollars. Now you owe me forty-eight.' He waved the knife menacingly. The man shrank back, not knowing that Imperno never fought with knives.

'No,' he said. 'No, do not touch me.' He fumbled in a pocket. 'I will give you lottery tickets. See — they are five-dollar tickets. I will give you ten and you keep the knife — that is a good bargain.'

'Lottery tickets are for fools like you,' said Imperno. 'I do not gamble.'

The man grinned slyly. 'Nor do I, my friend. I am a ticket agent.'

'Then you should not need to steal.'

The man shrugged. 'I have much trouble. A wife and seven children to keep. *Por Dios*, such trouble I have!'

'You are a liar. The likes of you do not have a wife and seven children. But I think maybe you have stolen some ticket money and do not want to see the police. I have wasted enough time on you. I will take ten tickets. Show me your ticket-seller's licence.'

The man pulled a grubbly pasteboard from his pocket.

'Rubo de Marco,' Imperno read. 'And the Carlotta brothers are your main agents. They are a pair of sharks! You are in good company. But I am sorry for you because, if you have stolen ticket money, the Carlotta brothers will not go to the police. They will slit your throat — slowly. Now vamoose, pronto!'

Rubo de Marco scuttled away and disappeared among the fish-sellers.

Imperno leaned against the wall and said to himself:

'Too easy. Much too easy. Of course, I am very good and strong in the fight, and Rubo is a little scared rat. But even so – it was too easy. Why?'

He glanced up and saw a portly fish-merchant waddling towards him.

'Shine, señor!' Imperno cried. 'Shine your worthy shoes, I beg you! My family is crying for food. Shine, señor!'

The merchant paused, observing the clean face and bright eyes of the pleading boy. It was tradition in the city for merchants to be charitable to shoe-shine boys. Many merchants had begun their own business lives as shoe-shine boys, and by smart dealing, bribery and general know-how had accumulated wealth. At the end of a prosperous day it was good for a man's soul to aid the poor.

'Set up your kit,' said the merchant. 'And if you make these shine, I will give you two dollars.'

'Right away, señor — many thanks.' Imperno squatted on his hunkers, set the small stand in front of him and began work.

It was hard work because the merchant's shoes were greasy with fish scales. But Imperno had learned about such tricks from the meat market where, if you didn't shine greasy shoes, you got a cuff across the head instead of money. It was all part of the fun and games of earning a living in the big city. So Imperno carried a small bottle of very strong spirit in his kit. This removed the grease and enabled him to make the shoes shine. Two days later, as the spirit worked into them, the shoes would split, but by then the owner had forgotten which shoe-shine boy had last cleaned the shoes. And even if he remembered — who could prove that Imperno used anything but polish and brush and hard labour?

When he saw the shining shoes, the fish-merchant flung two dollars on the ground and said:

'One day you will be rich like me. You work hard and well. That is the way to make money. Are those lottery tickets sticking out of your pocket?'

'Yes, señor.'

'Are you an agent?'

'A sub-agent, señor.'

'Who are your main agents?'

'Bondello and Company.'

'Ah! They are honest agents. Give me five dollars' worth.'

'Thank you, señor, thank you!' Imperno handed over the tickets, picked up seven dollars and watched the merchant waddle away, then muttered to himself: 'Fat slob! I will be rich one day, but not by cheating people with stinking fish!' Imperno grinned. 'Not a bad bit of business in a slack time. And I still have forty-five dollars' worth of lottery tickets to sell.' He took these out and inspected them carefully.

For a while Imperno squatted silently — very still. Then, gathering his kit, he sped away, dashed up the alley and didn't stop until he reached his small picture-postcard stand beneath the trees close by Maria Farez Gardens.

'Mama mia!' he panted. 'I will kill that rat Rubo! Oh, why was I such a greedy fool! Now I have sold forged lottery tickets to a fish-merchant who knows Bondello and Company. And they will know it was me because I am the only shoe-shine boy who is a sub-agent. I work hard to prove I am honest so that I get the sub-agency. Main agents cannot take a chance on sub-agents — they will never believe me. Of course, the

Carlotta brothers do not care because they work only on visitors. No local people buy their tickets. But do not panic, Imperno. You have made a mistake. Be still now and work this out to see what you must do.'

If Bondello discovered that Imperno had handled forged lottery tickets, not only would they take away his sub-agency but they would tell the police. Imperno sighed, knowing it would cost him money which he might not get back. But if he didn't spend it, then pretty soon he wouldn't be able to earn any more. So thinking, he made his decision.

Imperno went to see Nikko — little one-leg Nikko, who leaned on crutches in a corner of the Plaza del Torro and begged a good living from passers-by.

'It is the busy time for me, Imperno,' said Nikko. 'Many visitors are here now and the police have increased my bribe money. I would like to help you, but I lose money if I do.'

'I promise you will not lose money,' said Imperno. 'You will have all the profit you can make from the postcard stand, and be able to beg just as well from my stand.'

'Is this bad trouble you are in?' Nikko asked. He was a small, gentle-looking boy and one of Imperno's real friends.

'Yes. Bad trouble, Nikko. But I can get out of it if I have a few days free.'

Nikko shrugged and smiled. 'You will get out of it, amigo. You are so clever.'

'If I am so clever I would not be in it,' said Imperno bitterly. 'Will you help me?'

'You have helped me and we are friends, so how could I refuse?' said Nikko.

'Is Gorgio still living in the Stewpot?' Imperno asked.

'Yes — he and his gang will always live in the Devil's Stewpot. Where else would they feel at home?'

Imperno chuckled. 'That is true. Adios, amigo! I will see you soon.'

90

The Devil's Stewpot was a nest of narrow streets — a teeming quarter housing thieves and many of the boy-gangs.

'Hola!' Gorgio bellowed. 'Look who is here — the mighty Imperno! Good clothes he wears these days! They would fetch quite a few pesetas.'

Imperno moved fast. Bang, clip, zonk!

Gorgio collapsed, gasping. His friends drew back, giggling. Imperno grinned at them. He knew just how to handle these Stewpot boys. Always go for their leader. Gorgio was a big leader. He and Imperno had been friends in a strange city in the old days.

'Always the big mouth, eh, Gorgio?' said Imperno. 'And you smell worse than ever.'

'You and your fight tricks!' Gorgio spluttered. 'But it is good to see you. Have you come to join us?'

'Not yet,' said Imperno tactfully because Gorgio had a strange pride in his way of life. 'I have come to see if you can do a very special job. There is no one in the city who can do such a job but Gorgio.'

'Ah!' Gorgio puffed out his chest. 'But naturally! The Gorgio boys are the finest in the world. Who do you want robbed?'

'Nobody — not yet. First I must have the help of fine brains and clever trackers. For this I pay now.' Imperno passed Gorgio a roll of notes. 'Later there will be more money. But not if any of your boys talk, or if they do not work well.'

'They will not talk and they will work well,' said Gorgio. 'They know what will happen to them otherwise.' He glared around him. 'You hear me — you scum!'

'First I want Rubo de Marco,' said Imperno. 'Find him, follow him, and not let him out of sight day or night. Tell me where he goes, who he meets.'

'That poor trash!' Gorgio sneered. 'I thought this was important work?'

'Rubo is just a small piece. But he knows someone I want to meet, and that someone knows a man who is close to much money,' said Imperno.

'Ah! Now I see!' Gorgio chuckled. 'You were always a brainy one, Imperno! This is a plot you have — yes?'

'You could call it that.' Imperno grinned. He made more arrangements, then left Gorgio and the Devil's Stewpot. He had set his plan in motion. Now he must wait while Gorgio's boys combed the city for Rubo de Marco. They would find him all right. No doubt of that.

Imperno shared a lodging with Jocco, a taxi-driver older than himself who also had come from the mountains, so the two had much in common. Jocco was out with a fare and Imperno waited by the taxi stand, watching the crowds seething along the sidewalks.

Gorgio came up to him and said:

'That Rubo trash had gone to bed in his flea-pit. I have left two boys watching, but I think Rubo will not leave until the morning. He was drunk. Here is a list of the places he went to and the people he met. Well — not all of them because my boys did not know who he met inside two of the places he visited. But as one was the office of the Carlotta brothers, you can guess who he met there.'

Imperno studied the list.

'The wine shop and such places are not important unless he left them with anyone and went to another place.'

'No,' said Gorgio. 'You will see he met only other trash like himself. The second place I have marked with a cross. It is in a small square at the back of Avenue Gonzales, beyond the President's statue, nearly opposite the fish-sellers' quarter.' Gorgio leered at Imperno. 'There is a small printing press there! I will see you tomorrow?'

'Perhaps. I will send a message, or come and see you.'

'And there will be more money?' Gorgio asked.

Imperno nodded. 'There will be more money.'

'Bueno! Now I must go and put my lazy scum to work while the night is young.' Gorgio hurried off to organise his sneak-thief gang who roamed the city, stealing saleable articles from parked cars.

When Jocco returned, Imperno said:

'I am ready.'

'You know where to go?' Jocco asked.

'The Square of the Four Angels.'

'I know it. Climb in,' said Jocco.

The square was dim-lit, huddled in mellow age behind the wide Avenue whose neon lights flared the sky above the city roofs. Jocco parked the taxi on a dark corner next to a telephone kiosk, switched off lights and whispered:

'You are sure of this? That Gorgio may be twisting you.'

Imperno laughed softly. 'He would twist me if there was no money, but he will not twist me before he gets paid in full — because he knows he would not get paid. It is simple honesty.'

'That is not a word he understands, but it makes sense,' Jocco agreed.

'Do you know this business place of Garcia Lombardo?' Imperno asked.

'There is no Garcia Lombardo. The business was bought by Paddy Connors, an Irishman who came down from working on the ranches.'

Imperno chuckled. 'Taxi-drivers know all the gossip.'

'I know more,' said Jocco. 'And it will help you, amigo, because it makes another little piece of a puzzle to drop in place for you.' Jocco had a passion for doing jig-saw puzzles. 'The Carlotta brothers have five sisters. Paddy Connors married the youngest. And the Carlottas run a main lottery ticket agency.'

'But they would not be so foolish as to risk a family link-up with a forged-ticket printer,' said Imperno.

'They might think it worth the risk. There is big money to be made. And anyway — it is not *their* printing business, is it?'

'Or Paddy Connors may be running it without their knowledge, then using sub-agents like Rubo to pass the forged tickets,' said Imperno.

'You do not even know if they print tickets in Lombardo's old place,' said Jocco. 'You are spending a lot of money on a few guesses, amigo, and time is running out for you. There is a lottery draw for prizes at noon tomorrow — or rather, today. By then, your fish-merchant will be squealing — if he has not already squealed.'

'I know, I know,' Imperno snapped. 'But if I had not talked with you, how would I know about Paddy Connors and the Carlottas' sister? There is a time to move and a time to stay still. And while I talk — I think.'

'What do you think?' Jocco asked.

'That this small printing shop is too dark in its windows. See the other buildings? The lights reflect inside the windows of small offices. There are no blinds and the sun-shades are drawn up. Now look at Lombardo's. Those windows are blank, like dead men's eyes. I think they are covered from inside. I think they would not dare print forged tickets in daytime in case any police or stranger walked in. They would print posters but not tickets. So I think they are working there now. So what do I do?' Imperno opened the taxi door quietly and slid out. 'One toot of the horn for danger. Two for police. O.K.?'

'O.K., amigo,' Jocco agreed.

Imperno sped, silent-footed on rubber-soled shoes, across the square. He padded softly around the building, then into the narrow alley between it and the next-door office. He paused, listening for a moment, then leapt up, grabbed a pipe running down the wall and, monkey-lide, clambered up to a partly-open window. He eased the window open, climbed in and almost fell into the toilet pan. The toilet door opened on to a passage.

Imperno tip-toed along the passage to where yellow light beamed through a half-open door. Cautiously he looked into a small room. A heavy blanket was fixed over a board nailed across the window. The air flowing through the door was hot and tanged with sweat and the smell of oily metal.

A small, shiny machine fixed on rubber blocks filled the centre of the room, its operation so silent that only the hissing whirr of the take-off rack could be heard — like a distant hand rustling a newspaper in a sleeping room. Neat piles of milticoloured lottery tickets were stacked on a desk top. A man sat at the desk sorting the tickets into bundles, marking each bundle with a tag after referring to a filing index.

Another man watched the machine, removed and stacked the tickets as they flowed from the take-off rack. Sweat beaded the faces of both men working in this airless room, but they worked intently, not speaking. The man at the desk was of medium height, thick-shouldered, sandy-haired. Imperno judged him to be Paddy Connors. The other man was small, dark and paunchy, with stubby ink-stained fingers. He looked hot and tired.

Imperno turned, treading as if on egg-shells, back to the toilet, climbed through the window and lowered himself down the pipe.

Jocco said: 'Well — are you still guessing?'

'Not any more. I have no change, Jocco, because I did not want it to jingle in my pocket. Give me some coins for the telephone, please.'

'Here you are. What now?'

'I phone, and then I go back and start a fight.'

'I come with you,' said Jocco. 'How many in there?'

'Only two. If I am in much trouble I will try to smash

a window,' said Imperno. 'Then you come running. Otherwise, you stay out of it. O.K.?'

'If you say so, amigo! But you must have help.'

Imperno laughed. 'I am phoning someone who will hurry to help. I only hope he moves fast!'

Imperno dialled the number.

'Who calls?' said a woman's voice.

'I am Imperno Quartaro. I am a sub-agent of Bondello and Company.'

'So? Is this a time to call, you dolt?'

'A thousand apologies, beautiful Therese!'

'You know me?' She sounded surprised.

'Only that you are beautiful,' said Imperno, who knew she weighed two hundred and twenty pounds and had a face like a pickled cabbage. 'And that your soul is pure and kind. And also that I love and honour Señor Enrico Bondello, so I dare to phone him now to warn him of great danger.'

'Oh well — I suppose I must call him. Wait, Imperno Quartaro.'

Imperno waited and sweated. It was all nonsense how a man had to flatter a woman, but he had learned it was so much easier than arguing with them.

Enrico Bondello came on the line, thick-voiced, suspicious.

'I know you,' he said. 'You are bright and willing, but if this is a joke I will make you a very sad and sorry boy. What is it?'

'Señor Bondello, I am glad you remember me because you tell me I may one day be an agent and have my own ticket office, and I work hard to prove you are right to trust me.'

'So why this sort of talk in the middle of the night?'

'For your interests, señor,' said Imperno. 'For days and night I have been searching for the source of forged lottery tickets. I know how you hate such crooks.'

The voice grew sharp and clear. 'You are sure, Imperno—quite sure?'

'Yes, señor. And I need your help. I am going to catch the forgers red-handed. They are in...' Imperno gave clear directions, then continued: 'I will climb in again and tip-toe down to unlock the front door. But if they catch me, I may get hurt. This I do not mind because I know I am fighting for the good name of Bondello and Company, who one day will make me a full agent so that I can earn more money for them and for myself. But, señor Enrico, hurry—please hurry!'

Imperno hung up the telephone quickly. He grinned as he muttered to himself: 'You will hurry, señor, even though you are fat and soft with rich living. You will hurry because the government will give you a reward for catching forgers of their State Lottery tickets. It will be a secret reward, and you will not tell me because I could not get it anyway. But you will phone your high-up police friends, who will be praised for being so smart and given a medal and more money.' Imperno paused to lean on the taxi door.

'Do you enjoy talking to yourself?' Jocco asked.

'Very much,' said Imperno. 'That way I learn many things.'

'You are crazy! What are you waiting for?'

'For little fat rich men to wake up. Or for them to receive messages in night clubs or wherever they might be. When they receive these messages they will send out orders to their strong-arm men, and the police high-ups will give orders to the sergeants. I think maybe you should go now, Jocco.'

'What about you? How can I help you if I go?'

Imperno smiled. 'I shall have plenty of help soon. It is all a matter of timing.' He thought for a moment. 'Yes, I think you should go now, and I too will make my move. See you later, amigo!' He was gone before Jocco could answer.

Jocco shrugged. 'Crazy kid! Oh well — he knows what he wants.' Jocco drove out of the Square of the Four Angels and

Imperno slammed full force into the fat stomach

on to the crowded Avenue Gonzales, where he soon picked up a profitable fare.

Imperno entered the building in the same way. The light still beamed from the half-open door. This guided his way down the stairs, where he unlocked the front door and gently eased it ajar, then trod softly upstairs again.

He walked calmly into the hot little room.

'Hola!' said Imperno. 'Got any tickets to sell?'

The sandy-haired man at the desk froze, statue-like, with his hands over the filing index. The dark fat man tending the machine whirled, pop-eyed, mouth agape. Then his hand reached for a spanner lying across a ledge of the machine.

Imperno charged forward, head down. He slammed full force into the fat stomach. Air rushed from the man's open mouth with a long sighing *aaah!* He bent double. Imperno hit him on the back of the neck. The fat man folded on to the floor like a shapeless sawdust doll.

Imperno stepped back, looked towards the desk and found himself a nose-length away from a vicious-looking round black hole. At the other end of the hole was a hand. In between was the smooth, blue-black sheen of a gun.

'And what the divil d'ye think ye're up to?' a soft-toned surprised voice asked. 'Is it a game ye're playing now?'

Imperno's gaze moved from the gun to the arm, then to the face.

'If you shoot me — you die, señor. The police are on their way. Let the little fat man take the blame. Go while there is still time.'

Panic flashed into the man's eyes. Imperno rammed home his advantage.

'Go, Paddy Connors,' he urged. 'And do not trust men like Rubo de Marco again.'

The name seemed to convince Paddy Connors. He half turned away. Imperno snatched up the spanner and slashed it across the bunched knuckles of the Irishman's gun-hand. The gun fired as it fell. The bullet went *kerzonk* into the floor an inch from Imperno's big toe.

Imperno lowered his head and charged again. The impact flung Paddy Connors against the desk corner. He yelped with pain as the sharp wood jammed into his back. Imperno grabbed a large plastic machine cover draped on a chair-back, flung it over Connors' head and shoulders and spun him around. Then he kept him moving on stumbling feet, half crippled by the injured back, until by luck Connors fell into the open doorway of the toilet. Imperno didn't intend this, but gave silent thanks as he slammed the door shut, after whipping out the key from inside while Connors was groping over the toilet. Imperno raced back to the room. The little fat man still lay on the floor, painfully sleeping. Swiftly Imperno searched the room and, just in time, found what he was sure must be there — a wallet full of money. He extracted some, put it in the desk drawer, then stuffed the wallet inside his shirt, tight against his trousers, as the noise of heavy feet thudded up the stairs. Imperno flung himself against the fat man in a flurry of arms and legs.

A sergeant and two policemen pounded into the room, guns drawn. Imperno scrambled up, panting.

'Sergeant Bozzato!' he cried. *'Por Dios,* I thought you would never come! I have overpowered this villain. The other is locked in the toilet. He had a gun!'

Sergeant Brazzato waved a hand. 'Go get him,' he ordered the two policemen. When they had left the room he surveyed Imperno with a suspicious gaze. 'Imperno Quartaro strikes again!' he said, heavily sarcastic. 'That you should know such top men is not decent. That you should fight so good yet not like violence is a mystery. But what is worst of all is that I am ordered to protect you and not to question you, and see you are escorted safely to the house of Señor Bondello. How is it that one so young can know so much?'

Imperno shrugged. 'I am an innocent boy, Sergeant Señor Brazzato, and you are an honourable policeman. We both do our duty as best we can, as you will see if you open the desk drawer before your men return.'

The sergeant pulled open the drawer. One hand moved, slick and fast, from drawer to pocket.

'We understand each other, amigo.' He smiled a fat smile as the policemen returned with a struggling, handcuffed Paddy Connors. 'Leave him here,' the sergeant ordered. 'Take Señor Quartaro to the car and escort him to you-know-where. Send up four men from the wagon.'

Imperno turned at the doorway. 'They are all forged, amigo,' he said softly. 'So do not risk it!'

Sergeant Brazzato removed his hand from the pile of tickets.

And that was how Imperno Quartaro became the youngest lottery ticket agent in the city, with his own office and his own sign on the window.

As Gorgio said when he was paid — generously: 'I don't know how he does it, but he does it!'

Or as Señor Enrico Bondello's wife said: 'Such charm and honesty and hard work do not often go together in one boy.'

To which Señor Bondello grunted: 'Yes, my dear.' But under his breath added: '*Por Dios!* I should hope not!'

Gentlemen of the Sealed Knot

by GEOFFREY TREASE

It all began in that moment when I suddenly became quite certain that I was being watched.

I spun round on my skates and stood there, in the middle of the frozen canal, and looked round warily. The Dutch boys might be up to their tricks again. They often were. You could hardly blame them for taking it out of a solitary English boy when they got the chance. After all, England and Holland had been at war a year or two ago, and they still spoke of our Cromwell as though he were a bogey-man.

I stared round. The canal was lifted high above the frost-grey fields, and I could see a full mile each way across that dull Dutch countryside, until the haze grew too thick to pierce. And in all that landscape nothing stirred: the windmills stood along the dykes, not a sail turning; the willows and poplars might have been wrought iron, for not a branch so much as creaked or quivered in the breathless air.

'Imagination,' I muttered, but I did not believe it. Half-heartedly I tried another figure on my skates. I made rather a mess of it. If the Dutch boys had been watching, crouched down behind the canal-bank, they would have jumped up then, hooting with laughter. They couldn't have resisted it. I could never get them to realise that metal skates were still a complete novelty in England, that most people at home still amused themselves by tying bits of bone to their shoes, and that it wasn't fair to expect the same skill from us on the ice.

No, that last effort of mine would have brought the Bresken

lads to their feet, holding their sides and making rude remarks about Englishmen who cut their king's head off but couldn't cut a simple figure on skates.

Yet I still had that eerie sensation that I was being watched. I did another quick jump round, thinking that if it was somebody behind me I would take him by surprise. And this time I caught him — if 'caught' is the word. For he made no attempt to duck down again, but stood there, very tall in a high black hat and a long black cloak, like some giant raven perched on the dyke.

I gasped. I could hardly have been more surprised if the Devil himself had suddenly appeared out of that empty landscape. For a moment we stared at each other. His eyes were dark and brooding, deep set in a swarthy face — yet somehow it was not a sinister face, and there was a kindliness in it. It broke into a smile now, and the man spoke. His voice was quiet, low and musical, even though he spoke in Dutch.

I could only make out something about Englishmen, and answered, haltingly: 'Yes, Mynheer, I am English. I am afraid I cannot speak Dutch very well.'

His eyebrows went up. Then it was my turn to show surprise again, for his next words were in fluent English. He shot out a claw-like hand, beckoning me to the edge of the ice, and peered down into my face. He spoke urgently and, for all his quietness, like one used to command.

'What is your name, boy? What are you doing here? Englishmen seem as common as windmills hereabouts!'

That puzzled me. 'My name's Ralph Selden, sir. I don't know of any other Englishmen here except my father — and he's away at Leyden on business.'

'Selden... Of course, I remember. Your father is William Selden of Cambridge.' He nodded approvingly. 'He came to Holland four months ago to study methods of drainage and dyke-building, so that he may apply them in our own Fens.

His mission has the warmest approval of the Lord Protector.'

It was incredible. Father was not famous or anything, yet this stranger had every detail at his finger-tips. I began to exclaim. He checked me.

'It is my business to know about Englishmen abroad. Europe is full of wandering Englishmen — traitors who plot with any foreigner to ruin the Commonwealth. Tell me, boy —' he gripped my arm, and his fingers were like steel through his leather glove — 'have you heard of the Sealed Knot?'

'The Sealed Knot?' I shook my head.

He let go my arm. 'It's a conspiracy of the old Cavaliers. They stick at nothing. They tried to murder the Lord Protector as he took his Saturday afternoon ride to Hampton Court. They plotted to seize the port of Hull and let in the Spanish fleet.'

'I know nothing about all that, sir.' The Civil War had finished when I was quite small, and I hadn't realised its fires were still smouldering underground.

'But you are English,' said the man almost fiercely, 'and Cromwell has made England a great country again. Would you want to see her go down once more to rack and ruin?'

'No, sir —'

'Listen. There is something you can do, Ralph Selden.' He pointed to where the lights of the village were beginning to glimmer through the twilight haze. 'Three Englishmen rode into Bresken an hour ago. They have a horse to be re-shod, and they have ordered dinner, so they will be there some time. I would give a great deal to know where they are going, and why. To overhear five minutes of their private talk —'

'Wouldn't that be... spying?'

'There are times when honest men must spy — to stop treason and murder, to save innocent lives...' I saw that, and nodded. He smiled down at me and went on in a milder tone. 'Call me a spy if you like, boy. I prefer to call myself an agent of the English Government.' He swept off his hat and bowed solemnly — I had to laugh, it was so funny to see that towering figure bend towards me. 'Permit me to introduce myself, Ralph Selden — Doctor Pharaoh, once of the University of Cambridge, and now of any part of the globe where England has cause to send me! Just now she has sent me to Bresken in Holland, but I think it is the Lord who has sent *you* here to be my helper.'

'Your helper?' I echoed. 'How?'

He chuckled. 'I have one great disadvantage in this work — I am a big man, and, once seen, easily remembered. If I walk into that inn I shall be recognised. Our English gentlemen will keep mum. I shall get nothing for my pains — unless it be a bullet at the first lonely spot on the road when we all move on.'

'They'd do that?'

'They stick at nothing. Only a month or two ago, at Cologne, where the young Prince weaves his plots in exile, they caught one of my friends.'

'What did they do to him?'

'Took him into a wood and shot him.'

I thought for a moment. 'I expect you'd like *me* to go to the inn, and find out anything I can?'

Doctor Pharaoh nodded. 'And report to me at that small tavern at the far end of the village, the "Golden Lion". And forget — otherwise — that you have ever seen me or heard my name.'

'I understand, sir.'

And so we parted in the frosty dusk. He was gone like a shadow, and by the time I had unstrapped my skates and stepped over the dyke it was hard to believe that he had ever been there.

The great inn at Bresken was quieter than usual, for the

roads were almost as slippery as the ice-bound canals, and nobody was travelling who could avoid it. Even so, there was a good buzz and bustle, for it was a popular meeting-place with the local merchants and farmers, and it was easy for a boy to slip into a quiet corner unnoticed.

If anyone had challenged me, I should have said that I was waiting to deliver a message from my father to one of the millers, when he came in; but in actual fact no one gave me a second glance.

I picked out our three Englishmen at once. Their ringleted hair, their ribbons and laces, their silk-lined boot-tops, all marked them out from that assembly of plainly dressed Dutchmen. Yet, when I studied their faces, bending to meet across the table, I saw that in spite of their fancy clothes and curls there was nothing womanish about them.

I saw the firm jaws and narrowed eyes of men who, as Doctor Pharaoh had said, would stick at nothing. One was portly, red-faced and scar-slashed, a hard-drinking, hard-swearing cavalry officer. Another, the youngest of the three, was lean and pale, with eyes that blazed madly, when he showed excitement, in the light of the candles. But the obvious leader of the group, and the most dangerous, whom the others addressed as Sir James, was a little, oldish, sandy fellow, with the coldest, cruellest face I have ever seen. He made me think of a stoat.

Their dinner was getting near its end. The young man was saying: 'The horses should be ready to move on in another hour.'

'No hurry,' said the red-faced man. 'The wine here is good.'

'That will be your last glass,' Sir James told him firmly. 'Cool heads till the work is done.'

'Cool?' snorted his companion. 'We shall be frozen by the time we reach Tielpoort. We need something to keep the cold out.' But I noticed that his hand fell away from the bottle and he made no further move to refill his glass.

The young man seemed nervous. 'I suppose we are quite certain Wytham will spend tonight in Tielpoort?'

'Where else? He was leaving The Hague this morning. He is in a hurry. That means an early start tomorrow, before dawn. All the better. We shall get him as he steps into his coach. It will be all the easier to slip away if it is still dark.'

'I'm not afraid, Sir James.' But I could see that the young man was as nervous as a cat. He stared round the great room, at the plump Dutchmen warming their breeches and smoking their pipes around the blazing fire, at the maids bustling in and out with drinks and dishes, at the landlord's children playing with a hound in one corner, at myself sitting there with my hat pulled down over my brows, trying to look small and half-asleep. 'I suppose,' I heard him mutter, 'none of these people understand English?'

'If they did,' said the red-faced gentleman irritably, 'what would it matter? Why should they interfere? Anyhow, in a few hours now, it'll be too late for anyone to interfere.' None the less Sir James switched the conversation into French and I could follow it no more.

That sould have been a warning to me. For, if it was only Dutchmen they were afraid of, French was no safer than English. But, at the time, I did not stop to think out the full meaning of the move. I knew that I should overhear nothing more, and, Heaven knows, I had heard enough. Someone named Wytham was to be murdered at Tielpoort, first thing in the morning. Wytham? Suddenly the name seemed to click in my brain. Of course — Lord Wytham, the new English Ambassador to Holland! The blood rushed to my cheeks as I realised the full importance of the news.

I had already risen to my feet, trying to act casually, like a boy who was bored and tired of waiting to deliver his

I sat there, trying to look small and half-asleep

message. But now I was so anxious to carry my news to Doctor Pharaoh that I moved more hastily. I collided with one of the serving-girls so that she nearly dropped her tray, and beer went slopping all over my sleeve. I muttered an apology, and she smiled and dabbed my arm with her cloth; then I made my escape juts as quickly as I could.

In the doorway I turned and stole a glance at the Englishmen's table. Sir James and the young man were talking hard. But the red-faced fellow had gone.

*　　*　　*　　*

I stepped out into the cobbled yard. The night air stung my hot cheeks. My mind was racing ahead of my stumbling feet: in imagination, I was already at the far end of the village, reporting to Doctor Pharaoh at the 'Golden Lion'. I was taken completely by surprise when a voice addressed me from the blackness of the archway.

'Just a moment, young fellow.'

Instinctively, I paused and turned. And in that moment I was seized in a powerful grip and dragged into the shadows. I smelt hot, wine-laden breath on my face. I knew then, though I could see nothing, that it was the red-faced fellow.

'I thought as much,' he growled. 'You understand English.'

'He *is* English.'

Two figures loomed out of the night, and for an instant I hoped for rescue, and started to cry out, but a leathery hand was clapped over my mouth, and I realised that the newcomers were the other conspirators.

It was Sir James who had spoken. He went on: 'I have just asked that maid. The boy is staying in Bresken. His father is an engineer, studying the dyke-building.' He turned to me. 'Where were you going?'

The rough hand moved to let me answer: 'Home, sir.'

'What other Englishmen are there in this district?'

'None, sir. And my father is away just now.'

There was silence while they considered. Then the young man said anxiously: 'What shall we do with him? He must have heard.'

The red-faced man chuckled brutally. 'Let him study the canals like his Dad. A small hole in the ice, and no questions asked.'

'*No!*' said the young one in a horrified tone. 'We're gentlemen, not murderers! Wytham is bad enough... but we do that for the cause.'

'Quiet, both of you,' ordered Sir James. We all stood there in the inky shadow. The hand was over my mouth again, the iron grip never relaxed from the arm twisted behind my back. He thought for a few moments longer. Then he said: 'You must not be so squeamish, Anthony. The servants of the Sealed Knot must do whatever is necessary. But the death of this boy is not necessary — it will only hinder our cause by making fresh enemies. Tie him up, gag him firmly, and shut him up in one of these outhouses. By the time he is found we shall have done our work, and be miles on our road to — where we are going.'

'All right,' growled Red-face sulkily. 'But he'd have made a neat hole in the ice!'

* * * *

The next few hours were about the worst I have ever spent. How often, playing with other boys, I had been bound and gagged — and how often, after a few squirmings and wrigglings, had I got free from their amateurish knots! This time it was quite different.

I lay helpless in a pitch-black outhouse, half-filled with sawn logs of firewood, mighty hard to lie on. They might at least (I thought to myself bitterly) have stowed me away in the hayloft! I had no idea why the Royalist conspiracy had chosen the name of the Sealed Knot, but in this case it was most fitting. The cords at my wrists and ankles held firm against all my efforts.

The discomfort was bad enough, but I knew it could be only a matter of hours before some inn-servant found me—probably first thing in the morning. It was cold, but for a long time I was hardly aware of that: my useless struggles kept me warm. The worst thing was the knowledge that a man's life depended on me. I knew nothing of Lord Wytham as a person, I cared nothing for the politics of Royalist and Commonwealth men, but I knew that murder was wrong. And if I lay there till a servant found me in the morning, Lord Wytham was a dead man.

Now and again I heard footsteps scrape and slither across the frozen yard, or saw the glint of a lantern through the cracks of the door. I strained at my gag. I could only mumble faintly. Then I managed, by working my legs to and fro, to start a miniature landslide of logs. Part of the heap came rumbling down with a loud noise, and I felt sure that someone would come to investigate, but silence fell again, and nobody came near.

Yet, in the end, it was well they had shut me in the wood-shed and not amid the comfortable hay. There would have been no hatchet in the hayloft. As it was, I suddenly discovered it, and, what was more, the tip of the blade was firmly em-bedded in the large block on which the servant split the logs!

This was marvellous luck. I could not have done much with a loose hatchet, but this one offered me a blade, fixed quite rigidly, in a position which I could reach with my hands tied behind me. It was not easy. A hatchet used only for splitting firewood is seldom razor-keen, and it cost me a good many minutes of desperate sawing before I felt the tightness at my wrists go suddenly, leaving me with only a few loops of slackened cord.

After that it was easy. Out came the sodden handkerchief from between my teeth, a few seconds were spared to massage the ache from wrists and arms, and another minute freed my ankles. The door of the shed had neither lock nor bolt, only a latch. I burst out into the yard, almost falling full length on the slippery cobbles. The first thing I saw was the full moon coming up over the gabled roof, and I knew then how late it must be. I must have spent hours in that shed. And, as I hurried down the street, I saw that nearly all the lights were out.

* * * *

The 'Golden Lion' was a small, low-class tavern, and I had never set foot inside it. Nor have I, to this day, for there was no need. A great horse, almost black, stood saddled at the door, and Doctor Pharaoh had his foot in the stirrup.

'The boy!' he muttered under his breath, and put his foot down again. 'I'd given you up. I've just heard — the men slipped away towards Leyden hours and hours ago. I'm after them.'

'They're not going to Leyden,' I panted. 'That's a blind. They're going to Tielpoort.'

'Tielpoort? The opposite direction! Why?'

'The English Ambassador is sleeping there tonight. They mean to assassinate him — early tomorrow morning — as he walks out to his coach.' I stammered out my story as quickly as I could.

He said grimly: 'Civil War is a cruel thing, Ralph Selden. You see where it leads? Englishman against Englishmen. It did not stop at Naseby, nor at Worcester. It goes on — in the colonies, at the courts of foreign princes, underground, shots in the dark, conspiracies, spyings... but this is no time to philosophise. Tielpoort, you said? A long way.'

113

Only then did I start calculating, setting the distance against the time. 'You can't do it,' I groaned.

'I must do it.'

'Not with the roads in this state. They're like glass.'

He swung his vast bulk into the saddle. 'Sir James and his friends will do it.'

'But they've had hours of start. They could walk their horses. *You* can't.'

'I must trust in the Lord,' he said simply. 'Goodbye, Ralph Selden, you've done a good night's work.'

He touched the mare, and she started forward, and down the moonlit street they clattered at a speed which made me wince. I walked after them, simply because it was the way to the farm where we were lodged, and I wanted to find my skates where Red-face had kicked them when he seized me under the archway. They were still there all right, and I walked on out of Bresken, suddenly conscious how cold and hungry and tired I was. My adventure had ended as abruptly as it had started.

*   *   *   *

But it proved otherwise.

As I passed from the village street into the open country and saw the long, moonlit road striped with the shadows of the poplars, I was aware of another dark shadow just in front, a patch which moved as I drew nearer. I heard a low groan from the ditch, and hesitated, scared lest some new danger lurked there. I felt I had had enough for one night. Then I saw that the moving shadow was Doctor Pharaoh's black mare, and, as I hurried forward again, the man himself stumbled to his feet. He recognised me at once.

'You were right, boy,' he said between his teeth, and I knew he was in pain, 'the road is like glass. Hold her a moment, will you? I think my arm is broken.' And to my amazement

I saw he was trying to climb into the saddle again.

'You can't ride like that, sir!'

'I must.' But his right arm hung useless, and he was a great, heavy man. I had no strength to help him up.

The moon was riding high in an almost cloudless heaven. The silvered landscape lay under it, bright as day. I knew it must be very late now. It was a roundabout route to Tielpoort — the road bent this way and that, avoiding marshes and unbridged canals. I knew it was no use my offering to ride in his place. No horseman could now reach Tielpoort before dawn. I said so, as he paused in his struggle to mount, and leant panting and sweating against the mare's flank.

'Then the Ambassador is done for!' he groaned. 'Think boy, is there no other way?'

Then in a twinkling, the idea came. 'Yes, sir! I've just thought — the canal! It runs to Tielpoort, straight as a die! Half the distance of the road —'

'I can't ride along a canal —'

'It's frozen —'

'And more slippery than the road!'

'I don't mean to ride,' I said impatiently. 'I mean *skate*'.

As I said that, I knew for certain that it must be I who went to Tielpoort. There could be few Englishmen in the world with enough experience of skating to cover all those miles. I was not sure I could do it myself. But I could try.

Doctor Pharaoh wasted no time in argument. He asked one or two sensible questions, and then the matter was settled. To my relief, he had provisions in his saddle-bag, and, as I listened to his instruction, I was able to eat, and sip the spirit-and-water he carried in his flask. 'Take it,' he said, 'and the food — but only a sip, mind, when you feel chilled.' We said goodbye then, rather solemnly, he mumbling some text from the Bible, and I ran down across the fields, my feet scrunching the frozen furrows, to where the canal lay between its high banks, a narrow white stripe running to the far horizon.

I knelt, strapped on my skates, and started, wondering very much if I should ever reach the end of my journey, and what taht end would be.

* * * *

The Dutch, of course, travelled long distances on their skates. I had never gone farther than a mile or two from home, though I suppose, in a long afternoon's skating, I must have covered a good distance up and down. But I had never done anything like this before.

It was an eerie journey. The whole world was asleep except myself. Not a light glimmered from the villages. The stark poplars stood up like skeletons, the windmills spread their motionless arms like crucifixes. And on and on, unbending as a moonbeam, the great canal stretched from horizon to horizon. If I had been the man in the moon, I could not have felt more lonely.

On, on... mile after mile... under bridges, over the desolate salt-marshes, once through a sleeping town with high, curved gables and paved quays, and a churchspire catching the light like a dagger... on, on, with aching legs and thumping heart — just a minute's pause to sit quivering on the dyke, to tear ravenously at bread and meat, to sip the fiery drink in the Doctor's flask... then on again, on, on...

The moon was sinking. Longer and longer were the crossed shadows of the windmills. My pace slackened. There was a great ache in my ankles, my thighs, in every part of my weary body. Then I remembered those three faces plotting murder over the candle-lit table at the inn, and I forced myself forward again.

Forward! The moon was nearly down. Only its upper rim

gleamed yellow above the horizon. Then even that was gone, and icy darkness flooded the landscape, and I knew I had barely an hour to dawn.

At least there was no fear of missing my way. Smaller drains and ditches forked left and right, but the main canal ran ever forward, and even without the moon it was possible to see that ghostly grey causeway stretching ever onwards. Was that a light, pricking the gloom like a golden star, perhaps a mile in front? Yes! And there was another. A third over there to the left...

The world was waking up again. I was approaching a town. Heaven be praised, it must be Tielpoort, no other!

Ten minutes later I was unfastening my skates on the broad, tree-lined quay of the deserted fish-market.

*   *   *   *

It was not hard to find the principal inn where the English Ambassador had slept. Its galleried courtyard was already astir. Lanterns bobbed everywhere. Even as I dragged my weary legs under the archway, the ostlers were harnessing four powerful Flemish beasts to a heavy coach.

I plucked a servant by the sleeve and asked for the Ambassador, only to be brushed aside with an impatient laugh. Then I tackled a lanky, cross-looking fellow, a secretary to judge from the papers in his hand.

'Are you crazy?' he said roughly. Then with surprise: 'Why, you're English!'

'I must see the Ambassador,' I whispered. 'At once.'

He gave me a narrow look, summing me up. Then, without further dispute he led me by way of a staircase to a handsome upper room, where a small white-haired gentleman was eating hurriedly as he stood, already cloaked and hatted for the road.

I bowed as I had been taught to do to a nobleman. 'My lord, I have a message — from Doctor Pharaoh.'

The old gentleman started. 'Pharaoh? That faithful watch-dog. Close the door, Mr Benson, and stand against it. Well, boy?'

My knees felt suddenly like water. I clutched at a chair-back. 'Three men are waiting to shoot you as you go out to your coach, my lord. They are agents of the Sealed Knot. Sir James Borrowdale and two others.'

The secretary exclaimed. Lord Wytham nodded as if he was not entirely surprised. Then he said in a calm tone: 'My pistols, Mr Benson.'

'Surely, my lord, you will not risk yourself —'

'Mr Benson,' said the old gentleman with dignity, 'here in Holland I represent England. England does not slip out by back ways, nor does she cower indoors.'

'But wait, while I have these men arrested, my lord —'

'Who will arrest them? We are not at home. And on what charge can they be arrested before they have fired a shot? Warn the escort, Mr Benson, but do not give the alarm. Leave the rest to me.'

The last scene of the drama I watched from the safety of the inn-gallery, peering down into the courtyard. The coach was drawn up near the foot of the outside staircase. Early as the hour was, the courtyard was full of townspeople curious to see Cromwell's Ambassador. The escort, four armed men, kept a space clear from the stairs to the coach-step. I scanned the faces of the crowd eagerly. At once I picked up Red-face, then the blazing eyes of the pale young man, then, a pace or two away, Sir James…

Everyone was turned towards the main staircace, as first the Ambassador's boxes were carried down and then Mr Benson descended, with a backward glance as though expecting to see his master just behind. Yet, when the Ambassador appeared, no one saw him but myself.

He had come down another way, entered his coach from the opposite side, and now stood framed in its open doorway. A pistol glinted in each hand. He spoke quietly, and every head spun round in amazement.

'Well, Sir James, have you something to say to me?'

Their pistols snapped almost together. I heard Sir James's bullet shatter the window of the coach. The next moment the whole courtyard was in an uproar, as escort and conspirators battled to reach one another through the panic-stricken, neutral crowd.

They got away, the three gentlemen of the Sealed Knot. I fancy that Lord Wytham preferred them to escape, once they had shown their hand. They had horses ready outside, and galloped away over the fields into the dawn. Only Red-face's horse stumbled, and I had the great satisfaction of seeing him thrown head-first into a duck-pond — and it was no small hole in the ice *he* made. He came out, cursing and dripping, remounted and fled after the others before his pursuers could catch up with him.

I was wiping the tears of laughter from my eyes when I heard the quiet voice of the Ambassador at my side:

'I think, my boy, England owes you a good breakfast — and perhaps a little more.'

The Wild Ones

by REX DIXON

'For the last time, Cougar Calastro, take the good price I offer. Take it and git. You ain't no room to grow around this section. So why be stubborn?'

'Mebbe you're the stubborn one, Josh Sone — lording it mighty high! But your old man done built his ranch, same as me, so how come you think you got rights to force me to sell?'

'If you had sense you'd see my rights. Them Nose Point Hills are the natural boundary south of my J. S. Circle land. Your Double C land can't graze more'n two hundred head. Like I say — you ain't no room to grow.'

The J. S. Circle riders grouped around Josh Sone nodded and muttered. Most of them would have easier work if J. S. Circle owned the Nose Point Hills. The foreman, Clint Dell, said: 'You and me have grown a mite older working these hyar ranges, Cougar. Take Josh's price and buy yourself a spread down the trail a-ways. Let that boy of yourn have somep'n to raise himself on. You owe Cub that much, don't you? And his mother too.'

Cub Calastro sat hitch-hipped on the fence.

'What my pa does is sure enough right with me,' said Cub.

'I don't hold with stubborn men,' said Mrs Calastro, then laughed. 'I guess you're stubborn and my menfolk jest strong willed. It's gettin' dark, Josh. Why not ride off before that temper of yourn rises with the moon?'

'Don't bait him, Ma,' said Cougar Calastro. 'It ain't Josh's fault he gits moon-crazy.'

Cub moved forward — tall, sinewy cub of his hard-muscled father, his jeering smile scarcely visible in the falling dark —

and said: 'Yeah, you do that. Reckon like rides with like. Josh ain't alone when it comes to gittin' a mite moon-crazy.'

'If you don't aim to talk sense, then quit talking,' Cougar snarled.

'Aw, let him yap,' said one of the riders. 'It ain't no more'n a little bitty cub yelping.'

Cub sprang forward and pulled the man from his horse. The animal reared and plunged. For seconds the group of riders was split and milling around the two struggling figures. There was no sign of drawn guns, yet suddenly a shot rang out — staccato in its single action. Cub and the man stopped fighting. The man climbed back on his horse.

The silence grew tense as Cougar strode towards his wife, lying huddled on the ground. He knelt beside her, then slowly rose to his feet.

'She's dead!' His voice was cold, flat — empty of emotion, yet its very emptiness held the full charge of the searing pain that filled his mind. 'My wife is dead,' said Cougar. 'Which of you fired that gun?'

'No!' Josh Sone cried. 'No, Calastro, no! It was an accident. The horses milled around. Someone's gun went off. My God! I'm sorry — sorry!'

'Who fired the gun?' said Cougar again.

'Tell him! Tell him!' Cub sobbed. 'I'll kill you — all of you! I'll kill you!' He ran for the gun resting on its pegs in the house.

'I ain't stopping him,' said Cougar. 'If I had my gun, you'd be dead right now, Josh Sone. And from this night I ride double-holstered. I'll kill any J. S. riders I see on my land. And I'll find who fired the gun. And when I do — he'll die.'

'I'll send the sheriff out,' said Josh Sone.

'He'll not give me back my wife.'

They heard Cub pounding back, saw his shadowy figure, saw the early star-glow glinting on the gun-barrel.

122

'Ride!' Josh Sone yelled. 'Let's ride!'

The riders bunched, wheeled their horses and rode off fast. Cub panted to a halt, snugged the gun stock into his shoulder and fired. He went on firing until the Winchester magazine was empty. Then he threw down the gun and knelt by his mother's side.

From that moment father and son didn't speak much.

It was dawn before Sheriff Keller rode out from Trail City. He looked at the grave and rough-carved cross beneath the live oak, with its veils of Spanish moss drooping like weeping greybeards above. Then he glanced up to see Cougar Calastro, double-holstered, had come quietly to face him.

'A bad business, Calastro. Sure 'am sorry,' said Keller.

'My business,' said Cougar. 'Git off my land.'

'There's things I have to do — legal things.'

'Ain't nothing you can do. Ain't nothing to be done that I can't do.'

The sheriff pointed to Cougar's guns. 'A vengeance killing ain't going to help no one either.'

'It's a murderer who fired the bullet that killed my ma,' said Cub from back of the sheriff, the rifle now heft in the crook of his arm. 'Justice ain't vengeance.'

The sheriff raised his hands pleadingly towards Cub's father. 'Not the boy too, Calastro,' he said. 'At least don't make *him* gun-happy.'

'Ain't no one happy around here. Why don't you git? We'll tend to our own business in our own way.'

'There'll be a court hearing. Do you have the bullet?'

Cougar nodded. 'I have the bullet.'

'Give it me — it's evidence. We may be able to trace the gun,' said the sheriff.

'Evidence for talking. That ain't the way it's going to be,' said Cougar.

'Take time, Calastro. Take time, an' let your grief simmer·

down a mite. Let me handle this.'

Cougar's hand flashed down and up. The gun levelled menacingly. 'I said git. Now git!'

The sheriff shrugged. 'Folks named you Cougar right from first you came here. Lean, tough and ornery — they said. Like a cougar — allus roaming, ready to pounce and keeping himself on a lone trail. In all these years they ain't changed toward you and you ain't wanted 'em to change. And you raised your son in your image. So be it. That's the way you are. But if you kill — then I'm coming after you, Calastro, same as I would after a killer mountain lion.' The sheriff went to his horse, mounted and rode away, not looking back.

'You, and me, son — we talk a mite. Then I go.'

'Yes, Pa.'

No why or where to, or can I come along — just 'Yes, Pa.' Not because Cub was meek but because to him this tall quiet-voiced man had always been Cub's kind of man. Not just a father he had to obey. There was that too, of course, but it was only part of the boy's true feelings.

'Keller will keep his word,' said Cougar. 'But what I have to do *must* be done. You got argument?'

'No, Pa. I'd do it if you didn't.'

'They may hang me, they may jail me. Either way it's going to hurt you, son. You reckon you're man enough?'

The boy nodded. 'I reckon.' He stood tall and straight — nigh as tall as his father. And he knew that from one minute after the shot had been fired he had become a man. This is the way he felt.

Cougar pulled a thin chain from around his neck. A small key glinted as he swung the chain over Cub's head.

'All I got is yours, son. You know part of what I've been working for all these years, and why I couldn't sell. The steel box under the hearth-stone in the house — that's the key. As of now it's yours. I ain't asking you to decide whether you go on working as I've done, or sell out. It's your life. Reckon that's all. My horse is saddled.'

Cougar held out his hand. Father and son gripped hands, looking deep into each other's eyes. Then Cougar turned, walked to his horse, mounted and rode away.

At the top of the rise he halted, turned in the saddle and waved. Cub hadn't moved until he now raised one hand high and held it there as his father rode on over the rise and disappeared from view.

Cub returned to the lonely house, barred the door, covered the windows, lit the tallow-oil lamp and levered the heavy stone to one side. He didn't touch the box even though it was the first time he'd seen it. There was a crest cut on the top. It was old, very old, obviously made by a craftsman. The key-hole was flush, not raised to take a padlock. Next to the box was an oil-silk package. Cub took this out, opened it and found a small leather-bound book. Inside the cover was written: General Damon Calastro — His Journal. Cub flipped the yellowed pages. Two clean-looking papers fell out. One was a letter from his father. The other a sealed envelope. Cub read the letter.

My dear Son,

The Journal of my grandfather will explain why I have stayed here — even why I came here at all — why I dared not tell our secret to a living soul. The greed of men is often beyond friendship. Remember that and be silent as I was silent.

Sealed in the box is a map, and a copy of the same map is marked by me to show exactly where I have searched for our heritage — yours now, my son. The heritage of the Calastros. Some will say it does not exist. I have spent over fifteen years proving my belief that it does. You must decide your own belief.

There is money in the box, enough for your needs for several months. I do not charge you to follow my steps. But if you do, then I give you further details in the sealed envelope to help you. I leave you a free men. The choice is yours.

Your loving Father.'

Cub read the Journal from cover to cover. It wasn't long, but the writing had faded and was spidery and hard to read. General Calastro had been a trusted friend of Emperor Maximilian of Mexico and the Journal told of his adventures whilst escaping from the revolution with three wagons of treasure. Two wagons were lost when crossing a river. The third struggled on. General Calastro described the journey.

'Now come we to a mountain having a shape much like the nose of a man pointing toward the east. I have but five companions out of the forty who accompanied me. Three of these are sick. I myself am ill from lack of sleep and proper food. We are in poor condition to fight off further attacks from Indians. My plan must be to burn the wagon, bury the boxes, then ride for the north and safety. This, God willing, I will do. The Emperor will never forgive me, but all is lost and in this way I may save some part of my means. It is the only way.'

There followed some notes in Cub's father's writing, explaining how General Calastro died in Fort Worth, Texas. A box containing his personal effects was handed to his son's wife as his son was a prisoner in Mexico. This box was then passed down to Cub's father.

Cub opened the box and spent a long time studying the maps and other documents which proved the Calastro rights. His studies were disturbed by the sound of thrumming — like distant thunder, yet it wasn't the storm season. Cub replaced the box and Journal, re-set the stone and went outside.

It was dark now, for he had spent some hours in the house. He lay on the ground keening his ears in the way his father had taught him.

'It's a running herd sure enough,' said Cub to himself. 'The J.S. is gathering for trail — mebbe a thousand head on their home ranges. But they surely ain't trailing at night — nor running 'em!'

Next day he found out why, when Sheriff Keller rode up. 'Pa ain't at home' said Cub.

'I know where your pa is,' said the sheriff. 'In jail, back in Trail City. Durned fool! Why did he have to do it?'

Cub stared steadily. 'My pa ain't never done nothing that ain't right. So he got that murdering coyote, huh? How come?'

'He stampeded the J.S. trail herd last night. All the hands rushed to help head 'em off. Your pa nipped into the bunk-house and searched till he found the gun. He knew the bullet came from an old Sharps rifle. Ain't many of'em around. So he waited, then called out the man who owned the gun and shot him.'

'Not cold,' said Cub. 'Not killing like that. Not Pa.'

'Nope,' the sheriff admitted. 'He gave Shaw a small chance to draw. But Shaw was tired from chasing cattle all night. And your pa drew both guns. Shaw didn't have a chance.'

'Nor did my ma,' said Cub. 'You've done said what you came to say — now git!'

'Like father, like son. You Calastros are hard, ain't you?'

'Mebbe we've reason.'

'It don't pay, son. Jest give folks a chance to help you.'

'Like Josh Sone and his men helped my ma? Like you're helping Pa?' Cub choked back a sob. He was a man now, and men don't cry. 'Helping to hang him?'

'He won't hang,' said the sheriff. 'But it'll be prison for him.

The judge will decide. You can visit your pa if you want. But watch for trouble when you ride into town. The dead man had plenty of friends.'

Cub loosened the stock-whip thong, flicked his wrist and sent the whip cracking out. The tip snicked a piece out of the sheriff's hat-brim.

'Could've been your nose, or your ear,' said Cub. 'Trouble they want — trouble they git. See what I mean?'

The sheriff sighed. 'Suit yourself, son. I've got the Cougar. I ain't time to spend taming his Cub. Them as act like wild ones are treated as wild ones. See you in town.'

Cub rode into town later. Folks stared at him. Some said, 'Howdy, son.' Others glared. Cub could feel the strange mixture of tension and sympathy, as if the town was divided in feelings for and against him.

The court hearing was short. It was a clear case of shooting. All the judge had to decide was whether the man Cougar Calastro killed did actually own a Sharps rifle, and whether Cougar gave him a chance to defend himself.

'I reckon this fella Shaw did own the rifle,' said the judge. 'I reckon it was the same gun that was fired accidentally and killed poor Mrs Calastro. But you, Calastro, had no right to take the law in your own hands. If Shaw hadn't worn a gun, you'd be guilty of murder. He did wear a gun but was slow to use it, and you didn't give him time to defend himself. So I reckon you're guilty of manslaughter and you'll go to prison for a term of not less than one year and not more than five in the State City Penitentiary. Case is closed.'

Cougar nodded curtly and walked, head high, from the court. Cub saw him a few minutes later.

'Better than I expected,' said Cougar. 'I'll do mebbe two years before parole.'

'I'll be at the gate when you come out,' said Cub.

His father smiled. 'Do that, son. Did you open the box yet?'

Cub nodded. 'Spent nigh on a night of studying, Pa.'

'I've spent many a night. It's there somewhere — and it belongs to us — some place in Nose Point Hills. Remember, son, we run a bitty ranch jest to make enough to live, but ranching ain't our real work. That's what we can't tell no one. I've carried the secret all these years. Now I guess the load's on you.'

'I'll carry it, Pa.'

'Go now,' said Cougar. 'Write me?'

'Sure will. So long, Pa.'

Out in the street Cub's way was barred by three J. S. Circle riders.

'Fair warning,' said one. 'We're going to run you outa town. And if we sight you on J. S. land, we'll make you sorry you was born.' A bullet hit the ground in front of Cub's foot.

Cub lifted the stock-whip he carried on a slip-thong attached to his belt. His arm moved faster than a gunhand. The whip snaked out, its tip cut across the man's hand, spinning the gun away. Then the whip snaked and cracked, writhing and whirling around the three men, its tip flicking and stinging, and preventing any gun-draw. Their hats went flying. Shirt buttons were flicked off.

'Now *you* git,' said Cub, 'or I'll cut you in ribbons.'

Sheriff Keller came up. He faced the men, gun drawn.

'I told you hombres — no trouble,' he said. 'It's all over. Debts are paid in full. Leave the boy be, or so help me, I'll lock you all up for drawing a gun on an unarmed person.' He turned to Cub. 'And you, boy — you ride outa town right now. Go work your ranch and sweat the hate outa you.'

'I got no hate,' said Cub. 'Jest let me be.' He strode to the hitching rail, mounted his horse and rode down the main street, head high, tall in the saddle, the stock-whip held looped around one arm, moving menacingly.

Cub rode out of town and into a new world of an empty

house, lonely days and many night hours spent in studying maps and making his own plans of the Nose Point Hills. One day he rode south to San Rosata across the border; a town in which his father sold their few head of cattle twice a year. Cub hired two Mexicans as ranch hands. Both were sons of friends of Cougar's, so Cub had no doubts in doing this.

But the J. S. riders had many doubts about hiring Mexicans, whom they neither liked nor trusted, so even more bad feeling grew up over what, in truth, was none of their business. There was no actual fighting, but for over six months Cub and his hired hands had to work hard to keep their cattle from straying over the Nose Point Hills side of the boundary between the ranches to avoid trouble.

Cub spent much time in the hills, searching for the signs given in the old map. He found the place where his great-grandfather, General Calastro, had written the last notes in his Journal. Part luck, part skill, aided by a heavy rainstorm which uprooted trees and washed down piles of earth on the southern slopes. Under the earth was a rocky surface which formed a natural track up the hillside. Cub spent days checking its course, cutting down trees and digging away piles of rotted leaves.

These trees would have been small shrubs when General Calastro crossed the Nose Point Hills. Cub had been searching for a track that would take a wagon — forgetting that the trees had grown so much since all those years ago. But now he knew he had found the way the General had crossed the hills. Somewhere along it he'd burned the wagon and buried the treasure.

Then, suddenly, it was all made simple for him.

The J. S. riders came chasing one of their breed bulls that had gone mad in a storm and headed into the hills. The fore-man, Clint Dell, met Cub on the southern slopes.

'I'm asking the right to search over your land,' he said

gruffly. 'Ain't wasting no more bad blood between us, so I'm asking real polite-like.'

'Go ahead,' said Cub. 'Breed bulls are purty valuable critturs. Why don't Josh Sone ask me?'

'Josh ain't here. He's been ill this past month. I'm in charge of the J. S.'

'More like he's drunk,' said Cub. 'Best hurry—there's a storm a-comin'.'

Storm clouds, rolling black around them, broke with fierce lightning and thunder just as the J. S. riders had roped the bull. Rain poured down like steel rods, bowing the shoulders with its weight. The bull bellowed and lunged. The horses squealed and slithered. And suddenly the whole caboosh of'em went a-sliding and a-stumbling down the slope as the earth gave way under the force of rain and trampling hooves. But the J. S. riders held the bull and after a time rode off with it, leaving Cub to survey this latest earth-shift.

The rain eased. The sun came out and steam covered the hillside. When this cleared Cub saw what he knew must be the end of his father's and his own search. Old, charred pieces of wood and some rusty metal told their own story. This was the trail of General Calastro, these were the remains of his wagon.

It took Cub another week of careful searching before he found signs that something had been buried. Even then, he didn't dig at once but went working the cattle for a spell. Cub didn't want to spend unbroken time in the hills and have one of the Mexicans come looking for him, and so discover all the digging.

'Be silent,' his father had said. Cub was both silent and cautious. And patient too — which was hardest of all. Then he helped round up a small herd of market beef and sent the two Mexicans to trail them to San Rosata. Not until he was alone again did Cub take shovels and gear and pack-horse into the hills.

The three boxes were buried deep, carefully wrapped in oiled cloths and sacking. They were the same type as the one under his own hearth-stone, with the same crest on the lids. Final proof of ownership, if proof were needed, was that the Calastro key opened each box.

Cub loaded them on the pack-horse, filled in the ground, scattered fallen trees over the area, then rode his horse around many times to stamp down the loose earth.

At home he opened the boxes. One held only documents, such as deeds to houses and lands in Mexico, a Last Will and Testament of General Damon Calastro, some letters from the Emperor Maximilian, and a few pieces of jewellery. Another was filled with gold coins. The third box held dozens of small packages wrapped in oiled silk. Each package contained precious stones — diamonds, pearls, rubies, sapphires. A few were set in gold rings, bracelets and necklaces, but most were naked stones, each worth a fortune.

The finding of this fortune didn't stir Cub to great excitement. It made him feel only that he had kept faith with his father. He had found the Calastro heritage. Cub now opened the sealed envelope from the family box. In it his father had written names and addresses of a lawyer and a bank in State City. Cub didn't delay. He saddled his own and the pack-horse, loaded the boxes, collected food and water for the journey and set off for State City. He arrived there three days later and went direct to the lawyer's office, dumping the boxes on that surprised man's desk as if it was a Wells Fargo freight office.

In a few hours Cub Calastro knew what it was like to be suddenly rich. The lawyer booked him in at the finest hotel in town. Tailors came with fine suits of clothes and linen, but Cub wasted no time on such falderals. Still in his range clothes, dusty and sweat-soaked, he made the lawyer go with him to the State prison. Not until then did Cub feel free to do

The three boxes were buried deep

as *he* pleased — not until he had faced his father and said:

'That's, it, Pa — we've done it! We don't have to take no more from that Josh Sone — not ever.' Then he added: 'Pa, the lawyer says we're rich. Can I have jest one thing?'

'Anything you say, son — jest anything at all.'

Cub said it. His father looked at the lawyer and asked: 'Can you fix that, Mr Holroyd?'

The lawyer nodded. 'I think it can be done, just as the boy wants. Might take a little while.'

It took five weeks. Then, dressed in fine clothes and riding a spanking bay horse, Cub rode back. He rode through the main street of Trail City, swinging his stock-whip and smiling, raising his hat to the ladies, who stared as if their eyes would pop out.

Cub rode clear over the J. S. Circle lands and up to the ranch house. Josh Sone sat on the porch with Clint Dell standing near by.

'You want to call your riders to throw me off your lands, Josh Sone?' Cub asked.

Clint laughed while Josh Sone glared silently.

'You ain't been around lately, boy, else you'd have heard the news,' said Clint. 'The J. S. ranch has been taken over — bought out by a mystery buyer back East.'

'Yeah — I know it.' Cub pulled a paper from his pocket and waved it gently. 'This hyar is the title paper to the J. S. Circle ranch. As of noon today I own it.' He uncoiled the stock-whip and cracked it casually. 'You're on my property, Josh Sone. Climb on your horse and git before I cut off your ears!'

It didn't sound much. It didn't sound nearly as fine as Cub planned it would. Which was funny, because his pa had never thought of doing this. But Cub had dreamed of doing it for as long as he could remember. Perhaps it was because Ma wasn't there to hear it. Cub almost thought he heard her laugh — and suddenly he felt fine!

Battle on Storm Island

by ROBERT BATEMAN

Tom Challoner swung the wheel hard over to bring the *Viking III* round the end of the breakwater. His father looked ahead at the fierce seas surging beyond. Pete Mansell was standing by to hitch on two new cans of fuel for the big sturdy outboard engines which were thrusting the *Viking III* through the water at thirty knots.

It looked like a tough assignment, but the Challoner Speedboat Service was used to beating the clock and the weather. There had been no warning — just a sudden S.O.S. message from right out at the tail-end of the long string of islands, an S.O.S. from Professor Lawley, who lived on Storm Island with his daughter Mary.

'It was not often that they had a call to visit Storm Island,' Tom thought as he battled to control the *Viking III* and bring her round the bank of jagged black rocks which fringed the first of the islands. Professor Lawley did not like visitors. There was nothing on Storm Island except his house and his laboratory — the long, low, windowless building in which he and Mary carried out some kind of mysterious research in secret.

Ahead, the string of islands was just visible through the dense clouds of spray thrown up by the heavy bow slamming into the seas. Bracken Island, Granite Island, The Shoals, and finally Storm Island, looking dark and sinister on the horizon.

The seas were even higher now. They slammed viciously against the bows as the *Viking III* fought to keep her course. Tom listened to Pete's engines. In rough seas you always kept one ear alert for the engines. Your life depended on them.

Tom's father was inside the cabin, warming up the radio.

135

He held up the microphone. 'Hullo, Storm Island, hullo Professor Lawley. Can you hear me? Can you hear me? Over to you, over.'

Tom ducked his head to look into the cabin. 'Any reply?'

His father shook his head. 'Whatever the trouble is, it's probably keeping him away from the set. But surely he's left Mary on watch?' Once again he picked up the mike. 'Hullo, Storm Island. *Viking III* calling. Can you hear me? Hullo, Storm Island. Am waiting for your answer. Over to you, over.'

The moment he switched the set to the receiving position there was a loud, booming reply. 'Lawley here. Avoid enemy boat. Repeat, avoid enemy boat. Keep radio silent from now on, because they have direction-finder. Over and out.'

Tom reached down from the wheel again, and stared into his father's astonished face. 'What in the world's all that about? Has the old man gone off his nut?'

His father shrugged his shoulders. 'Search me! Lawley's always been a weird old bird.'

Tom looked up only just in time. Round the steep shore of Granite Island came the black bows of a boat travelling at terrific speed, and heading straight towards them.

'Hey!' he shouted. 'Look at that! I've never seen her before, have you?'

Pete Mansell turned from his crouching position in the stern. 'She's ex-Navy,' he bellowed. 'Fast as a whippet, and tough, too. I don't know who owns her. I've not seen her before, either.'

The black bows were now only two hundred yards away, and swinging slightly to intercept. Tom beckoned to his father. 'She's heading straight for us! I don't like it, Dad. Maybe old Lawley wasn't playing the fool after all?'

His father came out of the cabin. 'Give me the wheel, Tom. There's one easy way of finding out whether she's after us.

Change course and see if she follows.' He turned the wheel slightly, so that the *Viking III* swung away a little to starboard in the direction of The Shoals.

Only a second passed before Tom shouted, 'She's after us, Dad. They've altered course to cross our bows.'

His father looked quickly from the big ex-Navy boat to The Shoals and back again. 'It's another three miles to Storm Island.'

'She'll catch up with us before we've gone half that distance! Look! Just watch that bow wave.'

'I know. Reckon she can manage an extra two knots above our speed. But she can't board us. Not in this sea. Remember, we can twist and turn twice as fast.' The *Viking III* was still going at top speed, but the pursuer was now only seventy-five yards astern. 'Wait until she catches up and then I'll show you.'

They were past The Shoals now, with the steep, dark slope of Storm Island just in sight, almost masked by driving spray. But Tom was not looking ahead. He was watching the other boat as her bows crept closer and closer. He could see three men in the huge cockpit. One of them suddenly spoke through an amplifier. '*Viking III*, *Viking III*, we are coming alongside. Shut off your engines.'

Toms' father gave a loud snort. 'What, in this sea?' he muttered. 'We'd be swamped in ten seconds. He must be crazy.'

The man aboard the black boat spoke again. '*Viking III*, you have been warned. Shut off your engines or we shall ram you.'

Tom's father waved his fist defiantly. 'Quick Tom, nip into the cabin. Call up the shore station and tell them there's a madman out here.'

'That won't help. There isn't a coastguard boat for forty miles. Anyway, that black brute can go faster than anything

I've ever seen along this coast.' In spite of this, he went into the cabin and switched on the transmitter.

Just as he picked up the microphone, from outside came a rapid burst of shooting. Startled, he put his head out, pulling it back again just in time to avoid being hit by the mast and aerial as they crashed down.

'Do not attempt to send signals,' said the voice from the other vessel. 'The next time I shoot it will not be at your mast but at your hull. So stop your engines.'

Pete Mansell, crouching in the stern beside the engines, looked round for instructions.

Tom had a sudden idea. 'Distress rockets! If I send them up somebody on Granite Island might see them.' Hurriedly he grabbed the rocket pistol from the rack inside the cabin and climbed back into the cockpit.

'Look out, Tom!' yelled his father 'He's going to shoot you.'

Tom ducked just as the man aboard the black boat put his machine-gun to his shoulder. Then there was a cheer from Pete. 'The gun's jammed, Mr Challoner! It won't fire.'

Immediately Tom's father swung the wheel hard over. The *Viking III* twisted hard to port, so violently that water slopped over the gunwale into the cockpit and the starboard engine screamed at high speed as its propeller lifted out of the water. As they completed a U-turn and came level with the cockpit of the black boat, Tom aimed the clumsy signal pistol and fired. The signal rocket went straight for the cockpit, hitting the man with the machine-gun, and then dropping down below the wheel where it flared violently. The helmsman backed away, letting go of the wheel, and the black boat promptly spun off course and headed away towards The Shoals.

'Well done, Tom! That's given us a real chance.' His father whipped the wheel round again, and they raced for Storm

Island at top speed, crashing down into the trough between every wave, then rising swiftly as the next came rolling, white-crested, towards them.

Uneasily Tom watched the other boat. In the cockpit he could see one man fighting with a fire-extinguisher to douse the rocket, while another was throttling down the big inboard engine. Everything depended on how long it would take them to get going again. With every second that passed, the *Viking III* narrowed the distance towards Storm Island and the little jetty where the Professor and Mary would be waiting.

'Here they come again, Dad!' He shouted the warning as soon as he saw the first faint trace of bow wave which showed that the black boat was on the move again.

But the black boat had no hope now of catching them before they reached the jetty. And once ashore, even if the man with the machine-gun managed to put it back in action, surely the Professor had some means of defence himself?

They rounded the huge grey rock which sheltered the small bay in which Professor Lawley had his landing jetty. For a moment there was no sign of either the Professor or Mary. There was no smoke from the chimney of his house, high on the hill overlooking the bay.

Then, with a rifle in his hands, the Professor came out from behind a stone wall at the end of the jetty. As the *Viking III* came alongside he grabbed the rope which Tom's father flung to him.

'Did the *Black Gull* chase you?'

'The big ex-Navy boat? She nearly sank us. They tried to board us, and then shot down our aerial. What's the idea, Professor? Have you got any more guns? The'll be here in a minute.'

Professor Lawley gave a short bark of a laugh. 'They won't come round that big rock. They did once — this morning — and fired their machine-gun, but I was behind the wall.' He waved the rifle. 'This gun's got telescopic sights. I hit their fuel tank first shot, and they haven't come back again.' He helt out a hand to Tom's father. 'Come ashore. Mary's in the boathouse making tea.'

He was as calm and unruffled as if nothing at all was happening. Tom stared at him in amazement.

Ashore, they went over to the boathouse in which the Professor kept his own boat — an old dinghy with a low-powered engine, quite useless for escaping from the *Black Gull*. A kettle was boiling on a paraffin stove. Mary looked up, smiling. 'I knew you'd get here in time,' she said to Tom.

Profesor Lawley glanced out of the boathouse window. There was still no sign of the *Black Gull*. 'I'd better explain,' he said.

Tom's father grinned at him. 'I was wondering when you'd get around to that! It's not every day we get shot at here among the islands. What's the idea?'

'Ever heard of Larsen Fenner?'

Tom's father shook his head. So did Tom and Pete.

'He's in electronics — same as myself. There's a lot of secret work being done in electronics. The first man with a new idea can make a fortune. That's why Mary and I came here — for secrecy. Fenner's working on the same project — portable videotape.'

Tom looked at him blankly. 'What on earth is that?'

'A portable tape-recorder you can carry in your pocket, but which records pictures as well as sound. The camera's in your buttonhole. Or police can fit it to a car windscreen, and get evidence about the criminals they're chasing.'

'Whew!' Pete burst out. 'Sounds pretty marvellous. Imagine seeing the Derby from the horse's viewpoint!'

Professor Lawley nodded. 'You've got the idea. Well, I've nearly perfected the portable videotape — and Fenner knows it! He's determined to steal it, even if he has to kill me.'

140

'He doesn't seem to mind killing me, too,' muttered Tom. 'What are we going to do?'

Tom's father looked thoughtful. 'We could radio for help and then just sit tight.'

'No. That signal I sent you was our last.' He pointed to the remains of a shed just outside the boathouse. 'That's the radio hut. Just as I finished speaking to you the *Black Gull* came round the point and machine-gunned it. There must have been tracer bullets; it caught fire.'

'Then we'll have to get away in *Viking III*. We can't stay here fending them off for ever.'

Professor Lawley nodded. 'You're right. Luckily there's nowhere else on the island where they can get ashore, but we haven't much food. We were due for a trip to the mainland for supplies. I thought perhaps we might be able to dodge them after dark.'

'It's not so much a question of day or night,' said Tom's father. 'It's wind and sea that matter. The rougher the sea, the more advantage they have. No, what we've got to do is create a diversion round the far side of the island — something which will make them go round to investigate. Then we might get a one-mile start before they discover we've gone.'

'If we're lucky,' said Mary suddenly. 'Larsen Fenner's no fool. And he's a good shot with that machine-gun of his.'

'He'll be an *angry* good shot, too!' said Pete. 'Tom scored a direct hit on him with the signal rocket. It won't have done much damage, but I bet it's made him hopping mad.'

'A diversion,' muttered Professor Lawley. 'Have you got any more signal rockets?'

Tom nodded. 'Five left.'

'Who's fast over rough country?'

Tom nodded again. 'I'm not too bad.'

'Right, then. Here, Mary take the rifle in case the *Black Gull* comes back this way. Everybody get aboard the *Viking III*.

141

Tom and I will go over the hill and I'll show him where to stand while he fires off the rockets. The *Black Gull* will come round the island to see what's going on. The moment Tom sees her he runs back and we leave. How's that for a plan?'

Tom's father stood up. 'I don't think we've any other choice. We'd better get this invention of yours loaded aboard first.'

Any idea Tom had of complicated masses of wires and equipment vanished when they climbed the hill to the laboratory and the Professor opened the door. The work benches were clear. There was nothing in sight except a suitcase.

'Everything's in there,' Professor Lawley said. 'The actual models, and the plans for mass production. Everything else I've destroyed. Even if they search the island they won't find anything that'll help them.' He pointed to the suitcase. 'I'll pick it up on my way back. Now I'll show you where to fire the rockets.'

Storm Island was about a mile and a half across. The centre was a high rocky pinnacle, round which there was a path made by the Professor and Mary on their walks. On the far side was a gentle grassy slope leading down to a sheer granite cliff. The Professor led Tom down to the edge of the cliff. 'Here's the best spot. Fire all five rockets, and then wait. I imagine the *Black Gull* will appear round the island in about five minutes. Larsen doesn't take any chances. If he thinks something may be going on he'll waste no time investigating.' He turned, and began to walk back up the slope. 'Give me five minutes' start before you fire the rockets. Good luck!'

Left on his own, Tom crouched down in the long grass at the edge of the cliff. Below him, the sea was pounding on the jagged rocks with a deafening roar. The open sea stretched to the horizon. Storm Island was the last dot of land; beyond it the sea stretched unbroken across thousands of miles to America.

There was no sign of the *Black Gull*. Probably she was at

anchor, sheltering in one of the inlets where there was deep water. One of the three men on board would be on constant lookout duty; the moment the first signal rocket went up, the anchor would be raised.

He stood up. The five minutes asked for by Professor Lawley must be over by now, surely? He raised the pistol, and fired.

The rocket soared high into the grey sky, then exploded in a bright flare. Immediately Tom reloaded and fired again.

By the time he was reloading for the fifth and final rocket, there was a distant roar of engines. Quickly he shifted to a spot from which he could see without being seen, and could run undetected up the slope towards the hilltop. A moment after he dropped into cover, the nose of the *Black Gull* appeared round the headland. The bows were churning up a huge wake as she raced into view at top speed, and in the cockpit he could see Larsen Fenner peering at the clifftop through binoculars.

Tom grinned to himself. Fenner would need X-ray eyes, not binoculars, to see him running, crouched down, through the long grass. He turned, and began moving swiftly uphill.

Behind him he heard Fenner's voice again through the amplifier. 'Professor Lawley, give up the fight; I have enough fuel and supplies to starve you out. Surrender and I promise you safe conduct.'

Tom ran another hundred yards, then heard an angry bellow from Fenner. 'All right, Lawley. If you choose to be a fool, then look out!' Machine-gun fire thundered against the cliff.

So Fenner was armed again? Tom had no idea of the range of the gun, but now it was essential that the *Viking III* got away with a long start. It would be no fun to sit in the heavily-laden boat pursued by Fenner firing off bursts of tracer every time he could find them in his sights.

Tom was on the hilltop now, skirting it carefully to avoid being seen from the deck of the *Black Gull*. Then, on the far side, he looked down the steep slope to the jetty, where *Viking III* lay secured by a single rope.

He shouted and waved. Below him, the signal was seen; he heard the roar as *Viking III*'s twin outboards started up, and Professor Lawley jumped on to the quay to stand by the rope. Tom was gasping now; even though he was in good training, the uphill climb to the summit of the island had winded him, and the journey down was at a jolting run, with every footfall perilous because of the loose surface of the path.

His knees were rubbery with exhaustion when he reached the jetty. Hands reached out from the boat to haul him aboard; Professor Lawley let go the rope and jumped in after him, and the *Viking III*'s helm went hard over, bringing her round to face the homeward journey. Up went the bows as the powerful outboards bit deep into the water — calm water at this point, still in the shelter of the inlet.

'Hold on tight!' shouted Tom's father as they butted into the first of the heavy seas outside. *Viking III* rose high in the air, then slammed down again with bone-shattering force, flinging Mary across the cockpit. Tom caught her as she pitched across the gunwale, and hauled her back aboard. Her face was white with panic. Tom pointed out the footholds in the cockpit planking, and showed her how to thrust her shoes into them and grip when the boat rose with the next wave. Then he swung round and looked astern at the tall cliffs, and more important still, the twin capes, round one of which the *Black Gull* must appear.

'Any sign?' shouted his father.

'Not yet. Those rockets have fooled him.'

'He won't stay fooled for long,' said Professor Lawley grimly. 'Not Fenner.' Then, 'Look, here he comes!'

At almost unbelievable speed, the bows of the *Black Gull* shot out from the side of the island and raced towards them. 'How far ahead are we?' Tom's father bellowed.

'Half a mile,' Tom guessed. 'Certainly no more than that.'

His father's face set tight. Tom knew what he was thinking — that at the speed the *Black Gull* was travelling, by the time they reached The Shoals she could be alongside. And to Tom's surprise, the bow swung slightly.

'Dad! You're heading straight for The Shoals!'

His father said nothing. He was crouched over the wheel, with the spray pouring over the top of the windshield into his face. The change of course had put the *Viking III* into a cross-sea, and he had to fight not to be swept broadside on every time a wave caught them on the quarter. Looking astern, Tom could see the *Black Gull* gaining fast, creaming through the seas, untroubled by the cross-currents because of her greater size and power. He stared at his father, wondering what in the world had got into him. It was as if he *wanted* the *Viking III* to be overtaken.

From astern, a few hundred yards away, came a warning burst of machine-gun fire. Tom's father turned his head scornfully. 'Well, it's his ammunition not ours!'

Professor Lawley steadied himself and tried to fire back with the rifle, but after two attempts he shrugged his shoulders and gave up. It was impossible to aim with any kind of accuracy while the *Viking III* was rolling, pitching, and heaving herself up on to the crest of every wave.

Suddenly Tom jumped up. 'Dad! You're heading straight on to The Shoals!' He grabbed his father's arm. 'You'll put us on the rocks.' He looked ahead in horror as the *Viking III* raced towards the long line of rocks and sandbanks which stretched for half a mile. His father was aiming right for the centre, his face set with concentration.

There was another burst of fire, this time with the range too short to be comfortable. A neat row of holes appeared down one side of the cabin, sending a shower of broken glass across the floor.

'Tell them to hang on tight!' said Tom's father quietly. 'Here we go!'

Another touch of the wheel, and the *Viking III* was aimed at a narrow gap in The Shoals — a gap no more than twenty feet wide. Tom stared at it in surprise. He had been past The Shoals dozens of times, but he had never noticed it before.

Then they were into the gap, lifting on a wave.

And at that moment Tom heard an angry jarring noise from below his feet! Pete heard it too, and with a tremendous effort he reached behind him and rocked the two engines upwards so that their propellers came almost clear of the water. A split second later they were out of the gap, in open sea again, just as the *Black Gull* fired again. A long burst of fire raked the cabin top. Tracer bullets set the thin timbers alight; Professor Lawley fought his way in through the smoke and came out again with the fire-extinguisher, which he hammered on a thwart until the fierce jet of foam shot out from its nozzle towards the flames.

Then, astern, there was a tremendous rending, tearing sound as the *Black Gull* hit. She reared up almost on end, her bottom torn away for half her length. Through the broad gash dropped a man; the other two toppled off the deck into the boiling seas.

'Throttle down, Pete!' shouted Tom's father, bringing the wheel round. He turned the *Viking III* in a tight circle, and brought her to within twenty feet of the gap. 'Know your tides, Tom!'

Tom goggled at him. 'But there's no gap in The Shoals, even at high tide!'

'No proper gap. But the water covers the rocks a few inches deep. I took a chance — we went over on a wave. I knew the *Black Gull* must draw twice as much water as we do. She couldn't make it.'

They were reaching into the water now to grab the three

146

The three exhausted men were struggling in the fierce sea

exhausted men, who were struggling to stay afloat in the fierce sea.

Fenner collapsed on the floor of the cockpit. Professor Lawley looked down at him with a grim smile. 'Pity,' he said. 'You won't be doing any more inventing for about the next ten years. I'll miss you. A rival's useful — keeps me up to the mark.'

The *Viking III* was now in smoother water, with the mainland dead ahead. The colour was coming back into Mary's cheeks. Over the three men stood the Professor, with his rifle pointed at Fenner, but none of them showed any sign of resistance. All seemed faintly surprised to find themselves still alive.

Professor Lawley looked into the cabin to see that his precious suitcase was still safe. Then he nodded to Tom, his father, and Pete. 'Thanks,' he said quite calmly, as though a sea battle happened to him every day. 'Anything I can do for you any time, just let me know.'

It was an invitation Tom could not resist. 'Well, there *is* something,' he said quietly. 'As soon as you have one to spare, I'd like one of those portable videotapes.'

His father stared at him. 'Whatever d'you want that for?'

Tom grinned. 'Simple enough. Think of the publicity, Dad! We'll be the only boat in the world that can offer passengers a full sound and picture show of their journey!'

Weird Sister

by HOWARD JONES

Well, I'm in a regular pickle, and no mistake. It's a humiliating thought for an older brother, but the sooner Mother and Father return from their holiday cruise in the Mediterranean, the better for all concerned. Mother's the only person who can really cope with Felicity Jane.

They'll blame me, of course. Or, at least, Father will. I can almost hear his voice now: 'Sitting there all night and half the day!' he'll say, looking down his nose. "Pon me word, where's your sense of responsibility, boy?' And Mother will give me one of her wistful looks and say: 'But you're her brother — why did you let her do it?'

And being Mother, and so wonderfully practical, she'll soon have Felicity Jane running around with dewy eyes and full of apologies to everyone for the trouble she's caused. And because Felicity Jane is — well, what she is, we'll all say: 'There, there, don't cry now, it was just a little girl's harmless prank, wasn't it?'

I suppose that in a way I *am* to blame for this silly mess I'm in. I mean, if only I'd done something about Felicity Jane last week, if only I'd taken that wretched book away from her and pitched it into the kitchen stove or on to Jobling's bonfire... If only I'd locked her in her room the morning Jobling's birch broom mysteriously vanished... If only — but there, what's the use of recriminations now? The damage has been done, and it's no use crying over spilt milk, as they say.

Talking of milk, if there's any spilt about the house just now, I'm liable to lap it up. That's an odd reflection and I dare say it puzzles you. However, I'll make my meaning quite clear by and by.

You'll probably take me for a frightful ass when you've read what I have to say. But I'm not, really I'm not. It's simply that I can't cope with Felicity Jane. I wish you knew her, I'm sure you'd sympathise with me. (Though I can't help thinking that when you've heard my story, you may be very glad that you *don't* know her.)

She's just twelve years and six months old, with a roses-and-cream complexion, enormous sea-green eyes, and long chestnut pigtails. Honestly, Felicity Jane is as pretty as a picture, though I say it who shouldn't. And she's clever, very clever.

She absolutely sails through all her exams; and only the other day, Miss Plonket, the Head Mistress at the High School, declared she's quite the brainiest child to pass through her hands in forty years of teaching.

Ever since she was so-high, my kid sister has been a regular bookworm, reading anything and everything she could lay her hands on. Come to think of it, all this trouble really started with books; or rather, a particular book.

It was the first Saturday after Mother and Father had left for their cruise, I remember. That morning I happened to be whitening my cricket pads in the garden shed when Felicity Jane, sweet as cherry pie, came to me begging a loan of fifty pence so that she could go to the sale at Mrs Mason's cottage in Meadowsweet Lane.

This was the first I'd heard about the sale. But I knew old Widow Mason and her tumbledown cottage very well. She was a queer, crabbed, scruffy old woman — a bit of a miser, so they said, and judging from her ancient clothes, and the height of the weeds in her garden, and the loose tiles and cracked panes in her cottage windows, you could very easily believe it.

'Mrs Mason's leaving the district for keeps,' said Felicity Jane. 'That's why she's selling up everything — absolutely everything. Her furniture and china, her curtains and linen...'

'Just a lot of old junk,' I said.

'... and her pictures and her books and her carpets,' said Felicity Jane. 'Absolutely *everything*. There's no knowing what treasures she's got hidden away, and if you ask me' — which I didn't — 'if you ask me, there'll be some wonderful bargains to be picked up for next to nothing.'

Well, she prattled on in this way for a solid ten minutes while I was trying to get my pads respectably white. And, of course, in the end I lent her ten bob. I confess it was my secret hope t at she'd bring back a piece of valuable old china — a Dresden cherub, say, or a Chelsea shepherdess; or, failing that, something useful, like a sturdy old wheelback chair which would fit comfortably into my room.

She had left me in peace shortly before eleven o'clock when the sale was due to open. At twenty past eleven she came staggering back along the garden path, weighed down by a pile of old books bound together with a frayed length of picture cord.

Honestly, you've never seen such a useless lot of rubbish in all your life.

There was a book in English — at least, in a sort of English. The binding was entirely missing, but the title was displayed in a very queer, tilted sort of print on the fly-leaf:

> *HOCUS-POCUS, beinge the Opus*
> *Mirabilis or Secrete Recipes of*
> *the Female Necromancer Mathilde*
> *Malprax; confessed by her before her*
> *recent notorious Tryall;*
> *Which is to say, Her Booke Revealing*
> *Rare and Varied Magickal Artes,*
> *and likewise the Fabrickation of Certaine*
> *Charmes and the Weavinge of Useful*
> *Potente Spelles.*

I glanced through this wretched book. But what with the paper being all stained and yellow, and the 'f's and the 's's all alike, it gave me quite a headache. Or perhaps it was my bad temper that gave me the headache, because I really was put out that Felicity Jane should waste her fifty pence — I mean, my fifty pence — on rubbish such as this.

There were picture books without pictures, dictionaries in obscure languages with half the pages missing. There were books without covers and covers without books. There were books in Latin, French, in Greek, all with the pages stained and nibbled and torn and dog-eared.

Naturally, I rated her pretty soundly. But she protested that old books were often very valuable, even when the bindings were missing; and that for all I knew she had picked up a fortune.

Now all this happened a fortnight ago last Saturday. I had all but forgotten those wretched books and my wasted fifty pence, though I should have known better, I admit. Because, for all her charms, Felicity Jane is a very determined young person, and you never can tell what sort of mischief is brewing in the back of her mind.

She had carried the books up to her room, and there she spent a great deal of time, with the door closed firmly upon the outside world. Yet I suspected nothing, not even when Jobling, our gardener, complained bitterly that some interfering busybody had borrowed his birch broom from the woodshed; and had either pinched it for keeps, which he strongly suspected, or forgotten to replace it, which he doubted.

In fact, I had absolutely no inkling of trouble brewing until Sergeant Burrows telephoned from the local police station yesterday morning.

'Is that Mr Twistleton-Brown?' said Sergeant Burrows in a husky sort of voice. And when I told him I was Timothy Twistleton-Brown, he said quickly: 'Ah, um, ah! Fetch your father quick, young gent, will ye?'

I said that at that moment Father was cruising somewhere off Sicily and couldn't be fetched. Sergeant Burrows was silent for a bit, then he said: 'Ah, um, ah! Then I take it in a sense *you're* responsible for a juvenile female party name o' Felicity Jane Twistleton-Brown.'

I agreed that I was.

'In that case,' said Sergeant Burrows, 'I must inform you that in one hour from now the said juvenile party is to be brought before a magistrate...'

'How ridiculous!' I cried.

'... on a charge of creating a serious public mischief,' said Sergeant Burrows. 'You'll learn all about it if you come along to court, young gent.' And he added — a little apprehensively, so I thought — 'Though it takes a bit of believing, blow me down if it don't!'

I dashed up to Felicity Jane's room. The casement window stood wide open. In the middle of the carpet lay an open book — that wretched Hocus-Pocus book with the 'f's and 's's all confused. And there, on the rug beneath the window, were a few birch twigs which *might* have come from Jobling's broom.

The bed had not been slept in.

These clues should have told me a great deal, I suppose. But my mind was in confusion, I could think only of my poor little sister in the cruel clutches of the police, of the urgency of reaching the court to bail her out, or to testify to her sweet and simple nature. I grabbed my bicycle from the garage, and as I pedalled like fury up the road, I rehearsed to myself the words I would repeat to the magistrate.

'A very warm-hearted child, my lord.' (But was a magistrate a lord, an honour, or a worship? Might be better just to call him 'sir'...) 'A very good scholar, sir, top of her class in everything for the last three years!'... 'Fond of animals? She literally wouldn't harm a fly, sir!'... 'Always polite and not in the least greedy, sir — couldn't you let her off with a caution?'

Yes, but let her off from *what*? 'It takes a bit of believing,' Sergeant Burrows had said. And at the recollection of that ominous message, gloom seized me once again, my heart descended to the depths.

Dusty and perspiring, I reached the courtroom just as Felicity Jane's name was called. She spotted me at once; she grinned and winked an eye at me, clearly enjoying the novelty of the proceedings. The magistrate, a stout gentleman with tortoiseshell spectacles and bushy white whiskers, beamed down from the bench, his finger-tips pressed together — rather like a genial old toad, I thought.

In the well of the court, facing Felicity Jane but pretending not to notice her, stood Police Constable Blower, who has directed traffic at Market Cross longer than most people can remember. He dabbed at his glistening bald head with a spotted handkerchief, studied the ceiling, and shifted uneasily from foot to foot, as if he doubted whether the floorboards would bear his considerable weight.

'Constable Blower's evidence, your worship,' called the clerk, a little man with an enormous wing collar, bobbing up from a pile of papers and bobbing down again. The magistrate nodded and leant forward, curving his fingers round his right ear. Constable Blower blew his nose, produced a notebook, and declared, in a loud, deep voice:

'Your wazzip! At eight a.m. today — being market morning, your wazzip — I was directing the traffic at Market Cross, as is required. At eight-five a.m. precise, I observed the young defendant proceeding towards me from the direction of 'Igh Street. She were astride a broomstick.'

'My good man,' said his worship gruffly, leaning forward a little more. 'My good man, you really must speak up. Don't mouth your words.'

154

'I b'ain't mouthing nothing,' said Blower. 'I'm a-telling the plain truth, as the law requires.'

'You're mouthing your words. Just for the moment I thought you said the defendant was astride a broomstick.'

'Just what I *did* say,' bellowed Blower. 'She were astride this 'ere very broomstick which I now produce in hevidence.' And he dived beneath the clerk's table and held up Jobling's birch broom.

His worship blinked behind his spectacles.

'Um, a complete broom, not merely a broomstick. Be more precise in your facts, Blower. In any case, there is no law against a child playing with a broomstick. What was she doing with this particular broomstick?'

'She were flying about on it, your wazzip.'

'Flying about? On a broomstick?'

'Flying about,' said Blower doggedly. 'On a broomstick. When I first observes her, she were a little above the rooftops. I estimates her speed at twenty miles per hower.'

'Twenty miles per hower — I mean, hour,' said the magistrate looking vaguely at Blower and then at Felicity Jane, who responded with her most enchanting smile. Then he said: 'Perhaps at that time of the morning the light was not very good.'

'Broad daylight,' said Blower. 'A fine, sunny morning, that it were.'

'Perhaps your eyesight is defective, Blower?'

'Look 'ere,' said Blower, 'I'm a-telling you what I saw, plain and straightforward. There's not a copper in the county with better eyes 'n mine, though I says it myself. If you doubts me word, just ask the police surgeon.'

'The police surgeon? Was *he* with you? Did *he* observe this child flying, as you say, on a broomstick?'

'No, no, no!' cried Blower. 'He weren't there so far as I'm aware.'

'Then why bring him up? Keep strictly to the facts, Blower. Proceed.'

Blower took a deep breath. 'As I was a-saying,' he resumed, 'I observed the defendant flying towards me astride a broomstick from the direction of 'Igh Street. And as I was a-saying, 'tis market morning, there were a deal of traffic to contend with. The appearance of the defendant on a broomstick caused a great deal of chaos, concern, and consternation. As the defendant floated towards me...'

'Floated?' said his worship. 'Just now you said she was flying. Was she floating or was she flying, Blower? Come, make up your mind!'

'She were flying with a sort of floating motion,' insisted Blower. 'As she approached, I hollered to her to come down. She replied: "Arf a mo" — or some such words, your wazzip — "Arf a mo, I'm just getting the hang of it!" And with that she circled the Market Cross three times, waving and grinning at me. Finally, she came down — none too smoothly, neither — just abaft Mrs Carter's apple stall. I immediately took her into custody and charged her with creating a public mischief.'

For a little while there was silence. His worship shifted his spectacles over the broad bridge of his nose and smoothed his long white moustaches. At length he remarked, to nobody in particular: 'A fine sunny morning — exactly! A trick of light and shade, no doubt! A mirage! An illusion!'

'I beg your pardon, sir,' said Felicity Jane, speaking up for the first time. 'I beg your pardon, but that's not quite fair. I've known Constable Blower for ages and ages, he's a very kind and honest gentleman. Everything he has said is true.'

His worship gave another tug at his spectacles and said pleasantly: 'Perhaps you'd like to tell us all about it, my dear?'

'As a matter of fact, I would, sir,' said Felicity Jane. 'As

a matter of fact, I've only just learned to fly on a broomstick —
it's rather tricky, like learning to skate, only harder, you know.
As a matter of fact, I was out practising all last night, and I
think I'm pretty good just now, if you'll excuse me saying so.
I'm terribly sorry about causing public mischief, and I hope
Constable Blower doesn't think I was *rude* to him.'

'I am sure he doesn't,' said his worship, pleasantly. 'Tell us
about last night, my dear. Where did you go, for instance?'

'As a matter of fact,' said Felicity Jane, 'I don't know
exactly where I went. There was no moon, sir, it was pitch
dark, you see. But, as a matter of fact, I *do* remember coasting
over Whitesheet Hill and the chalk quarry. Oh yes, and I went
over Bobhanger Wood so close I could have touched the tree-
tops. And, as a matter of fact, I was rather scared, sir — the
owls were hooting, you see, and it was very, very dark.'

'Quite a nightmare! said his worship; and it was clear
from the smug look on his face that he didn't believe a word
of it. I saw a little pink flush rise in Felicity Jane's cheeks —
and with her, that's *always* a danger sign.

'But I *can* fly on the broomstick!' she yelled. 'I *did* fly over
Whitesheet and Bobhanger. I *did* fly over High Street and
three times round Market Cross! And, as a matter of fact, sir,
if you don't believe me, I can jolly well prove it!'

'There, there!' said his worship soothingly. 'You mustn't
upset yourself. I propose to remand you for one week, and if
you promise faithfully...' He broke off, then added, in sharper
tones, to the clerk: 'Kindly oblige me by removing that
broomstick from the defendant's reach.'

But he was too late. Felicity Jane had already seized the
broom and was soaring ceilingwards. Twice she circled the
courtroom, then, with a wave of her hand, she passed
through the open door. His worship shuddered and covered
his face with his hands. The clerk moaned and vanished
under his table. Only Constable Blower was completely

157

unmoved. He stood with his hands on his hips, staring at the window, a satisfied smile on his big brown face.

In the ensuing pandemonium, I took the opportunity to slip away. When I reached home, Felicity Jane was in her room, lying flat on her stomach, her nose deep in the Hocus-Pocus book. The birch broom was propped up in a corner. I pitched it through the window, and said: 'Felicity Jane, I am now going to burn that book.'

'Oh, no!' she cried.

'I am going to burn that wretched book!' I said. 'Give it to me at once.'

'You know,' said Felicity Jane, thoughtfully, 'what I *ought* to have is a cat. A nice, sleek, black cat. I think you'd make a very good cat. Would you mind very much? Just for a few days, you know.'

She smiled at me with her great green eyes. Her lips moved gently. 'Puss, puss!' she said. 'Nice puss!'

Last night she was out again on the broomstick. I ought to have stopped her, I suppose — after all, I *am* her brother. But I found it much more entertaining sitting at home — by the mouse-hole under the kitchen sink.

Yes, the sooner Mother and Father return home, the better for all concerned, especially me. As I said before, Mother's the only one who can *really* cope with Felicity Jane.

The Case of the Gilt Mirror

It was there, in its place, when Bill came in to tea one Thursday afternoon. It hung, this splendid mirror in a moulded, gilt frame, over the mantelpiece. It was oval in shape and leaned slightly away from the wall, so that the tea-table and much of the room reflected themselves pleasantly in its shining glass. Bill walked up to it and stared at himself in its polished depths, his cap slightly cocked sideways, his thin face wearing its little comical grin. His mother bustled in with the teapot and looked at him with a smile.

'I didn't buy that for vain young gentlemen to admire themselves in it,' she said.

'No?' said Bill, looking at her in the glass. 'What did you buy it for, then?'

'It is nice, isn't it, Bill?' she said. 'And the gilt frame is beautiful.'

'It is,' said Bill, examining it. 'I should think it's valuable, too. You must have paid a lot for it. What's Dad going to say?'

'He'll be very pleased. We've been looking for a mirror like that for some time. And it was very cheap.'

'Where did you get it?'

'There's a second-hand shop just before you come to Tooting Broadway. I was that way this afternoon, and I went in to inquire for a glass. They had several — not very elegant ones — and I was just going to leave when the lady, a very pleasant, helpful person, brought this one out. It was exactly what I wanted and I just had to have it.'

'A good buy,' said Bill, throwing his cap on a chair and sitting at the table.

'A good buy,' mimicked Mrs Holmes. 'You children all talk nowadays as if you were about fifty with all the experience in the world. And how many times have I got to tell you to hang your cap up and not throw it on chairs?'

'Oh, all right, Mother,' said Bill, in a resigned voice, but even as he rose to put matters right Mrs Holmes hung the offending cap up herself. Bill grinned and sat down again. She was a kindly mother, more bark than bite.

When Mr Holmes came in to tea he admired the purchase, as well he might, and commended his wife's wisdom in acquiring so beautiful an article for so little money. The family had settled down for the evening, Mr Holmes to his pipe and his newspaper, Mrs Holmes to her mending and Bill to the rewriting of an essay for Mr Snooks, when there came a shy little knock at the front door.

Mrs Holmes looked up at her husband, who glanced back at her over the top his newspaper.

'Who can that be?' she said.

Mr Holmes shook his head.

'Are you expecting Tony?' asked Mrs Holmes.

'Not at the front door,' said Bill.

The shy little tap came again.

'What's wrong,' suggested Bill, 'with answering the door?'

'Nothing,' said his father. 'You thought of it. You try it.'

When Bill opened the door, there in the lamp-light stood an old man with a moustache and beard, a long overcoat, and a black hat, which he took off and held in his hand as soon as the door opened.

'Good evening,' he said, making a little bow. 'I am sorry to give you trouble, but I must know — does a Mrs Holmes live here?'

'Yes,' said Bill. 'She does. She's my mother. Do you want to see her?'

The old man smiled and spoke so politely and charmingly.

'Oh,' he said. 'I am glad. Yes, please. If I could see her for only just a little time.'

'Step inside,' said Bill. 'I'll call her.'

'Oh, thank you, thank you,' said the old man. 'I am sorry to give you so much trouble. My name is Trien — Charles Trien. I will not detain her a minute — perhaps two. Not more.'

Mrs Holmes came into the front room where Mr Trien stood; and he bowed very low to her, smiling and apologising for his intrusion.

'Good evening, Mrs Holmes, I believe. Forgive me, please. But I think you bought a mirror with a gilt frame from my shop today.'

'I certainly bought a mirror like that today. I didn't know it was from your shop.'

'Yes, yes. My good wife served you, is not that so?'

Bill was watching the old man with close interest, and behind all the politeness he could see an eagerness, a nervousness which it took old Mr Trien all his time to control.

'How did you know where we lived, Mr Trien?' he asked.

The old man turned to Bill with a smile and another little bow.

'Oh, that is so simple,' he said. 'In our business we take always the name and address of a customer. Your good mother will remember — yes.'

'Well, is there anything wrong?' asked Mrs Holmes, who feared that the old gentleman had repented of the price at which his wife had let the mirror go; she was resolved not to pay another shilling, come what might.

'Nothing wrong, no, not at all,' replied Mr Trien. 'But I am so sorry — my wife had no right to sell this article. It was reserved for another customer. It was not ours to sell any longer. It was already sold. I am so sorry. I feel so ashamed, but what can I do?'

'You mean you want me to let you have it back?' said Mrs Holmes.

'Oh, you are so kind,' said old Mr Trien, putting his hands together. 'And I shall let you choose any other in my shop and charge nothing, even if it shall be a greater price.'

'I didn't like any of the others,' said Mrs Holmes. 'This was absolutely the one I wanted.'

'Yes, of course,' said Mr Trien, more abjectly polite than ever.

'But you understand — my other customer — it is so bad for my business. Perhaps I can get you one just like it.'

'Well, can't you get the other customer one just like it?' said Mrs Holmes, who hated the thought of the bare place on the wall if she should part with this king of mirrors.

'Oh, dear — forgive me — you see, that one is not mine. It belongs to this other customer. You must see, dear Mrs Holmes, how bad it will be for me.'

'I must have a word with my husband about it,' said Mrs Holmes, looking very troubled.

'Of course, of course,' agreed Mr Trien. 'I am sure he will see my difficulty. He is no doubt a business man himself.'

But Mr Holmes did not see Mr Trien's difficulty. He only saw his wife's side and, after all, he was fond of his wife and not of Mr Trien. While the matter was explained to him by Mrs Holmes, to the accompaniment of nods and polite sounds and little bows from the old man, he looked very severe and filled his pipe.

'It comes to this, then,' he said. 'My wife bought an article at your shop all fair and square, paid for it, and brought it away, and now you want it back.'

This plain talking seemed to occasion Mr Trien some pain. He smiled apologetically and shifted his feet.

'Well, sir,' he said, 'the circumstances are very difficult —'

'You could get a replica if we parted with this one?'

162

'Oh yes, of course. A few days only,' said Mr Trien, delightedly rubbing his hands.

'You're absolutely sure of that?' asked Mr Holmes.

'My dear sir, I am absolutely certain to do it.'

'Well, then, get it for the other fellow,' said Mr Holmes. 'That's my last word. We're going to stick to this one, because my wife likes it and has paid for it, and it's legally hers.'

A little moan escaped the bearded lips of Mr Trien, to be followed by an earnest appeal to Mr Holmes to change his mind, but there was no result, and the old gentleman found himself outside the door, where he buzzed and bumbled for a moment like a disappointed bee and then vanished into the night. Bill, usually a polite enough lad, threw himself into a chair, and let out peal after peal of laughter.

'What's the matter with you?' demanded his father.

'He looked so funny — going and not wanting to go, being polite and wanting to be rude,' said Bill.

'I've never heard of such a thing,' said Mrs Holmes. 'Coming here and asking for his goods back. He won't go far in business like that. I shan't go there again, you may be sure.'

'A regular sauce, I call it,' said Mr Holmes. 'Anyhow, you've got your mirror, and there's an end of it.'

The next morning Bill woke with a heavy cold, and when his mother told him he must stay at home for the day he was not ill-pleased, though he protested loudly.

'Oh, Mother, what rot! I can't stay at home for a thing like a slight cold,' he said.

'You'll stay, not only for your own sake. It's not fair to other people to mix with them. That's the way colds spread,' she said firmly. 'Besides, it's not a slight cold. It's a heavy one. You'll stay in your room and I'll dose you so that you'll be all right in a day or two.'

Though he grumbled, Bill was already enjoying the thought of a whole day in his room, meals there and all, for he had plenty to do, cuttings to paste up, a new book to read, a book with the title *Modus Operandi — A Text-Book of Modern Methods of Crime Detection*, and plenty of odd office jobs for which he usually had little enough time. So when his fire was lit, his breakfast eaten, and the first dose of medicine taken, he settled down to a very pleasant day.

Outside the weather was lovely, the sky blue, the sun bright, and everything looked fresh and sharp; it was a pity to have a cold on such a day, but there you were, you couldn't pick and choose your times for bad colds.

About eleven Mrs Holmes bustled in with a tray bearing a cup of coffee and some biscuits.

'Here you are, Bill,' she said. 'Something to keep you going till lunch-time.'

She sat on the edge of the bed holding the tray, her kind, homely face full of pleasure, for she liked nursing Bill or his father, and didn't mind a bit their being ill in a small way.

'There's been such a nice man at the door, Bill,' she said. 'He wanted a job — any little job about the house — offered to dig the garden, anything for a shilling or so.' Bill knew his mother. He gave her a warning look.

'You didn't part with any money, did you?' he asked. 'You know what Dad says about your heart.'

'No. I didn't,' said Mrs Holmes firmly. Not quite firmly enough, however.

'Come on,' said Bill. 'What did you give him?'

'Only a cup of coffee and a sandwich.'

'You didn't ask him in, surely?'

'Well, I did. He wasn't like the usual caller. There was something about him — in spite of being a beggar, he was a gentleman.'

'You'll get your throat cut one day for certain,' said Bill, shaking his head. 'You don't know the first thing about these chaps. They might do anything.'

'Well, you're wrong. About this one, anyway. While he sat and had his coffee he told me about himself.'

'Oh, yes?' said Bill, with a grin. 'And it turned out he was cousin to the King of the Belgians.'

'No, it didn't. He's been an accountant — I could tell he'd been a professional man from his speech. He's had bad luck —'

'Don't tell me,' said Bill putting down his cup. 'I might believe it too.'

'You naughty boy,' said Mrs Holmes. 'You're like all the rest nowadays. You've no sympathy.'

'That's right, Mother,' said Bill. 'Nasty suspicious lot we are.'

'Yes, you are,' said Mrs Holmes. She put the sheets straight on the bed. 'Now keep covered up. I want you right by the morning.'

'Yes, Mother,' said Bill, picking up his book. When the door closed, and he heard his mother go into the kitchen, he shut his book, threw aside the bed-clothes, and took from behind the door a particular treasure — a pair of binoculars lent to him for as long as he liked by Tony Harries, to whose father they had once belonged. He had not had them long enough to test them out, and it occurred to him that now was a good time to do it — a bright day, the expanses of the common before his window, and leisure to stare at whatever presented itself.

They were wonderful glasses. Once Bill had got the right focus, the world within that magic-lit circle was trebly fascinating — the clearness of detail, the shapes of the leaves on distant clumps, the grass on far-away ground, the sudden appearance, almost within reach, of the features of a man, unaware of being watched, half a mile away.

Suddenly, the ideal object of scrutiny came into view,

something to watch from the moment of its appearance. It was the figure of a man carrying the impedimenta of an artist. Bill watched while he selected a position in front of a clump of bushes — to shield him from the wind, Bill supposed — set up his easel and board, put his stool up, and settled down to paint. Bill could clearly see his face — that of a dark young man with a raincoat and blue beret — and could watch all his movements. At first Bill was puzzled. There was a painter all right, and all the tools of the trade. But what could he be painting? Bill knew very little about such matters, but he observed that the sun was in the painter's eyes, and all there could be to paint was the row of houses of which Bill's home was one. Still, there was no accounting for artists and their tastes, more especially as some of the modern ones didn't produce a canvas that looked anything like the original, so perhaps subject didn't matter.

'Bill!' cried Mrs Holmes's voice, breaking into these reflections and this vigilance. 'What *are* you doing out of bed? You'll get pneumonia. And not even your dressing-gown on! Get into bed at once!'

Bill turned to his mother, who had come into the bedroom so quietly that in his interest in the artist he had not heard the door open.

'All right, Mother,' he said. 'The room's quite warm and I've only been out a minute. I was trying these glasses that Tony lent me.'

'Get into bed — *at once!*' cried Mrs Holmes. 'What next, I wonder?'

Bill skipped into bed, and pulled the clothes over himself. 'There,' he said. 'Will that do?'

'Yes. And stay there till I tell you to get up,' ordered Mrs Holmes, smiling at him nevertheless.

He held out the glasses to her.

'Have a look,' he said. 'They're wonderful glasses. There's

166

an artist chap out there. See if you can get him.'

Mrs Holmes took the binoculars and Bill watched her.

'Turn the screw thing till they suit your eyes,' he said. 'No, not that way — the other.'

Mrs Holmes obeyed, got the focus, and stared hard over the common.

'Got him?' asked Bill.

'Why, Bill — 'said Mrs Holmes.

'They're grand, aren't they?' said Bill. 'You can see his mind working.'

'Why, Bill —' repeated Mrs Holmes.

'Yes? What?'

'The artist — it's the man who called — the man I asked in for coffee,' said Mrs Holmes.

'What!' cried Bill.

'Yes. It is. I'm sure it is.'

'So he's not an accountant after all,' said Bill, grinning.

He jumped out of bed and took the glasses from his mother to have another look. And this time she did not protest, but merely draped his dressing-gown around his shoulders.

'I can't understand it at all,' she said. 'If he is really a painter, why didn't he say so? I suppose he does pictures as one way of getting a living.'

Bill made no reply, and kindly Mrs Holmes went downstairs again, troubled but little about the queer ways of menfolk. She felt she understood men too well to let them worry her.

Bill however continued to stare at the man seated in front of the easel, and the longer he stared, the more convinced he became that there was very little serious painting being done. The man's hands were not moving enough. Nor was his head. Only once did he seem to be working at the painting, and that was when a small boy approached to look on. Bill watched the boy come near, hands in pockets. Then he drew a step nearer, and Bill saw the man order him away with a sharp movement of his hand. The boy drifted resentfully away and all was as before.

When Mrs Holmes brought lunch up, Bill was stitting up meekly in bed, his newspaper-cutting book before him, his scissors and paste on the table beside him.

'Is he still there?' asked Mrs Holmes.

'I haven't looked for an hour,' replied Bill, 'But I'm sure he is.'

'You're right,' said Mrs Holmes, glancing out of the window. She watched the man for a while and then added: 'I've a good mind to go over and shame him. I don't like people who tell lies.'

'For goodness' sake,' cried Bill, nearly upsetting his tray in his excitement, 'don't do that. That would spoil it properly.'

'Spoil what, pray?' asked Mrs Holmes, glancing curiously at her son.

'Why — the joke,' mumbled Bill.

'I see no joke in deceiving decent people,' said Mrs Holmes severely.

'No. Well, promise you won't go near him,' said Bill.

'You needn't worry. I don't wish to see him again,' said Mrs Holmes. 'By the way, I'm going down to the shops this afternoon. You'll be all right for an hour, won't you?'

'Yes, of course. But when you go, do you mind going out at the back and through the garden to the lower road? It's just as quick.'

'Why on earth should I go that way? I never do.'

'Well — I want you to — today.'

'But why, Bill?'

Bill nodded to the window.

'That chap,' he said. 'I don't want him to know you've gone out.'

'Good gracious, Bill,' cried Mrs Holmes, 'you've got him on the brain. You don't mean you're afraid?'

'I am, a bit,' said Bill, hanging his head.

'Why, then, if you really mean that, of course I won't go at all.' Again Bill nearly overturned his tray.

'Oh, you must go. I insist on your going. Oh, Mother, don't be difficult. Do as I say, there's a dear. Go out at the back door, don't let anyone see you go and, above all, don't let anything — not even me — stop you going.'

'You funny boy,' said Mrs Holmes fondly. She had a habit of seeing Bill sometimes as if he were only three or four years old. This was one of these occasions, and much as Bill loved her he found this habit very, very trying. She came over to Bill and put her arm round his shoulders. 'There's nothing to be afraid of, my dear,' she said.

'Oh lor'!' said Bill silently. Aloud he said. 'Careful, Mother. You'll have the gravy on the sheet any minute now.'

No sooner had Mrs Holmes called goodbye to Bill, before she went on her shopping expedition, than he jumped out of bed, seized his binoculars, and rushed to the window. Sure enough, there sat the artist making no pretence of doing anything but enjoying a smoke. His eyes were fixed, it seemed, on the Holmes's house. Mrs Holmes had carried out Bill's instructions and gone out by the back door. There was silence in the house as Bill went downstairs into the familiar room in the afternoon stillness. Tea was laid ready on the table, the cat lay asleep in Mr Holmes's chair, the fire burned brightly, and the kettle sang softly on the side of the fireplace.

Bill took a chair from its place at the table, stood on it, and carefully lifted down the gilt mirror from the wall. He stood it against his father's chair, and the cat opened sleepy eyes, yawned, turned round, and went to sleep again. Bill took newspapers from the rack, spread them on the floor and laid the mirror face down on them. Suddenly he rose, locked the back door, drew the curtains across the window, and switched on the light.

He had hardly done what he came to do, and restored the room to its normal appearance, before someone tried the back door. He rushed silent-footed, his heart beating fast, into the room where Mr Trien had stood, the room whose windows faced the common. The painter was still there. He went into the other room and heard Tony's cheerful voice as he rattled the back door.

'Open up here,' he cried. 'What's the idea of locking a friend out?'

'Sorry, Tony,' he said. 'I didn't know it was locked.'

'Liar,' said Tony promptly. 'You did. You locked it yourself. I just met your mother and heard you had a cold. She told me I could get in at the back door when I said I'd come and visit the sick. So *she* didn't lock it. Your father's out, *so thero* — you must have locked it. Or was it the cat, hoping to get an undisturbed nap?'

Bill grinned.

'You're coming on, Tony,' he said.

'What were you up to?' asked Tony suspiciously. 'A man doesn't lock himself in for nothing.'

'You're getting so good, you tell me,' said Bill.

'Well, you're downstairs, when your mother thinks you're in bed. That's one thing.'

'I had to come down. I can't turn a key, even for a pal, while I'm lying in bed.'

'Oh, no,' said Tony knowingly. 'Oh, no. You locked that door as well as unlocked it. That won't wash.'

'Well, what did I lock it for!'

'I believe I could find out, you know,' said Tony.

'Go ahead,' said Bill.

'Show me your hands.'

Bill held them out. Tony looked at them, raised one to his nose, and sniffed.

'Just washed,' he said, 'with carbolic soap.'

170

'Right,' said Bill. 'What now?'

'Oh, I suppose it was some experiment you didn't want your mother to know about — making a duplicator perhaps — or maybe stealing jam.'

'That's the worst of your brain getting tired,' said Bill. 'Wild guesses, like a blindfolded man trying to hit a cat in a dark room with a broomstick.'

The binoculars were hanging round Bill's neck on their strap.

'Come and have a look through these glasses,' said Bill. He led Tony into the front room and gave him the glasses.

'They are good, I know,' said Tony, looking.

'What do you see?' asked Bill.

'Oh, there's a girl pushing a pram, a chap and a girl on horses, and a feller painting.'

Tony handed back the glasses, and they went back into the other room. As he sat down Tony picked up a scrap of torn newspaper, screwed it up and threw it into the fire. He nodded at the gilt mirror.

'Smartening the place up,' he said. 'That's a nice bit of mirror, if you'll allow me to say so.'

'My dear Harries,' said Bill solemnly, 'you have now picked up every single clue to tell you why I locked the door. Put them together with the same skill as you observed them and you have the answer.'

'There are moments, Holmes,' said Tony, 'when I should dearly love to kick you, hard and plenty. This is one of them. You began by telling me a lie —'

'Clue number one,' said Bill.

'You deflect me from my enquiry by getting me to look at a lot of twirps through good glasses worthy of a better task —'

'Clue number two,' said Bill.

'And finish up by insulting my intelligence. I have observed nothing because you have purposely prevented me from doing so. Forget it. I don't wish to know what you were doing. It was probably discreditable. But I'd still like to kick you — you superior ass!'

At which the two burst into roars of laughter, though not at quite the same joke. For a while they chatted together and then Bill electrified his patient friend by a question.

'Have you ever been present at a burglary?' he asked.

Tony's eyebrows shot up, and he stared through his spectacles at Bill.

'Actually present — no, I haven't — I don't follow you, Holmes,' he said.

'How would you like to be there when a burglary was attempted?' persisted Bill.

'Well — all right, I suppose,' said Tony. 'If it was safe, you know.'

'It's never very safe,' said Bill. 'But if you'd like it, I can pretty well guarantee you won't get hurt.'

'Well, of course, in that case —', said Tony. 'Look here, Holmes, what are you getting at? Where's this burglary going to take place?'

'In this house, tonight,' said Bill dramatically.

'Here! What rot! How do you know? Be serious for a minute, Holmes. What is all this about?'

'I'm pretty certain of it,' said Bill, 'and it ought to be rather fun. Would old Peter let you sleep here tonight? You can have the spare room. It's quite comfortable.'

'I'm sure it is,' said Tony, 'but what can I tell my father?'

'Tell him anything — tell him it's my birthday and I've a late party — you can think of something. And bring that sporting rifle of yours.'

'Good heavens, Holmes!' spluttered Tony. 'Who's going to use that?'

'You probably. You're quite a good shot. You've told me so several times.'

'You want me to shoot this burglar who you insist is coming?'

'Yes. If necessary. Why not?'

A grin broke the solemnity of Tony's face.

'I've always wanted a break like that,' he said. 'To shoot a burglar! It's a worthy deed. I'll do it, Holmes. So much more fun than shooting a rabbit.'

'There's more of the burglar, too,' said Bill. 'Not so much chance of missing him. Well done, Tony. Be here at nine. No later.'

'Why? Is the burglar coming at nine?'

'No. It'll be supper-time.'

*   *   *   *

It was simple enough to get the agreement of Bill's father to Tony's stopping the night, though the true reason was not given. All the early evening, Bill was restless and excited. He tried to curb it and show no sign. His cold seemed so much better that he was allowed to dress and come downstairs after tea, but he had great difficulty in settling down to any occupation. He read for a few minutes, closed his book, played with the cat, tapped the barometer, and behaved like someone waiting for a train or a postman.

'What's the matter with you, Bill?' asked his father. 'You're like a cat on hot bricks. You haven't sat still for five minutes since tea.'

'It's the cold,' said Mrs Holmes. 'He's probably a bit feverish. I'm not sure it was wise to let him come downstairs. Perhaps you'd better go back to bed after all.'

'No, no,' said Bill. 'I'm all right. Really I am.'

The risk of alarming his mother to the extent of causing her to clap him back in bed sent Bill back to his chair, and he summoned all his will-power to make himself stare unseeingly but convincingly at his book. How long he could have controlled his impatience can never be known, for at precisely seven o'clock something happened so totally unexpected, so far from Bill's mind, so finally settling, that for once he was taken by surprise. What was it? Why, nothing more dramatic than a shy little knock at the front door.

Well, thought Bill, 'I'm blowed.'

Mrs Holmes put down her sewing, and went to the door. Yes. It was Mr Trien, the old gentleman from the secondhand shop. Seeing Mrs Holmes, he swept off his black hat. At the gate stood a car, and under Mr Trien's arm was a gilt mirror. 'Good evening,' he said, smiling and bowing. 'It is Mr Trien. I called last night. I have been fortunate enough tŏ find for you a mirror the equal of the one you have — a little better indeed.' He tapped the mirror under his arm.

'That's very kind,' said Mrs Holmes. 'But you shouldn't have troubled. I'm quite satisfied with the one I have.'

'Oh, please,' said old Mr Trien very persuasively. 'Will you not look at it? Please? Now that I have brought it so far?'

The woman who gave out-of-work accountants coffee and sandwiches was not the woman to resist Mr Trien's charm. She asked him in, and soon he was showing Mr and Mrs Holmes and Bill the mirror he had brought.

'You see,' he said, 'they are not common mirrors, these. They are of a great age and very difficult to find. But the one I have brought you has better-quality gilt than the other. I would give this to my other customer, but he is expert and insists on the one he had already bought — the one you have. So now, will you give me back that one? If so, you will do good to yourselves, you will get me out of trouble, and please my other friend. Yes?'

The old man looked at them with kind, bright eyes; he trembled slightly with age (as Bill was doing from excitement) and so Mr and Mrs Holmes, feeling that all had been done that could be done by a very nice old gentleman, agreed to the exchange.

'Well,' said Mr Holmes, 'if my wife is satisfied, I've no objection.'

Mr Trien did not speak, but turned his eyes on Mrs Holmes. 'Quite,' said she, fingering the gilt of the new mirror. 'If anything I like this one better.'

'Oh,' said Mr Trien, exceeding all previous efforts in politeness, so that his voice sounded like a kind hand stroking one's hair. 'I knew you would like it better. I am so happy. Thank you. Thank you so much. Now — I must go — please, where is the other?'

He followed them into the other room, and Bill watched him while Mr Holmes got a chair and stood on it to take down the mirror. The chain caught for a second on the nail, and it looked as if Mr Trien would faint with anxiety.

'Oh, please,' he cried. 'Be careful — let me — I am so used to it. Oh, thank you.' He took it in his hands and breathed hard. Smilingly he added: 'They are so difficult to find. It would be terrible if this one should have been broken.' He looked around at them, bowed and smiled at each one. 'Now I shall go. Thank you so much. We are all happy, is it not so?' He went to the door and struggled with his hat.

'Let me put it on,' said Mr Holmes, taking the black hat, while old Mr Trien held fast to the mirror with both hands Suiting the action to the words, he placed it on the old man's head, where it sat awkwardly.

'Thank you. Thank you,' said Mr Trien. 'So kind. Good night. Good night.'

In a few moments he had put the mirror in the car and driven away.

'Well,' said Mr Holmes. 'That's that.'

'Oh, is it?' thought Bill.

'Funny old boy,' added Mr Holmes, taking up his paper.

'Wasn't it kind of him?' said Mrs Holmes, putting the new mirror in place. 'He's a nice old man, really.'

'Not half,' thought Bill, 'you just wait and see.'

* * * *

Three hours later Tony was sitting in Bill's bedroom, while the latter consumed a bowl of hot bread and milk. His rifle had just been hauled up through the window on a piece of string, and six cartridges stood on Bill's bedside table.

'I thought I smuggled the rifle in very well,' he said complacently.

'Put the light out,' said Bill.

The light went out, and Tony was gone.

Bill grinned in the darkness and was quickly asleep.

* * * *

Meanwhile, old Mr Trien had reached home. Like Mr Holmes, he too had a wife and son, and they gathered round him as he entered the dark shop with its crowded contents — tables, fenders, pictures, wardrobes, rolls of carpet — and its smell of dust.

'Have you got it?' asked Mrs Trien in a low voice.

She was younger than her husband; a tall, thin woman with her hair drawn back from her forehead. Her knobbly hands were tightly clasped and her face was sad.

'Yes, yes. With much trouble I have got it,' replied the old man crossly. 'Open the door there.'

The door led into an untidy living-room containing a table, a sofa, and some chairs, these two last being covered with green plush. The stock had overflowed into this living-room, and made it anything but a place to live in with comfort. Three or four clocks stood about, pictures rested against the wall, and a packing-case with straw falling out of it stood in a corner.

'Maria, you get the supper,' said old Trien. 'Josef you help me with this.'

He put the mirror face down on the table, and when Mrs Trien had gone into the kitchen his son and he began to take the plywood backing off the mirror, taking care not to scratch the gilt. When the back was almost off, the edge of something appeared and old Trien with trembling hands drew it out. He gazed at it thunderstruck. It was a picture from a grocer's illustrated calendar, and it was labelled: 'Neddy — a humble friend.' It was, in fact, a picture of a grey donkey in the shafts of a cart, gazing mildly at Mr Trien. A terrible spasm seized the old man. He clutched his head with both hands and sent up a great cry.

'Oh, oh!' he cried. 'This is what Eddy has done to me. Oh, oh!'

He staggered to the green plush sofa and sat there rocking to and fro in agony of mind. His son Josef lit a cigarette and coolly put the mirror together again.

'Stop that noise, Dad,' he said sharply.

'Oh, oh!' wailed old Trien. 'What can we do?'

Josef exhaled a cloud of smoke.

'We've had it,' he said shortly.

* * * *

Wimbledon Common lay under the stars. The lamps were all out and the dark houses stood wrapped in sleep. A low-lying mist hung in hollows here and there. A clock somewhere had just struck two. Suddenly Tony Harries, in the spare room at Bill's house, was wide awake, like a spring released. For a moment he did not realise where he was, but his heart was beating uncomfortably fast. He lay there in bed for some seconds and then, his brain taking the news very unwillingly, he felt certain he heard sounds from downstairs — gentle, stealthy sounds. His head went hot, his mouth became dry and his heart beat even more loudly. He had the sense not to turn on the lights, but even in the darkness he felt helpless without his spectacles. He put his hand out to the bedside table, felt about in the blackness, found them, and put them on his nose with a trembling hand. He sat up and listened intently. For a while there was silence and he almost hoped he had been mistaken. But the sounds, creeping, furtive, began again. He stepped out of bed. His legs felt so weak that he stumbled and nearly fell. He peered through a chink in his curtains out into the dark garden. All was silent there.

Suddenly a terrifying thing happened. His door began to open slowly. He stared, his eyes wide, his mouth open to scream.

'Sh!' came a whisper. 'It's me — Bill.'

The pyjama-clad figure of Bill Holmes slipped into the room, closing the door silently behind itself. 'Gosh,' said Tony, sweating. 'I'm glad you're here.' Bill made no reply. He drew the curtains back and, so slowly that the made no sound, he pushed up the window.

'So you *were* right,' whispered Tony.

Bill made no answer to this either. He, too, had heard the sounds, but they were, on his reasoning, inexplicable. The cold air flowed into the room, and Tony shivered. They had not long to wait. From the window below them emerged a dark figure.

'Gun!' said Bill in a whisper like a lash. Tony seized his rifle from its place against the wall. Bill pointed swiftly to the window. Tony raised the rifle and took aim at the dark figure as it stealthily crossed the garden.

'Let him have it!' said Bill fiercely.

Tony pressed the trigger and there came — not a blinding flash and a crash of explosion — but a little metallic click. Bill stared at Tony, who looked foolishly at the rifle and then at Bill.

The old man sent up a great cry

'I forgot to load it,' he said.

The dark figure had vanished from the garden. Bill pulled down the window and drew the curtains as silently as before. He turned on the light. Tony blinked at him in the brightness.

'If our lives had depended on that shot,' said Bill, 'we'd have been in a bad way now, shouldn't we?'

'Oughtn't you to have your dressing-gown on with that cold?' asked Tony. 'Here, put mine on.'

Bill silently let Tony help him on with the dressing-gown.

'I'm sorry, Bill,' said Tony.

'It doesn't matter,' said Bill. 'It's probably just as well. Only I've never seen anyone shoot a burglar. But you'd probably have missed him anyway, and then there'd have been all that noise for nothing.'

'What do we do now?' asked Tony, overlooking this slur on his shooting. 'Oughtn't we to see what he's stolen?'

'I know,' said Bill. 'But we might as well have a look round.'

'You know? But I thought you'd cut out the idea of a burglary at all. That's why I wasn't ready.'

'Come on downstairs,' said Bill, 'and not a sound, mind.'

They crept downstairs and entered the room where the mirror hung. The window was open, and the mirror lay in three pieces — glass, frame, and plywood backing. Otherwise all was as usual. Bill shut the window, using a handkerchief to do it.

'That catch,' he said. 'A baby could force it and get in here.'

He looked all round the room, but Tony could see only one thing.

'What's happened to the mirror?' he asked.

Bill, still careful not to touch anything with his fingers, first examined the mirror and then put it together.

'Gloves and rubber shoes,' he said. 'If ever you go cracking cribs, Tony, be sure to use them.'

'Did this chap?'

180

'He certainly did.'

Bill hung the mirror in its place over the mantelpiece.

'Well,' he said, 'that's that. For the moment.'

'What do we do now?' asked Tony.

'Go back to bed. Look, it's half past three. Time all good boys were in bed.'

'Yes. But — hasn't that chap taken anything?'

'Not a thing.'

'You haven't looked in the other rooms.'

'No need. It's all right, Tony.'

Tony was annoyed.

'Well, but — aren't you going to report it to the police?'

'No need for that either. They'll be here tomorrow or the next day or the day after that.'

'Look here, Holmes,' said Tony, 'why don't you come clean and tell me what you know? I want to see this thing cleared up.'

'It's going to clear itself up,' said Bill annoyingly.

'And what about your father and mother — we've got to tell them, haven't we?'

'If you breathe a word to them,' said Bill fiercely, 'I'll—I'll shoot you with your own rifle.'

'Oh well,' said Tony, shrugging his shoulders, 'it'll all come out in the wash, I suppose.'

'It will,' said Bill.

At the moment he spoke the inner door opened and Mr and Mrs Holmes appeared.

'What on earth —?' cried Mr Holmes.

'Hullo, Dad — and Mother!' said Bill.

'What are you doing down here in the middle of the night — and with a cold like you've got?' said Mrs Holmes. 'Really, it's a bit too much.'

'We thought we heard something down here,' said Bill innocently.

'It's all that reading you do,' said Mr Holmes, yawning. 'Well, get off to bed. And if you hear funny things in the night — or think you do — call me. Your mother'll like it better that way.'

'I should think so, indeed,' said Mrs Holmes 'Off you go. And you too, Tony. You'll look like a ghost in the morning.'

*   *   *   *

As the next day was a Saturday, neither Tony nor Bill was in a hurry. They breakfasted in bed, dressed in a leisurely way, and were chatting in Bill's bedroom when a car drew up at the front gate.

Bill looked out of his window.

'Mr Quilta!' he cried. 'Come on down.'

Bill and Tony thundered downstairs just as Mrs Holmes admitted the detective to the front room.

'Good morning,' Mrs Holmes,' he said. 'Hullo, young feller — and you too. I remember you. You came with us to rescue our young friend from the clutches of Mr Glinders. I wish I was a school-kid. Nothing to do on a Saturday morning but get in your mother's way. Well, I've no time to waste. Now, Mrs Holmes, I have reason to believe that you recently bought an article in a second-hand shop near Tooting Broadway.'

Bill and Tony, especially the former, listened with amusement to the clipped, brisk tones of Detective Quilta. He was very efficient. When he was not speaking he frowned and pursed his lips, as if no trifle could hope to escape his vigilant attention. When he was about to speak he took in little short stabs of air, as if he hardly trusted the air in large, free doses.

'Yes, that's right, Mr Quilta,' said Mrs Holmes. 'I hope there's nothing wrong.'

'A good deal, I'm afraid.'

'Oh, dear, I am sorry.'

'It was a mirror, I believe. A mirror with a gilt frame.'

'Yes. That's it.'

'Have you the article in question still in your possesion?'

'Yes. It was there a minute ago.'

'Then it'll still be there. May I see it, please?'

'Certainly. Come this way.'

The moment Quilta saw the mirror his eyes brightened. 'I must now take possession of the mirror, Mrs Holmes,' he said. 'I have to examine it.'

'Anything you wish, Mr Quilta.'

Bill watched, fascinated, as the mirror, in the powerful hands of Mr Quilta, was once more taken to pieces. When it lay on the table, glass, frame, and back, Mr Quilta's complacent expression changed to one like a thunder-cloud.

'Is this the mirror you bought, Mrs Holmes?' he demanded.

'Well, no, not the first one,' replied Bill's mother.

'Not the first one!' exclaimed Quilta. 'I must warn you that this is a very serious matter. Why did you not tell me that at first?'

Mrs Holmes explained. She had hardly finished before Quilta was out of the door and the police-car was gone in a cloud of blue smoke. Mrs Holmes sat heavily in a handy chair.

'What *is* all this about?' she said. 'I can't understand it.'

Bill grinned as if he were saying: 'I can.'

'Come on, Tony,' he said. 'Let's try to find a real rat with your rifle.'

'Fancy Mr Quilta going off like that,' said Mrs Holmes, 'with never a word. I don't know what to think.'

'Neither does he,' said Bill. 'But don't worry, Mother. He'll be back.'

Bill was right. Mr Quilta called again at tea-time. Bill's father and mother, Tony and he were sitting at the table when the police-car drew up again.

'Here it comes,' said Bill. 'Have some more cake, Tony.'

Mr Quilta was in a genial mood when he entered the room. He even accepted, very graciously, a cup of tea.

'Never join the C.I.D. is my advice to young boys,' he said, smiling at Tony and Bill.

'I thought you liked it, Mr Quilta,' said Bill offering him cake, which he declined.

'I'd rather smoke a cigarette, if I may,' he said. 'Yes. I do like the job. But we need pretty smart men nowadays. Crime is both an art and a science.'

'Painting and pinching,' said Bill to Tony aside.

'It's rude to whisper,' said Mr Quilta waggishly.

'It's sometimes ruder to say it out loud,' replied Bill.

'Smart youngster,' said Quilta to Mr Holmes, nodding at Bill. 'He ought to go far.'

'I hope so,' said Mr Holmes.

'As long as he doesn't go too far,' said Quilta warningly. 'Anyway, down to business. Now I'm going to take you all into my confidence. Not a word of what I tell you outside these four walls, mind.'

He glanced at them one by one as they promised not to reveal his secrets.

'Right,' he said. 'Now I'm doing this because I think you may be able to help me. Shouldn't do it otherwise. You know the detective's motto — least said soonest mended. You'll agree with that, young feller, being a bit of a sleuth yourself.'

'Absolutely,' said Bill.

'I'll say he agrees with it,' said Tony fervently.

'Right again. Well, now —' he leaned forward, put his cup on the table, and spoke in a low, intense voice. 'The man you bought your mirror from, Mrs Holmes, is a fence — that is —'

'A receiver of stolen goods,' said Bill.

'How well you know it!' said Quilta, shaking his head in assumed wonderment. 'If words were deeds, you wouldn't be Bill Holmes; you'd be Sherlock.'

'Do you mean that old man stole the mirror and then sold it to me?' said Mrs Holmes. 'I wouldn't have bought it if I'd suspected that.'

'Nothing so small as mirrors, Mrs Holmes,' said Quilta. 'He deals in thousands of pounds; not a few shillings. Now here's the story. He's an expert valuer, and he was called in to the flat of Robert Farre, the film producer, to value some articles, and there he saw a rare painting by an artist called Turner. You'll have heard of him?'

'No,' said Mrs Holmes. 'I —'

'Sunsets,' said Bill quickly. 'Get on with the story. I can't wait.'

'Well, it's little known and the point is, it's small enough to fit behind your mirror.'

'Oh,' breathed Mr Holmes, 'I see.'

'A few days after his visit the picture was gone — cut out of the frame.'

'So you thought —' said Mrs Holmes, 'that it was hidden in my mirror. But — it wasn't there, was it?'

'No, but you had two mirrors, Mrs Holmes.'

'Did you find it in the other?'

'We've got the other. You see what happened was this. Old Trien employed a young crook called Eddy Leere to get the picture. Then he hid it in your mirror — your first mirror, you understand — and in his absence from the shop his wife, an honest woman if ever there was one, sold it to you. He slipped up by not warning her. By this time the owner, Robert Farre, had notified the Yard of his loss, and so Eddy Leere learned its true value, and how old man Trien was double-crossing him — not giving him anything like a square deal. It's always good for us when rogues fall out.'

'Good heavens!' said Mrs Holmes, staggered at the events connected with her purchase.

'Fascinating,' said Mr Holmes lighting his pipe which he had allowed to go out.

'We've picked up Eddy, old Trien, and his son. Now, I'm going to surprise you. Your house was burgled last night.' Quilta leaned back and enjoyed the sensation his announcement had created.

'Yes,' said Quilta. 'Eddy Leere came here and examined that very mirror. And you never heard a thing. Just shows you, doesn't it?'

'Well —' began Mrs Holmes. 'The —'

There was a loud crash as Bill pushed Mr Quilta's cup and saucer off the table.

'Bill!' cried his mother. She picked up the pieces and took them outside, Bill helping her.

'Least said, soonest mended,' he hissed in the scullery. 'Let him do the talking, Mother.'

'Oh dear,' said Mrs Holmes. 'Everyone's gone mad. I'm sure they have.'

'What does surprise me,' Mr Holmes was saying, 'is that we found the mirror as usual this morning.'

'Oh, nothing in that,' said Quilta. 'He left it as he found it so as to delay any report to us. You'd have obviously told us if you'd known he'd been here.'

Mr Quilta took out another cigarette and lit it.

'Now this is where I want you, Mrs Holmes, to try to remember every detail about the first mirror.'

'Yes. I'll try,' said Mrs Holmes attentively.

'It all fits in as far as we've gone,' said Mr Quilta. 'We've got Leere, and old Trien, and his son under lock and key, but they swear they haven't got the picture.'

He grinned. 'Someone put a fast one over on old Trien,' he

went on. 'Put a picture of a donkey in the mirror his wife sold you. Nearly broke his heart, that did. He swears Eddy Leere did it to get even with him. Eddy says he's never even seen the picture since he gave it to the old man to hide till the trouble blew over. In short, that picture's vanished into thin air.'

Bill rose, opened a drawer in the chest beside the fire, felt under the paper lining and drew something out.

'Perhaps I can help you,' he said, handing the something to Mr Quilta. 'Is that it?'

Quilta stared at it, and the others in the room stared from him to Bill. Quilta rose, holding the picture.

'Where did you get this?' he asked hoarsely.

'Out of the mirror — the one my mother bought,' said Bill. 'Is it what you're looking for?'

'But how — what made you look into the mirror?' demanded Quilta.

'You always say you know what boys are,' said Bill innocently.

Quilta stared at him for a moment and then began to laugh. He laughed till it seemed he would be ill. The tears came into his eyes. 'Oh, dear,' he said. 'You must excuse me. To think of a nosey kid putting Eddy Leere and old Trien into a jam like this. You didn't by any chance put the picture of the donkey in instead, did you? Oh, do say you did — it'll make the story better.'

Bill solemnly produced from among the newspapers a grocer's calendar, and showed the place where the month of November was missing. Mr Quilta began to laugh again.

'I tell you, Mr Holmes,' he said, 'this boy will go far. On the stage, I shouldn't wonder.' He suddenly grew serious. 'I may tell you, young feller, you're going to be very lucky. The owner of this picture has put a reward of two hundred pounds on it.'

When Mr Quilta had departed with the picture, Tony lost no time in getting Bill to himself in the latter's bedroom.

'Now then,' he said, 'Let's have the story. You knew that picture was in the mirror, didn't you? You can't get away with that innocent "You-know-what-boys-are-Mister-Quilta" stuff with me.'

'I didn't know what I should find,' said Bill, 'but when old Trien was so keen to get it back, and when he sent his son to call here and spot where it was, and then watch the house, I thought it would be worth while examining the mirror. That's all.'

'What made you say there'd be a burglary and then that there wouldn't, when after all it turned out that there was?'

'I slipped up there,' confessed Bill. 'You see, that's why young Trien watched the house. He knew about Eddy Leere. I didn't. I banked on old Trien, having failed to get the mirror by persuasion, trying his hand at stealing it. He upset my reckoning by bringing along the second mirror. If I'd known about Eddy, I'd have stuck to my theory about a burglary.'

'I see. And that's what you were doing when you locked the back door — taking the picture out of the mirror.'

'Yes. Just finished when you came. I thought you were young Trien. It gave me a fright, I'll tell you.'

'What did you mean by saying that I'd got all the clues to what you'd been doing?'

'Easy. You saw the painter on the common, and you might have noticed he wasn't painting at all. You saw the new mirror and you picked up a bit of the newspaper on which I'd been resting it. That's all you wanted, wasn't it?'

'Yes. I suppose it was,' sighed Tony. 'But I'm not you, Holmes. That's all.'

'Well, that's not worth wanting to be, anyway,' said Bill.

'Oh, yes, it is,' said Tony promptly. 'Two hundred quid, from all I could hear. Lucky bloke! But tell me this. Why were you so determined not to tell anyone — not even your parents — anything about it?'

'Well, Tony, there was so much about the case I didn't know, and could only get to know by letting things happen. If I'd told anyone, it would have spoiled everything.'

'Yes,' said Tony. 'I suppose it would. But your plan had one weakness.'

'What was that?'

'It might have led to my shooting a man.'

'There was never any fear of that,' said Bill.

'Why not?' demanded Tony indignantly. 'I'm a very good shot.'

'Maybe,' said Bill. 'But you didn't forget to load the gun. I took the cartridge out. On second thoughts I reckoned it would be safer.'

'Bill!' Mrs Homes's voice called upstairs.

'Yes, Mother?'

'Time for your medicine. I want you right by Monday.'

'Righto. Just coming.'

Bill went downstairs, followed by a very meditative Tony. At the bottom of the stairs Bill stopped.

'There's one thing you haven't asked me,' he said.

'What's that?' asked Tony.

'How I knew that chap wasn't really painting.'

'Well — how did you know?'

'Because he hadn't got a brush. They're good glasses, Tony. Can I really hang on to them?'

'As long as you like, of course — well, I'm blowed. I never noticed that, you know. But it's obvious, isn't it?'

'I think it is,' said Bill, and went to take his medicine.

The Legacy

by AUBREY FEIST

In that bitter winter of 1216 there was civil war in England.
A French army, called in by the Magna Carta barons, bestrode
the south-east; but that grim old war-dog, Hubert de Burgh,
held Dover for the King, and behind the strong shield of
Midland fortresses William the Marshal kept watch and ward
over little Henry, John Lackland's son. On the Eve of the
Apostles Simon and Jude, the boy-king had been crowned at
Gloucester; and now the aged Marshal was free to deal with
other, more secret matters. He had summoned Chester; and
soon, with a soft jingle of mail, his friend came striding into
the hall, the golden wheatsheaves on his long surcoat glim-
mering in the smoky torchlight. Blunt and direct, he came
straight to the point.

'You have chosen your messenger for Dover?'

'I have. Stephen is going.'

'I guessed as much. Think again, my lord. Has he the
courage for such a task?'

'I am certain of it,' replied the Marshal. 'I have had the
training of him myself.'

Ranulf, Earl of Chester flushed, his fiery beard bristling.

'For the love o' the saints, my lord, send a *man*, not a stripling
or one and twenty — an unfledged squire, more at home in my
lady's bower than the tilt-yard!'

The most famous knight in Christendom, Regent of England
and Earl of Pembroke, could afford to be tolerant. The
Marshal smiled.

'The boy shall have this chance to win his spurs. His father
was my friend.'

191

'So! I understand.'

'Not quite, Ranulf. Stephen de Corselin is poor, but I have bred him on stories of my old comrade's brave deeds, and this precious legacy of valour is worth more than gold or lands. He has an imagination which foresees and magnifies every danger; but, with such an example to follow, he has been able to conquer fear and do perilous work as our link with the loyal barons in the south.'

'Because of his father?'

'So I believe. Such courage can be an inspiration.'

And then there came a clash of curtain-rings and the torchlight flickered on the steel cap of a man-at-arms.

'Stephen de Corselin, my lord.'

'Bid him enter.'

The young squire made his reverence on bended knee before his master. With his soft brown hair and sensitive face, he looked anything but a warrior, and life in that iron thirteenth century could be hard for such as he. Only his resolute mouth and steady eyes told of the spirit that dwelt within, but the Marshal saw those signs and nodded approval.

'You are ready, Stephen?'

'Yes, my lord. I go disguised as a minstrel.'

'And the parchment?'

'Destroyed — after I had learned its contents by heart.'

'Good!' said the Marshal, but Ranulf of Chester was not so easily satisfied.

'You know what you have to do, Sir Squire?'

'Make my way into Dover Castle with intelligence for de Burgh.'

'Ay, it is vital that he should know our plan for the onset on St Hilary's Day.'

'But — no — one — else, I charge you, Stephen!' The good old Marshal spoke so gravely that Stephen swore he would die rather than betray his trust; then he flinched a little as Chester broke in with a laugh — gruff but not unkindly.

'Die! Ha! By the Bones of the Saints, if you are taken, a quick death will be something to pray for! It is Sir Ivo d'Yf whom you have to fear. His castle is but a league from Dover. You have heard of this Black Dog of d'Yf, as they call him?'

'I have been told that he is cruel.'

'Cruel! Men say that he has branded his serfs — and even his wife — like cattle. Fall into *his* hands and he will force your secrets from you with fire and iron!'

Stephen moistened his lips. His palms were sweating.

'How can he have heard of me or my errand?'

Chester shrugged.

'The walls of Gloucester Keep have ears and men can be bought with money. The rebels may well have learned that a messenger is on his way to Dover.'

But William the Marshal laid a restraining hand on his friend's shoulder.

'Have done, Ranulf! The boy will ride more boldly without such cold comfort.' He turned to Stephen. 'And yet, I beseech you, pay good heed to his words, for, if you are captured by Ivo d'Yf, you will need all your courage.'

*   *   *   *

In a Kentish wood, one icy morning, Stephen wormed his way through the bracken. Weak and ill, his clothes hung in tatters, and his long hair was dark and sticky with dried blood from a sword-cut.

Everything had gone awry. A false guide — a sudden ambush — flight — till at last he lay panting in the fern, like some desperate beast that hunters have cornered. He could hear them hallooing and beating the woods for him; and when, cautiously, he raised his head, a crossbow bolt sang past his ears.

He sprang to his feet and ran for it — staggering, stumbling. But not for long. As he crashed through a thicket, he heard the drumming of hooves and horsemen came galloping down the glade — horsemen who bore on shield and surcoat the sable hound of d'Yf.

Half-dazed, Stephen floundered and turned to fly, but the crossbowmen were behind him. There was nothing for it but to stand at bay and rip out his dagger. He struck one blow for his life — a random blow which glanced off a shield; then they overwhelmed him and, to the jeering laughter of Ivo's men, he was tied to a stirrup-leather, jerked off his feet, and dragged down the glade.

So his ordeal began; and, before he fainted, he wondered whether the courage that was his birthright would steel him to silence. For he was going to die — dreadfully, in the dark, not sword in hand, as he was proud to think his father had died before him.

* * * *

Sir Ivo d'Yf had come to glut his eyes on the prisoner chained to the wall of his dungeon. A fat man with a red, shaven face. He spoke gently: 'We are going to kill you.'

'I am ready,' said Stephen, conscious of the tremor in his voice; and heard Sir Ivo chuckle huskily savouring his triumph.

'Do not be in too much of a hurry. We shall kill you — slowly, and what is left of you will be cast down that dry well over there... the light, FitzUrse! Our guest must see the lodging that is prepared for him.'

A grinning squire swung his torch and Stephen saw the black opening in one corner. He shuddered, a movement which did not escape those hard little eyes.

'You might ransom your life,' said Sir Ivo softly.

'How can I do that?'

Stephen struck one blow for his life

'I think you know how. We too have our spies... Yes, the Black Dog can bite, but if you pacify him with a bone —' He chuckled again at his jest. 'The message that William the Marshal sent to de Burgh. Tell me *that* and you shall go free. And no one will ever know.'

'I would rather die,' said Stephen.

'As you will.' Sir Ivo moved ponderously to the door. 'I leave you to think it over and to picture the death that you will die if you refuse my offer... When the Priory bell rings for Vespers, FitzUrse will come for your answer.' Then the door clanged behind him, and Stephen was alone with the rats and the darkness.

Although Sir Ivo did not know it, he could have devised nothing more cruel, for his captive's own fancy could torment him more than fire or steel. For hours his imagination ran riot; and when it was almost past endurance, he seemed to hear that husky voice whispering: 'No one will ever know!'

To surrender. To betray his trust. To buy life at the price of honour. It was a grievous temptation for one who dreaded pain as he did. But always at the back of his mind was the thought of his father — the crusader who had died gloriously before the walls of Acre. In handing on this legacy, the Marshal had given him a rule to live by; he had set a standard below which Stephen was resolved not to fall. So, although he was cold with fear at the thought of what lay before him, when FitzUrse came for his answer, he had the strength to send his defiance.

After that, they left him alone again for hours; then, when the first grey light came stealing through the little grating above the moat, he heard the grinding of bolts and braced himself for the ordeal. The dungeon door swung slowly open; and there, carrying a taper, was no jailer, nor executioner, but a haggard woman with haunted eyes and the mark of the branding-iron on her brow.

'I am going to set you free,' she whispered. 'That shall be my revenge.'

'But — but — who are you?'

'I am his wife.'

He could only stare at her and wonder.

No one has told the tale of that woman's wrongs; only of her bitter hatred. She was smiling bleakly as, with the key she had stolen, she unlocked Stephen's fetters; and when he staggered to his feet, she gave him a dagger.

'You may not need this. The postern is unlocked and I have bribed the warder —'

She had no time to say more, for a bellow of rage rang through the dungeon; and there was Sir Ivo straddling the doorway, a heavy battle-axe in his hand.

Stephen dodged the first blow, which splintered a stool and struck sparks from the stone floor; and for a space they circled warily, eyeing each other and breathing hard. At last, like a wild-cat, the prisoner sprang straight at his enemy's throat. The dagger flashed up and down, but Sir Ivo dashed it aside with a snort of laughter. Shortening his axe, he jabbled with the pommel and Stephen reeled; then, grasping his weapon with both hands, Sir Ivo swung it above his head, stepped back — and went straight down the well.

Shouts and dancing torches as FitzUrse came running, and with him armed retainers.

'Sir Ivo called!'

'His death-cry!' answered the woman, with burning eyes. 'The well is deep and it is there you must seek him. I command here now.'

FitzUrse was silent. The men looked at each other and more than one sighed with relief. For they, too, were newly released from bondage. The Black Dog had been a bad master.

History tells us how Stephen de Corselin delivered his message to de Burgh. When, in the Castle of Gloucester once more, he told his lord whad he had done, William the Marshal remembered his promise. He ordered his squire to keep vigil on Christmas Eve in the church of St Peter; and there in the morning, before them all, little King Henry should dub him knight.

When Stephen had gone, the Marshal turned to Chester.

'You were wrong, Ranulf. I bred him true. Many another would have broken. And yet, with so much at stake, should I have taken the risk? If Stephen had betrayed us —!'

Chester looked at him strangely. William the Marshal was a shrewd judge of men. Had he too had doubts? He ventured a question but the old warrior did not answer him directly.

'There is something else that troubles me, Ranulf,' he said. 'A true knight should never lie. It will cost me a heavy penance to rid my soul of that sin — yet if I have erred, it was for the boy's sake, and good has come of it... I have always taught him that he has inherited a legacy of courage.'

'That was no lie. Did not his father die before the walls of Acre?'

'He died, yes. But he was hanged for cowardice. Stephen must never know.'

Harvest of Pride

by ALAN C. JENKINS

The rowlocks creaked. The blades of the oars scattered showers of silver. Steadily, grey-headed Eriksson rowed out from the sloping sandy shore of the river, while Lars, young and eager, stood in the stern of the boat, shooting the dark-brown seine-net, one end of which was secured to a birch tree. The lead-weighted net sank evenly as Lars paid out the tarry meshes, then slowly it opened out as the line of corks along the top floated to the surface. The seine settled like a fence in the shallow river, gradually enfolding the unsuspecting fish gliding and finning about within the area it surrounded.

On shore the rest of the men waited gravely, arms folded or hands on hips. A thousand times they'd taken part in the seine-netting, yet each time there was the same suppressed excitement and hope behind their stolid exteriors, for their livelihood depended on the operation.

Slowly, Eriksson rowed out across the tranquil riverpool. He was so accustomed to rowing he did it as unconsciously and effortlessly as he walked. He stared out across the river and felt a deep contentment. It would be a good catch; he sensed that, mighty salmon; sprightly sea-trout. Within an hour or two of landing they'd be cleaned, packed, and sent off downriver by boat to the railhead. The fish swam in from the Atlantic and the money flowed into Eriksson's pockets and those of the fishermen who worked with him. It was hard work, but a good return. There would be a good living for his son Lars when Eriksson retired. If ever that day came!

Now Eriksson was resting on one oar, rowing only with the

other one to bring the boat back towards the shore to complete a half-moon. His two hands working in unison, Lars continued to pay out the net until the very end. So exactly had his father judged the distance that the last meshes went over the stern as the little boat grounded on the sandy shore.

Now the rest of the men Trygve, Nielsson, limping Ingmar, loud-mouthed Johannsson, came tramping down ready to help. Eagerly Lars clambered out into the water, holding the dragging-rope. He waded briskly in his rubber thigh-boots, hauling on the heavy meshes while Nielsson and Ingmar jostled round to help. Eriksson and the others hauled the boat out a little way and then, unlashing the second end of the rope from its birch-tree anchor, began to haul in, too.

At first they took it easy, savouring the prospects. Eriksson even took a moment's respite to apply a pinch of snuff to his nose. He sniffed gustily with pleasure and eyed the swirling water within the influence of the seine.

'There's a good shoal of fish in that net,' he remarked, with a shake of his iron-grey head. He made it sound as if he was trickling gold through his fingers and Lars smiled, glad at his father's pleasure and proud, too, that he was now working as a full member of the syndicate. He felt a strange secret thrill as his muscles tensed under the weight of the net.

'What are we waiting for then?' bawled Johannsson. He always shouted the loudest and did the least. Johannsson was always quick to blame other people when the catch disappointed; slow to lend a hand when it was needed most. As soon as the seine was hauled in you'd find Johannsson sloping off for a smoke, or yarning on the little jetty with the women-folk while the others hung up the nets to dry or started gutting the fish.

'Haul away, then!' shouted Eriksson cheerfully and the two groups of men began in unison to bend their backs, slowly, without hurrying. A haul and a pause, another haul and a pause, while the dripping meshes draped down gradually on the shore. The cork-floats bobbed, the water stirred, swirled ponderously as the men heaved with rugged rhythm, and there was not one man who did not gaze expectantly, trying to guess what harvest was being dragged together in that ever-tightening circle.

'I'd say you've got the rock of ages in that net, Eriksson!' grunted Ingmar, struggling gamely as ever with his lame foot.

'Haul on then, lads!' Eriksson encouraged, bending his old back like a birch tree in a gale. 'There's gold in that net, I'm telling you. An intense, exultant look showed on his weathered features as he worked and the men responded to his enthusiasm. Grunting, tramping backwards step by step, whipping the dripping meshes through their hands, they toiled on, eager to land the catch. Steadily the space enclosed by the seine was constricting. Lars's eyes lit up and he exchanged a silent grin with Ingmar, who had glanced round at him, for now the water thrashed and churned with leaping fish. It was a fine catch. One of those monsters must be at least a thirty-pounder. In a few moments now they'd be safely landed.

*　　*　　*　　*

But all that was a thing of the past. It no longer happened, except in the regretful thoughts of Lars or the surly reminiscenses of the men. No more did the vaulting salmon or the sturdy sea-trout come to Laxhavn. The harvest of the river had ceased.

It was nearly two years now since any of the seine-net teams along the stately river had hauled in a catch of any sort.

It had all started imperceptibly, as gradually as winter coming on. The leaves of the alders and birches turned to red and gold. A lacework of ice crept along the margin of the river. You began to put down the ear-flaps of your sealskin cap against the nipping wind which grew colder every day.

It had been just like that. The first sign had occurred one day when the men had been lounging on the shore examining the nets, drawing the tarry folds across their knees, carefully inspecting every single mesh. One hole in a seine-net and the richest catch you'd ever taken could ebb away like life-blood from a wound.

'What are those chaps doing?' Nielsson had speculated idly, taking the pipe from his mouth and indicating a couple of figures on the distant fells that overlooked the river.

'Hikers?' grunted someone, not very interested.

'They're measuring or something,' said Lars, the keenest sighted of them all. 'Surveyors. They've got a theodolite.'

'Map-making, that's what they're doing,' decided Johannsson, sitting on an upturned boat he was supposed to be caulking.

Nobody thought any more about it. There was too much to do, it was time to shoot the net again. But they would not have been so indifferent had they known what the two surveyors signified.

The next sign that something was in the offing was an odd paragraph or two in the local newspaper about certain plans of the State Electricity Generating Corporation. They had put forward a vast scheme for a hydro-electric project which would supply the whole of the Laxhavn district.

But few of the fishermen had time to read. Only when the local parliamentary deputy came down to address a meeting did the truth sink in. The river was going to be dammed. The livelihood of the seine-netting syndicates for several miles along the river was in danger. Laxhavn suddenly began to seethe like a nest of wood-ants.

Protest meetings were held. Petitions organised. The S.E. G.C. officials who came down to explain what the scheme would entail for the whole country had to be given police protection from the angry fishermen.

'Let them put down one barrow-load of cement and we'll smash it!' shouted Johannsson, shaking a gnarled fist and thrusting out his mottled face. But he would be the last to act, thought Lars bitterly, as he sat in a corner listening to the stormy talk. Johannsson would egg people on, but he'd be careful to hang back at the fringe of the crowd!

But not all the defiant words in the world were of any avail once the State moved into action. Courteously but firmly the explanations went on. The negotiations started.

'We'll listen to what they have to say,' said Eriksson. 'But that doesn't mean we'll compromise ourselves.'

Together with two other representatives of the seine-net fishermen and a local lawyer and the pastor, Eriksson went to meet the S.E.G.C. negotiating body. There couldn't be much argument. The Corporation simply wanted the fishermen out of the way. The Laxhavn hydro-electric scheme was a colossal affair. Compensating a few fishermen was chicken-feed compared with what was involved. Civilisation marched on, people could no longer be expected to put up with the old fish-oil lamps that had served them for generations. They demanded light, heat, power, or at least, so it was said by the planners.

Eriksson and the other fishermen came away from the negotiations feeling baffled. It all seemed too simple.

'How could we argue with them?' he said again and again, scratching his head. 'It's been made plain to us that there's nothing we can do to stop the scheme. All that remained was to agree on adequate compensation.'

Over that there was no difficulty. The Corporation agreed, indeed they suggested, a perpetual compensation for the fishermen, based on their average catches over the past twenty years. None of your lump-sum payments and that's that, but compensation going on indefinitely...

'It's money for old rope, boys!' Johannsson had shouted gleefully. 'Man, you did a fine job for us, Eriksson!'

But Lars hadn't liked it. There was a catch in it somewhere, he sighed, as he watched the commencement of the work on the hydro-electric scheme. It grieved him to see the mutilation of the valley where he'd grown up, to see the scars appear on the fellsides, see the endless churning convoys of contractors' lorries, hear the grinding noise of giant cement-mixers, the thud of pile-drivers.

But it wasn't this that worried him so much. Young and eager, he could see what a thrilling enterprise the hydro-electric scheme was. He knew it would benefit thousands of people and he was glad to get temporary work on the dam. He was proud to think he'd lent a hand, however insignificant, in building that curving, handsome, white giant of a barrage which, after two years' work, spanned the mighty river.

No, it wasn't this that worried Lars. It was the effect of it all on the fishermen of Laxhavn. Not that even Lars appreciated this until later on...

*   *   *   *

'Haul on then, lads!' Eriksson shouted, exactly as he had shouted in the past and the men bent their backs, hauled slowly on the seine-net, dragging its dripping splashing, meshes out of the river.

Nothing had changed. Or nothing seemed to have changed. But everyone knew it had. Lars, hauling along with the others at his father's command, stared sullenly at the glittering water that cascaded and swirled as the seine-net was hauled ashore. Hundreds of times in the past he had seen that scene enacted, but now it was different.

No longer did the men strain and grunt with eager anticipation, speculating on the catch. For every man-jack of them knew there was no catch. The net was empty and would remain empty. Not a single salmon or sea-trout came by Laxhavn now, since the dam was built. Yet the nets continued to be shot and hauled in, all along the stretch of the river, as in the past.

For that was the condition of the compensation the Corporation paid. The fishermen had to go through the motions of shooting their nets in order to qualify. Once they gave up, the compensation might cease. It was a typical, inane piece of red tape to satisfy somebody's legal quibble and to make certain that as men droppped out the compensation diminished.

Not that the fishermen minded. As long as they got their money they didn't mind enacting this futile little pantomime of the empty nets. No gutting, no packing. Same return for less work and gradually you could even skimp the net-shooting a bit, so that it became a sort of spree, the chance for a smoke and a gossip and the comforting thought of the money you were going to draw at the end of each month while the 'season' lasted.

'Has the cheque come this month all right, Eriksson?' bellowed Johannsson, not even pretending to take part in the hauling. He strolled away and lit a cigarette.

'Sure!' answered Lars's father. 'We'll go up to Olav's bar presently and have the share-out. Come on, now, boys, one more good haul and we'll land the catch. There's gold in that net!'

Lars's face clouded as he listened to Eriksson. He felt ashamed at this sordid pantomime. He said so later on as the men jostled around Eriksson, signing up for their share of the compensation.

'Keep it, Father!' he said angrily, when his turn came. 'I want none of it.' He pushed aside the coffee-cup and stood up.

'Too proud, eh, to touch filthy lucre?' Johannsson sneered. 'Maybe if you pulled your weight you'd feel entitled all right.'

'Yes, maybe I am too proud,' retorted Lars, slowly eyeing the massive figure that confronted him. Lars had filled out in the last two years. He looked like a sapling compared with the lumbering Johannsson, but his shoulders were powerful and he was light on his feet. 'All right, the State's taken away our livelihood, but there's no need for us to become demoralised and go through this pantomime of hauling in empty nets. We're becoming like a crowd of old women...'

'Speak for yourself, big head!' shouted Johannsson, thrusting out an arm and catching Lars by the shirt. 'You haven't worked for this as long as some of us.'

Lars knocked the fellow's arm away unceremoniously. Johannsson made another grab at him. Lars eyed him cool y, side-stepped and put a jab into his ribs. He merely wanted to warn Johannsson off. But Johannsson was now intent on showing who was master. While the others got out of the way or shouted to him to pack it up, he went blundering after Lars. A chair went over with a crash. Cups crashed on the floor. Johannsson aimed a violent blow at Lars's head. Lars ducked, knocked up the man's guard and planted his fist against his cheekbone, and the cuts on his knuckles gave him considerable satisfaction afterwards.

But now the other men had come between them.

'Cool down, Johannsson,' they warned. Eriksson jerked his head at Lars and slowly, still raw with the shame of that seine-net pantomime, Lars made his way out of the café.

*　　*　　*　　*

Lars went for a walk. A long one. He knew it was the best way of cooling off. No matter what the circumstances, whether you were fed up or angry or just out of sorts, there was something healing and soothing about Nature. A whiff of the pine woods, the sight of wild duck churning up some forest pool, the calm

Lars planted his fist against Johannsson's cheekbone

outline of the distant mountains with their glistening top-knot, all this was guaranteed to cure you.

But today the cure was a long time working. Lars was seething inwardly as he mooched on. He hated the indignity of it all, that empty farce turned them into a pack of beggars. He didn't give a straw for anyone like Johannsson, he was a waster anyway. But it hurt him that his father and old Nielsson should have to act like a crowd of mimes to get the dole the Corporation paid.

It hurt his pride even more to think that he, young and eager, was humbly taking his part in the pretence.

He strode on across the dam-road, past the dazzling white elegant power-houses and control rooms, felt the hum of activity, the roar of water in the sluices. He nodded at a passing engineer, took note of the man's lively gait, the implicit pride in his bearing. He bore no resentment against the engineers for disrupting the life of the Laxhavn fishermen. Life was complicated anyway and occasionally a minority had to suffer for the benefit of the many.

No, if anything, he envied that engineer the pride he clearly took in his work and it made the thought of the empty net pantomime seem even more bitter.

The fire was still in Lars's head as he clambered down the riverside track from the dam abutment. Hour after hour he walked, leaving the neat little red-painted wooden houses, plunging into the forestland along the lower stretches of the river.

Only when his legs began to ache did he halt. He had stuffed a couple of pieces of ryebread and some goat cheese in his lumber-shirt pocket and, while he sat on a fallen tree near a stream that flowed down towards the river, he began to munch these hungrily. Idly he glanced across the tall fireweed and the surrounding birch trees. This was a favourite spot of his. He often used to come here shooting black game.

Sometimes he and some of the chaps, Limping Ingmar and young Torgil, slept out in an old army hut a bit farther down. He'd often wondered why nobody used those two or three huts, they were still in good shape, concrete floors and all.

Then he remembered the fish-trap they'd built last summer. He grinned and, still chewing, sprang up and went clambering and slithering down the bank towards the stream.

It would be like old times to have a look at the trap. Built of wooden stakes and stones and sods, it was a simple affair with a cunning funnel-shaped entrance made of stripped willow wands and nylon threads. At times they'd caught one or two sizeable fish in it.

Now he sat on his hunkers and grunted contemptuously as he surveyed the derelict trap. A few minute fry flickered aimlessly here and there in the pool of water.

Abruptly, as he squatted there staring at the tiny fish, Lars stopped chewing. Something, he couldn't quite place it, was going on at the back of his mind. Hurriedly he finished the mouthful, bolting back the food as if it were an impediment to his mental processes. Then he rubbed his chin and, unconsciously, settled himself more comfortably against the bank, while fox-tailed bumble-bees burred in the fireweed. He'd got to think.

He realised that the idea hadn't just come to him. It must have been lying latent in his mind, and now the sight of those trout-fry had triggered it off.

It was that Englishman who had come rod-fishing two or three years ago. Lars had worked as his gillie for a couple of weeks, rowing him to and from the best salmon pools in the river. Mr Stevenson, his name had been, a big man in thick tweeds and a tweed hat full of flies, and he had lodged with Lars's aunt. When he learned that Lars did English at school, he'd lent him one or two sporting magazines. And it was through reading one of those that the idea had been born.

Now Lars remembered and clasped his knees in suppressed excitement. It was an article about fish-hatcheries, saying how so many of the world's rivers were understocked with good fish.

'I've even got planter friends overseas who send to Europe for trout-fry to stock their rivers,' Stevenson had said. 'Pity a few can't be shipped from these parts.'

Lars jumped up. His cheeks glowed. His eyes glinted. He scrambled up the bank, went crashing and blundering through the forest. A startled cow-elk that had been on her way down to drink turned in alarm and went churning away, but Lars took no notice. The army huts! He'd got to have a look at them. A ready-made site, alongside the river...

He tripped over a pine-root and fell headlong, painfully, but he was up again in an instant, his bruises ignored in the eager surge of the idea.

*   *   *   *

In secret Lars called a meeting. Not that there was anything furtive about the matter, but he just wanted to sound things out cautiously to begin with.

He concentrated on the young men and the youths of his acquaintance. No use asking the older chaps. Limping Ingmar, Torgil, young Gunnar of Sandviken, a few of the lads from the other seine-net teams.

To his gratification he found that most of them were as fed up as he was over the shame of hauling in the empty nets.

'It's degrading!' said Ingmar hotly, and his voice echoed in the long Nissen hut in the forest, where, appropriately, Lars had called the meeting. 'We might as well be on the dole!'

'It's the old men,' said Torgil. 'I suppose you can't blame them for taking it. After all, they've sweated their lives out at the seine-nets. It's only fair they should have some compensation.'

'But what's all the mystery about, Lars?' demanded Gunnar. 'You haven't brought us here just to belly-ache? We can do that at home all right, without getting blisters tramping all this way.'

'Fair enough,' grinned Lars, ruffling back his fair hair as he sat with swinging legs on a bench. 'This is what I propose...'

Briefly, coolly purposely controlling his own eagerness, he outlined the idea of the fish-hatchery. At first sceptical, but with growing interest, the others listened. Chins on fists, eyes frowning, they heard him through.

'We've been done down once,' Lars finished up, his voice almost hoarse by now. He'd never spoken so long in his life before, except perhaps when he once had to recite one of the sagas at a school prize-giving. 'Why can't we make a fresh start and stand on our own feet...?'

Of course there were objections, questions.

'Money? It doesn't grow on blueberry bushes, you know?'

'What about the know-how? Where would we sell the trout-fry?'

It was Limping Ingmar who triggered things off over the first point.

'I'm all for it,' he said, emphatically. 'What about the compensation money? I've got a fair bit tucked away and there'll be more to come. I'm willing to put it in the kitty...'

'That goes for me, too,' cried Erlend, who had kept quiet till now. 'It's a great idea, Lars!'

They were all young and enthusiastic. Difficulties there would be, of course. But they were made to be conquered. The meeting went on for hours and dusk had fallen when they made their way home.

Lars went into action at once. He and Ingmar and Gunnar borrowed Torre Svensen's car and drove over to Larvik to see the local representative of the Ministry of Fisheries; followed it up by, somewhat bashfully, visiting the bank manager. None of them had been inside a bank before and they were a bit overawed until they started talking to the manager.

But it was Grieg, the Ministry chap, who really got things moving. A few days later he telephoned Lars.

'Keep your fingers crossed,' he said, 'but I think it's going to work. I've put your case to the Ministry. They want a detailed scheme, but they're favourably disposed towards the idea of a grant. They'll even send along an instructor to help get you going...'

'The buildings?' Lars asked, anxiously. He knew that without the site they'd be sunk.

'I'm seeing the commandant at Skogheim tomorrow. If he knows the Ministry approves there won't be any difficulties there...'

'Fine! Thanks a lot, Mr Grieg. Soon as we can we're going to start in on doing up the huts. There are all sorts of things... he went on, the enthusiasm bubbling out of him like a stream.

'There are all sorts of difficulties, too, Lars,' Grieg cautioned, at the other end of the telephone. But the word snag didn't exist in Lars's vocabulary.

*　　*　　*　　*

To begin with everything went perfectly. The Ministry of Fisheries grant materialised all right. A generous one, too, Lars and his partners said gleefully. The Ministry of Fisheries expert was first class, too. He took enthusiastically to the job of advising the boys fully about equipping the hatchery, showed them how to 'strip' the parent fish, squeezing the eggs from the hen trout like toothpaste from a tube, getting the milt from the cock fish. He trained them in storing the precious larva, showed them how to sort out the 'eyed' from the 'blind' eggs.

On paper Lars and the other Laxhavn boys were developing into experts. In practice, they found how devastatingly difficult things could be. It was bad enough chafing at the time factor, fretting at the slow development of the trout-fry. It was nerve-racking to see how that once sizeable grant seemed to melt away in face of all the overheads such as electricity, transport, water-tanks and to on.

Even so, after month of effort and sacrifice, it really seemed as if the pay-off was coming. They'd got their first big customer in rospect and if this deal came off there was every possibility they'd begin to pay their way.

And then, just as Lars really thought they were on the verge of success, disease struck. They isolated the tank in question, kept their fingers crossed... and wat hed anxiously. Lars and Erlend groaned as they saw one morning that the disease had spread to the other tanks. Within a few d ys there wasn't a single alevin left alive in the whole hatchery.

'Sorry,' shrugged the prospective customer. 'I can't wait. I'll have to give someone else the order.'

It was indeed a blow beneath the belt. Some of the 'partners' showed signs of wavering. Even Lars was near despair.

But he gritted his teeth and once again took a walk through th forest to think things out, exactly as he had when he first had the idea of starting the hatcheries. As he sat brooding on the trials and tribulations of life he heard an outboard motor-boat chugging along the river. Lars watched it gloomily and saw that the three men in it were carrying rifles. Probably after elk, he shrugged, for the season had recently opened. The boat glided in towards the little landing-stage not far away and the men clambered out. They spoke casually to Lars and were making their way into the forest when one of them half turned and glanced sharply at Lars, a big grey-haired man in tweeds...

'Aren't you Lars Eriksson?' he asked in English. 'You don't

remember me? It's quite a time since we met.'

For a moment Lars stared blankly at the man, trying to take in the unaccustomed language. Then he leapt to his feet, grinning cheerfully.

'Of course,' he said, holding out a hand. 'You're Mr Stevenson. I used to act as gillie for you. When there were plenty of fish in the river,' he added bitterly.

'Yes, I heard all about that,' frowned Stevenson, while his companions waited curiously for him. 'I suppose you got yourself another job when the seine-netting packed up?'

The rest of the story is quickly told, but for Lars it was a graphic example of what a game of snakes and ladders life can be. One moment you're down, next moment you're shinning up a ladder. Before he finished recounting his attempt to set up the Laxhavn Trout Hatcheries the other men were listening as intently as Stevenson.

'Look here, Steve,' said one of them, a lean, sunburnt man, with a pipe eternally clutched between his teeth. 'It looks as if you've introduced me to the right chap...'

He was a planter on leave from India, one of the same people Stevenson had once told him sent to Europe for their trout-fry. He questioned Lars expertly, nodded approvingly at the expert answers he got, asked to see the hatchery.

Eventually, scarcely believing his ears, Lars heard him offer an order twice as big as the original one he had lost. While he was still grinning with delight and wonder at this sudden turn of fortune, the third man had something to say. He was an editor of one of the biggest Oslo dailies.

'There's a first-rate story here,' he said to Stevenson. 'Guts and enterprise...'

And he, too, began to question Lars closely, as Lars took the visitors round the hatcheries. That was how Laxhavn Trout Hatcheries really got off the ground. A whacking great order for umpteen thousand trout-fry to be despatched to

India, plus headlines in a national newspaper.

From then on the affair prospered. But the real reward as far as Lars was concerned was the fact that it had given him and his pals the chance to stand on their own feet again, instead of performing that undignified mummery of hauling in empty nets. They had been cheated of one harvest of the river. But in future the boys of Laxhavn would gather the harvest of pride. You could achieve anything — anything — if you had a mind to do so, provided, as the Oslo editor said, you had the guts and determination to see it through.

The Stowaway and the Hunted Stranger

by CHARLES KING

The *Pleiades* was seventeen hours out of Tilbury and clearing Land's End when Farrer discovered the stowaway.

He had gone on deck in the grey dawn with a stiff breeze blowing from the south-west and the sea showing its teeth. It was late June but cold. He trudged a couple of times around the deserted deck and then stood in the lee of one of the lifeboats slung on davits by the rail to smoke a cigarette. The sound from inside the lifeboat was a mere rustle of cloth against wood, but it was part of Farrer's job to hear such sounds.

He stood very still. When he heard the sound again, he slid the lighter back into his pocket and flicked the unlit cigarette over the rail. He turned quietly on the balls of his feet and reached up a hand to the tarpaulin which covered the lifeboat.

Someone had unfastened the lashings which held the corner of the tarpaulin in place. Farrer grinned to himself and glanced along the deck. It was deserted. He put one foot on the lower rung of the rail, one hand on the corner of the tarpaulin, and thrust himself upwards and whipped back the tarpaulin in a single swift movement.

There was a boy crouching at the bottom of the lifeboat. He had flattened himself there when the tarpaulin slid back. He had a weighty-looking sandwich in one hand and a torch in the other and the torch was still alight. He stared up at Farrer, wide-eyed and shocked but not afraid. He had a defiant look on his face.

Farrer grinned and said, 'Well, well. A stowaway.'

The boy just watched Farrer. He was about fifteen, Farrer judged, but he had a good-natured face and a keen jaw. He was wearing dungarees and a thick woollen sweater and there was a duffle coat crumpled up beside him. There was also a kit-bag with its neck open to show a vacuum flask and a thickish book inside it. The boy had planned this thing well. And he had the sense to keep quiet and wait for developments when he was in a tight corner.

Farrer said, 'You might have chosen a more original hiding-place.'

'There wasn't time,' The boy watched Farrer fiercely, but he switched off the torch. 'I only got aboard ten minutes before she sailed. There were people all over the place.'

'But it'll be six more days before we reach Nassau. You couldn't hope to hold out that long.'

'I was going to shift around. At night. I'd have found something.'

'Myself, I've always thought the best way would be to put some decent clothes on, carry a deck-chair, and just swan around the ship as though I'd got a first-class ticket in my pocket and not a care in the world.'

The boy looked at Farrer without smiling. He glanced at the sandwich and the torch in his hands and moved his shoulders bitterly. He said, 'It doesn't matter much, anyway. Now you've found me.'

Farrer turned his head and looked both ways along the deck. It was still deserted. He was a man who made up his mind quickly. He said, 'I'm going to put the tarpaulin back in place now and lash it down. You'll have to stay put for a while but we'll do something about that later. I'll smoke a cigarette and you can tell me why you stowed away.'

'You're not going to report me, then?'

'No, I am not.'

'Thanks,' the boy said.

Farrer liked that simple, adequate word and the way the boy said it, gratefully but not humbly. He liked the boy. Whatever he had stowed away for it would make no difference to Farrer's decision to help him, but he was interested.

He pulled the tarpaulin over the thwarts and lashed it in place. Then he eased himself down to the deck and got a cigarette out and lit it. He was just standing there casually in the lee of the lifeboat with the smoke shredding away from his fingers in the wind when the ship's officer walked past.

Farrer returned the man's 'Morning, sir', and agreed that the wind was fresh and watched him until he turned the corner of the deckhouse and disappeared. When the deck was empty again he leaned on the lifeboat and said softly, 'Fire away, youngster. Name?'

'Keith Douglas.'

'Go on, then.'

'My father's in the consular office in the Bahamas,' the boy said. He must have put his lips close to the lifeboat's hull because his voice was low but quite clear. 'I'm on holiday from school, Rossall's in Hertfordshire. I'm supposed to be spending the holidays with my uncle.'

'But you wanted to join your father in Nassau?'

'Well, yes, I did. But that's not why I stowed away. Dad would have paid my fare... if he'd wanted to.'

Farrer waited for a moment and said, 'If it's private, you don't need to tell me.'

'Oh it's not that. It's just that it sounds wet. But Dad has this idea that I've had it too easy, that I've been spoon-fed all my life and I take it for granted. He says I ought to learn to work my passage.'

Farrer grinned to himself. He could picture father Douglas saying that. But he wondered how any father could look at a boy like this one, the clear eyes and solid jaw, and get him

— his whole character — so utterly wrong.

'So you stowed away on the *Pleiades* to prove you could work your passage, eh?' he said.

'I told you it sounded wet.'

'I don't think it does. I'm just wondering whether you'll accept any help from me, that's all. If you want it that way, I'll just walk away and let you go it alone.'

He waited for the boy's answer curiously. Plenty of kids had guts, but the intelligence that should go with it, the knowledge of one's limitations and the readiness to accept them, that was rarer. It was rare even in Farrer's specialised line of business.

The boy said, simply, 'I'd be glad if you'd help me, sir.'

'I hoped you'd say that,' Farrer said. 'Right then, you'd better stay where you are for a couple of days. I'll find out when they check the lifeboats. And I'll look for another hiding-place. How's the food situation?'

'I've got sandwiches fot two more days, but they're pretty stale already.'

'I'll bring some food to you after dark tonight. All right?'

'Fine, sir.' The boy stirred inside the lifeboat, getting into a position he could hold comfortably for a few hours, Farrer guessed. The voice was fainter, muffled, when he spoke again. 'I don't know why you're doing this for me.'

Farrer flipped his cigarette over the rail and grinned. The same thought had occurred to him. He liked the boy and respected his reason for defying authority, but that was only part of the answer. He put out a hand and touched the wooden hull of the lifeboat.

'Maybe it's a form of insurance,' he said. 'Maybe there'll be somebody around to help me, one of these days, when I need him.'

At dawn on the fourth day out, Farrer told Keith Douglas that he would have to move that night. They were holding a full-scale lifeboat drill next day, and the tarpaulins would be stripped off and the boats slung overboard. He had found a new hiding-place, Farrer said. He would come for Keith at two o'clock in the morning and take him there.

Keith settled down in the well of the lifeboat with the hard-boiled egg and the rolls and milk that Farrer had brought him. He was not hungry but he ate. He tried to keep his mind off the twenty rotten hours he would have to spend in this boxed-up darkness before Farrer came to him again.

He thought about Farrer. All he had seen of Farrer was a lean profile against the moonlit sky, a lean hand passing the food under the tarpaulin. From those brief glimpses and the firm, lazy sound of Farrer's voice, Keith guessed he was in his late thirties, and a man who made his own decisions and stuck by them.

What Farrer did for a living was a mystery. He had called himself a businessman when Keith asked him the night before, but with just enough hesitation to suggest that the answer might have been different if Farrer had trusted him with it. Keith wished Farrer had trusted him. He thought Farrer was terrific.

What he would have done if Farrer hadn't helped him, Keith shuddered to think. Eight days in the lifeboat would have been murder. He had managed to scramble out for half an hour at a time on the second and third nights, scuttling around the deserted upper deck to ease the cramp in his muscles, but sooner or later he would have been driven out of hiding by hunger or sickness or claustrophobia, and then it would have been all up.

Farrer was one in a million, Keith thought, shifting his position at the end of the second hour and freezing again as the high yapping voices of a couple of female passengers passed by the lifeboat. Anyone else would have handed him straight over to the ship's officers. Even his father would have done that, not out of spite but because he believed in obedience to the rules. Most adults felt that way, in Keith's experience. But Farrer was the sort of man who made his own rules.

He hadn't overdone the help, either. He had come to the lifeboat just once in each twenty-four hours, bringing the food and talking for ten minutes and then going away again. He seemed to understand that too much help would have been as bad as too little. He had let Keith go it the hard way, alone, and that was what Keith had stowed away for in the first place, after all.

Keith squirmed into a new position in the muffled darkness of the lifeboat. Farrer had told him the wind had dropped and the barometer was rising, and it was certainly hot under the tarpaulin. The sun must be beating straight down on it. Keith gritted his teeth and tried to shut out the gruesome thought of the next sixteen hours and failed.

That fourth day in the lifeboat was almost unbearable. People kept bringing their deck-chairs close to the lifeboat, grumbling about the breeze, and the darkness under the tarpaulin was airless and foul. The only thing which kept Keith going was the thought of Farrer and the rendezvous he had with him that night.

It got dark outside and cool at last, and the deck emptied. Keith opened a corner of the tarpaulin and gulped in the blessed night air. At midnight he gathered his things together and crammed them into the kit-bag, slowly and carefully, and at two o'clock he loosened the tarpaulin again and peered out along the deck.

Farrer was there, a lean dark shape in the moonlight twenty yards away. He was leaning against the rail and smoking a cigarette. That was one of the things about Farrer, his absolute dependability. It made Keith think about wartime and officers synchronising their watches and split-second timing. Looking at Farrer in that moment, Keith thought that whatever he really did for a living it must be something that involved action.

He was right, too, dead right. Because the next moment, while he was still waiting for Farrer to signal him, Keith saw a man step out of the shadows of the deckhouse behind Farrer. The man was bulky and he wore a white tuxedo. He stood five yards from Farrer's back, and if Farrer heard him he must have thought he was just a belated passenger because he never looked around.

The bulky man moved suddenly, so suddenly that Keith had no time to cry out. A spot of moonlight glittered on his left hand, probably on a ring. He swept his left hand high up and down again in a vicious chopping blow at the back of Farrer's head.

Farrer sagged. His body jack-knifed across the rail and hung there motionless, face downward. Keith would have cried out in horror but his throat had locked. He just gripped the edge of the lifeboat with rigid fingers and watched the bulky man lean over Farrer's unconscious body and fumble at it.

The whole thing happened very quickly. Keith's mind was still grappling with shock when the bulky man crammed something into his breast pocket and stooped to Farrer's legs and heaved them upwards. The body tipped over the rail and fell towards the sea, arms and legs flung wide with the horrible effect of a parcel bursting open.

Keith gouged himself out from under the tarpaulin. He clawed over the bows of the lifeboat and fell on to the deck, his cramped legs buckling and incoherent sounds coming from his throat. The fall steadied him.

He looked swiftly along the deck. The bulky man had already disappeared and it was empty. Keith dragged himself sideways and clutched the lower rung of the rail and pushed his head through. Fifty or sixty feet below the sea slid past, a creamy ribbon of foam folding back on itself and arrowing away from the black wall of the ship's hull.

There was a patch of white floating farther out on the dark water that must have been Farrer's body. It was sliding fast astern. Keith had no time to see whether Farrer was struggling. He fumbled with the lifebelt which hung against the rail by his head, dragging it fiercely from its lashings and shouting desperately, 'Man overboard! Man overboard!'

He got the lifebelt free and swung it with all his strength over the rail. It splashed into the sea ten yards short of the white patch on the water and glimmered astern. It was no good diving after it, Keith knew in a flash. His only hope of saving Farrer was to warn the man on the bridge and get the ship turned around.

He ran forward along the deck to where dark mass of the bridge structure loomed overhead, forgetting the pain in his legs, yelling, 'Man overboard!' again and again. A light flashed suddenly on the wing of the bridge. A sharp voice cried, 'I see it, sir! A lifebelt! Starboard quarter!' Bells tinkled urgently up there and the deck hammered under Keith's feet as the screws trod down the water and churned astern.

Keith stopped shouting. Arc lamps were blazing along the liner's decks as it heeled in a sharp turn to starboard, the broad scar of its wake fanning out astern. People were crowding to the rail, crewmen and women in evening dress and men in pyjamas. There was nothing Keith could do now except wait.

He had put on his duffle coat in the lifeboat earlier, waiting for the rendezvous with Farrer. He pulled the hood of it over his head now and wedged himself into the lee of the lifeboat against the rail. There was not much chance of anyone noticing him among the confused mob of passengers on deck.

While the ship ploughed back on its course, quartering the dark sea with searchlights, he thought about the attack on

Farrer. Who was the bulky man in the white tuxedo? Why had he tried to kill Farrer? No words had been spoken. The bulky man had just stepped up behind Farrer and slugged him and then thrown his body overboard.

But before he had thrown the body overboard, Keith remembered, the killer had fumbled at Farrer's body and crammed something into his pocket. Was the motive for the attack just robbery? Keith shook his head decisively in the darkness. Farrer was not the sort of man to attract an aimless violence like that. If anyone tried to kill Farrer it would be because he hated Farrer, of feared him. Keith thought about that lean profile and lazy voice and knew that Farrer's enmity would be just as downright as his friendship.

The bellow of the ship's siren cut across Keith's thoughts. The deck was shuddering again as the screws threshed astern. The searchlights had coned on the water a hundred yards away on the starboard bow and people were shouting and pointing and a boat was being lowered.

Keith shuffled along the deck with the mob of excited passengers. He was three back in the crowd massed around the gangway when they brought Farrer aboard ten minutes later. All he could see of Farrer was an arm dangling over the side of the stretcher, a lean hand swaying loosely as the seaman carried him across the deck to the sick bay, but he heard the words passed back through the crowd, 'He's alive, he's alive.'

There were twin ventilators sprouting from the deck five yards from the white-painted door of the sick bay, with a narrow space between them. When the crowd of passengers shuffled away, chattering, Keith edged between the ventilators and hid there. He had to know more about Farrer's condition. He had to decide what to do next.

The obvious thing was to report the attack on Farrer to the ship's officers. That would mean giving himself up, and Keith was ready for that. But would he be believed? It was his word, the word of a boy and a stowaway, against the word of the man in the white tuxedo who was obviously a passenger and might be an important one. If Keith had got evidence against the man it might be different, but he knew nothing about him, not his name, not even what he looked like.

Keith clenched his fists in the pockets of his duffle coat. He knew what Farrer would have done. Farrer would have found out who the man in the white tuxedo was. He would have shadowed the man, dug out some evidence linking him with the victim of his attack, worked and waited until he could give the authorities some hard facts. The authorities liked facts.

In the moment Keith made up his mind, wondering grimly how he could start looking for the man in the white tuxedo, the door of the sick bay opened. A ship's officer came out, holding the door for a tall man who was obviously the doctor. They paused three yards from the dark space between the ventilators where Keith was hidden.

'He'll do,' the doctor said. 'But he was darned lucky.'

'I'll say. If that lifebelt hadn't been floating near him, we'd never have spotted him. That's a funny thing. I had the deck party repainting those lifebelts before we sailed.'

'The chap who threw the lifebelt overboard deserves some credit, eh?' The doctor stretched and yawned. 'Ah well, I'll turn in. You'll call me if I'm needed.'

'Right, Doc. Should we have somebody watching your patient?'

'Not all the time. He won't come to for an hour or so yet. But you might look in on him now and then.'

The doctor walked away up the deck. The officer turned and moved out of Keith's line of vision. Keith heard his footsteps stop suddenly behind the ventilators as he said, 'Ah, Mr Godolphin. Anxious about out man overboard?'

A deep, plummy voice said, 'Poor fellow. I saw you rescue him. How is he?'

226

'Unconscious still. The doc says he must have hit his head when he fell overboard. The shock of the water probably brought him to and he kept himself afloat till the boat picked him up. But he's lost a lot of blood from the wound and he passed out again.'

'But he'll survive?'

'Oh yes, the doc's stitched him up. He'll come to in a few hours.'

'Good, good.' The rich voice purred approval. 'Who is the poor fellow, by the way?'

'Farrer's his name. According to the purser he's a salesman for a computer firm. Travelling alone. Maybe he'll be able to tell us what happened when he comes to.'

'Ah yes. That would be most satisfactory. Well, I mustn't keep you from your duties. Good night, officer.'

'Good night, Mr Godolphin.'

The officer's footsteps echoed away down the deck. There was no other sound. The other man, this Mr Godolphin with his plummy voice and his concern for Farrer, must be standing still in the darkness outside the sick bay. Suddenly Keith wanted very much to see Mr Godolphin.

He eased out carefully from between the ventilators. He put a hand on the warm metal of the starboard ventilator and leaned around it, not moving his feet. The man was standing a bare two yards away, staring at the door of the sick bay with his fleshy profile silhouetted by the glow from the porthole. Keith froze in the shadows.

Mr Godolphin was a bulky man. A spot of light glittered on his left hand, probably on a ring. He was wearing a white tuxedo.

*   *   *   *

When Mr Godolphin moved away up the deck, Keith followed him. There had been a moment of fear, a sudden intense longing to skulk back to the lifeboat and hide there in the safe darkness until the ship reached Nassau and his father, and then Keith remembered Farrer's words.

'Maybe there'll be somebody around to help me, one of these days, when I need him,' Farrer had said.

Keith glided along the deck, using the shadow of the deckhouse, keeping Godolphin's bulky figure in sight twenty yards ahead. This man had tried to kill Farrer and he might try again, now he knew that Farrer would recover and perhaps talk. Farrer needed somebody to help him now, and Keith was around.

The ship was deserted, anyway. It was nearly three in the morning and isolated lights burned along the empty throbbing deck. There was no one in sight when Godolphin turned into the doorway to the first-class cabins and walked past the rows of locked doors. This business was between Godolphin and Farrer and Keith, and no one else would interfere until it was finished.

Flattened in the doorway to the boat-deck, Keith marked the cabin door which Godolphin unlocked and entered. When the door had closed again, Keith soft-footed along the corridor and straight past it without stopping. There was an empty pantry farther down on the opposite side. Keith hid in there. He kept the door narrowly open and watched Godolphin's cabin. He had to get inside that cabin somehow, but he had no idea how to manage it.

Godolphin settled that problem himself five minutes later by coming out of the cabin with an empty cigarette carton crumpled in his hand. He frowned, pulled the door shut behind him without locking it, and walked hurriedly away. He was going to get cigarettes, Keith guessed. He had changed the white tuxedo for a dark blazer.

Keith gave himself no time to think. Directly Godolphin had disappeared, he padded along the corridor to the cabin, opened the door, and slid inside.

A single lamp was burning in there. The cabin was big and full of shadows. There were pigskin suitcases heaped at the foot of the bunk, three of them. Clothes on hangers fiilled a deep cupboard on one bulkhead. Keith looked around desperately, knowing he had a minute or two at the most to find what he wanted, and the last thing he saw was the white tuxedo hanging behind the door.

He took two sharp steps to the door and rifled the tuxedo. There was a wallet in the breast pocket. He opened it and his fiingers shook. He had been looking for a link between Godolphin and Farrer, and this was it. This was Farrer's wallet. It had a leather flap inside it with a celluloid panel and a card under the panel with Farrer's photograph on it. Under the photograph was printed, *R. T. Farrer, Federal Bureau of Investigation, Narcotics Division, seconded from Special Branch, Scotland Yard.*

One side of the wallet was a thin notebook. Godolphin's name was scribbled on the first leaf with a column of dates underneath it. Against each date there was a place-name, Turin, Genoa, Paris, London, or a question mark. There were more question marks than names. Farrer was a detective investigating Godolphin, obviously, and it was something to do with narcotics, and Godolphin had found out and tried to kill Farrer. He had taken the wallet from Farrer's body before he tipped him overboard.

Keith snapped the wallet shut and stood listening. He heard nothing but he knew that Godolphin was coming back. He turned and slid across the cabin to the open cupboard and thrust himself deep into the clothes hanging inside there. He was hidden when the cabin door opened.

Godolphin shut the door and stood looking around the cabin, smoking. Keith could see him without moving, through a gap in the hanging clothes. He saw Godolphin turn towards the tuxedo and put out a hand to the breast pocket. Farrer's wallet was still in Keith's hand, and his fingers closed on it rigidly.

But Godolphin checked. He glanced at his wristwatch. He shook his head and scowled and turned towards the suitcases at the foot of the bunk. He dug out the bottom one and heaved it on to the bunk and unlocked it. He was hidden from Keith's view there and Keith was too scared to move for a moment.

The silence nerved him. He pushed the sleeve of a suit aside very carefully and shifted his head to the right. Godolphin was standing over the open suitcase. He was holding a hypodermic syringe up to the light and jabbing the needle into a phial. He was smiling as he did it.

The smile chilled Keith's neck. It was a killer's smile, moving the heavy mouth and cheeks but not reaching the eyes. Keith let the sleeve of the suit drop back. Whatever happened, Godolphin must not find him now. If he did, Farrer would die and Keith too. Keith knew, with ice in his bones, what Godolphin meant to do with that hypodermic needle.

He stood in the musty darkness among the clothes, listening to the faint sounds Godolphin made. He heard the tinkle of the empty phial dropped back into the suitcase. He heard the click of the lock as Godolphin closed the suitcase and locked it. He heard Godolphin's soft, heavy footsteps cross the cabin backwards and forwards, and then stop for a long heart-shaking moment, and then move to the door.

When the door had shut and the key turned in the lock, Keith slid out into the empty cabin. He stood for a moment looking around him. He was not really making up his mind, that was already done. There was nothing more to look for in here and it would be no good running for the ship's officers and raising the alarm. By the time he had explained what he was doing on the ship and tried to convince them he was telling the truth, Godolphin would have done what he meant to do and there would be no evidence.

Keith ran to the door. The lock was bolt-operated and he slid it softly back. He opened the door and peered out. The bulky figure of Godolphin was framed in the doorway to the deck at the end of the corridor. He had his left hand bunched in the pocket of his coat, protecting something in there. He stepped out to the deck as Keith watched him, and disappeared.

Keith slid along the corridor after him. He checked at the doorway to the deck, looking aft. He was right, Godolphin was moving that way. He was keeping to the shadows but the deck was deserted anyway. Keith had a sudden queer sense of the great ship trudging on across the windy vastness of the sea with its cargo of sleeping people and a murderer stalking his victim along the deck.

He slid out after Godolphin. He moved quickly, sure of the direction. He had no weapon and no idea of how he would tackle Godolphin when the moment came. He only knew that Godolphin had to be stopped and of all the hundreds of people on the ship, people who had a right to be aboard, passengers and crew, he, the stowaway, was the only one who could stop him.

Godolphin had moved fast. He was already inside the sick bay when Keith got there. Keith heard the soft sound of his footsteps moving there as he crept up to the door. He had a sudden horrible fear that he was too late and he just slammed open the door and blundered through it into the harsh glare of light inside.

Godolphin was stooping over the iron cot against the far wall. He had the hypodermic syringe raised in his left hand. Farrer was lying in the cot with a bandage on his head and his eyes shut and his bare arm outside the blanket. The needle of the hypodermic was three inches from his arm.

As Keith blundered into the sick bay, Godolphin swung around. He snarled. His eyes shone in the light as he glared at Keith. His breath made moist sounds in his throat.

Keith said, raggedly, 'You're not going to kill Farrer.'

'Who... are you?'

'It doesn't matter. I saw you hit Farrer. I saw you push him overboard. You're not going to get away with this...'

Godolphin said, softly, 'No? No?' and smiled. He started to move towards Keith, very slowly. He said, 'You saw too much, then.' He slid his left arm forward in front of his body, reaching out for Keith, and the light shivered along the hypodermic needle in his hand.

Farrer saw the light and heard voices. There was a fiendish ache in his head and he had no idea what position his body was lying in. He felt nothing except the pain behind his eyes but the voices were very clear. A deep, smooth voice, one of them, Godolphin's. And then a ragged young voice that pierced the fog in his brain.

Farrer put the bits together laboriously, lying there and listening to the voices. He was in the sick bay on the ship. The boat must have picked him up. He had been struggling in the sea. Before that he had been standing at the rail and waiting for young Keith to join him and then jagged light had suddenly exploded behind his eyes.

He still felt nothing in his body, but his brain was functioning. Keith was in the sick bay with Godolphin. Farrer tried to lift his head but his neck muscles were dead. He shut his eyes against the harsh glare of the light and focused on the voices.

Godolphin was saying, 'So you are a stowaway. How convenient. You will not be missed. Only Farrer and I know you are aboard and Farrer will soon be dead also.'

Keith's voice was fierce. 'You won't get away with this.'

'Oh, but I will. I have got away with it for more years than you have been alive. Farrer was a fool to meddle with me. You are a fool, too. You could have run through that door before I locked it...'

'I don't run. You're not going to kill Farrer. He helped me. I've only got to shout...'

'No one would hear you. And this drug acts very quickly. Come, we have wasted enough time...'

'No... no...'

Farrer wrenched his head off the pillow. He saw Keith trapped in the far corner of the sick bay with Godolphin crouched three feet away, menacing him. He saw the glitter of light in Godolphin's outstretched hand that was the hypodermic needle. He tried to move his body but it would not obey.

As the needle quested forward at Keith's shrinking body, Farrer wrung words out of his throat. 'Godolphin... you devil...'

Godolphin swung around. He stood half-turned towards the cot, his hand with the needle in it wavering in front of Keith, his mind working a split second slower than his eyes as he focused them viciously on Farrer. That split second was Keith's chance, Farrer knew, if the boy was cool enough to take it.

Keith took it. He slid forward. He raised both hands and chopped them hard down on Godolphin's left wrist. Godolphin screamed and dropped the hypodermic syringe and it smashed on the floor.

Keith lunged at Godolphin then, with both fists working, Godolphin made a harsh sound in his throat and put thick hands on Keith's neck. He flung Keith away across the floor and grabbed at something inside his coat as Keith crashed against the baseboard and lay there groaning. The sight of the gun in Godolphin's hand must have unlocked Farrer's limbs. He jack-knifed forward across the cot. Godolphin was aiming the gun with both hands at Keith's sprawled body and his finger was squeezing the trigger when Farrer's shoulder hit him.

The gun went off twice. One of the bullets ricocheted off the ceiling. Farrer clamped a hand on Godolphin's left wrist and dug his fingers into the soft flesh as they struggled on the floor. Godolphin screamed and the gun fell out of his hand. Farrer grabbed it by the barrel and brought it over sharply and hammered Godolphin with it once, twice.

Godolphin's body went limp. Farrer eased himself up on his forearms and just hung there, panting, the pain surging behind his eyes. He looked up after a moment and Keith was kneeling by the wall, looking across at him and trying to smile.

Farrer said the one simple, adequate word which had started this whole thing, the word Keith had used three nights ago on the deck in the shadows of the lifeboat, 'Thanks.'

After that there were trampling feet on the deck outside and shoulders breaking down the door and ship's officers piling into the sick bay.

With the last of his strength, as the gentle hands lifted him off Godolphin's unconscious body and the tide of pain engulfed him again, Farrer said, 'The boy.. he's been helping me... undercover... go easy with him until... I can explain...'

He explained two days later, the last day of the voyage, when the doctor finally let him stand on his own two feet and he walked to the captain's cabin under the bridge. Keith was there, spruced up and without the lines of tension in his face but looking shy. Farrer just put his hand on Keith's arm without saying anything, but the hand was enough.

Farrer told the captain and Keith that he had been shadowing Godolphin for nine months across the Near East and Europe. Godolphin was a courier for a group of international drug-runners. The Americans had uncovered a branch of the gang in the Caribbean and when Godolphin booked a passage on

234

the *Pleiades*, Farrer was seconded to the F. B. I. and instructed to follow him.

Godolphin must have discovered Farrer's identity after the ship had sailed and tried to get rid of him before the gang's contacts came aboard at Nassau and walked into the trap. Thanks to Keith, Farrer was still alive and Godolphin was locked up in the ship's cell, and with any luck the contacts would be trapped in Nassau after all.

When Farrer had finished talking, Keith had some explaining to do. He made it brief, but Farrer had been in enough tight corners himself to know just what the boy had gone through. He had been right about Keith when he found him hiding in the lifeboat. The insurance he had taken out had paid off.

Farrer tried to explain that to the captain when Keith told his story, but the captain cut him short. Stowing away on a seagoing ship was a serious crime, the captain said gravely, but he thought Keith had done enough in the circumstances to justify a free pardon. He had already put Keith in the next cabin to Farrer's and he proposed that Keith should travel at his company's expense for the remainder of the voyage.

The final explanation was made by Farrer to Keith's father when the *Pleiades* docked at Nassau next day. Farrer had stayed below in Godolphin's cabin when the ship tied up, and Godolphin's contacts, an American and a woman, had walked right into his hands. When he came on deck ten minutes later with the job sewn up, he saw Keith by the rail with his father.

Keith's father had been warned of his son's arrival by radio. He was a compact little man with a high colour and a stern moustache. He was just as Farrer had pictured him, and he was saying to Keith, 'What have you been up to, heh? That's what I want to know, what have you been up to?'

Farrer walked over to the pair of them. He put a lean arm around Keith's shoulder. He said to Keith's father, grinning, 'He's just been working his passage, Mr Douglas, that's all.'

The Tightrope

by IAN SERRAILLIER

One summer morning fifty years ago, in the Swiss watch-manufacturing town of Gresslau, a fifteen-year-old lad was on his way to the station to meet the train from Berne. He was freckled, sturdy-limbed and long in the leg, and he carried a violin case under his arm. His name was Franz Klöti.

The main street was decorated with bunting, flags and gay banners of welcome. A big orange poster outside the Cafe Silberhorn made the reason for these clear:

ON THURSDAY AFTERNOON NEXT A TIGHTROPE WILL BE SUSPENDED FROM A FOURTH-FLOOR WINDOW OF THE CAFÉ SILBERHORN TO THE BALCONY OF THE HOTEL BUNDERHOF OPPOSITE. AT SIX P. M. PRECISELY THE CELEBRATED ITALIAN TIGHTROPE WALKER POMPOZINI WILL WALK ACROSS WEATHER PERMITTING D.V. NO NET WILL BE PROVIDED.

Franz had read the poster at least a dozen times in the past week. Now, as he walked by, a bill-poster was pasting on a label marked TODAY.

Outside the station he paused to gaze at a hoarding splashed with a gaudy-coloured picture of Pompozini. The great man was superbly poised on a rope that spanned a chasm between two beetling crags — and he was pushing a wheelbarrow in front of him! Solid and self-assured, he looked as if the wildest gale could not knock him off.

Franz studied the features carefully, for it was Pompozini that he had come to meet. He had never seen him. He had made no appointment for today. Nor did he know for certain that Pompozini would be on the train. But it was the only one in the morning; and it seemed probable that, with all his apparatus to set up, the acrobat would not leave his arrival till as late as the afternoon.

Punctual to the minute, the electric train swept into the station and emptied its crowded carriages on to the platftorm. Everybody seemed to be getting out at Gresslau today. Hundreds of people were pushing and shoving their way to the barrier, all of them here to see the great performance.

'I shall never find him in all this crowd,' thought Franz, as he searched the excited faces. 'I can see nobody like the picture. And now they've all gone.'

The platform was empty.

Or was it?

At the far end Franz saw a pile of luggage, with an angry little man lost in the middle. He ran to him.

'Ten thousand curses on his stupid head! The imbecile — *imbecile!*' he shouted, the points of his moustache trembling.

The boy didn't inquire who was being referred to in such unflattering terms. Instead he looked at the name on one of the numerous labels and grinned. Yes, this was the man he was looking for. Now was the time to make his speech.

But it would not come. This is what he had *intended* to say: 'Mr Pompozini, all the world knows you're the greatest acrobat. Will you let me join your troupe? I'm in that line of business myself. I can walk the length of my bed-rail juggling with three tennis balls. I can swot up the hardest conjuring trick in half an hour. I can sing comic songs. I can play the violin balancing on two legs of a chair. I have mastered the xylophone and the wooden harp and the guitar and the mandolin and the tinkling glass carillon. I'm at your service, sir.'

But he was a little flustered, and all he could remember to say was 'At your service, sir.'

'And high time too!' snapped the little man, in a strong foreign accent. 'I bawl for a porter half an hour not stopping.'

'Oh I didn't mean that,' said Franz. But all the same he picked up two of the bags.

'And this one, with the apparatus!'

It was the biggest and heaviest, but he picked it up as well. As he struggled to the barrier, his spine almost cracked under the weight.

'Fetch me a taxi, boy. And tell the driver no luggage on the roof — it falls off — cannot lose my rope — two years ago it happens, I lose my best rope. Presto!'

Franz dumped the luggage and ran across the yard to find a taxi. The last one was just disappearing. There were no more left. But he hailed a carrier whom he knew and persuaded him to help.

'What, travel in a common lorry? Me, the great Pompozini? Pfff!'

'The driver says we can sit beside him on the seat and put the luggage in the back. It's the best I can manage. There won't be any taxis back for at least half an hour.'

'Very disagreeable. Well, I hope nobody recognises me.'

'Nobody will,' thought Franz. 'He's nothing like as wonderful as the poster.'

Swallowing his vanity, Pompozini stepped up beside the driver, exclaiming as he did so: 'Shades of Blondini, what would my impresario say!'

'I'm coming with you too,' said Franz. 'I'm not a porter,' he added, refusing the proffered tip.

Pompozini said nothing. Nevertheless, he made room for Franz on the seat, quite eagerly too.

They drove out of the station yard.

'Which hotel?' said the driver.

Pompozini pressed the palm of his hand to his head. 'Ach, I do not remember. My man he makes all the arrangements — the imbecile he does not meet me at Berne — I do not imagine what goes wrong — always he travels with me, *always* — to guard my luggage, to fix the apparatus, to —'

'Was it the Bunderhof?' said Franz. 'That's where the tight-rope's to be fixed.'

'That is it, that is it!'

'And you don't need to worry about your man. I'll take his place. You can't possibly manage all that stuff alone. I'll stay and fix the apparatus.'

'You save my life, boy,' said Pompozini, throwing an arm round his shoulders. 'What is your name?'

'Franz Klöti.'

'And what is your trade to be?'

'I want to join your troupe.'

Pompozini groaned. 'No, no, no! Everybody wishes to join my troupe. It is very disagreeable.'

'I have exceptional ability, sir.' Franz launched into the speech he had intended to make at the station.

At the finish Pompozini groaned more loudly than ever. 'Ach, the usual rigmarole. Perhaps the detail changes, perhaps a little more conjuring is the custom. Once a boy he comes to me — he is about your height, but he has the face of cold porridge, no freckles — I am foolish, I engage him. He has the first-class testimonials to saw ladies in two. I try him out on the stage at Milano — and that is what he does, he saws the lady in two — *psst*, like that! Blood all over the place — trial for murder — terrible fuss about nothing.' He mopped his brow with his handkerchief.

'I am more careful,' said Franz drily. 'And I'm an acrobat too. Mother says I shall be a great one.'

'Mothers always say that. And when I put the offspring through his paces, what do I find? That he is no more good than an old gentleman with the legs amputated. No, I never believe parents.'

'Father says I'll break my neck,' said Franz quickly.

'A pity you do not break it before you come to me today.'

'It's not for want of trying,' put in the driver, who had been listening carefully to the conversation. 'I used to live next door to the Klötis. Franz was always practising his tight rope walk along the fence. When he came level with my chicken run he always fell off. Three times I had to mend the roof of the henhouse. Then I went to live somewhere else.'

'I was only a nipper then,' said Franz. 'I never fall off now. I can walk along now playing the violin.'

'And the guitar and a couple of accordions as well — I know, I know,' said Pompozini.

'One accordion is enough to start with,' said Franz seriously. 'I've been trying that trick this week. Would you like to hear my violin?'

It was under the seat and he leaned down to reach it.

'Let it stay where it is. I cannot abide cat squeaks,' said Pompozini.

'You will let me join your troupe, won't you, sir?'

'No! I tell you I am full. Do not ask again, for I never change my mind.'

'You will,' said the driver.

'What is it you say?'

'I know Franz better than you do,' said the driver. But, catching a glimpse of Pompozini's blazing eyes, he added hastily, 'This is the Hotel Bunderhof, sir,' and pulled up at the kerb.

* * * *

They worked together through the lunch hour without a bite to eat. Pompozini never ate before a performance. Franz was ravenously hungry, but he didn't like to say so, there being so much to do. The trickiest job of all was the fixing of the rope. It had to be dead level, no uphill or downhill about it. And it must be taut as a banjo wire — 'If you pluck it,' said Pompozini, 'it should twang.' The acrobat supervised every detail of the arrangements himself, most of the afternoon standing out on the hotel balcony in the hot sun. He was precise, business-like, and quite unruffled, without a trace of the nervous irritability he had shown in the morning. He seemed a different man. Yet there was plenty to try his temper. Franz was very willing, but he had to have everything explained to him. Once was enough, but the hotel porter was so dim-witted that he had to be told everything three of four times. In addition there were constant interruptions from police, town officials, ticket-sellers, and whole herds of autograph-hunters. Pompozini bore with it all very patiently. He complained only once — about the heat.

All afternoon the trams clanked through the streets as usual. The pavements were jammed with people anxious for a glimpse of the great man. 'Pass along now, pass along, please!' cried the policemen continually, as they flourished their rubber truncheons.

By half past four the rope was ready, straight as a ruled line. Franz ran over to the café, where an elderly waiter with side-whiskers slipped half a dozen ham sandwiches into his hand. Returning to the hotel, he thought how high the rope looked and how thin — thin as cotton thread.

At five o'clock the street was closed to traffic and pedes-trians and all the shops shut. Fifty yards from either side of the hotel, barriers were erected. Here the ticket-sellers took their places, while on the café pavement a splendid gold-braided brass band appeared.

Soon after half past five the street was packed solid from side to side, from end to end. No room even for a mouse to squeeze his way. Windows everywhere were blobbed with white, expectant faces. There were even people on the roofs, perched on a ridge or astride a gable, and the café parapet was fringed with dangling legs.

POM! TA-ra-RA-ra-ra-ra! POM! POM! POM! thundered the brass band from far below.

'Franz, Mr Pomp-what's-it would like to see you in his room. Says it's urgent,' said the hotel porter.

Franz didn't want to lose his privileged position on the balcony. But he went all the same. He had a curious feeling that something had gone wrong.

They barged their way through the crowd.

The porter opened the door of bedroom 32.

Pompozini was standing in the middle of the room in full war-paint, splendid in close-fitting green tights bulging with muscles, a red-and-white striped blouse, and huge gold ear-rings. He was like a gorgeous, exotic flower on a green stalk. But as soon as the porter went out, the flower began to wilt and wither, and the pointed ends of the waxed moustachios began to droop. Pompozini was pale, his limbs were trembling.

'I am ill — I cannot go on, I *cannot go on*,' he said, pacing to and fro in considerable agitation. 'What it is I do not know — a touch of the sun, the vertigo? I am dizzy, diz-zy. I *cannot go on*.' He jerked out a hand to steady himself on a chair-back.

'But you must, sir. Everybody's paid his money now. They've come from as far away as Zurich to see you. If they're disappointed, they'll stampede like wild elephants.'

Tears began to roll down the great acrobat's cheeks.

'If I go on, I fall down, I kill myself. Once before this happens — in the Big Top at Castrovillari — I am dizzy, so, like this — the floor and the roof change places — I cannot go on. My partner he saves me, he goes on himself. My friend, you must help me — you say you are a great artiste. You prove it now — I give you anything you wish.'

At that moment the town clock struck six. A roar went up from the crowd outside. 'Pompozini! Pompozini! We want Pompozini!' they shouted, and the bedroom windows rattled.

'Then you must let me join your troupe — now,' said Franz steadily.

'You walk the rope?'

'Of course I will. I'm your partner now.'

'Ach, my dear partner! I kiss you on both cheeks,' exclaimed the acrobat in great excitement.

'May I borrow your shoes? Mine are too slippery for walking a rope.'

'I kiss my shoes too — for luck,' and Pompozini threw them to him.

'Where is the balance pole?'

'In the foyer behind the balcony. Go quickly now — they are shouting again. I dare not show myself — go quickly!'

A minute later, having removed his jacket and tucked his trousers into his socks, Franz was standing on the rail of the balcony with the balance pole grasped firmly in both hands. In front of him the tight rope stretched away across sixty feet of space to the fourth-floor window of the Café Silberhorn. Above him, the blue sky; below, the yawning chasm of the street. How much nearer the sky seemed than the white upturned faces of the crowd, tiny as confetti on a strip of carpet. But Franz was not afraid.

After the first gasp of surprise, the crowd seemed to have accepted the situation. There was a hush. Then a roll of drums, a gradual crescendo ending in a brisk tap as he stepped confidently on to the rope. After that, complete silence.

Yes, it was beautifully firm to the tread; the fixing had been done very thoroughly. Franz smiled happily as, with the self-assurance of an expert, he glided across. Better than walking along the bed-rail at home, or along the knife edge of the garden fence above an audience of scared hens. He began to sing a Swiss song, to yodel the refrain. He reached the middle of the rope. This was the supremely happy moment of his life, as he has remarked so often since. He stopped singing and surrendered himself wholly to his happiness. The thing he most remembers now about this moment was not the awestruck

Franz reached the middle of the rope

silence of the crowd, nor the vast emptiness under his feet, nor even the thrill of achievement. It was something quite trivial — the smell of magnolia as it rose to him from a near-by garden. It made his spirit soar.

Then it was that his other self, that madcap clowning self the world came to know so well, took hold of him.

'I'll turn round and go back,' he thought. 'I'll fetch my violin and walk across playing a tune.'

As he gently swivelled his shoulders and slid his feet round, the left tip of the pole dropped sharply. To recover his balance, he jerked the right tip down — too far down. He let go. Down it clattered into the shrieking crowd. As he fell he clutched at the rope, caught it, and clung on.

Far below his swinging feet the crowd yelled and stampeded, treading one another down in the frantic effort to get clear. Vainly trying to stem the panic, the band struck up a tune.

But Franz was calm. To the spectators it seemed almost as if this monkey work was part of the act, as if this was exactly what he had planned to do. He waited till his legs had stopped swinging and he had recovered his breath. Then, very slowly, hand over hand he hauled himself along the rope to the hotel balcony. As soon as he was within touching distance, a dozen hands reached down to lift him to safety.

That night it was not Pompozini who was fêted and carried shoulder-high through the town. It was fifteen-year-old Franz Klöti.

*　*　*　*

And that was how Franz, or the great Orinoco (to give him the name the world now knows him by), began his career. Few clowning acrobats can have enjoyed so sensational a start, and the many thousands who came as spectators have never forgotten it.

Pompozini kept his promise and let him join his troupe. For some years Franz toured Europe, first with Pompozini, then with other travelling shows, sleeping (if he were lucky) in a caravan but more often on a heap of straw. Success did not come easily. There were times when he was near to starving. But, whatever the state of his fortunes, he never lost his belief in himself. He went on working hard, experimenting, rehearsing new tricks, polishing up old ones, never doubting he would win through in the end. Before he was thirty he was the cleverest acrobat, the funniest and most musical clown in Europe. At forty he was world-famous and could command hundreds of pounds for a single performance.

He has retired now and lives on the Riviera in a splendid villa, the balcony of which is decorated with enormous clown masks welded into the ironwork. One of his many trasures is Pompozini's rope, the one used at Gresslau. And when the visitors ask him, as they often do, what was his greatest triumph, he tells them of that summer evening in his youth when he gave the townsfolk of Gresslau the biggest thrill of their lives.

On the White Fang

by EDWARD G. COWAN

In the evening air, reddened by setting sunlight, the snow-capped White Fang, all eleven thousand feet of it, bit deeply and cruelly into the arc of the sky. There were higher Alpine peaks, more famous ones — but the White Fang, clean and sharp in its outline, held the gaze in a strange and breath-taking manner, even as it held the gaze of the four young Englishmen now.

From the small balcony of the Grundtal climbing hut the four stared at the monster which reared above the pine slope. The warmth of the stove and sweet smell of brewing coffee contrasted with the stark beauty of the rising White Fang.

'The guide hasn't arrived, Tom. So what do we do?' asked Taff Annam.

He was small, dark and looked vaguely unhappy. The question was answered, not by Tom Hunter, but by Cliff Seeley, eager and with a schoolboyish grin.

'We have the maps, the photographs. How about making the climb for ourselves?' he said keenly. 'This is the big thrill. You know, the moment of truth.'

'I'm game!' answered Ron Grant, the fourth member.

The three turned inquiringly to Tom Hunter. He, perhaps, was the most experienced climber of all. He was quiet, stolid and now deep in thought.

'No! Give the guide another day,' he said slowly. 'There's something about the Fang. I feel it but can't put it into words.'

Taff nodded. He too felt that 'something'; perhaps it was because the sun-reddened peak gave the unpleasant suggestion of blood. The Fang reminded him of wild beasts and prey.

'The local folk reckon that something lives up there!' He stared hard at Cliff Seeley. 'My German wasn't good enough to understand them.'

'Good, the more reason for climbing. I rather fancy seeing an Alpine "Abominable Snowman",' Cliff Seeley grinned.

Again Tom shook his head. Taff agreed with the verdict but the other two stared at them, puzzled.

'Oh, for Pete's sake! The White Fang's been climbed before. If we take the eastern wall it's a cake-walk. I've checked a dozen accounts,' Cliff exclaimed. 'Hang it, we're not novices and our equipment is good.'

In the distance the White Fang seemed to mock them. To Taff, it seemed to know that anger was beginning to affect four close friends.

'Cliff, I'm not arguing. Mountaineering allows no mistakes, no showing off,' Tom said evenly. 'You never conquer a mountain, you climb it. But a mountain — any one — can always conquer a man.'

'Thanks! I particularly appreciated the bit about "show-offs",' Cliff retorted. 'I want to know what's up there. *Why* is the White Fang different?'

'Then we'll wait for the guide. Come on, let's have supper and turn in. Remember, I'm supposed to be the leader,' Tom smiled.

It was a forced smile, and the supper itself was not very cheerful. It came as a relief when the sleeping-bags were finally used.

Tom awoke in the small hours. The moon streamed in coldly and, beyond the windows, the White Fang seemed determined to attract his attention. He was far from imaginative but he detected an air of triumph about it. The mountain seemed to breathe; it was no longer a dead thing but alive.

'Cliff! Ron!'

He shouted the words and dragged himself free of the sleeping-bag. Taff Annam awoke and tumbled noisily into the gloom.

Two laden rucksacks were gone; so were Cliff Seeley and the shock-headed Ron Grant. Gone were half the ice-and rock-pitons; the nylon ropes; two Russian-type ice-axes with hammer-type head.

'Man, they're making the climb! A rope of two!' Taff's face was pale in the moonlight. 'They've gone to tackle the White Fang by themselves!'

Tom nodded, his own face without any expression. He and Taff moved together, collecting their equipment and checking it carefully. They donned the waterproof anoraks, warm but fitting loosely to give free movement of the arms.

Climbing-belts, ropes and metal rings for the pitons and snap-links; then rations and a final look at the maps. Neither spoke. They left the hut and moved out into snow-brilliant darkness. From four o'clock onwards in Alpine regions it was possible to climb.

'Head-torch? We may have to climb in real darkness,' Tom exclaimed quietly.

'Yes, I've brought it. Wonder how far they've got?' Taff replied.

There was no knowing; no knowing how much earlier Cliff and Ron had slipped away on their foolhardy venture. At any time a rope of two men was a grim business, the kind of climbing done only by mountain men who knew every mood of the wild peaks around them. A rope of four men would stand a much better chance.

'They'll make for the Eastern Approach. We'll reach it after one and a half miles. Don't hurry too much. We're too late to stop them anyway,' Tom warned.

'They'd never turn back. All we can do is to reach them and rope up with them,' Taff answered. 'As a party of four

251

we may not find it too bad.'

For suddenly he was afraid of the mountain. He had known it all along, known that White Fang awaited them; that they were its prey.

Just what was the belief of the local people? What lived on the White Fang? How he wished he could remember the German word which one mountaineer had said to another. A word to describe what most climbers of the White Fang were supposed to have met.

But soon there was little time for thinking. Unroped as yet, for the lower slopes of the Eastern Approach seemed straight-forward — and free climbing faster, they avoided the loose scree covered with sugar snow and began the ascent.

Travel was fast. The special rubber-soled climbing boots needed no crampons as yet. Moving close together, they climbed it the deathly silence up the great buttress which would soon lead to a rib. Tom knew it was the path their friends should have taken.

As Cliff had said earlier, it was easy — almost a cake-walk for experienced climbers — and now Tom almost began to doubt his earlier fears.

After all, did they really need a guide? Could he blame Cliff and Ron for being keen enough to test their own powers a little farther? Neither of them was a fool, and perhaps an over-active imagination had conjured up too alarming a picture.

Taff Annam was the one with imagination. High above them, veined in snow, the White Fang was looking down mockingly on the two ascending specks. He shuddered, though the anorak kept him warmer than might have seemed reasonable.

The very ease of this first ascent had something of treachery about it. It seemed to beckon them on, to try to lure them into climbing fast and carelessly.

Taff understood. The mountain knew that, because of their comrades ahead, they dared not turn back. They had to follow! It was an obligation, a duty — and the White Fang was laughing. They were trapped — already ensnared in some mirthless joke.

*   *   *   *

The dawn itself appeared magically and shafts of sunlight beat down with a quite startling warmth. Tom, standing in an almost upright position, strained his neck to glance upwards. In a way it was not surprising that he could make out no other two forms moving above them, for the mountain spread out like a giant. Marks, which would easily have been seen as main features by anyone standing back from the mountain, were no longer visible at all.

'Hadn't we better rope up?' Taff called from behind him.

'No need until we're on the rib,' Tom answered. 'I'll make a belay — using rope — to pull us both up to the rib. There's a rock projection that will hold the nylon loop.'

He thrust one foot forward, wedged a gloved hand into a crack and manipulated the rope with his free hand. The rope held and he tested it with weight.

Craaack!

With the sound of a revolver shot the rock outcrop tore from the rock-face. Half a hundredweight of the face crashed away into space. To Tom the whole world spun crazily with it. Clawing empty air, he sailed backwards, dragged by the unrelenting weight of his rucksack. Taff's cry of horror was drowned by the shrill rush of wind beating past his ears.

One complete somersault. The sun-melted ice slid beneath Tom's twisting, jolted body. He clawed frenziedly with fingers and toes. The glissade halted and his lungs seemed to explode with the force of the breath he sucked into them.

Hardly daring to move a single muscle, he began to check his position. He had been hurled on to a ledge where a brake of snow first halted the slide. Two hundred feet below, snow-covered rock slabs waited with sickening dizziness for his next fall.

Tom hung on and felt the blood ooze from strained fingers into the glove linings. His stomach was tight and cold, but above him moved the second human fly. Taff's speed was amazing, yet every movement was studied. Tom watched, concentrating on keeping his precarious hold.

Taff hammered a piton into the rock-face and belayed — tied — himself to it. Then he unfurled the two hundred foot long nylon rope. Tom moistened his lips. Time was no longer existent; he seemed to be outside it. He watched fascinated, while the agony in his hands became a cramp.

The loop of rope snaked down — and Tom, risking death, released his hold and clutched for it. His hands found it, as if by sheer instinct. Then Taff drove in a second piton, and — it was strangely matter-of-fact — Tom used the rope to climb back to where his friend stood.

The first rope lay snagged, so much tangled 'knitting'. It needed recoiling, then the rib again had to be reached.

'Tom, we'd better rope together now,' Taff repeated as if nothing had happened.

Tom drew another deep breath and nodded. He could find no words for what he wanted to say — not that it mattered. He knew that the very easiness of the lower slopes had lured him into that unwariness which so often spelled death on a mountain. On this mountain, in particular! Now he sensed everything that Taff Annam had felt.

The White Fang was amused. Now it lay dormant again, waiting and watching. So they climbed carefully, ascending by one rope-length pitched to the next. Pitons were driven in and the rope secured to them by snap-links. Every so often

254

*Clawing empty air, Tom sailed backwards
dragged by the weight of his rucksack*

an icicle snapped off and, tinkling strangely, pitched hundreds of feet down the rock.

To Taff, who moved last, came the precarious task of recovering the pitons whenever possible. Spiked crampons now had to be worn. The mountain was aware of them, yet seemed to ignore them. Strange coppery little clouds hung around it, and then followed tattered fingers of mist.

The ice was melting, no longer would it hold an ice piton firmly. Water ran stickily between the ice and the rock.

Still they climbed. Still they saw nothing of the other two climbers. Tom was aware that his nerves were tightening. Why was there no sign of the two other men?

Warily the pair thrust onward and upward. They were mounting a tower, and the ice-axe was needed to scrape away every surface before any hold — or even attempt at a hold — dared be made.

The mountain shook suddenly. It was the only description! For like some giant beast, it dislodged the loose rocks which, as others had found, it seemed to keep for a supply of ammunition. The sound of a rising wind was the first sign of the stone-fall. Roped to a piton, Tom and Taff pressed themselves close to the face and watched huge missiles wing down to the depths.

A small stone struck Taff, and blood seeped out through the clean hole in his anorak. It had pierced him as cleanly as the shot from a gun. A slight overhang saved them from the main falls, but waiting on that dizzy face was torture. Huge blocks would scream down, then bound outwards. White Fang was merely warning them what it could do if it tried.

Meanwhile, the mist crept up stealthily, hardly visible at first; then, by the time they first realised it, the danger it brought was upon them. Moisture on anoraks and gloves started to freeze; haloes of frost glittered chilly on their hoods.

The great face of the White Fang was changing — changing

like a sinister twist of expression. Once prominent features dwindled away into drifting white shadow. They were no longer sure of even the summit rearing above them, for other pinnacles could well be the same thing.

The cold was bitter, and continued movement the only safe measure. Both climbers recalled grim accounts of mountaineers who had been found frozen like dead flies to the very face of the rock. They dared not ease up, dared not let the cold gain a grip.

For seventeen hours they continued, their only pause being on a ledge barely ten inches wide. Rations were eaten sparingly, and moisture sucked from some of the snow in the crevices — yet only enough to moisten the mouth. To drink the actual snow water, mixed with rock dust, could cause a paralysing dysentery which under these conditions might spell the difference between life and death.

The night was bitter, and they camped on a sheltered terrace which was their only stroke of good fortune. Even so, the down-filled jackets hardly kept out the cold. They rubbed feet and hands to aid circulation, then thrust their feet into the depths of their rucksacks.

'It's not good. Strange about Cliff and Ron,' Taff voiced his thoughts. 'Should have seen them by now. At least we should have found their earlier tracks.'

'We'll press on as soon as possible. Things wil shake out,' Tom answered fiercely. 'They'll be O.K. Stop thinking — it's never much help.'

At dawn they recommenced the unending ordeal of ascending. They were weary, but determination kept them going — not that they had very much choice. Rotten snow, melting over bubbles of ice, gave a treacherous, deceptive surface which needed testing every inch of the way.

At midday they gained the summit. It was an eerie feeling, for the thin atmosphere of the White Fang brought a sensation that was almost unbeareble. The spike of the Fang glittered from the last thirty feet above them a spike of smooth ice, with a single handhold.

There was a tension in the air, a kind of expectancy. The White Fang was living — very much alive!

'Cliff and Ron. We ought to be able to see them — somewhere below,' Taff almost whispered.

'Yes!'

Tom had a sickness within him. They could see no one and both knew only too well what this meant.

Ron Grant and Cliff Seeley had wandered from the regular ascent route. The White Fang had fooled them — and — and—

Suddenly the shrill sound of a whistle — six blasts followed by silence and then six more blasts — echoed from those depths below them. The mountain tossed the sound around with hideous echoes.

'The Alpine distress signal!' Tom was clawing out his own whistle and answering.

He blew three blasts — silence — then three more.

Somewhere — unseen as yet — but somewhere, the two missing climbers were on the face of the White Fang — in trouble. The mountain had trapped them and, even now, they could be living the last hours of their lives.

'I knew it! Come on!' Taff said shakily.

He and Tom began tracing the sounds of the distant whistle. Each tried to keep his mind from the suspicion that the White Fang was even now reaching out for them too.

* * * *

They were a hundred feet down when they glimpsed the first clue in that haste-dangerous descent. Three thousand feet below, on a ghastly ice wall of the Eilenfrau glacier, a dark blotch caught their gaze. It stood out against ice and snow.

'A body!' Taff's cry was never fully completed.

'No, rucksacks! They must have been trying to tow them up after them — and something happened. Let's hope we're in time!' Tom cut in.

They changed position, moved to the rock-traverse and continued descending. In a series of rappels — roping down — they slid with double rope from one pitch to the next.

Then they saw their friends, both men wedged precariously in what was virtually a chimney. For Cliff, obviously leading, had climbed so far until unable to ascend or descend.

'Taff, they're alive! Both of them! The climbing beat them,' Tom shouted. 'If they're uninjured, there's more than a fighting chance for us all.'

Slowly, how terribly slowly, they worked their descent until almost above the two White-Fang-trapped men; not completely above them, for that might cause a stone-fall on to two helpless victims. So lowering a rope became a tricky and most dangerous affair.

Cliff took the rope. His face showed signs of frost-bite and he was wearing dark glasses. Fumbling, he roped on and tried to shout cheerily up.

Two pitons were driven by Taff and Tom into the ice-face and they belayed themselves to them. They took the strain while Cliff and Ron swung themselves clear of where they were trapped.

Things were going smoothly, and sheer action caused the menace of the White Fang to be temporarily forgotten. Ron, the last on that rescue line, now became the first to make the descents. Taff Annam became last man on a descending rope of four climbers.

Always the first two descending men had the two above to secure them. Taff, as the tail-ender, descended by the double rope unsecured. It was a relatively simple and straightforward rescue; no snags, no mishaps.

Yet no member of the quartet experienced any feeling of triumph. Ron Grant and Cliff Seeley were in bad shape, almost exhausted. One night's camp on a wide ledge only allowed them the grace of climbing afresh in a treacherous dawn shrouded in dusk.

Shadows from above the White Fang stretched out in long fingers — seemed to be following the climbers. Taff, who battled wildly against imagination, thought of the mountain as a giant cat allowing an injured mouse to try to drag itself out of sight.

'It won't allow it — the mountain's playing with us,' he could actually hear himself thinking. Strain had told on him. 'The White Fang will never let us escape.'

How far would it allow them to go? They were a party of two frost-bitten, exhausted men and two more who only kept going by will-power. The descent was mental torture; perhaps that was why the mountain still allowed them to live.

One hour, then another — and still the mountain was waiting. Far, far away below they could make out the tiny Alpine village of Gretz.

No one spoke at all. Tom Hunter strove not to allow his hopes to rise as he mentally pictured the village; nothing was worse than having rising hopes dashed. Steady! Now the next descent, and think of that only. The White Fang was watching, cruelly holding back until the moment when hopes had reason to rise.

A single flash of lightning — and, without any warning, the fury of a storm was upon them. White Fang had finally pounced! Swept by a rising gusty wind, snow and sleet lanced through tattered mists.

'This is it!'

Tom drove in a piton and sensed Taff making the same move above him. He could hear an axe madly hacking a deep step in the ice.

Into the howling wind crept a new note — an awesome hissing and whistling. Any mountaineer knew what it meant, and the four braced themselves and pressed flat to the face.

The White Fang, silent no longer, howled in the madness of its terrible triumph. Taff protected his head with his rucksack, for screaming particles of ice and rock danced down — the harbinger of an avalanche. A terrifying movement — slow at first, then quickening — was the prelude to the madness of fury which was suddenly unleashed.

Snow boiled past, sucking at the frail humans who clung to the ropes lashed to ice-pitons. It swirled and hissed, grasping and buffeting with an unendurable pressure; the sound was still like that of wild laughter. It strained at the ice-pitons; teased and worried the four clinging men.

Tom Hunter clung on doggedly and lived through what he wished was a nightmare. But it was real! Moreover, he knew the worst was to come.

They were already doomed. The wail of the wind and dancing cloud of ice granules told him the fall increasing. The ice-pitons trembled, awaiting the moment that the White Fang would choose for snatching them free and hurling four puny shapes to battered destruction. Everything was moving. The face itself was screened with tumbling white.

It became hard to breathe; lungs fought for air while aching muscles still worked despairingly. Tom remembered Cliff's earlier and now fateful remark about 'the moment of truth'.

This was that moment. The mountain had planned everything from the start, planned it while they were still in the hut. Perhaps even planned the non-arrival of the guide.

Tom closed his eyes and sensed the roaring, suffocating stream rushing down for him. The noise filled his ears, seemed to hypnotise him. He awaited that terrible moment when the suffocating weight would engulf him, and the frail, vibrating pitons tear free.

This would be death! Only one-half of his mind seemed to work; the other half was a detached and meaningless jumble of half-pictured incidents. Silly little things that had no reason at all.

He clung on, and an eternity passed within seconds. The roaring tube-train sound continued, then very slowly subsided; that was wrong. How could he still hear? Why had a tunnel of darkness not engulfed him and borne him away?

Tom opened his eyes. The cascade of ice crystals whirled past, but their very motion told him that the avalanche must have changed direction. Its force was spent, though that was not strange. What was miraculous was how its mighty, rushing force had somehow missed the four humans who had thought themselves in its path.

'It — it's over!' Taff's voice echoed shakily through the sudden, all so still silence.

Tom did not answer. There were four of them, four snow-powdered and very awed climbers. Yet they were alive. Each nodded to himself, silently echoing Taff's words.

There was a change. The White Fang seemed to have lost something. It was the same — and yet different. It was not a contradiction. The mountain, stark in its beauty, had turned back to a thing of inanimate rock.

It was a mountain — dangerous, beautiful — but without malice or any kind of life. Now it seemed that everything else must have been sheer imagination. Things had clicked back to the everyday risk and the normal.

'O. K., let's keep climbing!' Tom was almost surprised to hear himself say.

Nothing more would happen. He knew it as surely as if the future were spread out before him. They had not triumphed, it was just that they still lived and had in some way succeeded. Human courage had been tested to the full and had not been found wanting. So they climbed steadily, descending carefully but without the tenseness so unbearable before.

The rescue party met them on the loose scree when sheer exhaustion was taking its toll of the climbers. Three hours later, they were recovering in the small Alpine hospital where they would probably remain for the next couple of days.

'Glad you and Taff came after us,' Ron Grant said, gazing towards the vista of the White Fang in the distance. 'It was a tomfool trick of ours.'

'We all make mistakes,' Taff said, shrugging. 'That's the only way to learn, boys.'

'We are lucky! Shouldn't fancy it again,' Tom wryly grinned.

They all gazed at the view from the cool window. The White Fang seemed to watch them equally blankly. How could they ever have possibly thought it was 'alive'?

'Taff, I think I know what lives on the White Fang,' Cliff Seeley said unexpectedly. 'I've remembered the word used by the local mountaineers.'

Everyone looked at him sharply.

'It was "Furcht" — or something like it. FEAR! The German for "fear". Human fear!' Cliff continued. 'It makes sense to me. I know I met it. I think, so did Ron. You others can only tell for yourselves.'

It made sense. There were silent nods. In the distance the snow-capped White Fang, all eleven thousand feet of it, bit deeply and cruelly into the arc of the sky.

Fear. Human fear dwelled on the slopes of the White Fang!

The Beast by his True Name

THE STORY OF THE LAST WOLF IN SCOTLAND
by ALAN C. JENKINS

MacQueen of Pall-a'-Chrochain kept himself apart from other men. Like a hungry person who watches every crumb, he guarded against any unnecessary word falling from his lips.

His fellow highlanders in the rugged country of the Monadhliath mountains called him a man of iron. Or perhaps rather he resembled the boxwood that was the badge of his clan, a wood so hard it would not even float in water.

For he seemed to take a savage pleasure in meeting the fiercest weather and the most dangerous conditions. When other men would be huddling round the peat-fire harking to the north-easter screeching its maledictions through corrie and glen, MacQueen, shadowed by his two gaunt hunting dogs, Glas and Dubh, would be on the trail of the deer. Oblivious to discomfort, forgetful of hunger, he would plunge recklessly through the wildest torrents, fight his way through the wreathing snow.

As often as not the stars were his ceiling, a bundle of bracken or pine boughs his bed. For food, when there was niether venison nor salmon, he would be content with a mouthful of oatmeal cooked over a fire of twigs and washed down with water from the burn.

And by him lay his silent, watchful, devoted dogs, ready at a moment to resume the hunt. At a word from MacQueen they would as willingly have torn out the throat of a man as that of a deer.

Yet, though it was the deer MacQueen hunted, it seemed

as if he sought something else. He was a man driven on by an unrelenting purpose that haunted him like some grey shadow.

The more this eluded him, the more dour and withdrawn he became.

'Yet, man, I tell you, it wasn't always like this with him.'

They were talking in the Gaelic about MacQueen that evening at Angus Macintosh's place. A journeyman carpenter had come over from Inverness to work for the Laird's folk. Now, in the waning light, he was finishing a clothes chest and the men were watching him in admiration at his deft craftsmanship.

'I remember well the day, twelve years back and more,' Angus went on, flinging his plaid about him, for even by the fragrant peat-fire in the bothy the breath of winter reached, 'when he was a gay young blade, always willing to exchange a crack with the best.'

'What changed him, then?' the carpenter murmured absently. With firm strong strokes he was gouging out the date on the lid of the chest. January, 1743, he carved, stroke by patient stroke, blowing away the shavings of wood and fondly polishing the lid with a hand scarred by years of his craft.

'It was when the grey beast took his little daughter,' Angus explained, stirring the evening porridge as he squatted by the hearth, his bony knees gleaming beneath his kilt.

'Wolves?' the carpenter asked, glancing up abruptly. 'The wolves did that?'

'Whisht, man!' Angus frowned. 'Don't give the beast its true name. It is unlucky.' He stared darkly into the fire. 'Ay, the grey beast took the little child. The bairn could not even walk. From that day Mac Queen was a changed man. It was as if the smile on his face had been frozen like the waters of the loch.'

'But the wolves have gone since then?' the carpenter said. He began to rub the chest with beeswax. 'There are no more left in Scotland?'

'It is not so sure,' another man spoke from a corner of the room. He reached out with a long wooden spoon and helped himself to the porridge. He was one of the Chattans, the clan whose country bordered that of the Macintoshes. 'There's been talk lately of a grey beast in the glens beyond Findhorn...'

As he spoke, the door was suddenly flung open. The icy wind shrieked into the place and the men cowered in their plaids as if they were being attacked. Stooping under the lintel came a giant figure of a man. Six and a half feet tall and with shoulders that made one think of a sturdy oak, he had difficulty in entering the narrow doorway. At his heels, silent and aloof, padded two dogs, whose eyes turned to rubies in the glow of the fire.

'Peace on this house,' MacQueen said, as he stood waiting to be invited in.

'Be welcome, man, but shut the door,' Angus replied testily. 'We are only flesh and blood here. We feel the cold. But sit down by the hearth and take a sup of porridge from the dish there.'

'You are not often this way, MacQueen,' said the Chattan man, wiping his spoon on his kilt.

'A fine fat stag led me along the river,' Mac Queen answered curtly. 'It was many a mile before Glas and Dubh brought him down.' He flung back his plaid impatiently. 'Man, Angus, your place is like a baker's oven.'

Now Angus's wife had come in from milking the cow in the byre at the back of the dwelling. The room glowed vaguely from the lantern she carried.

'They are saying that it is true about the grey beast that has been seen in the hills,' she broke into the conversation unceremoniously. Her eyes were wide with anxiety as she surveyed the men. She set down the wooden pail and hurriedly shut the door.

'Where was it seen, woman of the house?' MacQueen demanded harshly, crouching intently. The dogs seemed to stiffen at his tone. 'Who is telling this news?'

'It was Kirsty Macintosh told me,' the woman said fearfully. She went and stood with a hand on her husband's shoulder, as if seeking protection. 'It is said that two bairns from Badenoch are missing. They were gathering firewood in the forest.'

'Ach, it is doubtless an old wives' tale,' scoffed the carpenter. He put away his tools and lowered himself with a sigh on to the chest. 'There are no wolves left but in folk's imagination.'

'What does a townsman know of such matters!' MacQueen rounded on him fiercely. The carpenter leant back in surprise as the huge figure threatened him. 'The beast has not yet been banished.'

'This one is maybe the last grey shepherd in Scotland,' the Chattan man suggested, with a placatory laugh. Everyone was gazing uneasily at MacQueen standing there vast and menacing in the wan light, his bonnet brushing the rafters even though he stooped awkwardly.

All at once the two dogs growled faintly and turned expectantly towards the door. From outside came the muffled thud of a horse's hooves. Then an urgent knock resounded and Angus got up to open the door. A muffled figure, his plaid flecked with grains of frost, came stamping inside, gasping in relief after battling with the wind that keened ceaselessly.

'Man! It is Donald Macintosh!' cried Angus's wife. 'It must be grave business that brings you riding all this way on such a night.'

'Ay, grave indeed!' panted the newcomer, blowing on his hands. He glanced at the assembled company and nodded in satisfaction as he saw MacQueen. 'I have come with a message from Lachlan, Laird of Macintosh...'

'What, man?' laughed the Chattan man. 'Is it the redcoats

of King George we will march against?'

'Not redcoats,' Donald answered. 'This is a grey coat we are summoned to fight. A grey beast in the mountains.'

'A wolf?' cried MacQueen, stepping forward and towering over the messenger. 'It is the beast himself has been seen?'

'Ay, and more than seen. It has killed the two bairns that were missing in the wood near the White Glen.'

The woman uttered a groan of horror. Even the carpenter looked uneasy, his earlier scepticism gone.

'This is true, man?' MacQueen spoke almost exultantly. 'Who saw the wolf and where?' He seemed almost more likely to strike Donald than question him, so urgent was his manner.

'It was some of the Laird's own boys saw the wolf. The Laird is convinced.'

'Where, man, where?'

'I tell you, near the White Glen beyond the Findhorn.'

'The Laird will summon a hunt?' asked the Chattan man, getting to his feet.

'Ay. It is to summon you to a tainchel that I am here,' explained Donald. 'Every man must come. We meet at Badachro at dawn tomorrow. MacQueen, Lachlan ordered me especially to summon you to attend with your dogs. You are the best hunter of us all. You will be there?'

MacQueen was silent. He stood looking through Donald as if he did not see him. All eyes were turned on him. Even the dogs, sensing something was afoot, watched him furtively.

'You will be there at the tainchel betimes?' Donald Mac-intosh prompted. 'It is twelve miles from Badachro to the White Glen. You will need to be there at a good hour.'

MacQueen glanced down absently at the man.

'Ay,' he murmured, his eyes hooded. 'I shall be there.'

Long before dawn had brought hope to the eastern horizon, MacQueen went loping across the iron-hard undulating snow, Glas and Dubh flanking him on either side, their long, sagacious heads wreathed in an aura of breath.

Like some delicately ornamented cloth, the snow glittered and winked with a thousand jewels of frost stitched on by some invisible hand. The deerskin shoes of MacQueen and the splayed paws of the hunting dogs left only a light tracery as they went. Their shadows were far more prominent, stalking long and black before them, for the three-quarter moon was low in the sky now, sinking beyond the Great Glen far to the west. The stars were stealing back again for a while.

Tirelessly, unfalteringly, MacQueen of Pall-a'-Chrochain went jogging, his bare knees impervious to the cold, his nostrils pricking in the frost, his face immobile as carved stone beneath the bonnet pulled down over his brow. Impatiently from time to time he twitched the red and grey plaid on his shoulder. In the other hand he carried his hunting-spear. At the top of his rough stocking the haft of his knife winked as if in answer to the frost.

Hour after hour he and the dogs threaded their way. Along ice-fringed burn, through naked wood, whose branches were limned against the snow in an intricate filigree, they pressed on, purposefully but unhurriedly. In Glen-na-Muik a herd of deer went foraging, scraping at the snow-withered turf. Glas and Dubh seemed to look up questioningly at their master. But MacQueen shook his head.

For once the deer were not his quarry.

*　*　*　*

At Badachro the clansmen stamped their feet and swung their arms. It was still bitterly cold, even though the rising sun was now casting a golden tinge across the snow.

'We are wasting precious time,' somebody grumbled, huddling in his plaid.

'I have my kine to milk,' said another. 'Why should we kick out heels here because MacQueen does not come?'

They muttered in little groups, cursing the cold and the delay, discussing the wolf and the terrible fate of the two children. Every man had his own opinion as to where the wolf had come from. Those who had found the gruesome remains were closely questioned.

'But where is MacQueen?' It all came back to that. The news of a wolf after so long seemed to have unnerved the men. All knew there was neither hunter nor tracker the equal of MacQueen. Not even the Laird's hunting-dogs could match Glas and Dubh.

'Where is MacQueen?' Lachlan, Laird of Macintosh, echoed the general complaint. He turned his pony and rode through the crowd of men to seek out Donald. His man followed behind, bearing the Laird's muzzle-loader on his shoulder. 'You are sure MacQueen understood the message? He promised to attend the tainchel?'

'I took the message, Lachlan,' Donald protested. 'Ask Angus Macintosh here. It was in his house that MacQueen was. Before him and others he said he would come with his dogs...'

'If I knew where he lay last night I would send men to drag him from his bed,' the Laird cried angrily. Sullenly the men waited, burning inwardly with resentment at MacQueen, though outwardly they shivered in the cold.

*   *   *   *

The tracks in the White Glen were nearly a day old. Their edges were blurred and sunken. But there was no mistaking them. As the first hint of daylight chinked through the stunted

birch trees, MacQueen squatted down to regard them. His
dogs nudged at his side, as if eager to tell him that they, too,
could read.

For a long while MacQueen squatted there, gazing at the
tracks in the snow. It was as if he were perusing the page of
a book, a book which told a stark tale. The lines on his wind-
roughened face were deep as scars. His blue eyse were the tone
office.

He levered himself up with his hunting-spear, flung the
plaid back over his shoulder and made his way on, still reading
the story the padmarks of the wolf told him. But it was an
unfinished story. It was he who would write the final chapter
in it. The muscles in his cheeks knotted angrily at the possibility
that it might not be he. Such a thought urged him on again
and he broke into the same steady lope as he skirted the dark
forest. A solitary blackcock got up with a clatter of wings.
A pine-marten vaulted through the branches.

Not even the dogs pricked an ear now. They shared their
master's iron purpose. Never would they swerve from the way
until he did.

With the patience of a woman unravelling a tangled skein
of wool, MacQueen followed the trail of the wolf. It doubled,
twisted, faltered, jinked. Sometimes it even vanished in a
scurry of prints round some rock scree. Several times he had
to cast back on his steps. Three times he had to cross treacherous burns, stumbling through ice-cold torrents, slipping
hazardously on icy rocks. Wherever the wolf had crossed
water, both trail and scent were lost, and at one point even
the resolute MacQueen feared he might be cheated of his
quarry.

But as he paused for breath at a place where a waterfall,
now partially masked in ice, tumbled in a white scarf over the
lip of a corrie whose sheer side rose massively against the sky,
Glas uttered a whimper.

'So, girl?' MacQueen muttered, following after her with Dubh. He knew that the bitch only cried like that when she was on a keen scent. He saw too now that a fresh set of tracks had appeared. Evidently the wolf had doubled back and had now — recently — passed that way along the top of the corrie.

Leaning on his hunting-spear he surveyed the place. It was like a dark, hungry maw opening up in the hillside, fringed with a tangle of blaeberry scrub and rowan saplings. While the dogs ranged lithely ahead, he began to climb round towards the lip of the cliff. He scarcely glanced at the tracks now; instinctively he knew that the climax of the hunt was near.

He was hurrying now. The bitter wind made his teeth ache. His lashes were heavy with frost. But the wind was right. If the wolf were lairing in the rocks up there it would not have taken the scent of its pursuers. Glas and Dubh were seized with the urgency of the hunt. Swiftly the man followed, nimble and neat despite his great stature.

Near at hand a golden eagle went keening away from the bloody carcase of a red deer hind that the wolf had evidently feasted on. MacQueen could tell from the stink of the entrails that the deer had been killed very recently. Nor had the blood on the snow yet lost its colour.

Sweating despite the cold, he half ran, half clambered on. It all happened suddenly, taking even him by surprise for all his anticipation. The brittle air was startled by a hideous outburst of snarling. It was like an explosion of shattering intensity, so that the wits were momentarily numbed.

The dogs converged on a third grey shape that had appeared. Glas and Dubh and the wolf abruptly merged into one chaotic, scrambling, many-limbed, several-headed body, rolling and sprawling, struggling, biting, scratching.

Shouting triumphantly, MacQueen panted closer, hunting-spear at the ready but unable to use it yet for fear of killing his own dogs. Gobbets of snow and soil spattered over him from the struggling animals. A long unbroken bubbling snarl rose from their throats.

The fighting mass rolled and slid and scuttered dangerously nearer the edge of the corrie. Dubh was fighting desperately to throw off the wolf, which was on top of him. The dog managed to twist clear, tried to scramble to its feet and resume the battle, but then lost its footing and went slithering backwards over the cliff.

Now Glas was left to face the wolf on her own. Free of the encumbrance of Dubh, who had been attacking it from beneath, the wolf turned all its attention on Glas. Savagely, powerfully, it darted in and seized the bitch behind the jaw, so that she could not use her own fangs.

Already she was torn in several places. Her ragged coat was frothed with blood.

Even Glas's endurance was not unbounded. She wrenched herself away from the wolf and tried to skulk out of range, seeking a respite from the fury of the desperate animal. Now, with a wild cry, MacQueen rushed in, poised to thrust with his spear. As he did so, his foot slipped on the frozen snow and he stumbled.

The wolf would have fled. But now it sprang at the man as he went down on his knees. The impetus of the animal bore MacQueen over on his side. The spear had been jolted from his grasp. Snarling, foaming, knowing that its life was at stake, the wolf strove to get at the man's face and throat.

MacQueen got his hands in its fur, fighting with all his strength to hold the creature off. He could see the amber-coloured pupils, feel its breath, reeking of the meat it had so recently gorged, see the gleaming fangs, ivory yellow in contrast with the snow.

He fought with one hand now, his fingers pressing and scrabbling against the frenzied onslaught. With his other hand he groped for the knife in his stocking...

274

The impetus of the animal bore MacQueen over on his side

After they had waited an hour or more, the Laird decided that they must start the hunt without MacQueen. The men were in an ill-humour as they trudged off into the hills. Moreover they were angry for the Laird's sake. Lachlan of Macintosh himself had sent the summons to the tainchel and it was an effront to their chieftain that this man, who was not a Macintosh, should disregard it.

When they had gone as far as Cleebrae one of the men in front uttered a shout and pointed.

'MacQueen comes now, yonder!'

Sure enough, there on the glistening hillside a giant figure had limped into view, fllanked by two dogs, one of which could scarcely drag itself along, while the other's head was bowed in exhaustion.

For a moment MacQueen paused as he gazed down on the straggling party that had now begun to utter vehement reproaches. Then, bracing himself, he marched towards them, the limp gone from his tread, his head upright, an arrogant look on his drawn face.

In their anger the men did not notice at first the bloody coats of the dogs, nor the dishevelled appearance of MacQueen's plaid and kilt. They were intent only on upbraiding him for his failure to turn up at the appointed time. But MacQueen, making no response, pushed past them, while the other dogs looked askance at Glas and Dubh.

In the meantime the Laird had hung back on his pony. He had decided it was more seemly to let MacQueen come to him and make his excuses.

'MacQueen of Pall-a'-Chrochain,' he cried peremptorily, as the hunter approached, 'you will do well to beg my pardon.'

'What was the hurry?' MacQueen asked insolently, twitching his plaid about him.

'Shame on you, man, for insulting the Laird!' one of the men shouted, while the others jostled about MacQueen with

276

a chorus of abuse. 'He deserves to be whipped, Lachlan of Macintosh!'

Calmly MacQueen let them have their shrill say. Then, in his own good time, he lifted the plaid and revealed a bloody, grinning head. He held it out towards Lachlan so that the Laird's pony rolled its eyes and backed away in terror.

With a mirthless laugh MacQueen flung the wolf's head on the snow among the crowding highlanders.

'There it is for you!' he said and pushed his way through the crowd. Followed by the weary, wounded Glas and Dubh, he strode slowly away with never another glance or word. Vengeance was a thing MacQueen of Pall-a'-Chrochain had not been prepared to share with any man.

Thus was killed the last wolf in Scotland. Only then did men dare to speak of the beast by its true name.

From Dude Ranch to Ghost Town

by GORDON GRINSTEAD

I was thrilled when Dad told me that Mr Gaskarth was
flying to Canada on behalf of a client and wanted to take me
with him.

You see, Mr Gaskarth is Dad's solicitor, and this client
happened to be my cousin, Stephen Corrigan. Steve was the
black sheep of the family. He was rather wild — a ne'er-do-
well, if you like — but I had always liked him. He was mad on
fire-arms and used to give me toy pistols when I was a kid.
I called him Stick-at-Nothing Steve and he called me Billy
the Kid.

But he had gone to America after he was sent down from
college; and now, with the proverbial luck of the prodigal son,
he had unexpectedly inherited a large fortune from an old
uncle in England. The trouble was, he knew nothing about
his windfall, and nobody knew where he was; so Mr Gaskarth,
after making some transatlantic inquiries, decided to go and
look for him, as such a big sum was involved — a million,
I believe. He had last been heard of heading for Saskatchewan
(he probably made the States too hot to hold him), so that
narrowed the field down a bit, and Mr Gaskarth had high
hopes of tracing the young heir before another chap — some
remote relation called Jonas Saltash — collected the 'lolly'
instead, by the terms of the will.

That was where I came in. I had known Cousin Steve as
well as anybody, and Mr Gaskarth wanted me to identify him
when found.

So here I was, on a ranch in the foothills of the Rockies — all among the cowboys and redskins — me, Billy the Kid! I was so excited that I could hardly wait to eat my cornflakes before rushing out to look at the horses the morning after we arrived. Flying the Atlantic and then riding on the Canadian Pacific Railway across a whole continent had been thrilling enough, but this was even better — or so I thought at first.

The Canadian police at Montreal had been rather cagey when Mr Gaskarth started asking questions about Stephen Corrigan, but in the end they told us to inquire at the Lakeside Ranch, not far from Medicine Hat, where he had last been seen. The boss of this outfit, a grey-headed man who looked like the Sheriff of Calamity Gulch, was even less helpful than the cops. He admitted that Mr Corrigan had stayed there, but he had left rather suddenly, under some sort of cloud, it seemed, without leaving a forwarding address. (This sounded only too like Stick-at-Nothing Steve!)

'Do you expect him back?' asked the solicitor.

The boss shook his head. 'No, sirree! He left a few things behind but —' he hesitated — 'I doubt if he'll come back for em. He skipped over the border — to Montana — and good riddance to him! If you aim to stop with us, sir, I should be mighty obliged if you'd not mention Mr Corrigan's name to my guests.' And that was all he would say about Steve!

Mr Gaskarth was disappointed, as well as mystified, but he wasn't half so fed up with Lakeside Ranch as I was. It wasn't a real ranch at all. It turned out to be what they call a Dude Ranch, more like a hotel really, where wealthy people came for their holidays and played at being cowboys. Some of them couldn't even ride!

A few of the younger visitors went trail-riding in the mountains, with guides, but even they were glad enough to get the ache out of their bones in the evening by sitting down to watch a western on the telly. The rest of the 'dudes' were quite content with a little quiet fishing or a game of poker in a bogus saloon known as 'The Bar-Eight', which had silly notices saying 'Park your shooting irons with the barkeep' and 'Don't serve fire-water to the Injuns'. The real cowboys out on the range didn't carry guns and they used jeeps instead of mustangs to round up the cattle, while the few Indians we saw came from a reservation near by, just to sell us pottery and basketwork. I can tell you, it wasn't my idea of the Wild West.

I wouldn't have wanted to stay if a rather nice American, who had arrived about the same time as we had, hadn't offered to teach me to ride. He was a stout, middle-aged man, in a big white sombrero, but he always wore a baggy lounge suit with it, unlike all those fake 'cowboys' who went swaggering about in huge stetsons and sheepskin chaps, like so many Wyatt Earps except for their fat tummies. But Captain Lockwood — that was his name — could really sit a horse. He even had a shot at mounting one of the broncos which the real cowpokes rode in the occasional rodeos they put on for the benefit of tourists; and he laughed like anything when he was bucked off in the dust of the corral. He was tough all right!

While he was putting me through my paces — on a quiet pony, of course — he questioned me pretty closely about what had brought an English boy like me to the West. But I had been told not to talk about Steve, so I kept mum.

Mr Gaskarth himself was not quite so discreet. He went around secretly pumping the 'dudes' in the hope that they would throw some light on the mystery of Steve's disappearance. He was soon let into the scandal by one Mr Ashton a small dark man to whom I took an instant dislike. I don't know why, I just didn't trust him. He was always showing his teeth in an insincere smile, even when there was nothing to laugh at.

'I hear you're looking for Steve Corrigan, sir,' he said,

peering rather furtively over one shoulder. 'Take it from me, you're wasting your time! I should advise you to chuck it and go home.' Mr Gaskarth looked surprised. 'That feller won't come back for his property, believe me.'

'What makes you say that, Mr Ashton?'

'Well, one of the things he left behind him was a dead body. Another was his revolver.' Mr Gaskarth's yees nearly popped out of his head, and I pricked up my ears. 'That's why they don't like to talk about him here — it's not good for business,' went on Mr Ashton, with his cynical smile. 'It seems an F.B.I. man — that's an American detective, you know — followed him from Montana to ask him a few awkward questions.'

'Well?' cried Mr Gaskarth, for the other had paused.

'Corrigan shot him!'

I cried out in horror and disbelief, but before Mr Gaskarth could express his dismay a deep voice cut in from behind us.

'I wouldn't say that, sir.' It was my friend Captain Lockwood, who had overheard the conversation. 'It ain't been proved yet.'

'May I ask what *you* know about it?' demanded Mr Ashton, swinging round. 'You weren't here at the time.'

'No sir, but I happen to be a Federal agent myself. Homicide!' (I heard later that he had also been making inquiries among the guests.) 'It's true that Corrigan left his gun behind. One chamber was empty and the slug from it was found in Lieutenant Barker's heart. I agree it looks bad for him, but I guess a man ain't guilty until a jury finds him so, and a judge convicts him. That's law. I'm investigating the case personally.'

'What did the detective want to ask him?' inquired Mr Gaskarth, mopping his brow.

'Nothing very serious — just a few queries about his passport, and a licence for five-arms. But they say that guy's rather quick on the draw.'

'Trigger happy, you might say,' murmured Mr Ashton.

I had been silent all this while, for I was feeling pretty shaken. I remembered Steve's interest in guns, but I just couldn't see him as a murderer.

'What's *your* opinion of your cousin, son?' asked Captain Lockwood, glancing shrewdly at me.

I didn't ask him how he knew about our relationship. In fact, he knew quite a lot about all of us. 'I — I don't believe Steve would kill anybody, sir,' I stammered. 'He was a bit of a dare-devil, and always keen on pistols and shooting, but —'

'There you are,' said Mr Ashton, and, shrugging his shoulders with a significant smile, he turned on his heel and left us.

'This don't make any difference to *your* mission, sir,' said Captain Lockwood to Mr Gaskarth. 'You got your duty to do same as me. I'll let you know if we get word of your client's whereabouts. He's probably hiding out some place in the Bad Lands.'

'Thanks, officer,' muttered the solicitor, who seemed in a daze. He retired to his room after that to think it over, and I had plenty to brood about, too. Somehow this shocking crime made the Dude Ranch seem sillier and more unreal than ever. But we had booked for a week, so we just stayed on as if nothing had happened.

A few days later Captain Lockwood approached us as we were leaning over the rail of the corral with the other guests watching a real cowboy rope a steer.

'How do you feel about a trip to the States on my expense account, gentlemen?' he asked us amiably. 'I'm following up some clues I've gotten from the office, and if you put yourselves in my hands maybe I could lead you to your unfortunate client.'

'H'm. I wonder if it wouldn't be wiser to let events take their course now, Captain?' hesitated Mr Gaskarth. 'I'm not sure that I ought to expose Billy here to any danger. The man's a killer!'

'It's too late to back out now, sir. If he's on a murder rap he may *need* that money you say he has inherited. And, frankly, I could use this bright lad of yours to help us identify him.'

Well, you can guess how excited I felt about all this! I wasn't sorry to leave that Dude Ranch, and the chance of seeing some real gun-play, with a genuine detective, seemed a terrific kick at the time. The idea of my cousin being a killer was rather disturbing, but somehow it didn't seem quite real to me — yet. It was more like a story I was living. Then we had another surprise. Mr Ashton, who had somehow got wind of our departure, offered to join us.

'What's your interest in this case, sir?' asked the captain bluntly.

'I'd just like to see justice done,' Mr Ashton replied with an enigmatic smile. 'I'm an Englishman too, and I could also identify the murderer for you.'

That was how all three of us came to be travelling south through the United States of America on the trail of a gunman. It was a colossal and often tedious journey, and I won't describe it in detail. Montana, Wyoming, Colorado, New Mexico — I saw them all, mostly through the windows of railway carriages. At every stop Captain Lockwood would make inquiries of the local police, while Mr Gaskarth kept in touch with his London office by occasional cablse. One he received at Amarillo, the Texan oil-town, made him more than usually thoughtful, but like a true lawyer he kept his own counsel.

It was in the old Texan Panhandle that we got our first definite news of our man. A helicopter crew checking fences and water-holes from the air had reported a gun-fight going on in an abandoned 'ghost town' in the desert. This was real cowboy country. Miles of purple sage, rolling away as far as the eye could see, and ringed by rugged mountains. We had fetched up at a lost little cattle town in the middle of the prairie, and we soon contacted the sheriff, a tall, sleepy Texan who seemed bored with the whole thing.

'Yeah, there's some crazy limey hiding out in Bogey Town, about thirty miles from hyar,' he drawled, chewing on a cheroot. 'I guess he's on the run. He tuk to the hills the moment I started asking questions about him. Bogey Town don't belong to nobody — it's bin desarted since the old railroad by-passed it — and he's kinda staked a claim thah, like a squatter. But it ain't worth my while to round up a posse and winkle him out. A gang of desperadoes — old enemies of his, I reckon — are gunning for him, and it looks like they'll do our dirty work for us.'

'But that's not the law, Sheriff,' objected Lockwood.

'It's gun law, Captain, and gun law still goes in Texas. If I was you I'd let sleeping coyotes lie. That hombre's real mean. Got some chip on his shoulder, I guess. He's mighty quick on the draw, and he shoots at sight.'

But this warning didn't deter Captain Lockwood from doing his duty. He hired horses, and we all rode out to Bogey Town. Boy, was I thrilled! Mr Gaskarth had wanted to leave me behind, but the captain said I'd be all right if I obeyed orders and kept out of range if there was any shooting.

We rode all day through the brooding sage-brush until we reached parched canyon country. It was like a lost world — bare, desolate, and rocky. The first signs of life we noticed were the buzzards circling above the rafters of some ruined roofs. The second was a sudden fusillade of shots as we came in sight of the old ghost town!

Our leader raised his hand, and we reined in our weary horses in the shelter of a crumbling barn on the edge of the derelict settlement.

So this was Bogey Town. It was like a film-set in a western.

There was something eerie and sinister about it — utterly different from the lively, if make-believe, bustle of that Dude Ranch at Lakeside. After the abrupt burst of shots the dusty main street was so still and empty in the blazing sun that it was — frightening. The rotting timbers of the old-time shanties, some still plastered with peeling notices advertising 'Jake's Store', 'Gambling' or 'Saloon', were collapsing into decay; but the solid stone courthouse (and Bogey Town jail) in the middle of the square was still standing. Puffs of smoke emerging from a barricaded window, and a ragged Union Jack fluttering forlornly from the flat roof, told us that this was the outlaw's lair. The last touch of defiance was just like Stick-at-Nothing Steve.

Then I saw something else which made my blood run cold. A dead man in cowboy rig lay in a spreading pool of blood outside the door, with his gun still in his hand, as if he had been shot while making a desperate attempt to storm the building. Just as we had arrived! This wasn't *playing* at cowboys. This was for real.

Captain Lockwood dismounted. 'I'm afraid it's true about your client, Mr Gaskarth,' he said grimly; and he drew a heavy automatic from the shoulder-holster he wore under his jacket. 'He's a killer.'

'So was the fellow who tried to get him, sir,' I put in quickly, although I felt slightly sick and faint.

'Maybe, son, maybe.' He tilted his sombrero over his keen eyes, to shade them from the sun-glare. 'Where's the rest of the gang?'

We all stared across the deserted square, and could just make out three men lurking in the shade of a ruined shack at the end of the street, opposite the beleaguered courthouse, but out of range, I should imagine. They were as still — and menacing — as statues. The barrel of a sawn-off shotgun glittered in the sun.

'Deadlock!' murmured Captain Lockwood thoughtfully. 'I wonder why Corrigan fell foul of those roughnecks? Your cousin sure is a trouble-shooter, Billy! We gotta handle this careful-like, before somebody else gets hurt.'

As he spoke Mr Ashton, who had also climbed down from his mustang, whipped out a pistol and fired it into the air. Before we had recovered from the shock (which made us all duck for cover) he was walking perkily across the square, towards the gunmen, shouting 'Friend!' and waving his handkerchief like a flag of truce.

'Come back, you fool!' shouted Captain Lockwood.

But it was too late. There was another shot, this time from the courthouse, but the bullet only kicked up the dust at Ashton's heels, and sent him scurrying like a rabbit to the shack, where he was safe. We saw him in breathless conference with the gunmen, who had held their fire when they saw him coming and heard his shout. It was too far away from us to hear what they were saying.

'The man must be mad,' muttered Captain Lockwood. 'What the blazes does he think he's doing? He could have been caught between a cross-fire and killed. I'd better talk to those hoodlums myself, before there's any more bloodshed. Here, hold my hoss, son, and don't follow me, on your life!'

He threw the reins to me, and then, with his gun at the ready, made a rapid dart to the shelter of a broken veranda. He was too downy a bird to take any risks like Mr Ashton. He crept, slowly and cautiously, from ruin to ruin, pausing behind each pillar or post, or empty water-butt, and only breaking cover in sudden bursts of speed which took him to the next point of safety. I don't think he was spotted either from the courthouse or by the gunmen besieging it.

But while we watched him with wildly beating hearts, I suddenly saw Mr Ashton leave his new companions, and, crouching almost double, run lightly across the street. He had taken an angle which was not immediately visible from the courthouse. I saw at once that he meant to attack it from the rear, and by the way he held his gun I knew that he meant business. He was showing his teeth in a mirthless grin.

Mr Gaskarth, who was very pale, was so intent on following Captain Lockwood's stealthy progress along the street that he failed to notice me drop softly from the saddle, and tether both horses to a hitching post by the old barn.

Scared as I was — and I don't mind confessing it — I meant to join in this three-cornered gun-fight. The captain had only told me not to follow *him*. It wouldn't be disobeying orders if I went to warn Steve of his danger. I wasn't going to stand by while my cousin, guilty or not, was trapped by this mysterious man who seemed to have taken sides wigh his enemies. Even an outlaw is entitled to a fair trial.

I waited a while, because I hoped that Steve would spot the man before he reached the corner of the courthouse. He would probably have done so, too, at one stage, but the three gunmen by the shack chose this moment, when Ashton was exposed, to step out of cover and let off a volley of shots which sent the chips flying from the stone wall and smashed through the boards of the window. The fire was instantly returned from within. There was a sharp crack, and a spurt of flame, but the gunmen stepped smartly back into cover again, although one of them had a neat hole drilled through his stetson. They had achieved their object of distracting Steve's attention. It was obviously a prearranged plan. Mr Ashton vanished unseen round the back of the building.

At the same time I left the barn and ran like lightning towards the other end of the courthouse. I heard Mr Gaskarth shout, but I didn't stop to hear what he said. I was too excited now to be scared, and in too much of a hurry to think of anything — except that I *must* reach Steve before Ashton did.

Panting and stumbling, I staggered round the side of the

grim block-house, hugging the flaking wall and looking desperately for some entrance. I didn't want to come face to face with
Ashton! To my relief, I saw a window above me. It was a mere
slit in the wall, much too small to admit a man's body, which
was probably why it had been left unguarded; but I thought
I could just manage to squeeze through it. I took a grip of the
sill with my fingers and hauled myself up. My shoulders
followed my head through the opening, and I found myself
staring into the main room.

There was no time to take in many details, but I noticed
that it was roughly furnished with a camp bed, a table and
a chair; and there were other signs of habitation including
a box of ammunition and a rifle propped up in a corner.

Steve Corrigan was flattened against the wall by the window
with his eye on a chink in the splintered slats through which
he had been firing at his besiegers. A thin curl of smoke was
still rising from the muzzle of his revolver, and the room was
acrid with the smell of gunpowder. Empty cartridge cases lay
scattered at his feet. I recognised my cousin at once. He was
older, of course, and he looked haggard and unshaven, but
there was the old dancing light in his crazy blue eyes and
a half-smile playing about his lips as if he was almost enjoying
himself.

'Steve!' I said softly. He whipped round, and his gun came
up like lightning. 'Don't shoot!' I shrieked. 'It's me!'

'Gosh! It's Billy the Kid!' he gasped incredulously, and
lowered the barrel as if he could hardly believe his eyes. The
tense look faded from his face, and he broke into the old
familiar grin — daring, reckless, but friendly. 'What in the
name of wonder are *you* doing here!'

I scrambled through the opening and dropped into the
room.

'I can't tell you now, Steve,' I blurted out hurriedly. 'I've
come to warn you. There's another chap trying to cut you off

from behind. He left the others and slipped round the back while they kept you busy. If he can get in he'll shoot. He's armed.'

'He's welcome,' said Stick-at-Nothing Steve lightly. He glanced quickly through the window to see that the coast was clear and then, thrusting his revolver back into its holster, came towards me with his hand outstretched in greeting. I noticed that he carried two guns, slung low from a cartridge belt buckled over his hips. With his loosely-knotted scarf and red shirt, his full-cut riding breeches and high boots, he looked a real swaggering desperado; and his next words showed that he was still the dare-devil adventurer of my hero-worshipping days.

'The more the merrier, Billy boy! I barricade the whole place at night, but in the daytime I leave the back door ajar – with a pail balanced on top of it — just to tempt 'em in.' He chuckled, and pointed to the inner door of the room, which opened into a dark passage. 'I'm quicker on the trigger than any of 'em, and your friend won't get very far once I hear that pail drop!'

'Why are they after you, Steve?' I asked. 'What have you done to them?'

'That's a long story, and maybe I'll tell you if I get out of this alive,' he said carelessly. 'But what about you? Don't tell me you came all the way from England to warn me that somebody was going to shoot me in the back. Somebody must have brought you here, for some very good reason.'

'That's right, Steve, and it's good news,' I cried eagerly. 'You've come into a fortune. Your Uncle Charlie died last year, and Mr Gaskarth — the lawyer, you know — has been looking for you ever since to tell you that the old boy left you a million!'

To my astonishment, Steve threw back his head and laughed aloud. 'Now isn't that just my luck!' he exclaimed. 'A millionaire at last, and I'm on the run from the law and being shot up by hoodlums. When I come into my inheritance I shall either be in the electric chair or riddled with bullets.' He gave a bitter, rueful smile. 'Either way I look like being the richest man in the cemetery.'

'Yes, that's another thing, and it's not so good, Steve,' I went on earnestly, and I suppose I looked troubled, for he darted an affectionate glance at me. 'An American detective, Captain Lockwood, also came with us, and he's got a warrant for your arrest!'

There was a long silence. He knew what I meant at once.

'I didn't kill that man at Lakeside, Billy,' he said at last, and something in his tone made my heart lift with relief. 'I don't know who did, but it wasn't me.' He looked me straight in the eyes, and I saw that his, which were usually dancing with mischief, were serious and sincere. 'You believe that, don't you?'

'Yes,' I said simply; and I did.

'Thanks, pal,' went on Steve, squeezing my arm. 'It's good to feel there's *someone* on my side. I've been a fool, Billy boy. Let my life be a warning to you! Mind you, I've got into plenty of scrapes and fights in my time, but I'd never *shot* anyone before those ruffians outside started gunning for me. But back at Lakeside —' he hesitated — 'Well, that poor chap who got killed *had* been pestering me — and it *was* my gun they found — although I didn't pull the trigger — I swear it, Billy!'

'Then why did you bolt?' I couldn't help asking.

'A fellow called Ashton who was staying there advised me to get out while the going was good,' he said slowly. 'With my reputation I was bound to be charged with murder. Everybody was against me — except that fellow Ashton. He was a friend in need.'

Suddenly I saw a great light.

'I wouldn't be so sure of that, Steve,' I cried excitedly.

'It's that fellow Ashton who is creeping round the back to kill you right now!'

Steve stared; but there was no time for further talk. A sudden clatter from the rear of the building, which told us that the pail had fallen from the door, made him leap aside. His guns seemed to jump from their holsters into his hands. With a quick movement of one arm he shoved me against the wall, so that I should be out of the line of fire from the door. He was only just in time. There was a scamper of feet in the passage — Ashton had walked into the trap but had decided to make a rush for it — and the next moment the door flew open, and our enemy was on the threshold, gun in hand.

My heart stood still at the murderous expression on his dark, triumphant face. Then the room seemed to rock and re-echo with the thunderous crash of fire-arms. Both men had pressed triggers almost simultaneously. But Steve was just that fraction of a second faster, and the pistol exploded in Ashton's hand and flew across the room in fragments. The man staggered back, and nearly fell. Even in that moment he was showing his teeth in a grin — but it was a grin of rage and anguish as his shattered gun-hand dropped bleeding to his side.

'Stay where you are — no tricks!' rapped out Steve, and, leaving the reeling man to clutch at the door for support, he darted back to the window.

For his quick ear had caught another burst of fire from outside. From where I stood cowering against the wall, with my hands over my ears, I could see through the bullet-torn slats that the hoodlums had taken advantage of the gunfight inside to open fire on the courthouse again. The three of them were racing across the square with blazing guns.

I saw Captain Lockwood step out from the shack and shoot low from the hip; and one of the villains pitched forward and sprawled on his face in the dust, clutching frantically at an ankle. Another whipped round to raise his sawn-off shotgun

Ashton's gun-hand dropped bleeding to his side

and draw a bead on the detective. I expected to see my friend shot at short range while he stooped over the fallen man. But at the same time my cousin fired through the window. His aim was perfect. The shotgun spun into the air, and the ruffian was dancing round, biting his wounded wrist. The third villain threw down his weapon and put up his hands in surrender as Captain Lockwood walked slowly towards him.

All this has taken some time to tell, but in actual fact it was all over in a matter of seconds.

The next thing I can remember was Mr Gaskarth clutching my arm and asking me if I was all right. He was supposed to be guarding the three hoodlums, but it was not really necessary. They were squatting on the floor of the courthouse, looking very sick and sorry for themselves. As for Ashton, that would-be assassin had collapsed in a dead faint.

Captain Lockwood was standing, hands on hips, in front of Steve, and shaking his head at him with a comic expression that was something between sad disapproval and grudging admiration.

'Tut-tut, Mr Corrigan, you've sure given us a long ride for our money!' he said amiably.

Steve held out the revolvers to him by the barrels. 'I suppose you'll want these, Captain,' he said with an impudent grin. 'I don't expect I shall need them where I'm going.'

'I hope not,' replied the detective gravely. 'If you'd only give up playing with fire-arms you might make a success of your life yet.'

Steve raised his eyebrows. 'What! In the pen?' he asked ironically. 'If you can't pin that Lakeside murder on me, I've no doubt this customer will be only too happy to oblige when he comes round.' He indicated the unconscious Ashton. 'He seems to have a grudge against me, like so many other people.'

'You underestimate the law, Mr Corrigan,' said Captain Lockwood. 'I have evidence that you were fishing on the lake at the time. The fingerprints we found on your gun were certainly not yours — and we have plenty of specimens of those, believe you me — but I've a notion they'll turn out to belong to this gentleman. We're having them checked at headquarters now. You see, Jonas Saltash had a special reason for killing that F.B.I. man and implicating you in the crime.'

'Jonas Saltash?'

'Yes, that's Ashton's real name, Stephen,' put in Mr Gaskarth. 'He was the next-of-kin, and would have inherited your uncle's fortune if —' he coughed — 'anything had happened to you. Such as sudden death, for instance.'

'Oh, Steve!' I rushed across and clasped my cousin's hand. 'You're innocent! And you've come into your money, too! Isn't it marvellous?'

Mr Gaskarth gave another discreet little cough. 'One moment. I'm afraid Billy has been speaking out of turn,' he went on uncomfortably. 'You're not exactly a millionaire after all. I had a cable when we were at Amarillo which — er — unfortunately makes it quite clear that certain debts, and other unexpected charges will — er —'

'Cut out the legal mumbo-jumbo, please!' interrupted Steve. 'How much do I get?'

'Well — ah — no more than a thousand pounds, I fear.'

'That's enough!' My cousin's blue eyes lit up with his old gay enthusiasm. 'I'd rather have it this way. When I was hiding out here from the law I discovered there's *oil* on this land,' he explained. 'That's why those hoodlums were after me. They wanted to stake their claim here. Now I can buy Bogey Town and work the wells myself. Of course, I'll need a law-yer —' Mr Gaskarth shook his head in alarm — 'and maybe a private sleuth for protection —'

'Count me out,' chuckled Lockwood. 'But you can keep your guns, boy, although I'd advise you to use blanks in future.'

'— and a loyal partner,' finished Steve, turning to me and

rumpling my hair affectionately. 'How about it, Billy the Kid?'

I grinned in embarrassment. 'Sorry, Steve. I've had enough of Dude Ranches and ghost towns. And I've got my G.C.E. to do. You'll have to stick it yourself, Stick-at-Nothing Steve, and the best of British luck to you!'

The Mystery of Spaniard's Cove

by JOHN DAVIES

The small sloop *Sea Wanderer* was making her way into a lone cove on the Dorset coast. The breeze had died as the sun went down, and she was puttering in with her sail furled. The sound of her engine carried clearly through the still evening air.

Up in her bows stood a stocky, well-built boy with gingery hair. He was wearing jeans and a T-shirt. Another boy, similarly dressed but fair-haired and slimmer, was standing in the little yacht's cockpit.

The fair-haired boy reached a hand down to the engine controls. The sloop began to lose way. He waved, and the other boy let the anchor go. Above the sound of the now idling engine came the rattle of the anchor-chain running out.

Then the anchor was down. The engine spat and stopped. The two boys went below. *Sea Wanderer* lay at rest on a sea as calm as a millpond. She was quite motionless. And silent.

The silence did not last long. A cheerful whistling started up in her cabin, accompanied by a rattling of post and pans. Then a wonderful fragrance wafted out into the twilight.

Bangers!

After a suitable interval there came the sound of washing-up.

*   *   *   *

'You ate five,' Tony said. 'Think they'll hold you until breakfast?'

'Funny fellow,' Peter said. 'You ate six.'

'I'm bigger than you are.'

'I don't know about that. Greedier, maybe.'

They had a bit of a scuffle then, which in the small cabin seemed like a fight between two young elephants, and didn't help much with the washing-up. Luckily nothing got broken.

When they had finished the chores, they went out and sat on the cabin top. Night had fallen now, but the sky was clear. A full moon was just rising. The surrounding cliffs frowned darkly down, but the cove itself was filled with a ghostly light. A solitary seabird broke the silence with a shrill, unearthly cry.

Tony gazed around him.

'Spaniard's Cove,' he murmured. 'Why "Spaniard's"?'

'It's an old story,' Peter said. 'Hundreds of years ago a ship-wrecked chap got ashore here. But he couldn't get up the cliffs, simply because there isn't any way up. And no boats came into the cove in those days. He wasn't found till years later, when he was just a skeleton — though he must have been alive when he landed, because he was found right up under the cliffs, above the tideline.' He paused. 'They identified him as a Spaniard, from a ring he was wearing. They reckoned he must have been off one of the Armada ships which were sunk not far from here.'

Tony was silent for a while.

'It's a smashing place,' he said at last. 'But it sort of gives me the creeps. And I'm not surprised, after that story.'

Tony was the stocky, red-headed one of the pair. He was a Londoner, and all this was new to him. He and Peter had become friends at school the previous term, and Peter had asked him down to stay during the summer holidays. He was glad he had come, too! He was having quite the best holiday of his life.

It wasn't new to Peter. He lived in Westhampton, the little Dorset port, some twenty miles away, which they had set sail from that morning. *Sea Wanderer* belonged to him, and he had been sailing pretty well all his life. But even he often felt the sea's mystery — as, indeed, he did tonight.

They continued to sit there for a while, and then Peter went below to look out his skin-diving gear. He was an expert diver, and he was hoping to do some spear-fishing in the cove next day. Tony was going to have a go too. He didn't know much about it as yet, but he was very keen. And he was as good a swimmer as Peter was himself.

Peter lit the oil lamp in the cabin, and a soft yellow light shone out through the portholes. Tona stirred himself and, stepping down into the cockpit, began tinkering with the engine. There wasn't much light there, but he scarcely needed to see, because he was an expert with engines. He had already got *Sea Wanderer's* little single-cylinder job to run better than it had ever done before. But he still wasn't satisfied.

Peter, in the cabin, suddenly heard a faint 'popping' sound. At first he thought Tony had started the engine to test it, but the noise grew rapidly louder. Then a shouted 'Hey!' of alarm from Tony brought him quickly to the cabin hatch.

He got there just as the noise became a ragged roar. Looking up, he saw a plane skimming seawards only a few feet above the top of the cliffs.

It was a small monoplane, and it was obviously in trouble. It dived steeply towards the sea until it seemed as though it must come down right on top of *Sea Wanderer*. Then it climbed just as abruptly, appeared to stall, fell away in an almost vertical banking turn, and crashed into the sea not more than a couple of hundred yards away!

'What the —?' Tony exclaimed.

Peter scrambled out of the cabin hatch.

'We've got to get there — fast!' he snapped.

Tony jumped down into the boat, grabbed the starting handle and put it on. The engine fired at the first swing.

Peter rushed forward and hauled up the anchor. In less than a minute *Sea Wanderer* was heading at full speed for the spot where the plane had crashed.

As they drew near, Peter handed the tiller over to Tony. 'You take her,' he said. 'I want to get my binoculars.' He dived into the cabin and reappeared with the glasses. They were excellent for night work, and showed up the sea and the rocks ahead in sharp detail.

'There!' Peter exclaimed. 'I can see the tail sticking up among those rocks, just offshore!' Then he drew in his breath sharply. 'And somebody's got out alive! I can see him on the beach!'

He had spotted a dark figure moving across the pale curve of sand. He kept the binoculars on the man until he was lost against the black background of the cliffs.

Now they were close enough to see the tail of the plane with the naked eye. It was tilted at a crazy angle, and had clearly broken off from the fuselage. There was no sign of anything else. The rest of the wreck must be lying in the deep water between the rocks.

Peter swept the small expanse of beach again with the binoculars, but there was no sign of life there.

'We'd better drop anchor and get ashore,' he said. 'That chap may be hurt.'

They anchored quickly and, jumping into the little dinghy *Sea Wanderer* was towing, rowed ashore as fast as they could. The dinghy grounded on the beach and, jumping out, they hauled the boat up so that it wouldn't float away. Then they stood motionless, side by side, staring and listening. After the grating of the dinghy's keel on the sand, everything was as silent as the grave. And the beach seemed to be deserted.

'Ahoy, there!' Peter called out. 'Where are you?'

The only reply was a hollow echo from the dark, high cliffs.

'Perhaps he's too badly hurt to answer,' Tony said. 'He could be lying unconscious somewhere.'

'Let's look for him, then,' Peter said. 'He disappeared up there, under the cliffs.'

It didn't take them long to look. The beach was only a narrow strip of sand, and it wasn't more than a hundred yards from end to end. The beach itself was plainly in view, and they searched right along the shadows under the cliffs.

There was no one there.

Baffled, they went slowly back towards the dinghy.

'You must have imagined you saw someone,' Tony said.

'Did I?' Peter retorted. 'Well — I'm not imagining those!'

He pointed. Just in front of him there were footprints in the sand.

'They're not ours,' he said. 'They're too big, and we didn't go that way. They're fresh too. The tide's only just uncovered this bit.'

Tony was staring in the direction in which the footprints led.

'We'd better follow them,' he said.

The footprints led to a smooth, low rock which was still half awash. There they ended. There was no one on the rock, and the sand beyond it was smooth.

Tony shivered slightly.

'It's — a bit queer, isn't it?' he said. He couldn't help recalling the story Peter had told him; the story of the skeleton with the Spanish ring.

'It's *very* queer,' Peter said. 'I just don't understand it.'

'So — what do we do now!'

'I don't know.' Peter shrugged. 'About the only thing we can do is go back aboard, and have another look round in the morning.'

They returned to the dinghy and rowed back out to *Sea Wanderer*. Peter made the dinghy fast astern and turned to go below, with Tony close behind him.

Peter was halfway into the cabin when he checked suddenly.

There was someone there.

A swarthy, thickset man was sitting on the port bunk, facing the cabin hatch. He was dripping wet, and Peter knew at once that this must be the man they had been looking for on the beach. They hadn't been able to find him because he had swum out to *Sea Wanderer!*

But he was only vaguely aware of this. His attention was riveted on the thing in the man's hand; something that glinted wickedly in the soft lamplight.

It was a heavy revolver, and it seemed to Peter that he was looking straight down the barrel.

The man stared at Peter. Then he gestured with the gun. He didn't speak, but his meaning was plain. Dazedly, Peter moved forward into the cabin. He had only one really conscious thought: *If only I could have warned Tony!* But he had been taken completely by surprise, and it was too late. Tony was already following him in through the hatchway.

Tony froze there, just as Peter had done.

'I guess you weren't expecting me either,' the gunman said. His voice was a growl. 'Get in here with your pal, before this thing goes off.'

* * * *

Sea Wanderer was heading out to sea. Peter was steering, with Tony sitting slumped beside him in the cockpit. Their unwelcome passenger was leaning in the hatchway, watching them, the gun still in his hand.

He had given Peter a course to steer, and every now and then his eyes flickered for a moment towards the dim glow of light in the compass bowl.

Neither Peter nor Tony had any idea where they were

going, or what lay ahead. But one thing they did know. They were in a lot of trouble.

After a while the gunman began turning every now and then to peer into the night. Every time he did so, the same thought leaped into both the boys' minds — could they jump him? But they both realised that it would be silly to try anything. The gun made it much too risky.

Suddenly their captor gave a low exclamation of satisfaction, and, looking past him, Peter saw a faint red light, out beyond *Sea Wanderer's* bows. A little later he could make out a pale white shape under the light. A boat.

Five minutes after that, *Sea Wanderer* came alongside a powerful, white-hulled motor-cruiser. There were two men aft in her well. The boys were bundled roughly aboard and, before they had a chance to wonder what was going to happen next, found themselves shoved into the cruiser's forepeak and the door locked upon them.

The forepeak was small and made more cramped by the gear stowed there. It was lit by a low-powered bulb recessed into the deckhead. Peter, being a sailor, instinctively looked round him in the dim light. There was the usual stuff that you might expect to find there — several heavy coils of rope, a heap of anchor-chain, a spare anchor. There was also a sealed tin box of distress flares, and the rueful thought flashed through his mind: *We're in distress all right, but these aren't much use to us!*

He sat wearily down with his back against the starboard side of the boat. Tony dropped down opposite him. They looked at each other.

'I'm sorry, Tony,' Peter said.

'Sorry?' Tony said. 'What for?'

'I ought to have warned you before he got you too.'

'Don't be daft,' Tony said. 'You didn't have a chance.'

They fell silent after that. They could hear voices on the

other side of the locked door, but they couldn't make out what was being said.

Then there were no more voices, and suddenly the light in the deck-head went out. Peter looked at the luminous dial of his watch, and was amazed to see that it was two o'clock in the morning.

All at once he felt desperately tired, and lay down as best he could on his side of the small, cramped compartment. Tony did the same. They were both certain they wouldn't sleep a wink. But it was pretty obvious that nothing more was going to happen until the morning, and, now that the danger and the excitement were temporarily over, exhaustion finally got the better of them.

*   *   *   *

When Peter awoke, the motor-cruiser was under way. He sat up stiffly and looked around him. There were no portholes in the forepeak, but a gleam of sunlight was slanting down through the small circular aperture through which the anchor-cable ran down from the deck above.

It was daylight. Morning. He looked at his watch. Early morning. Only just five o'clock.

A minute of so later Tony sat up, groaning and looking round him as though he couldn't remember where he was. Then it all came back to him. He groaned again and shifted his position on the hard deck.

'I don't think much of the accommodation on this cruise,' he said.

'Nor do I,' Peter said.

'Why don't we ask for our money back?'

It was a pretty feeble joke, but somehow it made them feel better. And at any rate it was daylight again. Nothing was ever quite so bad in daylight.

Suddenly Peter felt ravenously hungry. As though to

tantalise him, the smell of cooking began filtering in through the door.

Tony was feeling the same. He had a very healthy appetite under almost any circumstances.

'I could do with some of that,' he said.

'So could I,' Peter said, 'but we're not likely to get any.'

But he was wrong.

Even as he spoke, a key grated in the lock. Both the boys stiffened as the door opened.

It was their captor of the night before.

'Come on — out of it!' he ordered them. 'Look lively!'

They stumbled through into the saloon.

'Do you want anything to eat?'

'Yes,' Peter said.

'Yes,' said Tony.

'O. K. Sit over there. And don't try anything. There are three of us, and the other two aren't any more fussy than I am about what we do with you.'

The two boys sat down at the saloon table. The smell of cooking was wafting mouth-wateringly in from the galley, and a little later the 'cook' came in. He was a small, pale, ferrety-faced man. He was carrying two plates, which he slapped down on the table. On each there were three thick rashers of bacon. There was a ragged loaf of bread on the table, and he pushed that across. Then he turned to the other man.

'You want coffee, Muller?' he said.

'Yes,' Muller said.

'Here?'

'Yes. I reckon I'd better watch our guests' table manners.'

The food, rough as it was, tasted marvellous. And, in a way, it was a good omen. *They can't be meaning to bump us off*, Peter told himself as he ate. *Not yet anyway, or they wouldn't bother to feed us.*

He also thought he detected a change in the man named

Muller. He was still pretty tough, but not quite so threatening as he had been the night before.

Muller sat drinking his coffee, watching them eat.

'O.K.,' he said suddenly, 'whose is the skin-diving stuff?'

Peter hesitated. But there didn't seem any point in not telling him.

'Mine,' he said.

'You good at diving?'

'Yes.' There wasn't any reason for not telling him that either.

'O.K.,' Muller said again, and now his manner seemed almost friendly. 'Maybe you're going to get a lucky break after all.'

Peter looked at him.

'What do you eman by that?' he demanded.

'Never mind. Wait and see.'

There was silence after that. The two boys finished eating. Soon after they'd done so, the cruiser's engines cut out, and they heard the rattling of her anchor-chain. Instinctively, Peter glanced towards the nearest porthole.

Muller noticed him do so.

'Want to know where we are?' he said. 'Why don't you go out and have a look?'

Peter stood up. It would be a relief to get out into the open. Tony got up too. Muller didn't stop him.

As he came out into the well of the cruiser, the first thing Peter saw was his skin-diving gear lying on one of the locker-seats there. Then, looking around him, he saw where they were. They were back in Spaniard's Cove. There, sticking up out of the rocks only a few yards away, was the tail of the crashed plane!

He saw *Sea Wanderer* too, lying just a little way away. He guessed that the little yacht had been an embarrassment to the men on the cruiser. They couldn't just cut her adrift, in case anyone saw her, so they had towed her back to the cove and anchored her there.

Muller and the ferrety-faced man, whose name was Minelli, followed the boys out, and then a third man came down from the wheelhouse. He was big and tough, with the weatherbeaten face of a sailor. Muller called him Joe.

'Surprised?' Muller asked. He put a hand on Peter's shoulder. 'Now look, chum — we haven't got anything against you, or your pal. We don't want to do you any harm. And we won't — so long as you play ball with us.'

Peter wasn't deceived by Muller's manner.

'What do you want?' he asked shortly.

Muller jerked his head.

'Something down there in the plane,' he said. Just a little something. You say you're a good diver. All right — you fetch this little thing up, and you can just get in your boat over there and sail away. You and your friend, and no hard feelings.'

'And — if I don't?' Peter asked.

Muller reached slowly inside his jacket to where the bulge of his shoulder-holster showed through the cloth.

'You wouldn't be so silly, would you?' he said.

Peter knew he hadn't any choice.

'All right,' he said abruptly. 'What is it you want me to look for?'

It was a cylinder, Muller said. About three feet long by four inches in diameter. It was made of aluminium, and it would probably be floating up against the top of the plane, since it was watertight and there was 'nothing much' in it. There was a small canister attached to it by a short length of line. Muller didn't explain what this was.

Peter got into his diving gear. When he was ready, he climbed up on to the cruiser's gunwale.

'Good luck, Pete!' Tony called out.

Peter spotted the fuselage of the plane on the sea-bed

Tony was looking very worried. Peter waved a hand to reassure him, then slipped over the side into the sea. He swam slowly until he was over where he thought the rest of the wrecked plane must be lying. He couldn't see anything as he peered down through his mask, but he knew the water was deep there.

He dived, going down through pale to darker green. At first there was nothing to be seen except a steep, smooth slope of rock on his right hand. Then he spotted it.

The fuselage of the plane was lying on the sandy sea-bed. One wing was completely missing, and only a stub of the other was left. He could see the jagged hole where the tail had broken off.

He swam cautiously in through the hole. It wasn't a pleasant thing to do, because there wasn't much room. The fabric of the plane seemed very close, and there wasn't enough light to see properly.

After a moment or two he backed out, surfaced, and swam back to the motor-cruiser. Muller was leaning over the side.

'Any luck?' Muller asked eagerly.

Peter didn't bother to answer him.

'I need a torch,' he said.

Muller's head disappeared. A few moments later he was back again with a heavy, rubber-covered torch. Peter took it, swam back, and dived a second time. He swam in through the hole again feeling a lot happier with the torch — until he switched it on. Its powerful beam lit up the inside of the plane with a ghastly glare, and out of the glare a pale, slack-mouthed face leered sightlessly at him.

It was a dead man, hanging weightlessly, slewed round in the pilot's seat as though he had been struggling to get out of it when he died.

The sight was so horrible that Peter almost panicked. But with an effort he pulled himself together.

He found the cylinder a minute or so later. It was floating up against the top of the fuselage, as Muller had thought it might be. He spotted the small canister attached to it, and at once recognised it as a lamp of the kind that is worn on some lifejackets, and which lights up when it comes into contact with the water, so that the wearer of the jacket can be spotted.

He guessed then what the original plan must have been. The plane was to have rendezvoused with the motor-cruiser offshore and dropped the cylinder near it. The cylinder would have floated, and the light attached to it would have enabled the men on the cruiser to spot it and pick it up.

The whole thing was a clever smuggling operation. Or it would have been, if it had worked!

He grabbed the cylinder and swam out of the plane. He was very glad to get out, but he didn't surface immediately. Instead he sank to the bottom and, squatting on the sea-bed, examined his find curiously. He knew that it must contain something of great importance.

A little later he surfaced and swam towards the motor-cruiser. A yell of triumph came from her as the men in her well saw that he had the cylinder. When he reached the cruiser's side, Muller and Minelli grabbed him under the armpits and heaved him aboard.

'All right,' Muller said, snatching the cylinder, 'now get back up fo'rard! Both of you!'

Peter and Tony stared at him. Muller was clutching the cylinder in one hand. In the other was his gun.

'You heard what I said!' Muller growled. He jabbed the muzzle of the gun in Peter's ribs.

There was nothing Peter could do. He stumbled in through the doorway which led into the saloon. As he did so he cast a despairing look around him, instinctively seeking help. But, apart from a long, low, grey shape several miles away, the whole wide expanse of sea was empty.

Then he and Tony were back in their forepeak prison again. The key turned in the lock, and as it did so the cruiser's engines roared into life.

'The so-and-sos!' Tony exclaimed bitterly. 'They —'

But Peter wasn't listening.

'We've got to get out of here quick!' he exclaimed. 'Heaven knows where they're taking us. And if they have a good look at that thing I fetched up for them, they're not going to be a bit pleased!'

'What do you mean?'

'Never mind now.' Peter was looking desperately around him, and suddenly he pointed to the spare anchor lying on the deck. 'That! Do you think you could bash the door down with that?'

'I could have a good try,' Tony said. 'But —?'

'Once we're out,' Peter went on quickly, 'get aft as fast as you can, and then — straight over the side! Swim for it! O.K.?' He had pulled out the box of distress flares as he was speaking, and now he began tearing at the waterproof tape which sealed the lid. He wrenched the lid open, snatched up a couple of flares and the crude pistol that was supplied for firing them.

Tony was watching him, bewildered. He was holding the heavy anchor firmly in both hands, like a battering-ram.

'O.K.!' Peter snapped. 'Let's go!'

The cruiser was surging along at top speed. Tony drew a deep breath and charged the door. It burst open with a splintering crash and he dashed through it. Minelli was just getting up from one of the seats in the saloon, a look of surprise and alarm on his face. Tony flung the anchor at him. He raced aft, out into the well, and went over the side in a high, clean dive.

Peter was hard on his heels. As he came out into the well, he raised the pistol and fired. There was a dull explosion and

311

a red flare blossomed in the sky above the racing boat. Yells were coming from the wheelhouse. Someone was clattering down the ladder. Peter hastily fitted the other flare and fired it high, after the other. Then he plunged after Tony.

The cruiser's wake rolled him over. He surfaced, gasping, and stared around him. He saw Tony treading water only a little way away.

The cruiser was a good hundred yards from them now — but she was turning. She was coming back! They saw her alter course through a complete half-circle until her high, knife-like bows were pointing straight at them.

She was going to run them down, and there was nothing they could do. It would be impossible to escape by swimming.

On came the cruiser, roaring flat out, until it seemed that her bows were towering right over them. But then, amazingly, and at the very last moment, she veered sharply away. Round she went, in a tight, slithering turn that smothered both the boys in foam. Then she steadied and roared off into the distance.

Scarcely able to believe what had happened, Peter turned his head. The long, grey shape he had noticed earlier was a lot closer now. He saw that she was a destroyer. She must have spotted the flares and decided to investigate.

So — it had been a chance in a million that his plan would work. But it had!

* * * *

Westhampton was too small a port for H.M.S. *Wrathful* to enter, so she lay off and sent her motor-boat in. There were three passengers in the boat. One of these was the destroyer's captain, Commander John Forbes, D.S.O., R.N. The other two were Peter and Tony. Commander Forbes had a brief-case with him.

Inspector Palmer, chief of the Westhampton police, was

waiting for them on the quay. A police car took them straight to his office.

'Now,' he said, 'let's sort this out.' He glanced at the two boys. 'You two seem to have done a pretty good job.'

'We had a lot of luck,' Peter said.

'You've got these three scallywags safe?' Inspector Palmer asked Commander Forbes. He had already had a radio message from the destroyer, but it had been only a brief one.

'They're safe enough,' Commander Forbes said. 'They're under close arrest on my ship. We can hand them over to you any time you like.'

H.M.S. *Wrathful* had picked up Peter and Tony. Then it had overtaken and captured the motor-cruiser. Muller and his two accomplices had been transferred to the destroyer, while the motor-cruiser herself had been brought into West-hampton by a naval prize crew.

Somehow, though, Inspector Palmer didn't seem as pleased as he ought to have been.

'The trouble is,' he said, 'we've got those blokes, but we haven't got what they were trying to smuggle out.' He turned to the destroyer captain, frowning, 'I gather the cylinder was empty when you got hold of it?'

'That's right,' Commander Forbes said.

He couldn't quite suppress a smile as he spoke, and the Inspector noticed it. 'What's so funny about that?' he demanded irritably. 'For your information, there was something very important in that thing.'

'I know,' Commander Forbes said calmly. 'It contained a complete set of drawings for a new type of nuclear engine which has been developed for the British Government by the Research Division of the Ministry of Defence.'

The Inspector's face was comical with surprise.

'How the blazes do you know that?' he said. 'Nobody's supposed to know —'

'That's why I didn't mention the drawings in my radio signal,' Commander Forbes said.

'But how do you *know*?'

'Because of young Peter here,' the Commander said. 'He found the cylinder, didn't he, down there in the plane? And he guessed that it must contain something pretty important; so — well, he opened it up while he was still down there. He took the drawings and stowed them away inside the plane, and then he sealed the cylinder again as well as he could before he surfaced and handed it over —'

'But —'

'He went down for them again about a couple of hours ago, from my motor-boat,' Commander Forbes said. He opened his brief-case and took out a number of large folded sheets of blotting-paper. 'Here they are. They're still a bit damp, I'm afraid.'

The Inspector was speechless. When he had recovered himself, he asked a good many more questions.

'All right,' he said finally, 'That's that, for the time being at any rate.' He turned to Peter.

'You did an even better job than I thought! We may want you and your friend to give us some further information, though, so I must ask you to remain in touch —'

'What about my boat?' Peter asked. 'She's still out there in Spaniard's Cove.' He was worried about *Sea Wanderer*, lying there at anchor with no one on board.

'Well,' the Inspector said, 'you can fetch her, af you like. I shan't want you for a day or two anyway.'

'My motor-boat will take you out to her,' Commander Forbes said.

*　　*　　*　　*

Later that same afternoon, Peter and Tony stood waving on *Sea Wanderer*'s deck as the destroyer's motor-boat sped away.

Then Peter turned to his friend.

'What do you think?' he said. 'Shall we stay the night here, or start back straight away?'

Tony looked around him. The great cliffs of Spaniard's Cove were as dark and forbidding as ever. The tail of the wrecked plane still stuck up among the rocks.

He grimaced.

'With a dead man down there, and a ghost on the beach,' he said, 'I shouldn't mind a change of scenery. So why don't we get cracking?'

Toddy Proves his Point

by ROBERT MARTIN

'He *will* argue,' said Toddy's father.

'Yes — he gets it from you,' said Toddy's mother. 'But perhaps he'll grow out of it.'

'He does not get it from me, and I doubt if he'll grow out of it. And I don't see how he can argue over this... Ah, Toddy!'

''Lo, Dad!' Todhunter Brown was cheerful. One of the most annoying things about Todhunter Brown was that he was always cheerful. 'What's new?'

'Not the Vicar's collar,' said Toddy's father.

'Oh that!'

'Yes — oh that!' said Toddy's mother. 'How could you, Toddy?'

'Well, it was quite easy really. I waited until he was going down that rough slope from the churchyard, then I tripped him so that he fell on the grass.'

'We do not want to hear *how* you carried out this absurd and quite inexcusable attack,' said Toddy's father. 'We want to know why?'

'Attack?' said Toddy indignantly. 'I didn't attack him.'

'But you just said you tripped him!'

'He fell over my foot. If you want to talk about attacking — well, I reckon he attacked my foot.'

'Toddy!'

'Yes, Dad?'

'Stop arguing.'

'Why? I only said...'

'Shut up.'

'O.K.'

'Now tell me why?'

'You don't half make it difficult.' Toddy sighed. 'If I shut up, how can I tell you anything?'

'All your father wants to know is why you found it necessary to cause the Vicar to fall over,' said Toddy's mother with a patience born of much practice in dealing with her son.

'Ah!' said Toddy. 'Now that is very well put, if I may say so.'

'You may.'

'You see?' said Toddy to his father. 'Mum makes it simple.'

'And you must think I'm simple,' said Toddy's father. 'Simple in the head. All this yatta-t-yatta doesn't impress me a bit. You deliberately made the Vicar fall. Why?'

'Bunch says they've got elastic and he pulls 'em on over his head. I said they had a special back fitting. I was right — they have.'

'Can we leave your pal Bunch out of this?'

'Not really. You see, it was Bunch who said they had elastic...'

'Elastic what, dear?' said his mother.

'Collars,' said Toddy. 'No elastic. A little socket thing, they have. Very neat.'

Toddy's father gazed wide-eyed at his son.

'Do you mean to tell me that you tripped the Vicar just so that you could see how his collar fitted?' he asked in a disbelieving voice.

'Why couldn't you just ask him?' said Toddy's mother.

Toddy sighed, deep and long.

'But Dad told me the only way to learn things was to find out for myself. And anyway, Bunch bet me I wouldn't find out without asking. So you see I didn't attack the Rev. And after all, it isn't my fault if he didn't see my foot, is it?'

'You will apologise to the Vicar,' said Toddy's father.

'I have,' said Toddy. 'I apologised at the time. I brushed his coat too.'

'You are fined two shillings,' said Toddy's father. 'And three days ago I fined you a shilling for putting my tobacco in the fridge freezer to prove your opinion that frozen tobacco would smoke cool in hot weather.'

'Well, how was I to know it would go all soggy!'

'If you keep on at this rate, you'll not have any pocket money left.'

'I know,' said Toddy glumly. 'Life's pretty hard these days. I don't care much for this fining system, Dad. Couldn't you just give me a belt round the backside?'

'Don't talk like that in front of your mother or else you *will* get it.'

'Mum doesn't mind,' said Toddy cheerfully. 'She's always threatening to tell you to give me a good belt round the backside — aren't you, Mum?'

'Leave me out of it,' said his mother. 'And anyway, the fining system works better. At least it makes you think twice before you start another of your crazy tests. You really are the limit, Toddy. Why didn't you ask us about vicars' collars? It's — it's such a silly thing.'

'Did you know?' Toddy asked bluntly.

'Well — I had a good idea,'

'But you didn't really know,' Toddy insisted.

'That's enough argument,' said his father. 'I'm off to work and your mother wants you to help her with the shopping.'

'Aw, Mum! Do I have to?'

'You have to,' said his mother. 'Why should I carry heavy parcels when I've got a genius like you to help? Come on!'

As they drove to the shops, Toddy's mother said:

'Not raining now, but these wet roads splash the car with mud. You can clean and polish it when we get back.'

'Aw, Mum!'

'It might be worth five bob to you.'

'Only "might"?' said Toddy suspiciously. 'That's a bit of a niggly offer, isn't it?'

'Payment by results,' said his mother. 'Last time you got paid in advance and the car looked worse than when it was dirty.'

'I was experimenting with a new method of polishing.'

'Which didn't work.'

'No — not quite. But I won't experiment this time. So can I have it in advance, please?'

'No, you cannot. It's about time you learned to do a job properly — oh, look at that fool!'

Another car swung around the corner on the wrong side of the road. Toddy's mother braked hard and turned the steering wheel sharply. The little Mini skidded wildly on the greasy road. The other car got clear and drove away out of sight. The Mini spun, slithered, and had almost straightened out safely when its rear end hit a lamp-post.

'Yeow!' Toddy exlaimed. 'Mit der crunch! You all right, Mum?'

'Yes, dear. Are you?'

'Yes, I'm O.K. I felt the skid start and grabbed the dashboard. It wasn't really your fault. A bit too hard on the brake — that's what did it.'

'You're such a help,' said Toddy's mother sarcastically. 'Now get out and see what damage there is.'

Toddy hopped out, inspected the rear end and clambered back into the car.

'Not to worry, Mum. Just biffed the rear panel a bit, that's all.'

'Thank goodness! Your father would be livid if I lost him his no-claim bonus. I'll call at the garage on our way.'

After the garage call, Toddy's mother said:

'Just biffed it a bit, eh? You'd think I'd wrecked the car!'

320

'How much?' Toddy asked.

'Twenty pounds, and I'll have to pay it out of the house-keeping!'

'Poor old Mum! I'll tell Dad I made you put the brake on suddenly — then he'll blame me.'

'No you won't. You'll tell the truth and not try to help me — you'll only make it worse.'

Toddy's friend Bunch came to the garage whilst Toddy was washing the car.

'Women drivers!' said Bunch, kicking the bashed rear end. 'My dad says they're a menace.'

'My mum's a good driver,' said Toddy. 'As good as your old man any day. A man driver came around a corner on the wrong side. Mum put the Mini into a skid to miss him.'

'Gertcha!' said Bunch. 'She's not that good a driver. Bet she skidded because she slammed on her brakes too hard. A wet road and bad tyres and — zoom kerplonk!'

'I'll kerplonk you,' said Toddy. 'Calling my mum a menace and saying we've got bad tyres. New tyres, they are.'

'Not non-skid tyres. Any tyres that aren't non-skid are bad tyres.'

'Just because your old man sells special PX4 tyres, it doesn't mean they're perfect,' said Toddy. 'I bet I could make your old PX4 tyres skid if I wanted to.'

'Bet you couldn't.'

'Bet I could. Bet you a hundred thousand pounds I could!'

'Yeah!' Bunch sneered. 'How about real money? Bet you five bob you couldn't. Anyway, how are you going to prove it? You can drive your Mini on a private road, but not on the main road, and you'd have to buy a set of PX4s to prove it.'

'I'll think of something. I don't *have* to drive myself. Any car with PX4 tyres will do. If I can make it skid you owe me five bob.'

'You'd better pay me now,' said Bunch. 'I can do with an

extra five bob to spend at the County Fair. I lost two bob to you over the Vicar's collar.'

'And I lost two bob through it,' said Toddy. 'So I can do with your five bob. The Vicar coughed to Dad and Dad put the bit on me.'

That's rough,' said Bunch. 'Not my fault, though. What time are you going to the County Fair?'

'Early. Mum's got a stall — well, she's helping on the handicraft stall, so we'll be there early and stay all day.' Toddy paused in polishing the car. 'Hey, Bunch — d'you reckon the Honourable T.T. nit will be there?'

'Ho yaas!' Bunch scoffed. 'The Honourable Trevor Trevor and his Honourable Flippin' County family always attend the County Fair, doncherknow! He's a right stinker — him and his flash driving in that big Jaguar car.'

'That's what I mean,' said Toddy. 'T.T.'s Jag has PX4 tyres.'

'Don't I know it!' said Bunch. 'And he ain't paid for 'em yet.' He scowled at Toddy. 'The T.T. nit wouldn't let *you* drive his Jag, if that's what you're thinking.'

'He wouldn't need to,' said Toddy smugly. 'I've got an idea.'

'What sort of idea?'

'You'll see. It always rains when the County Fair is on.'

'You hope!' Bunch retorted. 'PX4s are the best in the wet. But anyway, my dad says it's going to be fine, so you'll have to think a bit harder, mate!'

Bunch was right. It didn't rain for the County Fair. The weather was hot and the ground hard with solid-packed earth.

The County Fair was a big event, held mainly for farmers and farm machinery makers to exhibit cattle and other beasts and farm gear. But like so many such fairs, it had a large section for games and sports, and many tents full of flowers, vegetables, home-made jams and cakes and handicrafts. All

322

these sections entered competitions, and the Country Fair held something of interest to everyone. They even had a Bonny Baby and a Knobbly Knees competition as well as a competition to decide the County Fair Beauty Queen.

Thousands of people came in thousands of cars and coaches, so of course there had to be big car parks. Entrance money for cars and people drew in thousands of pounds, and many more thousands of pounds were spent on the stalls and in the food and drink tents. So for a lively local lad, the County Fair offered a great variety of fun and games, plus quite a few chances of earning some handy pocket money.

Toddy usually attached himself to the Members' Car Park because it was there that the most tips could be earned by helping people to park their cars. In wet weather he could earn ten bob a time helping the tractor driver to hitch a rope on to cars which had stuck in the mud. And the tractor driver also got paid for pulling out the cars. It was a nice little racket for them, but hot sunny weather was no help at all, so Toddy scouted around for other ways to pick up a few tips.

But to be honest, he didn't really bother about tips on this day. Toddy wanted an excuse to stay in the car park for long enough to prove his point to Bunch over the PX4 tyres. And he couldn't stay around without making a show of helping the car park attendant.

Toddy's mother had parked the family car close to the gate entrance to the car park. Joe, the attendant, had said:

'O.K., Toddy, if you want to help, then you fill those spaces with small cars and send the others on to me further down. And stop anyone parking opposite the gate — those spaces are reserved for committee members' cars.'

'There's only two spaces left,' said Toddy. 'All the committee people got here early.'

'One of 'em is for the Honourable Trevor Trevor,' said Joe. 'And he don't get nowhere early. And I've had orders to keep one space clear for one of the judges who's been held up in a traffic jam. So just you watch it, young Toddy, or you won't get the ten bob I've promised you.'

'O.K., Joe. I'll watch it,' Toddy promised, then said to himself: 'Ah, that suits me fine!'

The cars drove into the car park in a steady stream which kept Toddy busy directing them. He soon had filled the spaces with small cars and now sent all arrivals down the field to Joe.

A small blue car came in, driven by a clergyman.

'Go right down the field, sir,' said Toddy politely.

'I could squeeze the car into that space near the gate,' said the clergyman.

'Sorry, sir — no more cars this end.' Toddy leaned down to talk through the car's open window with his hand resting on the edge.

The clergyman smiled and pushed a folded pound note between Toddy's fingers.

'Look, son — I might have to leave early on an urgent call. I've got to have my car where I can get out quickly. Be a nice lad and let me park in that gap.'

Toddy hesitated. Tips were one thing. Bribery was something different. Toddy always reckoned to earn tips. But if a clergyman wanted to be so generous and if it *was* an urgent call — well, there wasn't really any harm in helping a clergyman.

'O.K., sir,' asid Toddy. 'Back up next to ours.'

'Oh, it's your car, is it?' the clergyman laughed. 'Keep the best places for yourself, eh? I don't blame you!' He reversed neatly into the small space, then climbed out, carrying a zipper bag. He was a small, brisk-moving man with large tinted glasses and a thick moustache, and these, combined with a rather large-brimmed hat, made it difficult to see whether he was young or old.

Toddy observed the white clerical collar with a tinge of regret for his lost two bob and felt even more satisfied with his pound tip. There seemed a sort of natural justice about it. Then the clergyman disappeared in the direction of the tents and Toddy forgot about him.

A blaring car hooter made him jump for his life out of the path of a Jaguar car which came swooping into the car park. It rocked to a halt, the driver grinning at Toddy.

'Look lively!' said the driver. 'Standing there daydreaming. You know me, don't you?'

'Yes, I know you — you big show-off nit,' said Toddy crossly. 'About two thousand cars have come in this field up to now and you're the only driver who has belted in at that speed — so of course it had to be the Honourable Trevor Trevor, didn't it?'

'Watch it, young 'un,' said the Honourable Trevor Trevor. 'Else I'll have you barred from the fair. We can do without you young layabouts.'

'Yeah?' said a voice from behind Toddy. 'And we can do without you old layabouts too!'

Toddy turned. 'Hiya, Bunch! Has this Honourable nit paid your dad for those tyres yet?'

'Hah!' said Bunch scornfully. 'His sort don't reckon to pay us working-class layabouts, y'know.'

The Honourable Trevor Trevor grew red in the face and zoomed the big Jag in a circle, then reversed it into his private parking space.

'Now look what you've done,' said Toddy to Bunch. 'You've gone and offended him.'

'Tut-tut!' said Bunch. 'How careless of me!'

They watched the elegantly dressed Honourable Trevor Trevor climb out of the Jag, collect a zipper bag from the rear seat and stalk off towards the tents.

'Coo!' said Bunch. 'It'd be fun, wouldn't it?'

'What would?'

'Jack up his car and take off the wheels. After all they're

325

still Dad's tyres, aren't they? That'd teach old T.T. nit a lesson.'

'Oh no you don't!' said Toddy. 'I'm going to prove that your tyres will skid. Anyway, he owes your dad the money — not you.'

'Ya!' Bunch retorted. 'You can't prove nothing — not on this dry ground.'

Toddy grinned. 'It son't be dry for long. There's a water stand-pipe over there, and Joe has agreed I can use a hose to spray all around here to keep the dust down. I'm going to soak the ground under the Jag's wheels. Then you can watch when the Honouragle T.T. drives off, because that's when I'll win my five bob.'

'How?'

'He'll skid,' said Toddy confidently. 'His PX4 tyres will skid on the greasy ground because T.T. always shows off and he'll try to zoom the Jag out of its space. Even if he doesn't zoom it, I reckon he'll still skid.'

'That's not a fair test.'

'Oh yes it is. You said PX4s were perfect and never skidded.'

Bunch was caught, and he knew it.

'O.K. — I'll watch for him coming out. Got to buzz now — I'm helping Dad on the Tractor Tyre stand.' Bunch scooted away.

Not long after this, the car park was full and late arrivals were directed to another field farther down the road. Toddy collected his cash from Joe and wandered off to tour the fair and stoke up with food and ice-cream. Before he went, he connected the hose and made a show of sprinkling the ground to lay the dust. No sense in soaking the ground under the Jag yet awhile because it would dry out too much before T.T. left.

During his tour through the fair, Toddy saw the Honourable T.T. and the clergyman who owned the small blue car talking earnestly at the rear of the Treasurer's tent. Toddy was faintly surptised that T.T. and the clergyman should know each other, but realised that people came from miles away to visit the County Fair and meet old friends.

By mid-afternoon Toddy had completed soaking the ground under and around the Jaguar car. He soaked it especially thoroughly in front of each wheel, so that the tyres would be moving forward on to slimy mud once they broke down the surface, then sprayed lightly around the whole area so as not to make it noticeable.

Checking the time, Toddy regretted that he'd been impatient because the Honourable T.T. might not leave for an hour or more yet. Toddy had reckoned T.T. would leave early because his type usually liked to get clear before the rush of general departure, but he really didn't know for sure.

He was just considering whether to soak the ground again when he saw the clergyman come hurrying across the car park, carrying his zipper bag. The clergyman climbed into his car and drove out on to the road, not noticing Toddy, who was squatting in the shade between two cars. He was gone before Toddy could reach the gate to direct him out.

Then, all of a sudden, things happened — fast.

Bunch came pelting up to Toddy, and gasped:

'Did you see him? Did you see him?'

'See who?'

'That clergyman bloke. He ran this way. They say it was him who coshed the Treasurer in the cash tent! He's swiped all the lolly!'

'He's gone — come on!' Toddy cried, and raced towards his family Mini. Bunch followed. They climbed in and Toddy started the engine.

'Hey!' said Bunch. 'You're not old enough to drive on the road, are you?'

'Forget it,' said Toddy. 'I can drive — and that's all we need to know. I saw which way that car went.' He put the

'What were you doing in it?' Toddy's mother demanded

car in gear, forgot the handbrake was on and stalled the engine.

'Clot!' said Bunch. 'Go on — get going!'

Once again Toddy started the car. This time it was Bunch who stopped him.

'Look!' Bunch yelled. 'The Honourable T.T. — and in a hurry too. Watch it, mate!'

Toddy was turning the car as the Honourable Trevor Trevor slammed his Jag's door and started the engine.

The big Jag engine roared, the wheels spun, the gears whined.

Toddy zoomed the car out of the direct path of the Jag. The Honourable Trevor Trevor gunned the motor. The Jag slid, lurched, shot forward, rear tyres thick with gooey mud.

The Jag slithered sideways. It slammed the Mini broadside on, then spun off, skidded the other way and rammed its nose hard into the gate-post. The Honourable Trevor Trevor appeared to be flung sideways, hitting his head as he fell.

Bunch rubbed his nose, which he'd bumped on the windscreen when the car was hit.

'Oh lor!' Toddy groaned. 'Mit der flippin' crunch with a vengeance, mate! Mum will murder me!'

'You and your skid tricks!' said Bunch. 'Now look at the mess we're in! Are you O.K.?'

Toddy nodded. 'Are you?'

'M'm — just a bonk on my conk. Coo, watch it, Toddy — here comes your mum!'

They climbed out with difficulty because only one door would open. One side of the Mini was badly damaged.

'What were you doing in it?' Toddy's mother demanded. 'Driving it — yes, of course you were driving it. Oh, Toddy, how could you! And did you cause this Jaguar to hit the post? I expect you did...'

'Aw, Mum, belt up a minute, will you?' Toddy interrupted. 'It isn't what you think. I was only...'

'Only trying to show off,' said his mother. 'Well, my lad, you've cooked yourself properly this time. You won't get any pocket money for the next fifty years. I don't know what your father will say.'

A County Fair official came up and asked: 'Did you see a man dressed as a clergyman come through here, Toddy?'

'Yes. I was going to chase him. He's in a small blue saloon.' Toddy told which way the man drove out and the official hurried to a police car in the road.

'What *is* going on?' said Toddy's mother.

'Don't you know?' said Bunch. 'Toddy was trying to chase the bloke who robbed the cash tent.'

'He was?'

'Sure he was.'

'Well, now, Toddy — why didn't you tell me.'

Toddy grinned. 'You were too busy being cross with me.'

His mother laughed. 'I did lead off a bit, didn't I? But, Toddy dear, our car is wrecked. Are you hurt?'

'No, Mum, but it looks as if the Honourable T.T. is,'

They went to join the crowd around the crashed Jaguar.

'He was just knocked out for a while, that's all,' said Joe.

'By golly, Toddy, that was a smart bit of driving you did. I've just told Mr Kirk about it.'

'Kirk!' Toddy exclaimed. 'He's the big boss of the fair! What did you want to go yapping to him for?'

Mr Kirk came up before Joe could reply.

'Ah, Toddy!' Mr Kirk boomed. He was that sort of man. Big, booming, jolly. 'Quick thinking on you part, eh? Don't know how you guessed that Trevor was mixed up in it too.'

'Eh?' said Toddy, blinking his eyes.

'Close your mouth, Toddy,' said his mother. 'You look like a fish out of water. What *did* happen, Mr Kirk?'

'A man dressed as a clergyman coshed our cashier and grabbed sackfuls of money — stuffed them in a zipper bag and disappeared into the crowds. He had a member's badge, else he couldn't have got near the tent — and that rat Trevor got the badge for him.'

'D'you mean the Honourable T.T. is the thief's accomplice? Toddy gasped.

Mr Kirk nodded. 'He's just this minute admitted it. Couldn't do anything else. We found the zipper bag full of our cash in his Jag.'

'But the clergyman had a zipper bag too,' said Toddy.

'That was a trick,' said Mr Kirk. 'No one would suspect Trevor, so they switched zipper bags. They'd share out later. Ah, well it's a great shame! Fine family, the Trevors, but no money, y'know. Must've been pretty desperate for cash. But you spoiled that little game *and* saved our cash. Great work, Toddy.'

Toddy came to life after being a little stunned by this twist of events.

'Thank you, sir,' he said politely. 'But, sir...'

'Yes, Toddy?'

'Well, sir — I had to use my mum's car and it's badly damaged, and...'

'And you're worried about who's going to pay for it, eh?'

'Yes, sir.'

Mr Kirk gazed across at the Mini. 'H'm — caught it on the side and back.'

'Oh, the back was...' Toddy's mother began, but Toddy dug his finger in her ribs.

'Mum means the back wasn't hit as hard as the side,' he said quickly.

'No matter,' said Mr Kirk. 'I give you my personal guarantee that the Fair Committee will pay for all the repairs. Make it like new and send the bill to us.'

'Thanks,' said Toddy. 'That's big of you.'

'Think nothing of it. We're proud of you. See you later.' Mr Kirk hurried away.

'Toddy!' his mother began. 'There's a bit of explaining.' Then she paused and smiled. 'Well, what I don't know is probably better than what you might tell me, so I don't think I'll ask. And twenty pounds for just a little bitty bump was an awful lot to pay out of the housekeeping!'

Toddy grinned. 'And Dad won't lose his no-claim bonus either!'

'It's all worked out very well, really.' said his mother.

'Things mostly do for Toddy,' said Bunch.

Toddy held out his hand. 'Come on — five bob you owe me!' He pointed to the skid marks made by the Jag. 'You and your PX4s!'

'You and your flippin' opinions!' Bunch growled. 'The lengths some people go to for money — it's indecent. Here, take it!'

Toddy laughed. 'Been quite a day. Come on, Mum, I'll buy you a smashing supper.'

'What about me?' Bunch asked. 'I eat too, y'know!'

'O.K.,' said Toddy. 'I want to see how that new fish-frier works. I've got an idea, Mum...'

Fire

by REGINALD MADDOCK

Vulf squatted beside old Berg to watch him shape the flint into a spear-blade. It was wonderful to see the bent hands change a lump of flint into a flaked and sharpened blade. It was wonderful too to see the showers of tiny light-points fly out of the fling each time Berg struck it.

'Those little lights,' Vulf said. 'They must be fires.'

He knew about fire. The spirits sent it. They lit it when they sent their fiery spears crashing out of the sky to strike a tree; or sometimes when the plains were dizzy under a hot sun they would start magic fires in the brush. It was from the spirits' fire that his people borrowed fire to roast the meat the hunters brought in.

'Those little lights *are* fires, aren't they, old father?' Vulf said.

Berg grunted. He knew young Vulf, whose father had been killed long before; killed when the great beasts charged out of the valley in which the hunters had trapped them. He struck the flint again and Vulf saw the light-points spray out of it and vanish like the stars that sometimes fell out of the sky.

'Why do they die so soon?' he asked. 'Is it because you don't feed them?'

Berg spat on his hands. Vulf was always asking questions. He was for ever wanting to know the things the spirits kept secret. He was one of the tribe, one of the People of the Plain, yet nobody understood him. Even Minta, his old mother, only sighed and shook her head at him.

'Fire's made by spirits, son,' he said. 'They make it for us and we keep it alive by feeding to it the timber it eats.'

'Just think, old father,' Vulf said, 'how it would be if men could make fire for themselves?'

'You'll anger the spirits,' Berg said. 'If they hear such talk they'll fill you with pains and cramps or blister you with sores.' He shook his head. 'It's bad to anger the spirits.'

Vulf wasn't listening. He was sitting on the heap of old flint-chippings and he was stroking the patchy fur of his loin-cloth and he was thinking. He didn't think as the other young men thought. Their thoughts were of hunting or fishing or dancing or girls, but Vulf's thoughts were of other things; the things old Croll the medicine-man thought of among the dark splashings in the Secret Cavern where he went to talk with the spirits.

'I wish I could make fire,' he whispered.

Berg heard him and glanced over his shoulder at the village; at the beehive huts with the naked children scuttering round them and the thin women working outside them.

'If Croll hears you he'll point the Magic Stick at you,' he said, 'and then your spirit'll never join the spirits of your ancestors.' He turned the flint over and studied the shape he was flaking out of shapelessness. 'It's out on the plain with the hunters you ought to be. You're never going to make a hunter like your father.'

'I don't want to hunt,' Vulf said. 'I want to make fire. Why shouldn't men be able to make fire?'

'Because only the spirits can make it. Man's magic isn't strong enough.'

Vulf sniffed. 'Your magic's strong enough to make spear-blades and axes. Who taught you how to make them?'

'My father; and his father taught him. Every tribe has its tool-makers and its hunters. Now that you've become a man you're supposed to be one of your hunters.'

'But who was the man who made the very first axe?'

Berg spat. 'No man made the first axe. There have always

been axes and men who made axes. There have always been hunters who brought in meat for the tribe and women who sewed skins for clothes and collected berries and roots and fed the fire when the tribe had one.'

'But there must have been a *first* axe!' Vulf said. His eyes were bright. 'And there must have been a man who made it. He would be the wisest man in the tribe.'

'The medicine-man's the wisest man in any tribe,' Berg said. 'Croll's our wisest man. It's the same with the other peoples in the land, the People of the River and the Forest People. Their wisest men are their medicine-men.'

'Yet none of them can make fire,' Vulf said. 'If men could make fire any time they needed it they'd always be able to roast their meat and they could drive away the freezing-spirits that sometimes stiffen the ground. The first man to make fire will be the greatest man in all the land.'

'He'll be dead,' Berg said. 'He'd have a spirit in him and Croll would tell the people that it was an evil spirit because he'd be afraid that the man's magic would be stronger than his.'

He struck the flint and a shower of light-points splashed across his hand.

'See them!' Vulf said. 'Little fires! If we could catch them and put them together we'd have a big fire.' He laughed. 'I'm going to do it!'

He looked up and there was old Croll coming down the hill from the Secret Cavern.

'Don't say a word about making fire!' old Berg whispered 'You'll find the Magic Stick pointing at you.'

Croll's feathered head was bobbing and Vulf thought that he walked like the long-legged birds that waded along the edge of the river.

He called out, 'I'm watching the little fires, medicine-man!'

Croll picked his way through the rocks and stopped on the slope above Vulf.

'How long is it since you became a man?' he asked.

Vulf was studying the feathers of Croll's head-dress. They were tattered and one of them had buckled against the rock-spikes that hung in groups from the roof of the Secret Cavern.

'Three moons have died since you became a man,' Croll went on, 'and three moons have been born and you haven't been out with the hunters once in that time. Yet you eat the meat the hunters bring in.'

Vulf scowled. 'You eat it and Berg eats it but you don't hunt.'

Croll's breath whistled through the gaps in his teeth.

Berg said, 'The medicine-man and me, Vulf, we do other things for the tribe.'

Vulf watched his fingers playing in the fur of his loin-cloth. He flicked a glance at Berg and saw the old man's eyes telling him to be silent.

'Without my magic the hunters would never kill,' Croll said, and his voice was like the wind round the house when the darkness was frozen. 'All day they hunt and all day I spend in the Secret Cavern so that they may kill and the people may eat. What does Vulf do all day?'

'He'll hunt, medicine-man,' Berg said. 'His father was a mighty hunter.'

Croll sniffed. 'Before he became a man this Vulf never played the hunting games with the other boys. Now that he's a man he doesn't hunt with the other men.'

'I'll do something for the people,' Vulf said, glaring up at the magic signs painted across Croll's forehead. 'I'll do something better than hunting.'

'Better than fetching in meat!' Croll cackled. 'What's better than meat?'

'Fire!' Vulf said. 'I'll make fire!'

In the silence he thought he heard the hill whispering his words back at him but he rushed on.

'Berg makes little fires. Every time he strikes his flint, fires fly out of it. I'm going to catch them and then I'll have a big fire.'

There were fires now in Croll's eyes.

'It's the way boys talk,' Berg said. He tossed a couple of discarded flints to Vulf. 'Boys like to watch me at work. Strike them, son, and show the medicine-man.'

Vulf picked up the flints but Croll said, 'This Vulf is claiming that his magic is as strong as the spirits' magic. For claiming this men have died. Wait till I talk with Varb, the chief, when we sit at the fire tonight.'

'He only means the little fires, medicine-man,' Berg said. 'Flints always make the little fires.'

'Why shouldn't men make fire?' Vulf said. 'They need it. Why should only the spirits be able to make it?'

Croll's bony finger pointed at him. 'There's an evil spirit in him!' The finger trembled. 'He must die. He'll bring evil to the tribe. All those with evil spirits should die.'

'We don't kill men,' Berg said. 'In the old days our people killed men of their own tribe but that was when they were no better than the beasts. Now we drive wrong-doers out of the tribe.'

Croll's pointing finger was dancing. 'There's an evil spirit in him! I can smell it!'

There were strange things to be seen in Croll's eyes. There were shadows and flickering lights in his eyes and Vulf saw them and was afraid. He sprang up and ran.

He ran down the slope and through the village, scattering the children who rolled in the dust, and he kept on running until he reached the little stream in the valley where the People of the Plain buried their dead. There he was with the spirits of his ancestors and he was no longer afraid. He was in a place taboo to the women and children. Only the men ever went to the Valley of the Dead.

He sat panting on a flat boulder and he looked at Berg's two flints, still in his hand. They were blue-black and they seemed to glow with a light of their own. He tapped one against the other and out rushed the little fires; an explosion of light-points that burned and died. He wondered if they died so quickly because they were not fed, as a man dies slowly when there is no meat. He forgot Croll and old Berg. He was thinking again and he forgot that he was alone.

He needed food for the little fires and his eyes searched about until he saw last year's moss wadded into a rock-crevice. It was dry and dusty. He pulled some of it out and made a heap of it and struck the flints together near to it. The little fires flew into the moss but they died. He kept on striking the flints and making great tribes of the little flying fires but none of them turned the moss into a big fire. He worked until he was sweating and dizzy, and at last he straightened his back and dropped the flints into the grass. He could hear the village children shouting over the hill.

He pushed the heap of dead moss with his toe and, as it rolled over, smoke came out of it like a sigh. He picked it up carefully. It was cold but part of it was scorch-blackened where the little fires had tried to devour it.

He leaned over to find the two flints and his heart was making a roaring sound in his head.

The roaring went on while he piled up the moss again and while he struck one flint hard against the other. He kept on striking, this time blowing the little fires gently on to the moss, and he didn't notice the sun swinging slowly across the sky and moving his shadow over the boulder. Only the birds saw what he was doing.

Back in the village the hunters had returned with the reindeer their spears had killed. The women had skinned it and cut it up and were now spitting it on pointed sticks to roast round the fire, which was beginning to climb up through the mountain of wood the children had collected during the day. The hunters sat on the dusty earth and stretched their legs and waited for the warmth of the fire and the meat it was roasting.

'Fire is good,' old Varb the chief said.

The men nodded and grunted and one of them said, 'So is meat and tonight we have both.'

'And the spirits gave them to us,' Croll said.

He was standing beside Varb and he had freshly painted the magic signs on his forehead and chest. The men knew that after the meat he would tell one of his best tales and later, while the women tapped music out of the hollow log, he would lead them in a dance round the fire.

'The spirits gave you the reindeer because I painted him for them in the Secret Cavern,' he droned. 'The spirits gave us the fire.'

'But it's the women and children who feed it and keep it alive,' a bent old woman said quietly.

'It's bad when the fire dies; when there's no wood or the rains come and kill the fire,' a man said. 'It's bad then. We're cold and we eat raw meat like the beasts.'

'The spirits give us fire and they take it away when we anger them,' Croll said. 'The fire is theirs to give. I tell you these things and you know that my words are true words.'

The men nodded and chanted,' We know, old father, we know.'

The fire was warm now and the scents from the meat were sweet in the men's nostrils and they felt good. They watched old Croll's bright eyes darting over them.

He said, 'There is one of our tribe who does not know. There is one who tries to be as terrible as the spirits; who wants to have magic stronger than mine.'

The men sat up.

'Who is this one?' somebody called.

'Name him,' Varb growled. 'I'll drive him out of the tribe.'

Croll smiled. 'He is Vulf, that son of nobody.'

'Vulf is my son,' the bent old woman whispered. 'He is the son of my man and he was a great hunter.'

The men were beginning to grin and to lie back on the earth. They knew Vulf. It was Vulf who always talked but never did anything; who liked to think; who watched the cloud-spirits race across the sky when he should have been chasing the girls round the houses. He was the strange one, the different one.

A man chuckled and shouted, 'Vulf, the fire-maker!' and Vulf said, 'I'm here,' and the hunters laughed.

He was standing near to the women, and the men saw him and laughed louder. He walked nearer to the fire and its light shone red in his eyes and the laughter stopped.

'The fire-maker!' a man said but there was fear in his voice.

The people were watching Vulf, wondering at the change in him. He was walking like a young chief.

'You all know how men need fire,' he said.

'And the spirits give it to us!' Croll shouted.

Vulf went on, 'You all know how there are times when the fire dies and we wait many moons for another. If the freezing-spirits come to us then we are so cold that we can't sleep in our houses.'

The men nodded. They knew the blueness of cold without fire.

'Think how it would be if men could make their own fires in those bad times,' Vulf said.

'Only the spirits can give fire!' Croll said.

His breath whistled through his teeth and the sound of it was like the sound of the wind among the rocks on top of the hill. The men shuddered.

'It's boys' talk, 'Berg said. 'Men can't make fire.'

'But a man can be driven out of the tribe for trying to,'

Croll said, 'and for saying he can make fire the tribe can kill him.'

'Why should he be killed for that, medicine-man?' Varb asked.

'Because he'd be claiming that his magic was as strong as the spirits' magic.' Croll leaned forward so that the hunters might see the lights in his eyes. 'The spirits give us fire and when we anger them they take it away. If we anger them too much we die.'

Old Minta covered her face with her hands. 'A man who could make fire!' she whispered, yet they all heard her. 'What kind of a man would he be?'

'He'd be a man with a spirit in him,' Croll said, 'and a man with a spirit in him is bad for the people. His magic is strong and evil and he must die. It is better for one man to die than for the tribe to die.'

'Fire can be made without any magic,' Vulf said. He held up two flints. 'The fire's in these. You've all seen it fly out of stones like these and if you catch it and feed it you have a fire. Watch, you men!'

He squatted down in front of them and they saw him arrange a little heap of the moss that grew in the shadows under rocks. They saw him pile twigs over the moss and bend over the pile and tap his flints together near to it, and their fear left them and they laughed.

'Vulf, the fire-maker!' somebody shouted and the men laughed so hard that many of them rolled on their backs in the dust. But Croll and the old women didn't laugh. They could feel more strongly than the hunters the power of Vulf's concentration.

Vulf didn't hear the laughter. He went on striking little fires out of the flints and gently blowing them into the moss and twigs. He didn't feel the waves of laughter that beat against his face; didn't notice when the laughing died away and there

They saw Vulf tap his flints together near the pile

was nothing more than a lonely snigger to disturb the clicking of the flints. He kept on working until at last he blew smoke out of the moss, and the hunters saw the smoke and some of them moaned.

Then the moss began to glow with a fire of its own and the hunters looked up at Croll. He was pointing the forked end of the Magic Stick at Vulf, and his lips were shaping unspoken words and the hunters knew the words.

'*Evil has come!*' Croll's lips formed. '*Kill the evil!*'

The men looked at Vulf and saw that he was still alive and that fire had taken hold of the twigs and was devouring them. Vulf was laughing.

'*Fire!*' he shouted.

'The hunters were on their feet. They were backing away from Vulf who was no longer the person they had known when he was a boy. Some of them were so afraid that they dared not look at him.

Croll leapt high in the air, his body stiff and his arm pointing. '*Kill!*' he screamed.

The men dashed into their houses, and the women and children chased after them. A young boy tripped and fell squealing, and his mother caught his arm and dragged him with her. But old Minta stayed, and Croll, still mouthing death, stayed, and Berg stayed, squatting near to Vulf and chewing a hunk of meat filched from its roasting-stick.

'Why are they afraid, old father?' Vulf said to Berg.

Berg looked at the plain beyond the houses where darkness was now pressing against the firelight.

'I'd be afraid if I weren't too old for fear,' he said. 'I'm old and I'm hungry.'

'Go, son!' Minta whispered.

'But what do they fear?' Vulf asked.

'You, man,' Berg said. 'There's a spirit inside you that's given you more magic than any man should have.' He pointed at the darkness. 'Do as the old mother says. Go! Men fear what they don't understand, and what men fear they kill. That's why the hunters are fetching their spears. Go to the People of the Forest and live with them and get rid of the spirit inside you. Never make fire again. Fire-making is spirits' work.'

Vulf turned from the old man to his mother and he looked past her at the village where he had always lived. From its shadows men were creeping, men who were strangers although he had known them all his life, and every man was carrying his spear. Vulf could see the blades, like flint teeth, glistening in the firelight.

'I wanted to give them fire,' he said.

'Only the spirits must give it,' Berg said.

Croll was prancing in front of the hunters, spitting '*Kill!*,' at them.

Vulf crept away to the edge of the light and then he began to run, and behind him the hunters howled and stopped bounding at the beginning of the darkness.

'I wanted to give them fire,' Vulf gasped to the spirits that thronged the night he was rushing through.

Day of the Jungle Knives

by ROBERT BATEMAN

It was hot, but they were used to it. Barry Blake had grown used to it after five years in Malaysia; his friends Lon Chee and Petal Pearl had always been used to it for they were Chinese-Malays, born on the edge of the jungle through which they were now struggling.

Barry wiped his face for the hundredth time, and pushed on, hacking his way with a heavy jungle knife. There was no path until they made it themselves. For a moment or two he wished he was back home in the village, helping his father at surgery.

He grinned to himself. In the jungle you grew up fast. As the son of a jungle doctor, by the time he was fourteen there was not much he did not know about being a male nurse.

But this was his day off — from lessons as well as work. It was a day he and his two friends had been waiting for — the chance to find the secret river with the deep, safe swimming pool.

It was there, somewhere in the jungle, because people had come back and talked about it. There were no crocodiles in the pool, and no deadly water insects. It was the one place in five hundred miles where you could swim without worrying.

'Whoever found it didn't leave much of a path,' Barry grumbled. The only clue to where the path had been was the way certain jungle branches twisted, showing where years ago they had been slashed out of the way by a traveller.

'Jungle not very patient,' grinned Lon Chee. 'Always in hurry to cover up again. Like angry man woken in night.' He moved closer. 'Let Lon Chee take turn. Lon Chee better than Barry in jungle.'

Barry flattened himself against the dense undergrowth to let Lon Chee squeeze past. Petal Pearl came up behind him. In her thornproof slacks she looked cool and comfortable. In her hair she had threaded bright jungle flowers. 'How you keep cool, beats me!' said Barry.

There was a sudden shout from Lon Chee. 'Barry! Strange thing Lon Chee find.' The Chinese boy brushed aside the leaves and branches. 'Look! New path crossing ours.' He touched a recently-cut branch. 'Sap still coming from wood. Perhaps others have same idea. All go swimming?'

Barry looked at his compass. 'Not if they keep to that path, they won't. The river's supposed to be to the west. That path runs north — and south, into bandit country.'

Lon Chee dropped on his knees, and looked at the ground. He picked up a twig and examined it, then stared at a patch of trampled leaves. 'Not many bandits.'

'How many?'

The Chinese boy held up one finger. 'First he go south to north, cutting path as he go. Then back again, north to south.'

There was a prickling feeling of uneasiness at the back of Barry's neck, as though in the jungle behind him there were rows of peering eyes. He turned, and looked at the blank wall of greenery.

'Very funny fellow, this bandit,' muttered Lon Chee, looking up and down the newly-discovered path. 'He come all alone, but he cut wide path.' He laughed. 'Very foolish — much hard work for nothing. He cut path wide enough for army.'

The words puzzled Barry, made him even more uneasy. He stepped past Lon Chee and went a short way up the northern path, then looked back.

There was no sign of his friends!

He had come round a bend. The bend continued, so that within a few more yards the bandit path was heading due east.

And to the east lay the unprotected village!

346

He went back, running in spite of the rough ground and broken roots underfoot. Lon Chee looked up in surprise. 'Running not for jungle. Running for cool day on seashore.'

But the sweat pouring down Barry's face was not because of the running. Quickly he explained about the path.

Petal Pearl stared at him in a panic. 'But only fifty people in village, Barry! No guns. Without guns, how can fight bandits?'

It was not Barry but Lon Chee who replied. 'Answer quite simple, Petal Pearl. Bandits cannot be fought in village, so bandits must be stopped before coming to village.' His face clouded. 'Yes, but how?'

'I want to *see* these bandits first,' said Barry. 'We don't know how many there are. They may not have guns themselves.'

Lon Chee shook his head vigorously. 'In Malaysia every bandit has gun. If no gun, then pretty soon soldier come put in jail.' He stood up. 'Now we go look and find bandit camp?'

Barry nodded.

'All right,' said Lon Chee. 'But go on soft feet. How you say it in English?'

'You mean walk carefully? Like a man walking on eggs?'

Lon Chee grinned. 'Very true! Only fool walk on eggs. All same fool walk down path looking for bandit camp.' He set off, with his back bent so that he could look at the ground and pick every footfall, avoiding places where there were dry leaves or twigs. Barry, following him, was not so clever at this, and soon trod on a stick which snapped like the noise of a rifle going off.

Lon Chee turned his head sharply. 'Which side you on, Barry? Ours or bandits?' He spoke in an angry whisper. 'Remember, if bandits catch us, not funny. Bandits all time hungry.' The Chinese boy managed to get his anger under control. 'Bandit look at you, Barry. You know what he think?

He think maybe pink English boy make good supper.'

Barry gulped. He knew that even though Lon Chee was grinning, he meant what he said. 'Hadn't we better send Petal Pearl back?' he asked.

Lon Chee wagged one finger from side to side. 'Old rule of Chinese generals before battle. Never split up army until have made plans.' He swung round and continued along the path, which was now going steeply downhill. From ahead came a sound like a fast-flowing stream or waterfall. With every step forward the noise became louder, until finally it was almost deafening. Lon Chee halted again, and beckoned Barry and Petal Pearl towards him.

They squatted together in the centre of the path. 'Wise bandit make camp by river bank,' Lon Chee said in a whisper only inches from their ears. 'Only fool goes long walk every time want bucket of water.' He got down flat in the middle of the path. 'Wise bandit also have guard on duty. So wise spy travel on stomach.'

Barry wriggled into place beside him; waited until Petal Pearl touched his shoe to signal she was ready, and then passed the signal on to Lon Chee. Smoothly, without effort, the Chinese boy wriggled along the path, which now turned and twisted every few yards in its steep drop to the bank of the stream.

It was at the fourth turn that Lon Chee put his head round, then froze. A split second later he hurriedly wriggled back again.

'What's the matter?' Barry whispered.

'A guard. Sitting in middle of path with rifle on knee.' Lon Chee waved them back round the next bend. When they were safely in hiding he said: 'Cannot cut new path. Too much noise.'

'Then how do we get past him?'

'Simple! If cannot go through bushes, must go *under* bushes.'

348

Lon Chee grinned. 'Lon Chee better than Barry in jungle.' Then he was off again, at right-angles to the path, wriggling in the undergrowth. The noise of the stream was loud enough to drown any sound he made, and behind him he left a hole, through which Barry and Petal Pearl could crawl without difficulty.

It was slow progress. Every few moments, ahead of Barry, Lon Chee halted and listened carefully to the sound of the stream to get his bearings.

Then, suddenly, instead of moving ahead, he hurriedly wriggled himself backwards. Barry jerked his head out of the way of the oncoming feet, and squeezed to one side so that the Chinese boy could get back beside him.

Before he could even ask what was the matter, the answer came from only a few feet in front.

'Voices!'

'Plenty talk by bandits,' whispered Lon Chee. 'They tell about making attack on village.'

'What are they saying?'

Lon Chee listened for several minutes, while Barry waited impatiently.

'One of them — perhaps he is chief of the bandits — says they should attack tonight. Other bandit say it is better to wait... Sssh! Let Lon Chee listen again.'

There was another long wait. Then Lon Chee went on, 'He say to wait because guide who made path is sick. But chief say they do not need guide, because path is already made.'

Barry frowned, thinking hard. 'Which are they going to do?'

'When bandit chief make up his mind, bandit who wish to live do not argue. Bandits will attack tonight. Will leave camp as soon as sun go down.' Lon Chee's face was frightened. 'Lon Chee know what will happen. Bandits will go to village with guns, and say they want food and money. If they do not get all they want, then they shoot everybody in village.'

Barry waited no longer. He wriggled back the way he had come, swiftly, but carefully in order not to kick Petal Pearl in the face. On the main path once again, he hurriedly turned a corner, to get well away from the guard before he started speaking. 'Lon Chee, can Petal Pearl find her way back to the village alone?'

'Petal Pearl can go anywhere alone,' said Lon Chee proudly. 'Lon Chee taught her. Lon Chee very good in jungle. Better than Barry!'

Barry swung round. From his shirt pocket he brought out a notebook and a pencil. He tore out a page and scribbled on it furiously. 'Petal Pearl, take this to my father. He will know what to do. Go back the way we came.'

'But...' Petal Pearl looked anxiously from one to the other. 'Petal Pearl cannot leave you and Lon Chee, not here, close to bandits.'

Barry managed to smile, though never in his life had he felt less like it. At any moment the guard might hear them, or come along the path as part of his regular patrol. 'We'll be all right, Petal Pearl. Just do as I ask — and go quickly!'

The Chinese girl took the sheet of paper, folded it carefully, and put it into the pocket of her slacks. Then she turned and began running swiftly but silently along the track, away from the stream and towards the place where their own rough path joined it.

Barry went back, knelt down, and disguised the entrance to the hole they had made by crawling on their stomachs. 'Right!' he whispered, 'Now we go too!'

They went for several hundred yards before Lon Chee caught Barry's shoulder and stopped him. 'Lon Chee not understand. On Barry's face is very clever look, but what Barry does has not been clever at all.'

They were far enough away from the bandit camp to be

able to speak normally. 'I'll tell you as we go,' said Barry. 'In that note I gave Petal Pearl I asked my father to fetch the troops and get them to follow her all the way back here.'

Lon Chee looked at him as if he was mad. 'But by then bandits will be in village! Troops should be *there* — to fight them.'

Barry shook his head. 'This path has been cut for many bandits. My father will be lucky if twenty soldiers are sent to the village. That's not enough. Twenty soldiers can beat the bandits only if they catch them by surprise.' He was running now, panting in the heat as he spoke. He jerked his thumb back along the path. 'That's where we'll have the ambush. At their own camp.'

Lon Chee's mouth dropped open. 'But by then it will be too late! That will be after bandits come back from vilage.'

Suddenly Barry halted by a gap in the side of the path. 'Is that where we came out before?'

Lon Chee nodded impatiently.

'Then the bandits are never going to reach the village!' Barry said, grinning. Quickly he covered up the narrow gap by stretching branches across it. 'Remember the bandit chief said the guide who made the path is ill?'

'Yes, but Lon Chee still do not understand.'

'Get out your jungle knife!' Barry produced his own, and began hacking away at the bushes beside ihm.

'What for?' Lon Chee brought out his own knife, but stood hesitating, not knowing what he was supposed to do.

'We're going to make a new path,' said Barry. 'We'll block the entrance to the old one. The new path will lead *away* from the village, in a big wide circle — back to the camp!'

Lon Chee stared at him. After a moment the terrified look went out of his face. He seemed to be thinking very hard. Then, 'Lon Chee understand,' he said, and began bending branches to hide the path they wanted to block.

It took him half an hour of hard work to disguise it. Lon Chee's expert hands wove branches and twigs into a thick barrier, from which leaves stuck out as if they had grown there naturally.

Barry had gone ahead, hacking the new path. By the time Lon Chee was ready to join him he was two hundred yards in front — but above, through the tops of the trees, the sun was sinking fast. In another hour it would drop below the skyline.

And then...

Barry's stomach turned over.

What would happen after sunset was something he would rather not think about. It was better of think of nothing but the next branch to be slashed, the next patch of dense undergrowth to be trampled down.

Lon Chee, too, was looking anxiously at the sunlight filtering through the trees. 'Lon Chee take turn,' he said. 'Lon Chee do cutting, Barry do trampling.'

The path lengthened. Barry checked its direction with his pocket compass, to make sure that it circled back towards the stream. Just as the sun finally went down, he decided they had come as close as they dare because of the noise. He held up his hand to signal Lon Chee, and then they both listened.

'Lon Chee not hear anything. Lon Chee think we far away from bandit camp.'

'Sssh!' Barry had a horrible suspicion that the Chinese boy might be right, that somehow his calculations with the compass had gone wrong, and that instead of a neat circle back towards the camp he had made a long path leading nowhere.

He jumped at the sudden shout not far away. It was followed immediately by a chorus of yells, and a pistol shot.

'Can you hear what they're shouting?' he asked Lon Chee.

'Oh, yes. Very loud and clear. Barry was right; we are close to camp. Shout was signal for bandits to get their guns. Pistol shot was signal to start marching.'

352

'Then it's our signal to start cutting again,' said Barry quickly. 'Once they're on the march they won't hear the noise we make.'

Now it was a wild race against time. Barry calculated that the bandits had a mile to go to the point at which the path had been diverted, and then another mile and a half along the circle to catch up with them. At the most that would take them forty minutes. In that time they must complete the path right to the heart of the camp, and then hide until Petal Pearl arrived with the soldiers.

Barry was streaming with sweat now as he hacked at the bushes and trampled the tangle of leaves and grass underfoot. He and Lon Chee were working side by side, in a hail of leaves and twigs from their fast-moving jungle knives. The backs of their hands were torn and bleeding from thorns, and their faces swollen from insect bites.

But in the distance they could hear the rushing water of the stream! It gave them new strength to cut faster. But now, Barry reckoned, the bandits would be past the diversion, and not much more than a mile behind them. Everything depended on how far the troops had got in their single-file trudge from he village along the narrow path they had made with Petal Pearl that morning.

'Barry! Look! The stream and the camp!'

The sight of the water and beside it the huts of the camp sent them running forward. It no longer mattered about cutting the path; by the time the bandits reached this point they would know, anyway, that they had been tricked.

Together they rushed into the small circle of mud huts. Too late Lon Chee shouted, 'Look out, Barry! The guide.'

He had forgotten all about the bandits' sick guide, who had been left behind. The man staggered out from one of the huts, with his rifle pointed at Lon Chee. For a moment it looked as if Lon Chee was going to rush at him and try to knock the gun out of his hand, but the guide said something in rapid Malay, and raised the barrel so that it was aimed directly at Lon Chee's chest.

'What does he say?' Barry shouted.

'Bandit say we stand together beside hut. Not move or he shoot us.'

Barry looked round him desperately, but he knew already there was no escape. If he tried to run for it, the bandit would certainly shoot his friend. With his hands above his head, he walked across the clearing in the centre of the camp, and stood beside Lon Chee against the mud wall of one of the huts. The bandit, clutching a dirty towel round his waist, squatted on the far side of the clearing, with the rifle held at the ready. Again he spoke to Lon Chee.

'What's he saying this time?'

'It is orders for you, Barry. He say English boy go into hut and bring out clothes.'

Barry looked at the bandit, who pointed to a hut a few yards away. Barry walked across to it, and went inside.

The only light was from a hole in the wall, for the door was covered by a blanket, which dropped back into place the moment he went inside. There was a bed made of blankets and boxes, and the bandit's clothes lay in an untidy heap on the end of it.

But before picking them up, he looked round swiftly in the faint hope that the bandit might have been careless enough to leave another gun in the hut.

From outside, Lon Chee shouted, 'Bandit say hurry up! If Barry not hurry, he shoot Lon Chee!'

The shout made Barry spin round, knocking over an oil lamp. The paraffin spilled across the floor and the bed. Barry acted faster than ever before in his life. He snatched up a box of matches lying beside the lamp, lit one, and tossed it into the pool of paraffin. Then he grabbed the bundle of clothes

Barry's leg shot out, tripping the bandit

and came out into the brilliant sunshine.

The bandit beckoned him across the clearing. The rifle muzzle moved warily back and forth between him and Lon Chee.

Barry put down the clothes, but did not move away, because in his present position he was blocking the bandit's view of the hut. Behing him he heard a crackle and a roar as inside the hut the bed burst into flames.

Only then, as smoke poured upwards, did the bandit jump to his feet with a yell of alarm. He hobbled towards the hut, right past Barry.

It was a chance too good to miss. Barry's leg shot out, tripping the bandit so that he sprawled forward into the dust. A split second later Lon Chee was on top of him, twisting at his hands to wrench away the rifle. It went off, just as the blazing hut collapsed only six feet away. A square of blazing thatch a yard across crashed down beside Lon Chee, who rolled away, swinging the rifle by the barrel to fend off the bandit.

From behind Barry, in the woods, came angry shouting; he turned, to see the bandits streaming towards him, looking dazedly at their blazing camp.

'Come on, Lon Chee!' he yelled. 'Run for it!'

The Chinese boy jabbed hard with the rifle-butt, catching his pursuer on the point of the jaw with a crack that could be heard above the din of the fire. But as he turned to run Lon Chee's clothes burst into flame. He stared in horror as a fierce jet of fire raced up the front of his shirt and singed his hair.

'Quick!' shouted Barry. 'The stream!'

They sprinted to the water's edge. Barry had a moment's glimpse of a sheet of water ahead, far wider than he had expected; then they both dived in, and swam hard under water until they felt their lungs would burst. Both came to the surface at the same moment, gasping for air. Barry glanced towards the bank twenty yards away. 'Dive!' he yelled, and heard a vicious spatter of bullets hit the water a split second after he went under.

*   *   *   *

At the bottom of his dive, he tried to think before coming to the surface. His hurried glance towards the bank had shown him that there were at least fifty bandits crowded there. This time, when they came up for air, the marksmen would be ready for them.

A face appeared only inches from his own. Air was bubbling out of Lon Chee's nose, and he was signalling with his hand that he would have to come to the surface.

This was it, then! Their second dive had carried them farther from the bank, but they were still within easy range of even the poorest marksman. Fifty marksmen, however poor, could not possibly miss.

He returned the thumb signal, and began to move upwards. Well, at least they would not have been shot for nothing. They had delayed the attack on the village, and now, with their camp burned down, perhaps the bandits would change their minds and not attack at all.

He shot out of the water, and took a tremendous gulp of air, expecting a hail of bullets.

He was under water again before he realised that not a single shot had been fired!

Once again he found Lon Chee's face in front of him, but this time the thumb signal was rapid and triumphant, and he could even see a tremendous grin on his friend's face. Puzzled, Barry kicked out with both feet, and came up once again into the middle of the huge pool.

And then they were both yelling and slapping each other

on the back! For at the water's edge the bandits were now huddled in a circle, surrounded by a body of soldiers who were covering them with automatic rifles. In front, waving to them across the water, was Petal Pearl!

They swam to the shore, slowly and easily, enjoying the cool of the water after the hours of heat and hard work. Petal Pearl reached down her hands to help them scramble up the steep bank. Dripping wet, they watched as in the camp the fire reached the bandit's fuel store, and a pillar of flame shot fifty feet into the sky.

Soldiers were busy roping the bandits together by the wrists, ready for the long march back to the village. The officer in charge came over to Barry and Lon Chee. He shook hands. 'You saved the lives of everybody in the village,' he said. 'Who thought of that clever trick with the path?' He looked at Lon Chee. 'You, I suppose? You've lived here all your life.'

Lon Chee shook his head. 'Not me — Barry.'

He glanced round, and grinned. 'Barry better in jungle than Lon Chee!'

It was the end of a proud boast which he had been making ever since they first met. But there was a mischievous look on his face. 'Does not matter! Does not matter at all. Now we have found our safe swimming pool.' He turned, and ran back towards the water's edge, shouting over his shoulder, 'Lon Chee better in water than Barry!'

Petal Pearl burst out laughing. Though she was fully dressed, she went to the edge of the bank, and toppled over slowly, in a graceful dive which hit the water so smoothly that it hardly made a ripple.

Barry could see just the faint outline of her as she swam underwater, far out into the centre of the pool — much farther than he could have bone without his lungs bursting. On she went, until he darted to the water's aldege in arm, fearing she had caught herself in weed or underwater roots.

Then, what seemed an incredible distance out from the shore, she came smoothly to the surface. She shouted, and the words came drifting across the pool towards him.

'Petal Pearl better in water than Barry *or* Lon Chee!'